THE CONNECTION
FORGING STEEL

THE CONNECTION FORGING STEEL

For information contact :
www.gastontking.com

Edited by Dean Roof and Belle Manuel
Cover designed by Evocative X from 99 Designs
ISBN : 979-8-9899752-0-4

First Edition : June 2024

9631

THE CONNECTION
FORGING STEEL

GASTON KING

20 24

GTK PUBLISHING

For Maya

MT. DIAMOND
CONSTRUCTION
SQUAD
RED PEAKS
THE LIFELESS DEPTHS
EXP
THE
CULT
SOUTH PORT D
IGNACIA

TION
D
THE NORTHERN BAY
GLASHELLER HEIGHTS
CAPITAL
TRANSFERRAL SQUAD
ION
THE SUNNY SEA

Contents

CHAPTER 1

Matching Behaviors

My eyes slowly opened as the burning wish to see my father encompassed my mind. Eight newly extinguished candles stared back at me. The momentary sadness seemed palpable until Rus plunged my face into the cake. I cheerfully wiped the coconut cream frosting out of my eyes as I looked up and saw the explosion of cake scattered across Grandpa's wooden dining room table. The energy of the party had escalated to a chaotic state.

My classmates started yelling and running wild as if a fox had gotten into the hen house. The last thing I wanted to do was put a stop to it. Grandpa opened the door to the backyard and shooed us out as if we were uninvited guests. Rus and I sprinted out onto the patio where we picked up our water guns and continued our all-out water war.

Roxanne followed soon after and delivered a powerful blow to all of the party members with a nearby garden hose. We all gallivanted through sprinklers and ran around my backyard for what felt like hours while the beautiful vermillion rays of sun began to fade.

A half hour later, fun sucking parents returned to reclaim my classmates. They all waved goodbye with smiling faces as their worried mothers wrapped each of them in warm, comforting, Egyptian cotton.

Rus and Roxanne were the last to remain. Both of my best friends made certain that I enjoyed my birthday. A favorable memory of the three of us gallivanting in Grandpa's backyard was branded onto my brain that day. Roxanne's father and Rus's mother arrived soon after and picked the two of them up, but not before we said our goodbyes. A lasting embrace, a newly stained dining room, and an exhausted Grandpa.

An hour later, we heard a guilty knock on the door.

Grandpa reluctantly opened the door. "Oh, I see you made it."

"Hey, Dad. I'm here to see Justin."

I joyfully sprinted to the door. "Dad, you're here!"

Grandpa stepped to the right and allowed me to dart past him and into a loving bear hug from my father.

"Hey, Justin, I'm sorry we missed your party, pal." His bright smile seemed to subside.

"It's okay! Did you bring Shadow? Can I see him?"

"Oh yeah, he's waiting in the zomorodi. Unfortunately, we can't stay. I just wanted to come by and see you for your big day."

My world sank. "You aren't staying? Not even for cake?"

Grandpa retorted, "It's okay, Justin. We'll have plenty of dessert to last us for weeks. You'll thank me later."

Noah Steele, leader of the Hero Regime, sighed deeply. "I wasn't going to miss the chance to give you your birthday present."

My father handed me a bright white box with a sparkling red ribbon that fully encapsulated the sides, tied together in the middle. I grabbed the box as my eyes gleamed with satisfaction and began to open it. I untied the bow, stripped it from its original poorly taped position and tore off the top of the box. Inside sat a nicely folded, identical uniform that matched my father's. It was an exact replica of the uniform he was currently wearing at that very moment.

"I had this one tailor made just for you. I hope it fits."

"Wow! So cool! Thanks, Dad!" I charged into him for another hug.

He awkwardly accepted my arms clasped around his waist as he patted me on the back before he inched toward his zomorodi. A sudden radio buzz came over the earpiece carefully hidden in his right ear.

"Calling all units, we have a 1014 in progress. Unauthorized personnel breaking into The Capital's Animal Food Bank. Please be advised suspects using arson and hostile forces."

"We've got to go. Please keep Justin safe."

"I always do."

I carefully watched as my father rejoined his fearsome male lion in his white zomorodi. The two ascended from the ground as a nearby fiery explosion occurred inside the midst of The Capital. My father and Shadow flew straight toward the chaos that erupted within The Capital of Ignacia. He had a knack for running straight into a fight.

My father lived for the excitement and the danger. He was more than my father; he was the leader of the Hero Regime. Which meant he was the man elected to put his life on the line every day. He never displayed any signs of weakness or the need for a suitable replacement to relieve him. But one day, I would be there for him. Until that day came, he had to serve as the defender of Ignacia.

I threw on the new uniform and chased after the high-powered, jet-infused vehicle down the dimly lit street. "Dad, wait!"

"Dusty, restrain Justin!" Grandpa yelled out.

Grandpa sent his American alligator, Dusty, after me. Grandpa activated his partner patch which gave Dusty the power to catch up to me. Dusty lunged after me and grabbed onto my new uniform.

No matter how hard I heaved forward, his massive jaws stopped me right in my tracks. I continued to inch forward as hard as I could until a loud tear broke the physical struggle.

The uniform had been torn in half as I collapsed on the ground in embarrassment. I watched my father soar off in the direction of the enemy through the night sky. Tears of momentary frustration filed my eyes as streetlamps illuminated the rocky road paved in front of me. All I wanted to do was to help him and be the hero my father wanted me to be.

Grandpa left the front door and started jogging toward me and Dusty. I was emotional and exhausted from running around with my friends. The same tears began to descend down my cheeks as my temper encompassed my headspace. Dusty felt remorse for what he had done as he laid his head on my lap. I became hysterical and shoved him off me. I got up, wiped away my tears and started running again in the torn uniform. I was moving faster and faster until my grandpa yelled out to me.

"Justin! Stop!"

I paused and turned around to face my grandpa as he continued jogging after me. I was stuck between my sense of logic and emotional stability. I'd let my longing to work alongside my father get the better of me. I turned around once more gasping for air and sat on the ground defeated.

Suddenly, ashes from the nearby burning buildings started to fill the night air. The smoke that followed removed any potential moisture from the air and caused my lungs to struggle. I coughed uncontrollably as my eyes continued to water. My grandfather swooped in, picked me up and brought me back to his home as I cried into his shoulder.

"Why? Why can't I help?" I cried, as snot seeped from my nose.

Grandpa started to breathe heavily as we reached the front door and sat me down. "You're not ready yet, Son."

"But, Grandpa, why? I'm strong. I can help him!"

Grandpa delivered me back inside our home and placed me on the living room sofa. "Yes, you are, Justin, and one day you will... I'm going to tell you a story. It's a heck of a story so listen well. It's called, *Herschel the Hero."*

I wiped my eyes. "Who's Herschel?"

"Listen, and you'll learn everything you need to know:

"A long time ago, there lived a young boy named Herschel. He lived in South Ignacia with his mother, father, and younger brother, Fred. The family had a happy life as farmers and they resided far away from the city life we have here in The Capital."

"Herschel and his family farmed croplands in hundreds of different acres. They grew the crops, sold the crops, and supported themselves off the land. Herschel's favorite cropland was the rice plantation that lay next to a nearby pond. He stopped by that little pond every day to see his friend, a large alligator that protected the crops from other animals. Each time Herschel visited his friend he rewarded this alligator with fresh meatballs from his mother's spaghetti. Life was very peaceful for Herschel, Fred, and their family on the farm. Until one day, a plague erupted from the north and began to eat away and destroy everything in its path."

"Grandpa, what's a plague?"

"An incurable virus, one that causes disease that slowly kills anyone or any living thing it comes in contact with. This plague started to eradicate all of the wildlife it came in contact with. From plants, food, crops, animals, and people alike."

"What about Herschel?!"

"Well, he knew that his friend was in trouble so before he went home, he raced back to the pond in hopes to save the alligator. But he was gone, the alligator was nowhere to be found. All that remained was a large white egg on the nearby shore.

"Herschel looked around, grabbed the egg, and immediately bolted back to his family. Herschel and Fred were stuffed away from the elements in a storage unit behind their house. Sadly, their parents were not as lucky. They were affected by the virus, trying to protect their children. The plague took everything from Herschel. His parents, his crops, his friend, and his home. Herschel and Fred were rescued just in the nick of time by men in hazmat suits. Those men who rescued the brothers were the first group of volunteers to take part in the Arc Project."

My mouth dropped. "Wow, the Arc Project... But what came out of the egg?"

"A baby alligator inched its way out during their time spent inside the storage unit. The alligator was very similar to the one Herschel had befriended in the rice croplands. Herschel instantly grew to love the alligator and decided to raise him as his own...I'm afraid we're getting off track, let's circle back and revisit the Arc Project–"

"Aw, a baby gator! Yeah, Rus said something about the Arc yesterday. What's that?"

"It was the last hope for restoring balance to Ignacia. It was first put in motion to save thousands of plants and animals from becoming extinct! A team of brave scientists banded together and devised a way to collect the surviving animals and people alike."

"Did it work? What happened next!?"

"Thankfully, they were successful. The team of scientists rescued and rehabilitated thousands of species of animals. They administered a vaccine that not only protected those from the virus but had a side effect that extended their lifespans. However, many animals were left without homes or ecosystems to return back to. The government had a heavy hand in deciding how mankind would move forward after surviving such a devastating ordeal."

"What's a vaccine?"

"It's like a cure. One that would help save everyone."

"Oh. So, Herschel and Fred both had the cure? What did they do?"

"Well, the members of the Arc Project had the cure. So, they decided to partner with them."

"They partnered with... who?"

"The members of the Arc Project partnered with the government so that we could partner with animals. You see, the people who ran the country decided that individuals within the Arc Project should be partnered with these animals but were only awarded a partner after surpassing a variety of tests. The challenges were particularly difficult, but they made each member exceptional in their own way."

"Grandpa, what happened to Herschel and Fred? What about the baby gator?"

"Herschel, his baby alligator, and younger brother Fred had nothing to go back to. The three had no choice but to do everything they could to join the Arc Project. The three of them worked incredibly hard to earn their own positions on the project as members. Once Herschel was on board, he knew there wasn't another partner he'd rather have than his young alligator. Fred joined the project and received a falcon as his partner. Of course, as time pressed on, the government transformed the Arc Project into the Wildlife Training Program or as we know it, the WT."

"Wow! Was the alligator strong like Dusty?"

Grandpa smiled. "Oh, yes, more than you know."

"So, how does the story end? Herschel and Fred got their animals, then what?"

"Well, they were placed into different divisions and sent to opposite ends of the country."

I sniffled and wiped my face. "Grandpa, what does that mean?"

"Divisions are categorized groups, groups that were designed to safely surround The Capital. The divisions that the government created are just like the ones we have today! There are Flyers over in East Ignacia with the Transferal Squad. Builders are placed in West Ignacia as the Construction Squad. Swimmers are placed up North in the Exploration Squad. Then, of course, there's the Hunters and Farmers in the Cultivation Squad."

"Where did Herschel and Fred go?"

"Herschel joined the Cultivation Squad and became a Hunter, while Fred joined the Transferal Squad and became a Flyer. However, they both trained very hard to grow and achieve a level of mastery until they were recruited by the top division, which were the ultimate protectors of Ignacia."

I yelled, "THE HERO REGIME! Oh, yeah! Just like Dad!"

"That's right, Justin, exactly like your father. That's where Herschel was lucky enough to work, to train, and went on to save thousands of animals and members alike. Herschel continued to grow until he became the top Hero and leader of the Hero Regime (HR). Henceforth he was called Herschel the Hero. He went on and built a life for himself, his alligator, and his brother. And they all lived happily ever after. The end."

I ran back to the dining room to retrieve one of my latest gifts. A bag of painted animal figurines. I pulled out an elephant. "So, if I want to join the WT, and I get an elephant for a partner—"

"You'd go to the Construction Squad in West Ignacia. However, Builders work around the clock with large mammals and reptiles. They're also made up of rhinos, large tortoises, and even gorillas."

I put the elephant back and pulled out an owl. "No, wait, maybe I'll have a great horned owl!"

"Well, Flyers are normally recognized for their wit, knowledge, and business orientation. They're transporters and notorious for traveling with imports and exports nationwide. Even though they're based in East Ignacia. But that may not–"

I put the owl back and fished out a beluga figurine. "I've always been good at swimming! Maybe I could have a beluga whale be my partner! That'd be amazing!"

Grandpa sighed to himself. "Just like your mother." Grandpa continued, "But if a WT member receives a fish, marine mammal, and or invertebrate from the ocean they will automatically be assigned to the Exploration Squad. Swimmers are generally stationed underwater in a variety of different submarines. The subs dock in the north port of Ignacia and are assigned to explore the remaining twenty percent of the ocean that has not yet been discovered."

"That's so cool! I can't wait! Grandpa, you're so smart. How did you learn all of this?"

Grandpa laughed. "Because, Justin, I, too, am a part of the WT. I was a Hunter in the Cultivation Squad. Half of the partnerships in that division are designed to hunt, while on the other side of the camp, trainers and partners are taught to tend to the farmlands in south Ignacia. They are called Farmers. The camp specializes in agriculture, botany, and medicinal herbs. Regardless, those who exhibit true strength and showcase an exemplary skill set as a pair can be recruited by the Hero Regime."

"Wow. That's going to be me! I'm going to be just like you and Dad!

"You will, Justin. One day we'll need your help protecting Ignacia and hunting down criminals who seek out to bring ruin to our newfound way of living. There have always been naysayers, but the AFA is different.

I stuttered, "The-the AF-FA?"

Grandpa spat on the ground. "The AFA is an organization built upon those who believe they are 'acting for animals.' That's their platform. When in reality, they just wish to return to the ways of the past. They have always wanted to return where we left off before the plague. No partnerships, no divisions. The AFA members don't want us to have lives with animals. They want to watch everything we've built collapse.

I placed the beluga figurine back and pulled out a white tiger and stood with determination. "I want a tiger! That way I can help Dad and be the new leader of the Hero Regime."

Grandpa laughed. "One day, it will be your turn, but be careful what you wish for. You wait, Justin. In a few years from now, you'll have what it takes to be a true leader. I'll make certain of it."

Shortly after, Grandpa revealed that his name was Herschel and that the story was all about him. Needless to say, I spent the next ten years trying to follow in his footsteps.

Only a select few in the world are recognized for their accomplishments: those who have impacted the country in such a positive way that others have no choice but to remember their names. Individuals that have made something greater of themselves by doing something significant and worthy with their lives. Many dream longingly to reach up and touch the stars, myself included. Too few are born into weightlessness and lack the ability to sail across the sky. Then there are those who are born with the power and resources to do pretty much whatever they want: I am nothing like those people.

I've waited my entire life to fill this internal void of loneliness. I've been jonesing for a chance to feel whole, to make a lasting bond with an animal of my own with whom I could potentially take on the world with. My parents and grandparents, leaders of the program, have told me stories of their relationships with their partners. It would be an honor to follow in their paths and have an animal partner of my own. I not only dreamed of it, but I had spent most of my life studying and preparing for it.

While my family was out living their lives and making names for themselves, I was working, stuck with homework or training in Grandpa's dojo. Friday, July 10, 3045, was the day I would turn eighteen. The day anyone was allowed to apply for the WT and attempt the application. I've been fortunate enough to do it all: saving money from delivering mail, facing off against my punching bag, and constantly studying my father's old animal anthology. It became more than a routine, it became my identity, and it was suffocating at times.

Joining the Hero Regime had been my dream for the past ten years. I've spent the majority of my time mastering my anthology, memorizing, and retaining everything about any and all animals. The more animals I could learn about, the stronger my future partner and I would become.

The date was Tuesday, July 7th, 3045, just three more days until my eighteenth birthday. My eyes started to open as the ceiling stared back at me. Today was a day to enjoy, one that allowed me to enjoy what was left of my summer vacation before I applied for the WT. That specific day was relatively important because Roxanne was going to show off her new WT partner at the park.

After throwing on a red WT t-shirt, black jeans, and black shoes, I scarfed down some leftover pizza Grandpa had made the night before. A secondary alarm started to vibrate from my phone. I checked my phone and saw it was already half past nine. A faint whisper emerged from my lips, "Shit."

Without a minute to lose, I threw on my pack, took a puff of my inhaler, and longboarded down the street to meet Rus and Roxanne. The rough and rugged roads made pedaling with urgency extremely difficult. Secretly, a part of me wanted to beat Rus there because Roxanne always made it a habit of being early. My right foot collided with the pavement while I maintained my balance on my left. Leaning forward and carefully positioning my feet on the board, I glided down the streets of the capitol with a comfortable yet smooth speed. Between the inconvenient traffic, vibrating bumpy roads, and the miles of Builders busy with construction, it took me half an hour before I arrived, resulting in tardiness.

A brief glimpse of Roxanne and Rus came across my line of sight as the two casually spoke to one another in the distance: the two watched other trainers and partners across the park. Roxanne was the mayor's daughter, and she was a quiet beauty that opened up most when she was around both of us. Rus and I met back in the early days of daycare. They were not our brightest days, but we found different ways to make the most of them.

For years Rus and I imagined we'd sail across the oceans of Ignacia, playing cops and robbers, and enjoying nap time all the same. A few years later we met Roxanne in grade school, where our lingering crushes on Roxanne first began; however, Rus was the only one who had the opportunity to date her. Roxanne and her new partner were both placed into the WT program the day prior. She was awarded a beautiful baby jaguar as her partner, and announced soon after his name was Diego.

Grandpa finished telling me the story of Roxanne's application exam results last night. He was raving about how overjoyed Roxanne was when she found out she'd been elected to the Cultivation Squad. Of course, she deserved her shot at joining the Hero Regime. She was positive, outgoing, and caring towards others. Roxanne was unlike anyone I'd ever met; she always saw the good in people and her perspective was a breath of fresh air. I always seemed to smile at the sight of her.

Russel yelled, "It's about time you showed up! What's up, JJ?"

I hopped off my green longboard to perform our well-rehearsed handshake. It was so strange, too: our birthdays were just one day apart. Once we learned that, we knew we were meant to be friends. Now we're newly-appointed friendly rivals, especially since our junior study courses.

Then again, Rus was always smarter in school and seemed to have the better grades. Rus's parents were both highly ranked Flyers, who traveled constantly. But they both always checked in and made sure Rus put his grades first.

"Look what the cat dragged in," I said.

"Hey, Diego, isn't just any cat: he's a jaguar!" Roxanne exclaimed.

I smiled and inspected the small jaguar cub lying next to Roxanne. He wore a small harness and thick, red leash. The harness read "Wildlife Training Do Not Pet!" A personalized harness was awarded to each new partner to showcase and allow any walkable animal into public spaces. Most newly partnered animals wore their harnesses until they received the off-leash certification. New animals weren't comfortable enough to go off leash until after a month or so.

Roxanne was sporting her new "Cultivation Squad" shamrock green uniform that read "JAGUAR" on the front and featured a black silhouette of a jaguar in the middle. She and Diego had both received partner patches, a man-made device designed to both physically and emotionally link the two wearers by synchronizing their vitals. I glanced around the multiple levels of the park and admired the different harnessed and unharnessed animals with their partner patches.

We noticed another classmate of ours quickly approaching us. He was sporting his newly appointed partner in the WT program as well. The kid's name was Todd Ramos, a student from Kilpatrick High. He and I were not particularly close. If anything, Todd was someone we did not wish to be seen with in public. His attitude was poor, and he was notorious for his black beanie and was always smoking something.

Todd took a puff of his electronic cigarette and announced himself, "Clear a path, ladies. Young crocodile coming through! And yes, Al does in fact bite."

Todd brushed me aside as he moseyed on by.

I met Todd during my early high school years. We even shared a variety of interests, which led us down a road to friendship. As time passed, however, we soon became mortal enemies. Everything I had, wore, or said was absorbed by Todd. He not only enveloped my style, but it seemed like he tried to become me. Since his father bought him anything he wanted, he never had to work a day in his life, and I didn't think he ever would. Todd walked his young crocodile on a similar harness as he sported his new shamrock green Cultivation Squad uniform. The design featured a silhouette outline of his reptile and above it read "CROCODILE."

A handful of graduated WT trainers looked over in the distance as Todd obnoxiously announced himself. The smoke from his vape pen seemed to upset the trainers and partners in the park. We were confused about how Todd was accepted into the Cultivation Squad in the first place. The nearby trainers attempted to calm down their partners until the smoke cleared. A lot of nearby trainers seemed to be working off leash behaviors with their partners.

Rus interjected, "Of course, Todd, we get it. You want space for you and your baby lizard? There's more than enough room here."

Todd took another puff, stopped in his tracks, and exhaled in Rus's face, "Looks like we've got Rustic Russel and his gang. Al and I have some training to do, so if you'd be so kind as to step aside?"

Rus stepped back and sarcastically bowed. Rus waved his hand grandly, courteously allowing him to pass, but just as Todd continued forward, I purposely stepped forward and blocked his path.

I smiled sarcastically, "Al was it? That's pretty funny."

Todd stopped in front of me, "What's funny?"

I laughed. "'Al' as in alligator? Only you would be smart enough to name a crocodile after an alligator."

Rus muttered under his breath, "And here we go."

Roxanne sighed and shook her head.

Todd took a puff and blew smoke in my face as he responded instantly, "Justin Steele. A worthier adversary. Especially with your dad as the big bad captain. You know that's big talk coming from a Steele. How long are you going to keep living in his shadow?"

I stepped closer, "As long as it takes to beat you."

We continued to stare into the black pits of each other's eyes, searching for a glimpse of self-doubt to exploit, but there was nothing. A faint hiss began to emerge from the mouth of his small crocodile. Todd was growing angry, and Al could feel it through his partner patch.

Todd smiled threateningly, "What's keeping me from letting him lose on you right now?"

Stepping closer I said, "Nothing. Go ahead and do it. I'm not going to stand here and let you push my friends around."

Al began to pull on his harness as he lunged forward aggressively attempting to bite my legs.

Rus stepped in and gently pushed Todd and me apart. He broke the tension, "Okay, let's not get carried away here. After all, we're in a park, and it's summer. Let's let what happened at school stay in school. Just leave the past in the past. Okay?" Rus always seemed to have my back with every difficult situation I faced.

Todd and I had our falling out two years ago. Afterward, he began a prank war, which included, but was not limited to, paint bombs, gas bombs, fart noises etc. I responded to his childish antics by turning his school supplies into gelatin. He did not take that lightly. Sometimes Todd went as far as creating animated cartoons of my father, undressed, and posted them around the school. For the past two years he'd attempted to humiliate me and my family every chance he could.

Roxanne chimed in, "Leave us alone, Todd. Save that sass for the Hunter's Camp."

Diego crouched low and steadily stalked Al, salivating at the thought of devouring him.

Todd acquiesced, "Another time, Steele. I'm interested to see what kind of partner you end up with anyhow. Or better yet, do us all a favor and stay at home with the suits."

Todd walked away with Al's leash in hand, smiling at his cocky comments.

Suits were members of society who did not make it into the WT program or chose not to. These interesting business-oriented individuals had to find another path in order to provide for themselves. Suits strictly conducted financial transactions to and for the Transferal Squad. Now most suits were recognized for their intellect, and use of psychology to get what they wanted for financial gain. According to Grandpa, all the suits really wanted was what they couldn't have: a partner and land to call their own. Suits were usually located in The Capital and East Ignacia.

Rus continued, “Such an odd dude, but it won’t be long now. Soon Justin and I will receive our own partners and join you, Roxanne. You wait and see. There’s a bald eagle in my future!”

Before all this commotion took place, I noticed a young woman sitting close by on a forest green park bench. I remembered her pale face well; her name was Laura Dean. She was top of her class at Kilpatrick High. Somebody I’d always admired from afar but never had the privilege or the courage to get to know. She graduated about three years ago and was awarded her whooping crane, Lilith, when she joined the WT. Lilith had grown exponentially and was almost unrecognizable: the large bird hunted for fish in a nearby pond. She successfully caught a large minnow, and flew back to Laura’s bench, watching as she read. Laura had been recruited by the Transferal Squad but wished to join the Cultivation Squad for a chance to join the Hero Regime. Newly admitted members always attempted to transfer; however, the process took months, sometimes years at a time to get approved which was precious time for the trainer to invest in their original division.

Rus pulled my attention back in. “What do you think you’ll get Friday?”

I smiled and shrugged. “I’m hoping for a big cat, but I’m not opposed to an alligator?”

Rus nodded. “Like father, like son.”

Roxanne scoffed. “I’m getting more of a clown fish energy from you. Oh wait! How about a praying mantis?”

Both Rus and Roxanne laughed as I rubbed my neck, trying not to blush. I contemplated my comeback, and that was when I first noticed something. I saw the way Roxanne looked up at Rus for a moment longer than usual. The two had this lingering chemistry since their relationship had ended. The two had dated briefly last year, but Rus broke it off to focus more on school.

Rus continued, “Whatever happens, we’ll make the most of it. No matter what. And, who knows, I may even walk out with a crystal claw of my own.”

I rolled my eyes in disbelief. "I'm pretty sure it doesn't work like that." I shrugged my shoulders. "Isn't it ... like a myth or something?"

Rus interrupted, "Justin, you've seen the photographs. The crystal claw is real. My grandfather, Jericho, and his flamingo were real!"

"Regardless of myths or memories, I look forward to working with both of you. I hope you both join us in the Cultivation Squad. It'll be crazy to think about what will come next," Roxanne charmingly concluded.

I asked, "Do you have your orders?"

Roxanne nodded. "Yep, we ship out for south Ignacia farmlands next Monday. Diego and I will have nine months to train, grow, and hunt before we have our chance to compete for a spot on the Hero Regime. I'm sure you both will be right behind me, as always."

I exhaled deeply. "Hopefully, but you never know. Truth be told, I haven't seen my pops in a while. Usually, it's just me and Grandpa. With criminals, meetings, traveling, press, it's an awesome time, according to Grandpa. You're just incredibly busy. It's crazy. I mean I'm thankful to have such a powerhouse of a family. It's just such a big shoe to fill. How am I supposed to live up to the hype?"

Rus grabbed my shoulder. "Hey, man, I know what you mean, but it'll all work out the way it's supposed to. I'll be right behind you on Saturday and complete the application myself."

Roxanne chimed in sarcastically, "We have too many birthdays to celebrate! Honestly, this is our chance to do something different and finally make a name for ourselves. I mean, we have no idea what waits for us 'out there,'" Roxanne muttered jokingly. "The members of the AFA are in for a rude awakening, right, Diego?"

Diego lifted his head from the ground, blinked twice, yawned, and laid his head down again. Rus and I laughed while Rus retorted, "You two may need to jumpstart that training."

I glanced around the park once more just as Laura Dean put away her book and rose from the bench. She carefully walked back toward the city with a somber energy. Her crane, Lilith, extended her wings before take-off and flew upward in an instant, following Laura from above, both smooth and in sync.

Lilith surveyed the area for any potential threats. There was an unspoken sense of trust and reliable nonverbal communication that spoke volumes about the two. Laura and Lilith had a palpable connection, one I've dreamt of having with a future animal partner. One of my greatest fears was that my partner and I wouldn't see eye to eye on matters or that they wouldn't like me.

Sometimes newly admitted members when awarded a new partner come out with two completely different wavelengths. The two must either find a way to proactively work together, or the animal would be returned, and the applicant would be forced to leave the program altogether.

There were a variety of trainers scattered throughout the park attempting to master different behaviors, skill sets, and adaptations for facing off against potential threats. Each pair wore their specific uniforms, sporting their squad and animal names. There was a gentleman near the pond wearing his blue uniform that read "Exploration Squad." He was training his Komodo dragon. The two were aggressively practicing in and out of water behaviors to transition from water combat to land combat. Mastering such a crucial maneuver, the sea-to-shore transition, can make the fatal difference in a fight against a potential enemy.

I watched this and became more inspired to jumpstart my dream of pursuing the Hero Regime. I spent the remainder of the day running around the park with Rus and Roxanne as we all attempted to help train Diego. We got lunch at a local food zomorodi parked alongside the national park. We reminisced about our glory days in high school. By the end of the day, Diego had finally warmed up to me.

Roxanne attempted to practice some simple behaviors with Diego, like responding to her call. For hours, she stood ten yards away from Diego, calling to him, "Diego, come here!" Diego appeared unamused and remained planted firmly on the ground. He suddenly heard the Komodo dragon swimming in the nearby pond. Diego lifted his head to see and sniffed the air, as he detected the lingering aroma radiating off the Komodo dragon. Roxanne glanced over to the pond and realized the potential worst-case scenario that could arise.

Roxanne muttered under her breath, which eventually turned into a yell, "Oh, no. Diego! Stop! STOP!"

I turned to look back. Instantly, Diego leaped into the small pond and swam toward the Komodo dragon. Before we knew it, Diego was attempting to take a bite out of the giant lizard. Both the Exploration Squad trainer and Roxanne leaped into the pond and pried the two apart. Once Roxanne removed Diego, Rus admitted sarcastically, "Well, uh, that's one way to learn his strengths–" Roxanne gasped for air. "And his weaknesses... like listening." Agitated, she carried Diego out of the pond and reattached the harness. She looked back and apologized to the trainer.

"Sorry!"

"Keep that jaguar of yours on a leash kid!"

"Will do, sorry again!"

I always enjoyed time with Rus and Roxanne. They always had a way of making me feel sane and valued. Unfortunately, the day had come to an end, and I safely boarded back home in time for overnight deliveries. Of course, I had hoped Grandpa was home so I could borrow his zomorodi. He'd just returned after a long day of making and breaking dreams for young people everywhere.

I walked inside the kitchen and found Grandpa sitting at the kitchen table watching the news.

"Can you believe this, Justin? What is Ignacia coming to? People are picketing in the streets naked, trying to get things done. I can't imagine getting anything done when everyone around you doesn't have any clothes on."

I laughed and waved at Dusty as he sat in the corner chewing on a set of cow ribs.

"Hi, Dusty! Grandpa, they're just trying to stand out, you know, send a message?"

"Mhm, if I was that guy I wouldn't want to stand out at all."

I shook my head and smiled. "I have to head to work and make some money. Have to save up more now to prepare to pay my own bills soon."

Grandpa lowered his glasses and stood. "Saving for what? Justin, the WT will provide you with everything you need."

"Not my own zomorodi."

"Well, wait until you're in my position and then they will. Just take things one day at a time."

I smirked. "I'm sure you said the same thing to Dad."

Herschel answered, jokingly, "I said a lot of things to your dad. Probably some that I shouldn't have."

I laughed and grabbed the keys to his vehicle, the 3046 black zomorodi with a red racing stripe along the left side. Zomorodis continued to grow over the past decade and have become the best form of transportation. Grandpa just happened to have the latest design in vehicular travel; he was lucky enough to be given one of the latest models. This slick vehicle traveled with a noiseless supercharged engine, air-powered hover drive, power drifting tires, and a dual suspension that made electric cars a thing of the past.

Grandpa called out, "Be careful working with those Flyers. Soon they might try to recruit you!"

"Oh, don't worry, they already have. I won't be working with them forever."

I waved goodbye and quickly changed shirts in the vehicle as I threw on my "IPS" work uniform and hat that read "Ignacia Postal Service."

I made my way into work half-awake, still tired from the night prior. I had stayed up studying the pros and cons of small reptiles. Each animal had its own power and its own skill set. A good trainer knew how to utilize each. Only a handful of trainers knew how to help any animal excel in order to reach its highest potential in any given situation. I happened to be related to two of them. I parked Grandpa's zomorodi, clocked in and checked in with Manny, my office manager.

"What's going on, Justin?"

Manny was a shorter gentleman dressed in a navy-blue button down and khaki pants with his small blue parakeet named Susan. The bird patiently sat on Manny's left shoulder as he worked in the office. He was a very comical, supportive, and respectful boss. He'd cut up with his coworkers and did his best to make the IPS a fun working environment.

I nodded my head and answered, "Hey, boss, I'm ready for another night on the town. What's the schedule look like tonight?"

"Just two for tonight. I've got one in East Ignacia and one downtown in The Capital. Take drone number five. It's fully charged and good to go."

I nodded. "Copy that. I'll get her back in one piece."

I carefully signed out the white headset and took it off from the charging unit of the break room. I walked through the halls, admiring offices, cubicles, and glass walls. I always enjoyed the view and found myself staring out into the city. The bright office lights dancing across the night sky left me speechless and in awe.

The Transferal Squad had a great set up with the IPS. The thought of potentially becoming a Flyer resonated in the back of my mind: traveling great distances, influencing positive work ethic, and taking part in professional business deals. Life seemed pretty great in the IPS.

Each night shift started off the same, a steep hike down to the assigned control rooms. The lucky number that evening just happened to cubicle number five. My fidgeting fingers opened the door as I switched on the fossilized vertical switch. In the center of the room sat a large computer monitor that was up and running. I took a seat in the grand white chair facing the monitor then fished the control gloves out of the charging stations. Once the gloves were synced to the chair, I plugged my headset into the computer to get a visual through the eyes of the drone. The long nights of training came back to me in a flash. I'd forgotten how long it took to land that job. Rus's parents had put in a good word for me, and I was fortunate enough to receive the position. The hours were nice, and the pay was phenomenal especially for a first job.

My gloves guided the drone to the loading dock while the factory hands loaded on two heavy packages. It certainly wasn't the maximum workload that the carrier was capable of withstanding. The drone was designed to be five feet in height, ranging about three feet in width. It came equipped with five mechanical attachments to latch onto packages and a propeller to safely fly over oncoming traffic.

Once both bulky packages were safely secured to the arm attachments, I ascended from the warehouse to take on the night. The grand chair came with headphones that each pilot could wear while delivering packages. Between deliveries I played smooth jazz music to help endure the evening. It was Grandpa's favorite music and it always seemed to help us both relax.

Usually, the smell of cardboard and sweat tended to overwhelm the scent of the headset, which reminded me of the stressful job at hand. I'd fly through the city just above traffic levels so that my drone deliveries were monitored by IPS and the police.

The police became the first integrated place of business in Ignacia. Members and nonmembers of the WT were selected or volunteered to serve with the police. It was full of fierce Hunters along with men and women who didn't have any animal partners at all. They worked together but were segregated by their own biases. It wasn't long until health care workers followed the trend and decided against joining the WT. Nurses and doctors spent so long working and caring for other patients that they didn't have the time or energy to care for a personal animal of their own. 20% of Ignacia was made up of individuals who didn't find a place in the WT, so they had to pave their own way in healthcare, business, or law enforcement.

The first stop was my largest box which seemed unbalanced as it hung off the first arm attachment. It was causing the drone to lean to the left ever so slightly to ensure the balance of the delivery. The mechanical pieces would shift back and forth even after maneuvering the package onto the drone. I'd always been bad with directions, so I had the system manually showcase bright red arrows inside the headset to direct me to the exact location. The guiding tool took me where I needed to go in the least amount of time. I arrived at my first stop, a beautiful, large-scale home in the hills of East Ignacia. I hesitantly flew over to the front door and began to gently descend. I safely removed the first set of attachments and laid the box in front of the door.

Just as I was about to return to the sky, the front door opened; a young man answered the door with a scarlet macaw on his left shoulder. He was a full-blown Flyer, white button-down shirt, and glasses. Very similar attire to my boss Manny. It appeared that he was having some form of business party or team building exercise with people awkwardly standing around in the background. I grabbed the microphone from my desk and pressed the red button on the side to access the mic. "Good evening, delivery from IPS. Nice Macaw!"

The man slightly smiled, nodded his head, picked up the package and said, "Thanks," in a quiet, polite manner.

I made my way back to the skies and began following the next set of red arrows in the system.

The people of Ignacia weren't always the most social beings, especially those enlisted in the WT program. Most members were so invested in their animal partner and the connection made between the two of them that everything else seemed obsolete. Members of the WT who were lucky enough to find a significant other were most likely in the program themselves and could relate to the amount of time it took to invest in their animal.

Even with the assistance of a partner patch, the energy and dedication required, in order to be fully in sync with an animal was tricky. The partner patch connected two sets of DNA from animal to human on an emotional, physical, and biological level. Both trainer and partner felt how the other was feeling at all times which made it easier to communicate and understand one another.

Some members spent their entire lives attempting to forge a strong bond with their animal. However, very few had the ability to achieve any real human relationship outside of their partner.

The sun had completely set, and rain was beginning to drizzle from the night sky. The next stop included three small boxes safely secured into one large box. Reportedly, it was from an online shopper. The directions were clear, to head downtown of The Capital past the crazy night life on a Saturday night. Of course, the benefit of flying a drone is that you could fly directly over traffic and not succumb to the dreary waiting game of a standstill. My goal was to quickly complete these deliveries so I could return home, and study more or maybe watch some TV, but I had to complete the task at hand. I continued forward, deep in thought, carefully maneuvering over the traffic.

Suddenly, I heard a loud yell, “Come on, let’s go!” from beneath.

Without warning, a tall, old school, black riot van bulldozed several zomorodis beneath me into a nearby building. The riot van clipped one of the arm attachments and sent my IPS drone spinning. The remaining package dropped on the side of the road alongside ongoing traffic.

Peripherally, I watched the van continue driving down the street unfazed by the devastation it had created. Once the spinning ceased, I stared in the middle of the road, breathing heavily, unsure whether or not I should pursue the van, collect the package, or wait until the police arrived. I began to hear loud honks from below as cars flashed their lights. Each person behind the devastation had collided into one another and sat in a standstill. Nobody was going anywhere until the police arrived.

In the meantime, I decided to survey the area to see if there were any survivors from the wreckage. A zomorodi had been decimated but revealed the shadow of a person inside. I could hear the EMT team sirens booming in the distance as the vehicle’s saving grace drew nearer. I didn’t want the driver to simply sit and possibly die alone. I decided to fly closer to the wreckage in an attempt to save the driver’s life. The concerned drivers who’d flashed their lights from behind started to step out of their vehicles to view the point of collision.

My drone drifted to the left side of the street toward the green zomorodi. The legal precautions on how to approach emergency situations like this rushed through my mind. For some reason, those rules were not going to stop me from checking to see if the passengers were safe.

When I arrived, I used the drone attachment hands to open the twisted vehicle door. A woman appeared to be lying on the steering wheel in the driver’s seat of the zomorodi. Scattered pieces of the vehicle’s shattered windshield glistened on the top of the dashboard. Glass covered the woman’s face and lap, as her face began to blur in the rain. She seemed unrecognizable from the wreckage.

A little dazed and confused myself, I decided to help the passenger and attempted to remove her from the vehicle. I carefully maneuvered the attachments under her arms and slowly pulled her out of the vehicle. The attachment arms were not designed to pick up a person, but with over a hundred hours of training under my belt, I wanted to try my best to get her out of the broken glass.

She had a partner patch on the right side of her arm, but I did not see any animal with her. The young woman was struggling to breathe as raindrops gently pushed the broken glass out of her face. I was just thankful that she was breathing.

I pressed the red button on my microphone and asked, "Hey, are you all right? Just keep breathing! Help is on the way, okay?"

Rain heavily poured down while blood trickled down the attachment arms of the drone. She remained unresponsive, and I was at a loss about what I should do.

Her nostrils moved steadily but with difficulty. Adrenaline continued pumping through my body. I cautiously maneuvered around the vehicle to get an accurate depiction of the zomorodi. Soon the EMT drivers arrived to pick her up from the scene. I heard the rescuers say that her breathing was weak, and she was unconscious. Her partner patch was beginning to blink.

Just as the EMT medics were making observations, a large bird touched down alongside the vehicle. The crane also seemed to have a partner patch on her right wing. It was difficult to see the crane in the severe rain, but I recognized them from the park. It was Lilith. Once the EMT drivers placed the woman on the stretcher and carried her inside the ambulance, the partner patch suddenly stopped flashing and fell off her arm.

I quietly asked, "Laura?"

The woman's patch bounced off the edge of the ambulance as they closed its doors and drove away. A low thunderous roar erupted from the night sky as the patch rolled on the ground toward the crane. Moments later the crane's partner patch disconnected from her wing. I was devastated by what I saw. The emotional and physical disconnection between a partner and a trainer. I gasped through my headpiece as my eyes began to water. This was not a good sign.

When a WT member or partner died and he or she was still connected to his or her partner, the patches awarded to the two would fall off almost simultaneously. Any and all connection between the member and his or her partner was disconnected, dissolved, and lost forever. Since there was no pulse or lifeline to connect the two, the patches became inoperative and disengaged themselves. Lilith took a final look back, expanded her wings, and ascended into the depths of the dark, stormy sky.

The drone propelled over traffic and loaded the last, poorly taped, box securely to my attachments, as drops of blood and rain ran down my mechanical arms. Usually loads were not this heavy, but the box became watered down as more rain continued. I decided to secure the package to the best of my ability and follow the red directional arrows. My eyes filled with tears of confusion and trauma as I pressed on to complete my final delivery.

It wasn't long until I sat flying over what appeared to be a closed, run-down bar. The old structure had no zomorodis, no customers and appeared to be in ruins. Hovering overhead, an "OPEN" sign sat pitch black in front of the cracked window. The thought of where to drop the box off confused me, but my directional arrows did not lie, and they pointed to that bar. A set of rusted double doors on the left side of the bar suddenly closed, so I assumed there was someone there who could assist. I nervously flew close enough to peer in through the grimy glass window.

A faint green light flickered on a table in the front of the bar. Without getting too close to be noticed, I saw two men, one large, bald man in a sleeveless black biker jacket while the other had a dark hood covering his face. There were no personal features that I could use to identify that shady character without getting closer. My fingers adjusted the volume up on my headset in hopes to pick up any noise or conversation between the two. The drone attachments eased open the door and quietly opened them without being detected. I entered the dimly lit room to drop the package off and leave, but I couldn't help but notice the massive set of claw marks alongside the hallway. An animal capable of strikes like that had to be big. It had to be both large and strong enough to slash through wooden walls. Something didn't seem right, and a part of me needed to know more. With the yellow button located on the side of my chair, I pressed it and activated the drone's stealth mode. The IPS installed this feature for the drone to project images from behind the drone to a screen in front of the machine. Instinctively, I decided to press the red record button as well and selected the video options from my controller. The two sinister voices seemed to be provocatively plotting some method of destruction.

The bald man spoke with a thick foreign accent, "We strike tomorrow. Cops are distracted, and the Regime will be too busy to intervene."

The hooded figure rejected the proposal. "Patience, Fedrov, our time will come, but it can't be tomorrow. It's not time yet. We're waiting for the miracle."

I zoomed in and began studying the two individuals—their heights, their width, their weight, anything I could use later to identify them. I was able to make out the bald gentleman's eye color without being seen. I knew almost for certain that the bald man was Artem Fedrov, one of Ignacia's most wanted war criminals from the AFA.

Suddenly, a large grizzly bear stumbled into the room carrying the wet package I had dropped off just moments ago.

Fedrov grinned. "Magnum, bring us the mail!" He gestured back to the hooded man. "The final piece of the puzzle has arrived. Though, I am surprised he didn't bring in the courier!" The massive grizzly took the package over and plopped it down in front of the two men. The wet box tore open, and three small boxes fell out. Fedrov kneeled down to pick up the boxes and placed them on the bar.

The hooded man looked to Fedrov. "Is this it? Inside here?"

Fedrov nodded, unloaded each box, and attached the three mechanical pieces together. "This is what Ronnie has been working on for the past month. It will play an important role in tomorrow's events. This is why it must be tomorrow!"

The hooded man spoke, "Listen, we removed the girl; that alone was too much noise." Fedrov reached below the table and with little effort tossed a bird carcass toward the gigantic bear. "We cannot afford for our plans to be revealed. She rejected our offer, and we do not take no for an answer. Such a pity. Laura would've been perfect."

Fedrov interjected, "Dinner time Magnum!" He peered back at the hooded man. "Let the kid try tomorrow. Let him show you what he has been training to do—"

"Laura!" I whispered.

They referenced Laura so callously, so angrily, I clenched my fists and, without hesitation, flew straight toward the hooded man. I wanted my mechanical arms to pin him down and rip his head off. The drone flew directly toward him but was stopped just inches away from revealing the hooded figure's identity. The man did not move or even flinch: a pair of jaws had stopped the drone in mid-flight. The same pair of jaws began crushing the drone, and broke the stealth mode projector, revealing the white, IPS branded drone.

The hooded man glared at the drone, as he began to recognize it. "Looks like we have ourselves a spy from the IPS."

Fedrov laughed. "Well, well, Magnum was in need of a new toy."

I heard a deep hissing sound coming from behind the hooded man as if something lay hidden in the shadows of the room. Fedrov grabbed the drone from Magnum's mouth and threw it to the floor. The drone landed alongside the bird carcass the hooded man had tossed aside. It was the same elegant crane that I'd seen earlier fly freely away into the clouds. The crane must've gone after her partner's killer.

Lilith's eyes remained rolled to the back of her head as death had consumed her.

Fedrov walked over, stared down at the drone, placed his face directly in front of the camera, and slyly snickered. "Next, we come for you. Bye-bye, little drone. Magnum, kill it."

The grizzly slowly stood on his back legs and slammed his front paws into the drone. The last thing I saw through my head piece was a giant set of Grizzly claws smashing the drone into pieces.

I pulled my headset off in a hurry and sat in my chair breathing heavily. The two men appeared to be more than criminals.

In reality, the two were AFA warlords who were plotting to destroy the peace that the WT had built. They were in possession of a homemade bomb or some other destructive weaponry.

Although I couldn't verify details about the hooded man, I recognized Artem Fedrov, one of the most heinous men in all of Ignacia, wanted for numerous crimes against humanity.

I peeled off my headset in shock. After a few minutes of trying to catch my breath, I stood up and walked with purpose back to the main office. I had failed in rescuing Lilith and Laura. I'd witnessed the traumatic separation of the two. That night was branded into my brain as one of the worst nights of my life. I tried to save them, even avenge them! But after ten years I still could not do anything to help. My drone had been destroyed by leaders of the AFA, and they were planning something. An evil act to decimate the WT program. Something else laid hidden on the horizon. And whatever they were planning, I had to run away and get out of sight.

I walked directly to Manny's office, placed my headset and IPS uniform on his desk, and said, emotionally exhausted, "I quit."

CHAPTER 2

Facing Fears

"Wait!" Manny shouted frantically as I turned to leave his office. "Wait, Justin!" He was almost running after me as I reached for the office doorknob.

When I turned around, Manny caught up to me and saw the peaky redness that blasted through my flushed face.

Manny continued, "I can't lose you. We're already short staffed as it is! What happened in there?"

"Artem Fedrov happened. Call the police. Everything you need is recorded in the chair. I'm sorry, Manny, something's happened, he's coming here, and I've got to get away."

"I'll call the cops, but they're going to want a statement. You can't leave now."

"Watch me."

I continued out the door to Grandpa's vehicle and navigated home. I was in shock from the amount of loss and death I'd just experienced. These two men were frighteningly different than anything I'd ever seen. They were another league of beings I'd heard horror stories about them throughout my childhood.

I parked the zomorodi and ran inside to tell Grandpa what I'd encountered. To my surprise, he was in front of the TV sleeping soundly and knocked out on his leather recliner. One of his favorite old late-night talk shows was playing as he slept. The fresh emotional trauma I'd just experience remained in my mind but made me feel powerless. I really needed to talk with him about what I'd seen, and I needed him to tell me that it would be okay. But instead of ruining his night, I went to bed with hopes of catching him up in the morning.

I sat at my desk, switched on my elephant desk lamp, and looked through the animal anthology my father bought me for my fifteenth birthday. My fingers forcefully flipped to the "Grizzly bear" section in the large book:

"Ursus arctos horribilis:

- Grizzly bears have the diet of an omnivore, allowing the animal to survive on both meat and vegetation.
- The average height of a grizzly bear is between four and eight feet.
- The largest grizzly bears are known as 'big browns' and can reach up to fifteen hundred pounds in weight.
- Adult grizzlies can run up to a maximum speed of forty miles per hour and can maintain that speed for two miles."

The thought of redirecting my focus seemed like a safe route to take. In hopes that studying would help get my mind off of things, but just as a field mouse escapes the clutches of a barn owl, I remained petrified and afraid of what could've happened. The thought of being in the same room with Fedrov and his Grizzly terrified me. I stepped away from my desk, slumped into bed and pulled the covers over my head.

"Just go to sleep. Please just go to sleep," I whispered to myself.

My eyes closed as I slowly began to drift, and suddenly a warm glaze of light fluttered over my face. When my eyes opened, I was greeted by a small bright ball of light that was circling me. The ball floated gracefully around me like a butterfly selecting a flower. It gravitated toward me with a sincere approach as it fluttered down on my right arm. It refused to linger for long and decided to gravitate toward the distant darkness.

Once my feet were on the ground, I found myself outside the same bar I escaped from just hours ago. The light floated toward the bar without a care in the world. Somehow, I felt responsible for this naïve ball of light and decided to run after it. Every ounce of my being would not allow this pure light to be tainted by the darkness that lay within. Without a second thought, I bolted after it, desperately reaching for it, but the light slowly faded into the set of double doors in the alley. My feet began to slide as I forced myself to stop before slamming my face into the doors.

The doors violently swung open, colliding with my face. The impact sent me flying back into the brick alley wall. I slowly stumbled to my feet, leaning against the wall for support. I blinked repeatedly, trying to figure out what stood before me. A monstrous entity fused with darkness reared over me. Its eyes were blood red as it bared its sharp fangs and let out a daunting roar. The creature stood ten feet tall on its hind legs with its bloodthirsty eyes locked on me. I quickly cowered and protectively raised my hands before me in fear of what appeared to be an enraged Grizzly.

I hesitantly glanced down to witness the same ball of light reemerge from my chest as it started to multiply in size. The light urgently grew and somehow took the shape of a giant grizzly bear. The bright bear outshined the dark Grizzly and stopped the darkness from bleeding out of the bar. The two entities stood tall, proud, and ready to die in attempts to destroy the other.

Both roared vigorously at one another. One chose to cause harm with hopes of destroying any threats while the other chose to protect and defend the innocent. The two lunged at one another as I fearfully cradled my face in my hands, attempting to hide from the great battle that lay within.

My eyes snapped open as I awoke to find myself in bed. I forced my body up from my lavender-scented pillows and attempted to catch my breath. A cold strand of sweat dripped down my nose and into my mouth. The salty aftertaste of confusion clouded my mind as to how I should address the events from the night prior. I felt conflicted and powerless. The events from last night had followed me into my dreams, creating a nightmare far more frightening than the actual event. I should've done more—I don't know what, but something else, anything. I should have called my dad immediately. Instead, I just came home and went to bed. What else could have been done? It wasn't my fault or my responsibility. I'm a delivery boy. Or at least, I was. Who am I to do anything now?

My hands sat glued to my face before reaching for my phone for the time, the phone illuminated "5:48 a.m.". I needed to get some air: The answers I needed would not be found on my bedroom ceiling. Those answers remained outside in the depths of The Capital.

The top half of my body had every intention to leave the bed, in hopes the morning numbness would quickly dissipate. But once I rose to my feet, I quickly discovered that I had unknowingly entangled my feet within my bed sheets, causing me to flop down on the white carpeted floor. Without warning, my face kissed the freshly vacuumed carpet beneath me.

My body sank into the floor. "Ow." A sad and confused sigh seeped from my lips. "I need to run."

I pushed myself up off the floor and decided to start my morning. After I threw on some running gear, slunk downstairs to the kitchen and ate a bowl of oatmeal with slices of banana. Followed by brushing my teeth and trying to feel somewhat put together.

After forcibly fitting each foot into their selected shoe, I started down the narrow driveway. The insatiable urge to run overcame me as I ran harder and faster. Nothing around me made sense and I wasn't really sure what to do with myself. I needed answers on how and why I did nothing about last night. Not to mention Laura and the haunting images of her unrecognizable face. Or the sight of Lilith's dead body on the floor before me.

I should've just carried on with my night. Picked up the box off the road and left it to the authorities. Why couldn't I just leave the box outside of the bar? Now I know those two men are up to something, and I should be the one to stop them. But how? What could I do?

It wasn't long before my quick pace brought me into the city. My feet lead me past the Builders, past the rhinos assisting the ironworkers erecting large building frames. The fabricated idea in my mind allowed me to increase my speed. It was the thought of moving with a similar sense of urgency that a normal trainer would. I wanted to prove that I had the mental and physical ability to be enough. Now, too, I had to run past the events of last night, if I could, or run until I couldn't think of them anymore.

Animals and trainers walked hand in hand, arm in arm and side by side throughout the city while I gripped my phone fearfully, suffering the internal struggle of self-doubt and self-loathing. Grandpa had Dusty, my father had Shadow, and my mother had her hands full with the Exploration Squad. But who did I have?

On top of everything, there was still one overwhelming question that bothered me. "Is this how we're supposed to feel without partners?"

After four miles of jogging and jumping through streets, back alleys, and shortcuts throughout the city, my body began to slow down. I had no choice but to walk and catch my breath. That was when my eyes peered over my left shoulder as I found myself outside the county courthouse.

My feet immediately stopped in their tracks at the sight of the towering white staircase. I caught myself staring at it longingly, awaiting and cherishing the day that would change everything: the day of the application exam into the WT. A subtle feeling of unworthiness overcame me as I made my way up the spotless staircase. My body stopped midway through the climb, and I turned around to redirect my focus on the city. Out of the corner of my eye was a tall figure that stood over me on the top of the stairs.

A familiar voice called out from behind me, "Justin, is that you?"

The sound of his voice was familiar and after a moment, I remembered the last time I heard it. It'd been over seven months since we last spoke. I knew exactly who the tall man was. My head hesitantly turned over my right shoulder, exhaled, and responded, "Hey, Dad."

My father angelically descended the courthouse stairs as I stood sweating through my gray hoodie with my entire body tinted red from the heat. He was sporting his new red and white Hero Regime uniform that read "LION" with a silhouette of a male lion. Each shoulder featured patches with his concentrations, "Cultivation Squad" "Level 1000" and "Hero Regime," all in gold lettering.

"What're you doing here?"

"We had another case this morning. Had to make sure we locked away another villain."

We spoke awkwardly trying to ignore the obvious fact that we never saw one another.

I hesitantly asked, "Oh. So, what'd they do?"

"Another incident of prying off partner patches."

"Seems to be a more common occurrence each day. How's Mom?" I nodded respectively.

He leaned on the handrail. "Yeah, Teresa is good, hanging in there. Her beluga, Shelly, is doing well."

"Mm... My birthday is tomorrow." I wishfully tested his memory.

He gave me a discerning look and raised two fingers. "Two more days isn't it? But you're celebrating tonight, aren't you?"

It was difficult to face him directly. "Just testing you. Should be fun. Roxanne and Rus will both be there."

"Maybe I'll stop by. How's Grandpa treating you?"

My eyes skated across the tall buildings within the city. "He's good. Same old guy making Ignacia a better place for animals and people alike."

The memory of the last time I saw my father was faint and blurry. The rare event took place about seven months prior. He'd stopped by Grandpa's house around 8 p.m. Christmas Day to drop off a present. He handed me a red gift bag, and I thankfully accepted it. I pulled back the green tissue paper and inside were his original red and black training gloves that he'd used during his days in the Hunter's Camp of the Cultivation Squad. He'd used them for numerous years. He trained with them and sported the gloves in adventures, challenges, and defeated many opponents.

Once he received his updated captain's uniform, he had no use for his outdated gloves anymore. They had been sitting on a shelf in my bedroom ever since.

He looked over at me regretfully. "You know growing up I wanted to be just like him."

I smiled. "You are. You and Grandpa actually have a lot in common."

"Sometimes. Sometimes, I try to be better," he responded condescendingly,

I hesitantly asked, "Dad, do you ever struggle with fighting off the darkness?"

"Are we talking about the AFA? Or something else, inside?" He pointed to his heart.

"Don't we all have light and dark inside us?"

"Yes, I suppose so."

"How do you fight off your darkness?"

"Sometimes, when I struggle with dark thoughts, and they get the better of me, I remember the first time I held Shadow."

A giant male lion made a brief grunt from atop the staircase, as Shadow confidently descended to Noah's side.

"How could you not? He makes you strong," I jealously responded.

"Yes, but it didn't start out that way..."

"Dad, last night, something happened. While I was out making deliveries..."

"Like what?"

"It was my last stop with the drone. It was at this run-down bar downtown off West Twenty-Fourth Street. I thought it was closed, but then I heard a noise, so I followed it with the delivery drone. Inside I saw two men. One of them had a hood up, but the other was Artem Fedrov."

"You saw Fedrov!" Noah yelled, both shocked and angry. "Wait, Justin, what did you deliver?"

"I don't know! I was just delivering a package and the next thing I knew—"

Shadow lifted his head and began sniffing the air. His ears shifted backward as he looked out into the city and began to growl.

"Justin, get up the stairs. We have to get you some—"

A sudden flash blasted past me just missing my face. The blast collided with the courthouse stairs, sending large fragments of cement through the air. The pressure alone from the missed shot sent me flying backward, causing me to slam into the white handrails.

We heard a voice in the distance making a sinister chuckle. People and animals in the nearby streets began running away, yelling for help while trying to avoid the two figures. A tall man in a black mask and black suit walked alongside what appeared to be a fully-grown, white liger, one of the animal kingdom's powerhouse crossbreeds of a lion and tiger.

The two casually walked down Main Street toward the county courthouse. The large animal wore sharp, black, metallic armor to defend itself. My father, Noah, rushed over to check on me. I looked up to see the dark figure approaching us. Noah stepped in front of me to face the enemy and remained close by ready to defend me.

The man in black spoke into his earpiece, "Phase One is complete. Engaging with Light Bearer." The man raised his hands and started to yell, "Hear me now, Light Bearer! The great, Noah Steele! You will remember the name Podidae! The man who attempted to revolutionize—"

"Who?" Noah annoyingly interjected.

"Podidae. The man with the—"

"Oh yes, yes, that's right! Guy had a thing for armadillos?" Noah interrupted.

"Leprosy. The sickness they carry, a virus that can and will destroy the very structure you've given so much to protect."

"Podidae went to jail, and if you're looking for a fight, so will you."

"Ha! I don't plan on seeing dear old Dad anytime soon," the man in black snickered.

Noah realized who the man was and stepped forward, "You were there when I stopped him. Listen, you don't have to go about trying to pick a fight in the street. You were just a boy. We can talk about this."

"No! That boy is dead." The man in black raised his hands and proclaimed, "I am Zeus. This is my partner Aries. We're here to resurrect Podidae's plan and get things back on track. Let's see what you can do in the next five minutes." Zeus pulled out a detonator to activate. He turned a key in the side of the remote and pushed a button to begin the five-minute countdown until detonation.

"We'll see about that." Noah turned back to face me. "Justin, get out of here. Shadow, on me."

Noah and Shadow both ran toward the two figures with ferocity in their eyes. He pressed his fingers into his wrists, activating his white, indestructible, forearm protectors. My father rushed towards Zeus as Shadow began circling the large liger, looking for an opening. Zeus pocketed the detonator and pulled out two katana blades, calculatingly slicing at Noah who blocked each strike.

Almost simultaneously, Shadow jumped on top of Aries, clawing at him, trying to locate a weak point. The armored beast remained undamaged as he grabbed Shadow with his paws and threw him off his back. Shadow flipped forward for an aerial recovery and landed on his feet. Aries roared loudly and cautiously paced around Shadow. As the liger readied for another attack, arms ferociously outstretched, he revealed a slight opening in his armor. The open fur was exposed on Aries' neck and chest, giving Shadow a slim chance of connecting a deadly blow.

Noah spoke into his earpiece, "Calling all HR members. We need backup outside the courthouse. We have a four twenty-two in progress. Armed and dangerous trainer with an armored liger partner. Response team, please report."

A quick response came over his earpiece, "No luck, sir! Handling a dangerous situation right now in sector three. A Builder's crane is going out of control. Tee minus twenty minutes for support."

"We need assistance now!" Noah yelled back. "There's a bomb hidden nearby. Expedite response!" He redirected his frustration towards me. "Justin, get moving! Check the surrounding area for the bomb."

I immediately jumped up and sprinted toward the next street over to search where the two had originated from. I crossed the first building just as Zeus peered over into the distance and his eyes found mine. Zeus immediately lunged after me, attempting to cut me off at the entrance of a nearby alleyway.

Noah saw Zeus's point of focus change and chased after him. I cut left into the next alleyway where I came across a similar looking box that I had delivered last night, sitting in the middle of a brown picketed fence in the alley. Zeus ran toward me. He suddenly appeared around the corner and was closing in on my location. I tried to turn around and face him, but my body gave out from the excessive running that morning.

I got a muscle spasm in my left thigh and dropped to the ground in pain. My leg tightened and squeezed the remaining air out of me. Zeus had finally reached me and was just a few feet away. He raised his swords high, ready to strike. I stared into the red crevices of his black mask as fear consumed me. My hands came together as I prayed and hoped that whatever happened next would be quick and painless. I blinked and moved my hands up in attempts to defend myself.

Out of the corner of my eye, I saw my father launch himself towards Zeus's back. My father's partner patch began to glow a bright red as he made direct contact with Zeus's spine. Dad sent Zeus out of the alleyway and into a nearby building. Noah gracefully landed in front of me.

My father offered me his hand. "Are you all right?" I nodded and slowly tried to stretch out my left leg until I forced myself to stand.

"Muscle spasm."

"Oh, that's all? Thought you may have lost your balance." My father smirked and patted me on the back. He noticed the package. "There it is huh?" he said and pointed toward the fence.

"It's just like the package I delivered. Is this what Zeus was trying to keep us away from?"

We unwrapped the package and found a large black briefcase inside. Noah pushed me behind him while he cautiously lifted the latches of the briefcase. Inside lay a variety of colored wires, and three mechanical attachments interconnected to a giant valve of what I assumed to be toxins. A large beeping timer counted down with four minutes and twenty-two seconds remaining. It looked like something out of an old spy movie.

Noah spoke before I could say anything. "All right, Podidae had a similar setup. The toxin is designed to short circuit all partner patches, solely destroying the bonds established for any trainer and partner nearby. He discovered that leprosy was the only virus that could destroy an animal to trainer connection from inside the partner patches. It also had a tendency to kill the user, so that was not ideal. Last time we drowned this sucker in the ocean; thus, the toxin never saw the light of day. Justin, bring this to the pond in front of the courthouse. It's deep enough so it should suffice."

"I'm on it."

"Are you sure? I don't want you cramping up—"

Before I could move, in the blink of an eye, Zeus reappeared in front of my father screaming,

"LIGHT BEARER!"

My father raised his right arm and activated his forearm protector. Again, he'd managed to stop both blades with just one hand. He barely moved a muscle while somehow deflecting the entire attack.

Then, masterfully calm, he asked, "Tell me. When you volunteered for this mission, did you think you would make it this far?"

"Maybe not. But we knew we could take you or your partner," Zeus smirked.

In the distance, a brief roar of pain echoed in the alleyway. My father paused briefly, pushed Zeus's swords off his protector and lunged forward, reaching for Zeus's throat. Without hesitation, my father gripped him with his left hand. Steadily tightening his grip more and more until Zeus' throat closed. Zeus began fighting back, hammering his fists on my father's forearm. Noah slammed Zeus's head into the wall and sprinted back to the courthouse. Zeus appeared unconscious and out of commission.

"Shadow, I'm coming! Justin, get that thing to the fountain!"

Noah started running faster and faster until he was out of my line of vision. I immediately picked up the briefcase and ran after him. Once I rounded the corner of the alleyway I saw Shadow lying on the ground facing Aries, struggling to move, let alone stand. Shadow had lacerations and bite marks scattered from his forelegs to his tail.

Aries raised his head high and roared loudly. The liger looked down on Shadow as he began to pounce from his back two legs. Aries was preparing for his final blow. Shadow accepted defeat and closed his eyes; he murmured softly as if it was his last. Noah slammed his left hand on top of his partner patch on his right shoulder. His legs moved like lightning and somehow made it between the two just in the nick of time.

My father stood his ground and raised his right fist, yelling, "Now let our strength combine. Get away from him! RIGHT NOOOARRR!"

It sounded as if Shadow's roar had come out of my father's own mouth. Noah's right fist drove directly into the same empty mid-section between Aries' armor powerfully thrusting the liger to the ground.

The liger struggled to breathe but started to move once more, rising on all four legs. The liger coughed up blood, gave a deadly glare, and growled at Noah as he bared his teeth. Noah was breathing heavily, sweating profusely, and Shadow was struggling to move. Zeus re-emerged from behind a nearby alleyway and continued limping toward my father with all of his remaining strength. I was getting closer to the pond while Zeus and Aries began to circle Noah and Shadow. A burst of adrenaline shot into my bloodstream while a look of fear began to form behind my eyes. I chucked the briefcase into the middle of the pond and continued sprinting toward the ongoing chaos just twenty-five yards away from me.

"NOW, ARIES. FINISH HIM!

The two darkened criminals closed in on their prey, while Zeus brandished his swords, drawing both blades toward my father's head. His partner, Aries, pounced forward, raising both sets of claws, bearing down on my father with all their combined weight. The leader of the Hero Regime instinctively activated his forearm protectors to block both deadly attacks.

Noah successfully parried the katanas but could not withstand the liger's strike. His arms trembled as the massive claws tore through his forearm, blood began trickling down onto the black pavement, while he caught sight of me fearfully running towards him in the distance.

"Justin, stay back!" my father yelled out.

I forced myself to run harder, closing the gap between us with every stride. Only a few yards remained before I reached the harrowing scene. The years of striving to make an impact on Grandpa's punching bag plagued my mind like a whisper of doubt. That's when it dawned on me, the haunting still frames from my nightmare were coming to life. But now wasn't the time for fear; it was time to fight. I could hear Grandpa Herschel's teachings echoing in my head as he coached me with intensity: 'Plant your feet. Find the strength inside. Put your heart in your fist. Don't just strike a heavy blow. Strike fear into your opponent and finish them!'

For a brief moment, I blinked and uncovered the same light from my dream. My eyes closed again for a split second, and I witnessed the bright illumination radiating from my clenched fist. I dug my feet into the road, drew in a deep breath, pulled my right arm back, and opened my eyes as I channeled every ounce of strength I had into Zeus's face.

"STOP IT!" I shouted at my enemy.

The impact successfully landed between Zeus's eyes. The impact alone sent him skidding backward ten yards across the pavement. The pain in my right hand was instant and began to grow, and the fear of facing a liger became my reality. I slowly glanced over just in the nick of time to witness an alligator dig his jaws into Aries's armored skull. I let out a deep sigh of relief when I saw Grandpa in the background standing on the Courthouse steps.

His alligator, Dusty, grabbed Aries's giant skull in his mouth and began to roll his body. The liger pulled away from Noah and scratched at the old, giant alligator.

Grandpa pressed his partner patch on his right shoulder and muttered, "Use my strength, old friend, and finish this."

Dusty's eyes began to glow as he withstood the scratches from Aries. Dusty's teeth suddenly changed color and shined with bright, metallic, steel-pointed edges. He tightened his grip onto Aries' skull until the liger lost consciousness from the pain. The bright red lights on Noah and Shadow's partner patches stopped blinking as the fight subsided.

Partner patches started to glow when a trainer's heart rate rose above one hundred and thirty beats per minute. This might have been caused by a challenge, training, or just working alongside your partner. When a trainer's heart rate returned to the lower rate of seventy beats per minute, the light on the partner patch began to fade.

Noah fell to the ground breathing heavily as I collapsed on the city's hot pavement. Zomorodis stopped in the road to witness the chaos. Grandpa hurriedly made his way down the courthouse staircase to assist me and Noah. I pushed myself to stand and limped over to help my father. My leg was immensely sore from sprinting with a muscle spasm. Dad raised his head and held his right arm still as he applied pressure to stop the bleeding.

"Where did you learn to hit like that?" Noah asked tiredly.

"Training with Grandpa."

"I guess you've got fists of steel," he said with a hint of pride.

"Just like a Steele," I boasted.

Noah started to stand just as Grandpa arrived. "Not a bad way to start the day. Well done, boys."

"I had him on the ropes." Noah breathed heavily.

"Seems to me it was Justin here who got the winning blow."

"Yes, he did," Noah replied proudly. "I suppose paramedics will be here soon."

"I've already called the police." Grandpa was always extremely thorough, especially when it came to covering the bases of a crime scene.

"But, Dad, you'll be there for dinner tonight?" I asked.

Grandpa and my father examined one another. The two shared a brief conversation with their eyes.

Grandpa sighed, walked over, as he placed his hand on my shoulder. "Justin, I'm not sure if your father will have time in his busy schedule to—"

"I've got time," Dad interjected. "Why not? I'll bring the Cold Goose."

Grandpa nodded. "I think it may be time for Justin to have his first round of Cold Goose. All right then it's settled. Dinner tonight at seven."

The paramedics, police, and members of the Hero Regime finally arrived shortly after to stitch up my father and Shadow while the authorities arrested Zeus and Aries. We still did not know where the two had come from. There were many questions and very few answers. What purpose did the plan serve? What was the real motive? I thoroughly explained to both Noah and Grandpa the events that occurred from the night prior. The two overreacted and yelled at me for venturing into dangerous territory alone and for quitting my job. Still, we decided to pile into Grandpa's zomorodi and visit the very same closed-down bar. We parked in the parking lot right outside the bar.

We exited the vehicle and cautiously approached the bar door. "HELLOOO?" Grandpa Herschel yelled.

My father back-handed Grandpa's shoulder. "What the heck was that for? You gave away our position! You've been out of the game too long, Pops."

Grandpa scratched his head and shrugged while the five of us proceeded through the front door of the bar. The lights were out, and it was pure black inside. Dad pulled out his phone and shined the flashlight from it. Dusty wiggled his way through the space while Shadow lowered his nose to the floor to smell the room. I followed and brought up the rear while the two top WT members led the way to locate any clues.

After a thorough sweep of the entire bar, the only thing we could locate was a dimly lit cigar. Grandpa walked through the double doors and discovered the remnants of my drone.

"They knew we were coming," Noah exclaimed angrily. "This was all planned, but I don't think they planned on Justin's drone."

"What are we searching for exactly?" I asked.

Noah sighed heavily. "Most of these drones come equipped with a camera that continues recording even after it is destroyed. Let me check this pile of rubble."

"Dad, all the footage has already been saved and submitted to the police. There's nothing left."

Noah examined the leftover remnants and located the memory slot where the disc lived, but he was unable to find a disc inside. He exhaled deeply. "Damnit. The memory card was removed."

"Now what do we do, Dad? There's no more proof!"

My father glanced over at me. "Now we wait. Wait for them to drop the ball again." Dad paused and fixated on the corner of the room and found a black horseshoe on the floor. He shined his light on the floor to reveal faint hoof tracks. "Justin, you said it was Fedrov and a hooded man, right?

"Yeah. Why?"

He lifted the horseshoe from the dirt. "Because this was no regular hooded man. This was the Dark Trainer."

The Dark Trainer was the leader of the AFA, the mastermind solely bent on taking down the WT. He planned and recruited criminals for decades. He's waited for the opportune moment to strike back and reclaim society. He believed if he abolished the WT, animals and humans could learn to create "true" and "natural" bonds instead of relying solely on partner patches. However, if we released animals and abolished the program, our natural ecosystems would fall into chaos.

We were taught in school that the Hunters of the Cultivation Squad were solely responsible for slowly rebuilding ecosystems. If we dropped the WT, everything would be undone, trainers wouldn't have jobs and society would crumble. The Dark Trainer had made death threats, bomb threats, financial demands and somehow remained undetected for years. He believed his voice was the sole voice of Ignacia and should be taken seriously. The Dark Trainer has been the most wanted criminal in Ignacia for almost thirty years. This trainer was the one responsible for killing Rus's grandfather, Jericho, and removing the last crystal claw.

Rus's grandfather Jericho was the last known crystal claw trainer. Jericho became the acting captain for the Hero Regime for fifteen years. In his later years, he achieved continuous high-ranking success. Supposedly, he was given a baby flamingo when he joined the WT program back when the program was transitioned from the Arc Project task force. The baby bird had a bright shiny crystallized foot. It was that same small flamingo that would go on to transform into some of the strongest and largest animals on the planet. The stories say his flamingo could transform into any and all animals. His partner served and protected him well, which helped Jericho receive the title of captain of The Hero Regime. Grandpa became his protégé and trained under him for many years. After Jericho passed, Herschel seemed like the only noteworthy candidate to follow.

With the two removed from power, the AFA had an opportunity to take down the WT. They did not, however, plan on the fighting force of the Cultivation Squad. Grandpa stepped up to the plate and challenged the Dark Trainer on several occasions. However, the Dark Trainer seemed to slip away and constantly avoid capture.

"Let's take a closer look here," Grandpa investigated the hoof prints more closely.

"Pops, focus on the hoof width. See how the print showcases those thick wall lines? Where else are you going to find that deep of an indentation at the tip?"

"Noah, even if it is him, we can't bring Justin into this. Not yet. He must be approved into the program first. Let's discuss more later."

"Fine. Between the HR and the police, we'll have it taken care of." Dad pulled out his phone and continued to take photos for evidence. After a couple of photos, Noah called the Hero Regime and the police for back up. Both teams sent patrolling officers shortly after to investigate the crime scene further and locate any more potential evidence of Fedrov and the Dark Trainer.

"You guys go on ahead," my father called out before Grandpa, Dusty, and I left. "I have to stay put until more members arrive to assist with the investigation. I'll meet you both at your place tonight."

I mustered a smile, somewhat happy to have had the opportunity to get these two in the same room again for a meal.

"Just bring the Cold Goose, all right?" Grandpa yelled back. "Don't forget. Seven o' clock!"

We climbed into Grandpa's zomorodi and tiredly closed the door with deep sighs.

"AC on high," I muttered to the zomorodi.

The vehicle turned the air conditioning on at the maximum level, outputting the cool air needed to waft the taste of victory out of our mouths. Dusty sat in the back, while Grandpa tossed him an uncooked steak from his black feeding pack. I rested my head back and closed my eyes, remembering the impact my fist made into Zeus's face. I rubbed my right fist with my left hand, feeling the painful skin splits from the hit. The joints and muscles inside my fist had turned purple, exhibiting broken blood vessels.

Grandpa whispered, "You broke his nose you know."

"I thought he was going to die."

"Who?"

"My father."

"Noah is one of the toughest fighters this country has ever seen. He would've been fine. But you."

"What about me?"

"It was incredibly foolish. What were you thinking!?"

"I guess I wasn't."

"What would've happened if Dusty hadn't been there? A fully-grown liger would've eaten you with a smile on its face."

"Probably."

"I didn't raise you to be cat food, Justin. You're meant for so much more."

"Like dog food?"

"Yes, like dog food." I smiled inwardly, but it slowly appeared outwardly on my face.

We continued our drive and eventually pulled back into our narrow driveway. Grandpa called the WT headquarters and reported the matter was a "family emergency." Needless to say, he was able to take the rest of the day off. He began decorating the kitchen and dining room, all while cooking tonight's dinner. He had a way of making everything look so easy and elegant, while I trudged up the staircase to my room to shower. I spent the remainder of the day exhausted forcing myself to read more of my animal anthology. I hurriedly flipped through the book to the section on ligers:

"Panthera leo x Panthera tigris:

- Ligers are created when a male lion breeds with a female tiger.
- They are called liger or ligress.
- This animal inherits a love for swimming from its mother as well as a variety of faint stripes on its body.
- A typical adult liger's height averages four and a half feet and weighs anywhere from seven hundred to twelve hundred pounds.
- A fit liger can reach up to speeds of fifty miles per hour, making this animal a deadly combination of speed and power.
- Most ligers only live a lifespan of thirteen to eighteen years."

I continued fighting my body and trying not to fall asleep. My willpower prevailed and allowed me to evade the same nightmare from last night. I thankfully remembered that I had two of the strongest leaders in the WT protecting me. Luckily, I was able to fixate my mind elsewhere, like remembering my friends would arrive in just a few hours. I also remembered that my father had a notorious habit of promising to be somewhere and breaking his promises, which was somewhat understandable. I mean, it came with the job. I suppose he received a pass since he's one of the leading protectors of the country. Regardless, I tried to allow myself to relax and let the night unfold naturally.

I pulled out the new black, fitted suit Grandpa had ordered for me for my birthday. The slick suit came with a black button-down shirt that shined with each ray of light that beamed over it. My getup came with black dress pants and black dress shoes to match. I assumed I wouldn't get another opportunity to celebrate with my dad, so I wanted to dress the part of someone who was worth celebrating. I came downstairs and noticed Grandpa going above and beyond by cooking all of my favorites from scratch: Massaman chicken curry, white rice, and spicy tuna sushi. He always enjoyed cooking and managed to pull out all the stops especially for holidays and special occasions. It felt good knowing he was bringing some positivity to the table tonight. It made me think the evening had a fighting chance.

Boy, was I wrong.

My dress shoes descended down each step of the carpeted staircase, inhaling the rich smells of the kitchen, "Something smells good in here!"

Grandpa smiled, "I hope so! We've got all the right stuff. Looking pretty sharp there."

I peered down to admire the suit, "Yeah, it was a gift, you know it might be my favorite one. Thank you."

Grandpa plated the serving dishes as I took the dishes from the kitchen counter to the dining room table. I began gathering silverware and napkins to help set the table for five. I glanced over at the clock and surprisingly discovered it was already 6:45 p.m.!

"Is it already six-forty-five? Where has the day gone?" I asked loudly.

"Well, you spent the majority of it sleeping and getting ready."

"I was actually studying more about ligers. I'm sorry, Grandpa. I should've helped more with dinner—"

"No, it's not that," he interrupted. "I enjoy this, and it brings me solace. I just hope your father shows. It's been a long time since he's eaten at this table. It's nice to know Rus and Roxanne will be joining us so we can all celebrate together. I had better get ready myself. Don't you get started until I get back."

Grandpa had lost faith in my father a long time ago. The two have bickered for years competing over the most ridiculous observations. During Dad's time in the Cultivation Squad, the two of them were known for spending hours bickering about what color the sun was.

I made sure the table was set and got the glasses out preparing for the sweet treat of a family tradition. My family had been drinking the cheapest red blend wine in history ever since Grandpa was a little boy and his father brought it home.

Grandpa would always share the sentimental value behind the wine. "It's not about the price or the brand or the size of the bottle. No, it's about the memories that come with it. The good, the bad, and the ugly."

Grandpa re-entered the kitchen from his downstairs master bedroom. He was wearing his Sunday best: a beautiful sky-blue sweater with khaki pants and a white collared shirt underneath. As he slowly pulled out his chair to join the dinner table, a funky mix of gator scales and uncooked meat joined the aroma of the room.

I scoffed. "Oh, wow, I didn't know you'd be wearing Dusty's personal scent tonight."

"Do you like it? It's my own personal concoction. I call it 'The Swamp.'"

"Smells like something died in a swamp."

The doorbell rang, and I quickly made my way to the front door. I laughed at how excited I was to have my friends over for dinner. A classic gesture and yet seemed completely underrated. I tried to collect myself and act as mature as possible, but I was all smiles from the start.

I opened the door to Rus and Roxanne smiling in the doorway. They held what appeared to be a homemade birthday cake inside a glass cake stand. The two collectively chimed, "Happy birthday!" I smiled while Roxanne came in for a hug. Rus carefully held the cake but still managed to rush toward me first. He managed to squeeze the life out of me in an intense embrace.

Roxanne stepped back, smiled teasingly, and commented, "I love your suit! Very stylish."

"Thank you, thank you. Gift from Grandpa. Uh, come on in," making a polite, inviting sweeping motion.

Rus had been inside our house many times; however, this was the first time Roxanne had returned since my eighth birthday party. Just in case, I went the extra mile and made sure any and all possibilities of showcasing my room were off the table and highly unachievable.

Rus, Roxanne, and Diego all cautiously entered the black and gray furnished living room notorious for Dusty's corner tucked away in the far-right side. Dusty's area included a large bed, a heat lamp, a tub full of water and a small empty trough containing leftover chicken bones. Dusty was resting peacefully under his giant heat lamp.

We turned left into the tall white kitchen, but not before Diego stopped and sniffed the surrounding area.

Roxanne pulled the baby jaguar from his harness and muttered, "Diego, walk on."

Diego turned to face Roxanne.

Suddenly, he raced towards her at a quick pace in order to catch up. As a reward Roxanne pulled out a small piece of meat from her feeding pack and hand-fed Diego.

"Positive reinforcement, nice! He's learning."

Roxanne exhaled cautiously, "For now, he's managed to cooperate more. But we still have a way to go."

Grandpa rose from his seat once we all entered the kitchen and greeted my friends as if they were his own. He hugged Rus and asked, "Ah, Russel, good to see you. What a lovely cake, we'll place it here on the kitchen counter. How're your folks?"

"Really good! Both busy as always." Rus nodded.

Grandpa patted him on the back. "Some things never change. Huh?" He redirected his line of vision on Roxanne. "Nice to see you again, little lady! Congrats again to you and Diego."

Roxanne placed Diego's leash in her left hand and reached out to shake with her right. "Thank you so much again, Mr. Steele. We're doing okay.

Actually, he's doing great today! He's just not playing very well with others at the moment."

Grandpa laughed and shook Roxanne's hand. "Don't worry about a thing! It won't last. Why, even Dusty wasn't the most well-behaved with other people at first. When he was a youthful adolescent, he snapped at almost everyone."

Dusty emerged from his corner in the living room and waddled toward Grandpa Herschel, who knelt down to pet the top of his head.

"But now he's greeting people every day. He's been particularly sweet for the past eighteen years."

The WT had made it a mission to rescue animals who faced extinction. Even after they were rescued from the plague, a variety of lifespans were shortened: the country was not survivable for people or animals alone. However, the scientists were able to create a vaccine that had a side effect which extended the lifespans of animals naturally. The vaccine was able to slow down each creature's metabolism, causing them to live longer.

A common Aldabra tortoise had the ability to live to be two hundred years old or so. Now the longest living animal on record in the WT was an Aldabra giant tortoise that was going on two hundred and fifty years old. Scientists started to breed, monitor, and record the lifespans for each animal that was rescued.

"Would you like Diego and Dusty to meet?" Grandpa kindly asked.

"Oh, no, I'm not sure that'd be the best idea," Roxanne hesitantly answered.

"Nonsense. It'll be fine, I promise," Grandpa Herschel encouraged.

I took a seat, and bragged, "Dusty took out a five-hundred-pound liger today. I think he can handle a baby jaguar."

Diego noticed Dusty approaching from the far side of the room. Diego lowered his body into a pouncing position, ready to strike. Dusty continued to waddle toward the baby jaguar. Diego jumped on top of Dusty's large set of jaws and pressed his sharp claws into the alligator. However, his claws were not able to break the thick skin of Grandpa's partner. Dusty opened his mouth high and began to shake Diego off.

Grandpa laughed, and everyone gradually took their seats. "He's got some good instincts," Grandpa jokingly remarked.

We all continued making conversation, trying to refrain from eating. After fifteen minutes of small talk Grandpa began to lose his patience waiting for my father to arrive. I exhaled deeply and looked up at Grandpa.

He took his hands and placed them together. "Why don't we all say grace?"

I gently clasped my hands together, praying my father would show.

Grandpa began his prayer, "Lord, we thank you for the many blessings you have bestowed upon this family. We pray you continue to give us the strength we need to work through the tough times to come. Allow us the patience to understand and to forgive those who have wronged us. And give Justin and Rus all the luck they need to pass their application tests with flying colors. In Ignacia's name we pray, amen."

"Thanks, Mr. Steele," Rus said humbly.

The front door suddenly closed, and the energy in the room shifted in that direction. We all turned to look as my father slowly entered the kitchen with a bottle of Cold Goose in one hand and a poorly wrapped box in the other. Shadow, slowly hobbled in with his new stitches and bandages, sniffing the kitchen and enjoying the unfamiliar scents. Dusty growled at Shadow while Diego scurried toward Shadow lovingly. Diego nestled up to Shadow while Shadow greeted the young cub with a nice head rub. Noah appeared to be wearing the exact same outfit from this morning. Truthfully, I didn't know how long he'd been wearing that uniform. My father laughed, "I see you all started without us." I stood and hugged him as Grandpa remained seated and started plating his food.

Roxanne quickly stood and nervously approached my father to introduce herself, "Wow, Noah Steele, hi! I'm Roxanne. I just joined the Cultivation Squad with my partner Diego. I've heard so much about you! It's nice to finally meet you."

My father smiled. "Yes, likewise. I wish you both the best of luck. You have some tough months ahead of you. But any friend of Justin's is a friend of mine. Good to see you again, Rus!"

Rus waved from his seat. "Good to see you, Mr. Steele!"

Grandpa pleasantly muttered, "Happy you decided to join us."

"There were a few more pressing matters I had to attend to, but we made it," my father scoffed. "And with the wine, as promised! Thanks for having us. Dad."

Dinner had just started, and I could already feel the tension rising. My father had placed the gift-wrapped box down on the kitchen counter and cracked open the wine. He poured five glasses of Cold Goose and passed out each one. This cheap red wine embodied celebrations in my family and helped ease the underlying combative energy in the air.

Dad retold the story of our brawl with Zeus and Aries. He then continued on about his latest excavations throughout the western part of Ignacia. We began devouring the amazing food Grandpa had perfected. My favorite had to be the curry. Grandpa always found a way to make it with just the right amount of spice and without any onion.

An hour went by, and I was still trying to do everything in my power to make this the least stressful dinner for everyone. Something seemed to be happening between Rus and Roxanne. They were sitting very close to one another, giggling, and smiling at each other while simultaneously whispering back and forth. Maybe it was just the wine, or maybe there was something more.

A small pain began to tighten in my stomach from watching the two. I wasn't sure if they'd gotten back together or if Rus was pulling at her heart strings. Either way, I was irritated. I tried to turn my attention back to Grandpa, but I could tell he was tired after a full day of cooking, decorating, and rescuing us from our deadly encounter. Dusty started to wobble over toward Rus, sniffing him. Diego attempted to spend as much time as possible sitting by Shadow and licking his wounds.

Grandpa was occupied, pretending to be interested in my father's third story of the evening in hopes of finding something more to talk about other than work. As the night went on, the conversation continued to flow. Everything was going pretty well and was tolerable. That is, until Dad started talking about North Ignacia, and his time spent visiting my mother, Teresa.

"We went skiing across the water, caught fresh seafood, and delivered most of it to the locals in need on the indie islands. Of course, we managed to save enough to take some home for ourselves and cook over an open fire. Seasoned it just how you would, Pops. Salt, pepper, lemon, and a bit of oregano. Teresa was in heaven and loved every minute of it."

"Speaking of which, it's time for dessert. Noah, could you help me in the kitchen please?" Grandpa gleefully interjected.

"Of course, Pops."

The two men exchanged abrasive whispers and murmurs. My father delivered five small dessert plates and forks back to the table while Grandpa removed the beautiful birthday cake Rus and Roxanne baked from the butler's pantry and reapproached the table. The two grinned proudly as they watched for my response. My face lit up and I was embarrassed by the kind gesture.

Grandpa placed the cake down directly in front of me as he lit the eighteen candles. He led the party in a brief "Happy Birthday" song. I blew out my candles as hard as I could; it took two breaths to blow them all out. The completion of this simple task brought everyone to applause and for the first time that evening made me feel whole again.

My father raised his glass. "I'd like to propose a toast. To my son, Justin. Son, you are the best and brightest son I could ever ask for. Happy birthday from me and your mom. She wishes she could be here."

"Aw well that's nice, Son. Truly it is..." Grandpa muttered sarcastically. "So, where exactly is his mother?"

A thick silence began to envelop the room. I became still and unsure of what he said exactly, but the energy in the air began to sink as the evening began to plummet. The air grew thicker than anything I'd ever experienced.

Dad calmly answered, smiling, "Um, well, as you know, Teresa lives on base now and is the new Director of Sea Development. So, she uh, doesn't receive much vacation time to–"

"No, no of course not," Grandpa cut Noah off again. "But she accrues *some* paid time off, does she not? Enough time to go water skiing with her husband?" The two locked eyes and did not break concentration from one another. Dusty slowly slithered back next to Grandpa as Shadow began to growl alongside my father.

Rus, sensing an awkward moment, tried to intercept. "So, Justin, you want to cut the cake and send me over a fat slice?" He jokingly sipped more of his wine.

"Please. It's fine, Dad. I promise," I whispered. "Grandpa, stop. It's okay that—"

Grandpa stood and addressed the table, "No, Justin, no, it's not. You see, that is the response you get from a respectful, polite, young man. One who is more loving and caring than you have ever been toward anyone in this family, Noah. You think you can just swoop in here with your fancy zomorodi and lion and that makes things all right? You've wasted years of your adult life defending the country, risking your life in the name of animals, trainers, and people alike. But I've got news for you. You haven't done a damn thing for this family since you received your title."

Dad stood, condescending. "Like father, like son." Noah raised his glass as if toasting his father.

Another silence came over the room as the two of them remained completely fixated on causing harm to the other.

My father was awarded the title of captain for the Hero Regime at the youngest age recorded in history, even a year before Jericho. Once Noah was awarded his lion cub as his partner in the WT program, he vowed to train insanely hard in order to stop any and all villains from harming the civilians of Ignacia.

After just sixty days of training as a hunter for the Cultivation Squad, the Hero Regime stepped in and recruited Noah on the spot. He was exempted from the challenge into the Hero Regime. Let the record show, all enlisted participants prior have been required to take a final, facing off against a member of the Hero Regime after a nine-month trial period. Noah and Shadow became one of the top three sets of combatants within the Hero Regime.

Of course, his father, Herschel, after being the underling to Jericho, became the captain and decided to take Noah on as his protégé. The two continuously bumped heads over the years. Herschel was more cautious and elusive as a leader for the Hero Regime while Noah was more stubborn and headstrong.

Four years passed. Noah became more agitated and frustrated with Herschel's teachings, so much so that he threatened to leave. Herschel offered him a sabbatical and asked Noah to take some time off. He presented Noah with two tickets to the northern Indie islands of Ignacia. Herschel ordered him to take Shadow and have some down time with the Exploration Squad. Noah hesitantly accepted and took Shadow on a mini-vacation to devote some time in another division. That's where Noah met my mother, Teresa.

Teresa was, at the time, Manager of Land Operations overseeing the restoration of island life. She was responsible for updating the mapping of the island on the surface.

Supposedly, as the story goes, the two met while Noah was surveying the island, and Teresa was taking a dip with her beluga, Shelly. Shadow ran toward the pair and stopped because he refused to swim. Shadow's tail began to swing left to right as Shelly squealed from the water. Teresa came up and raised her body out of the water like a full-blown mermaid.

Noah ended up spending the entire day getting to know her. The two would flirt and navigate the island together until they stumbled into the single remaining village. The limping structures had been desecrated and hit hard from a hurricane. The storm destroyed most of the island, so much so that the entire village was struggling without water or power.

Noah made it his newfound mission to help Teresa restore the village, starting with the power. Noah worked long hours restoring the power lines and fixing their control panels. After he restored electricity to those who had suffered tremendous loss, they referred to Noah as the "light bearer."

Noah returned with the support of the Exploration Squad at his back to aid in his claim to become the new captain of the Hero Regime. Herschel was caught off guard but agreed to his son's dare but only through a Challenge

Day Tournament. He offered Noah and Shadow the chance to train and contest him and his partner Dusty for the role of captain in one month's time.

After training for the following month while spending every other day with Teresa, Challenge Day finally arrived. Noah defeated several Hero Regime members before receiving the opportunity to face off against his father. Once Noah and Shadow stood facing Herschel, he and Shadow mastered their rapid combinations to out speed Dusty. Shadow would swat Dusty around, but once Dusty grabbed onto Shadow's paw, he would not let go.

Noah ran to the center of the brawl as his father met him in the middle. The two pressed their partner patches and collided head on with brutal strength. After an hour-long fight, Noah finally pinned Herschel. Noah and Shadow succeeded and moved forward with their newly earned roles. Herschel retired and sadly so did his way of thoughtful leadership. The Hero Regime became more proactive against members of the AFA and searched for ways to help all citizens around the clock.

Grandpa was offered a comfy desk job with the Animal Bridging Council for the WT. He humbly accepted the newly opened position but became distanced from Noah. Grandpa wasn't even invited to his son's wedding, which happened just four months later. When Noah found out Teresa was pregnant, he was excited; however, she decided she could not devotedly take care of a baby full time. Grandpa stepped up and offered his assistance. He spent hours, even days at a time caring for me, and he decided to help me every chance he could. Eventually, Grandpa became my full-time caregiver as he continued to assign future roles for the newly admitted members of the WT into society.

Grandpa responded to my father, "Are you sure you want to do this here?"

"You know, I've been waiting for something like this."

Both began to reach for their partner patches. Dusty and Shadow suddenly leaped toward one another across the dinner table. I instinctively jumped onto the table between them at the last possible moment and reached out my arms in an attempt to stop the two in their tracks. Both scratched at my new suit jacket as I closed my eyes, praying I didn't lose a limb. When I opened them, Dusty's jaws were pinched down in my right hand with Shadow's throat in my left.

I was astounded and confused as to how I'd managed to stop both beasts from attempting to kill one another. My eyes faced forward making direct eye contact with Roxanne. Amazed, her angelic hazel eyes stared back at me but slowly moved downward.

A moment passed as a squishy sound came from underneath my feet. I peered down and learned that I was standing in the cake Roxanne and Rus had made. However, with the combined weight of me, Shadow, and Dusty, it caused the entire glass table to shatter. After the heavy fall, it wasn't long before every party member was covered in the remaining food. I quickly rose to my feet and faced my relatives.

"I HOPE YOU BOTH ARE HAPPY," I yelled angrily. "You couldn't stand the idea of being in a room together, to enjoy a pleasant dinner, for my birthday. Why? WHY DID IT HAVE TO BE TONIGHT?"

Grandpa regretfully wiped food off his sleeves. "I'm sorry, Justin. I just lost control."

"I'm sorry, too, Son. I don't know what to say." I stepped in front of Grandpa as I faced Noah.

"You know, Dad, all I've ever wanted is for you to just try. But you and Mom couldn't do that as parents. You chose your animals over your own son. Grandpa is right. He's been there, and he's all I know." I continued facing him as Grandpa's right hand gently fell on my left shoulder.

Noah's eyes began to water as he stared at me longingly. I could see how guilty he felt for the years of neglect. He breathed deeply, held back the pain, paused for a moment, and finally mustered up the words to respond, "I-I'm sorry, Justin. Let's go, Shadow."

The two made their way out the door. We all watched silently until we heard the front door shut. I looked down at my suit, ruined by claw marks and cream cheese frosting. The remnants of the destroyed birthday cake lay scattered across the floor. Shaking my head, I surveyed the damage done to our dining room.

I sighed deeply. "Damnit."

CHAPTER 3

Becoming a Steele

My right fist swiftly connected with the three-hundred-pound punching bag that raced toward me. My bare feet danced across the moist mats covering the smoothed and sanded wooden floor. I quickly turned to face the remaining three bags that loomed around me one after the other. I jumped left to dodge the second bag. I placed my forearms in front of my face to deflect the third but lost focus as the fourth bag slammed into my face. The impact alone knocked me flat on my back. Grandpa remained outside the square of punching bags he positioned against me. He had launched each bag at me, pushing each one in a clockwise formation with sheer brute force.

Shaking his head, Grandpa entered the square, stopping each bag that crossed his path. He casually stood over me disappointedly and demanded, "Again."

I wiped away the blood seeping from inside my bottom lip and slowly stood. I slightly staggered to rise. "Can't I just spar with you?"

Grandpa chuckled. "You want to spar with me? Oh, Justin, you aren't ready for that. And besides, the point of this exercise is that you know how to defend yourself from an ambush of four enemies at once."

A deep sigh left my lips as I returned to my original stance. "The real test is tomorrow, you know, so if there are any last-minute training tips, I think now would be a good time to get into it."

My feet sat shoulder width apart as I held my hands up. Simultaneously, I kept my wrists and fingers relaxed and ready to block whatever bags that may come my way. An important exercise Grandpa always made me do was bounce in place in order to get my blood moving. My feet bounced around the mat ready for any punching bag he was going to throw at me.

Grandpa inhaled deeply and launched each bag at me one at a time. He clenched his fist and slammed it into the first bag. The bag came my way at the same speed as the last round, and I was able to safely dodge out of the way. The second bag swiftly followed, and I turned to connect my right fist directly in the butt of the bag.

I turned my head and noticed the third bag was aimed at my current position low on the floor. With little to no reaction time, the only choice I had was to leap upward in hopes of dodging; however, before landing successfully, I looked over and noticed Grandpa's right fist changing color. He brought his right hand backward and clenched his fingers into a shiny metal fist. He suddenly connected his metallic-colored fist into the bag. The collision between his hand and the fourth bag was unlike anything I'd ever seen.

The punching bag flew at me as if it were fired out of a rocket launcher. My body fell to the floor as if I'd been shot in order to dodge the monstrous attack. The bag moved at such an intense speed that I didn't have the reaction time to watch it sail over me. Getting up, I looked back and realized the fourth punching bag he'd hit had flown off its hinges and landed inside the wall of the dojo.

My mouth dropped. "What the hell was that?!"

Grandpa shook his hand quickly and smiled, "A little rusty, but you may have a point. I suppose now is as good a time as any."

Grandpa had always been a great storyteller especially when he retold stories of his glory days fighting among the Hero Regime. Some of his friends and members of the Hero Regime came over once or twice a month to visit, but after listening to their stories, I always assumed Grandpa was exaggerating some of the details for entertainment value.

A few months back my great Uncle Fred, the falconer, came to visit. Fred was Grandpa's younger brother, he started off as a Flyer in the Transferal Squad but was recruited into the Hero Regime. Once the news broke that Fred trained five falcons simultaneously, it was a no-brainer that he should be a walk-on to the Hero Regime. Grandpa and Fred both worked side by side under their new captain, Jericho, for the many years that followed.

The two had recently sat on the back porch outside the dojo. They shared a bottle of wine and a couple of cigars. I decided to join them and sat in on their conversations before heading to work that night. They spoke about the time Grandpa fought against the Dark Trainer, one on one. The Dark Trainer apparently wore heavy, black-plated armor and rode a fearsome black stallion.

"Hersh, you punched through his armor like it was wet toilet paper!" Fred commented.

The two spent hours reminiscing and the opportunity for me to ask about it was never afforded.

My eyes remained large with concern as I walked over and pried the punching bag out of the wall. Thoughts of panic and concern flooded my mind as I sat at the wall stunned and a bit confused. What wasn't Grandpa telling me? How was he still this powerful and at his age? I dragged the punching bag back with me.

My hands released the chain of the bag as it dropped to Grandpa's feet. "How did you do that?"

Grandpa sighed and began massaging his fist. "It's a long story. Go ahead and pop a squat."

A small grin grew over my face as I sat on the floor, crossed my legs, and straightened my back.

Grandpa grabbed a foldable chair in the corner of the room, brought it onto the mat, unfolded it and sat down. He placed his hands on his knees and looked directly at me. "Our family origins go back to the early days of Ignacia. So early, in fact, that we were the founders of the original crystal claw. And don't scoff or disbelieve the old 'tall tales' because they're real! The crystal claw, the legend, all of it. I know because our ancestors were there. As you know, my family started off as proud farmers living on the land in South Ignacia. Our family had lived on that farm for generations! Idyllically, we were living together in harmony because everything had a place. Everyone had a job to do, and there was structure in their day to day lives. But it didn't last.

During a bright, beautiful day, my great, great grandfather, Geo Steele, a young man in his mid-twenties or so, saw something falling out of the sky. It was this bright metallic vehicle that resembled some form of spacecraft. Supposedly, it had been beaten, battered, and thrown around the world's atmosphere. The bright burning ship sailed right over Geo's farm and crashed in the middle of the deep vegetation of the forest about fifty yards from his barn. He grabbed his shotgun and set out to examine the crash up close.

Geo noticed that the surrounding forest had been destroyed. Plants, leaves, and trees had all been turned into piles of ash. Once he located the vessel, he noticed how shiny the ship was in contrast to the dark piles of ash and dirt. It was like nothing he'd ever seen. Geo continued toward the ship until his right hand made contact with the vessel; instantly, it emitted an electromagnetic pulse and shocked him. He fell unconscious from the powerful bolt of electricity.

A couple of hours later, Geo woke up in a white, colorless room. The skinny farmer was lying on what appeared to be an operating table. He was no longer in pain, nor did he feel any negative repercussions from the shock. The farmer sat up and studied the room intently. Geo noticed there were no windows, no pictures, but what appeared to be four very bare walls, and one with a set of double doors. The doors slowly opened, and in the doorway stood a four-foot tall Endoparasitoid lifeform with two big black eyes, a small pale body with a large oval-shaped head. Its body had two stout arms with a set of bright crystal claws growing from each hand.

Geo stood, frightened and unsure of what to do. At first, he backed away, behind the table, putting distance between them. Neither made a sound. After a few moments of staring at the new life form, he tried to communicate with it. 'Who are you? What are you doing here? What do you want!?'

The life form muttered a delayed response. 'Who?'

'Do you understand me?' Geo continued.

The small alien responded instinctually. 'Do. You. Under. Stand. Me?'

Geo sighed. 'Okay, I'll take that as a no—'

'No,' the life form cut him off.

Geo straightened his posture and stood confidently. He tilted his head with curiosity as he examined the small creature. The creature did the same, simultaneously mirroring Geo, each studying the other, learning what they could about the being standing across from the other.

'Okay, let's try this. My name is George, but my friends call me Geo. What is your name?' Geo asked.

'Geo?' the small alien asked.

'Yes, my name is Geo.' He placed his right hand on his chest. 'Geo.'

The life form remarked, 'Geo?' and pointed at Geo from across the room.

Geo rubbed his hand through his dark hair in shock and awe. He began to wipe his face. He spoke aloud to himself, 'This can't be real. I mean, what am I even doing here? This is just some nightmare. I am not going to be probed by some little alien with sharp crystal claws. I need to get out of here and get back to the farm. My wife and the animals–'

'Animals? What. Are. Animals?'

'Can you understand me?'

'Well. Almost. It takes a moment for my internal voice module to update and formally understand any and all languages. Even one as antiquated as English.' His words became faster and more precise.

'How? How are you talking? You don't have a mouth?'

The small alien snickered. 'That may be true, but we're transporting a neural link to your Wernicke's area inside your brain so that you can hear my thoughts. Nobody can hear us communicate but you.'

"That was the first time a connection had been made between a human and a crystal claw. It wasn't intended for Jericho Zhang or their family line: it had always been meant for a Steele," Grandpa said.

I was star-struck. "Wait, but that still doesn't explain your fists."

Grandpa Herschel placed his left hand up, "Patience, Justin. I'm getting there. Where was I?"

'The two spent the day together communicating and learning more about one another. Geo had found someone to share his farm and his home with, and the alien life form had found a friend and a protector. By the end of the day, Geo had grown hungry, tired, and ready to get back to his farm.

'Do you have a name?' Geo asked.

'Well, on my planet everyone knows us as Paralifoid32189,' the life form muttered.

'Ha, okay how about something new? Something people around here can call you. What about Cici?'

'C.C.?'

'Yes, Cici. It's like a nickname for a sister. But the initials could also stand for crystal claw.'

The small alien examined their claws. 'Hmm, strange. They are made up of a different molecular structure, certainly not crystals. However, I have no problem with the name. Interesting, yet adequately elegant. I like it.'

'Cici, I have to get back to my farm. Would you like to come with me?'

'I do not know, Geo. It is a different world beyond our vessel, and based upon your initial response, there may not be room for us in it.'

'I'm sorry for the way I reacted. People fear change, the unknown, the unexplainable. But we can't just give up or feel out of place. We are intelligent beings. We can learn to adapt, especially if we have someone to help us. Still, even here, in my own native land and with my own familiar people, I feel out of place sometimes. I understand your hesitancy, but honestly, it's easier here, on my farm, where I only have to deal with animals most of the time, not people. You can trust me.'

Geo reached out his hand. 'I'll protect you. I promise.'

Cici paused for a moment and answered, 'If you're going to protect me, you're going to need the proper tools for the job.'

Geo carefully examined the life form as he reached out his hand, and Cici reached out their claw. Once the two connected, the claw pierced Geo's hand and a sharp metallic surge raced throughout his body. His tendons, his muscles, and his bones transformed into steel. He appeared to look as if nothing had happened, but inside he was as durable as a diamond.

Geo fell to the ground in pain. He could feel his body changing drastically inside. His weight intensified as if gravity pushed him down harder into the earth. He struggled to control his limbs as the weight gravitationally forced his body downward.

Shocked and fearful for his life, he yelled out, 'What is this? What's happening?'

'The Protector's Armor. It's a gift, one that will help you protect us from the world outside. One that will be passed down to your children's children.'

Geo's organs tightened and began to churn. With the new changes made to his body, he felt the weight forcing him down harder. The weight pushed directly on his chest, limiting his lungs as if he couldn't breathe from the weight of his own skin. His cells became stacked and solidified in place. Geo attempted to move by dragging his fingers through the soil. However, each arm had added almost another hundred pounds. Geo closed his eyes and focused on his breathing. He remembered his wife, her beautiful smiling face, his farm, his animals, and the need to get back.

Geo forced his palms into the floor and pushed himself up as hard as he could. The weight intensified in his arms and conjoined with his muscles. The gift became his newfound strength. What he thought was excruciating pain, grew to become his greatest tool."

Grandpa paused. "Eventually, the two left the ship together, and when Geo returned home, he noticed all the burnt vegetation from the crash had regrown into beautiful flowers and plant life. Geo learned to use his newfound power to plow the corn fields single handedly, he collected cattle with his bare hands, and most importantly he learned how to protect Cici, his wife, and eventually his family. Cici's gift of The Protector's Armor gave Geo a layer of internal steel-bodied armor and has been passed down to the first-born son in every other generation. My grandfather had it, I have it, and now you have it."

"Wait. So yesterday, when I punched Zeus, did I use my gift?"

"I'm not sure. I was too busy focusing on the liger trying to eat you. Regardless, I've been trying to help you find a way to access this power without me."

"Grandpa, wait. What happened with Cici? What did Geo do?"

Grandpa exhaled deeply. "They lived together for a long time. Geo was true to his word and protected Cici. After that, I don't know. Some say Cici left him and eventually moved on. Some say Geo scared Cici away. But according to our little family secret, the story goes that Cici stayed with Geo until he became old and gray. After that, they left human society and joined the animal kingdom. Cici found a way to manipulate their cells and transform into any animal on the planet. The only defining factor to tell if an animal has inherited the crystal claw gene is by examining each animal's hands, paws, or claws. If one of an animal's limbs is crystal, then it has inherited Cici's same gene, the same lifeform our ancestor befriended."

I glanced over my right hand, noticing that the bruising and cuts from the fight with Zeus had disappeared. The only battle scars that remained were the ones from fighting off the punching bags.

"I want to learn how to use it and stop the Dark Trainer. That is my new purpose."

Grandpa smiled. "Now you sound like your father. Sadly, he never inherited this gift. Even though he certainly acts like he did. All right, Justin, stand up and help me reset the bags."

Together we both arranged the four punching bags to face toward the wall of the dojo. They were all neatly placed in a row and ready to be hit as hard as possible. I mentally prepared to punch each bag harder than I ever had before. I remembered the shine in Grandpa's fist as he slowly brought his arm back. How did he do it? What was he thinking about? I wanted to master this ability to help others and defend the animals of Ignacia. I wouldn't stop until I became stronger.

"Remember your training," Grandpa calmly explained. "Allow your mind to go to that place. Visualize the enemy. Imagine they have your loved ones in harm's way. The only way to free them is to take the enemy out. Like this."

Grandpa closed his eyes, controlled his breath, and clenched his fist hard. That was when I saw it, I mean, really saw it. The tendons within his right hand slowly began to change. The metallic pigmentation of the steel started to shine and cover Grandpa's hand. His fist smashed the bag once more, and again it flew off the hinges straight into the wall.

Grandpa slowly and proudly turned to me, "Now, you try."

I was hesitant and responded jokingly, "Ha, okay, yeah. Nothing to it."

I threw a left-handed punch into the bag, but nothing happened. I threw a right-handed punch into the bag, but nothing happened.

"Why isn't it working?"

"Justin, you just learned you have this ability. These things take time, sometimes decades, to master. Today let's focus on accessing just a small portion of the power you have inside."

My patience was running thin, but I closed my eyes and took a deep breath. I had to clench my right fist like I did before. I replayed the story in my mind. The story of my ancestor befriending the alien and receiving the internal armor.

My fingers tightened as I opened my eyes and yelled at the bag, "RAAAAAAH!"

The stored energy from my fist was released into the bag and the impact was hard enough to make the bag swing upward. However, it did not fly off the hinges. The bag swung up but was coming back down toward me with a much higher velocity. I was out of options, so I brought my forearms up in front of me to deflect the blow. The three-hundred-pound bag had gained traction with an extra push from gravity.

The bag made contact with my forearms with a loud thud. It was the same sound of someone being slammed into a matted floor. The slam of the bag to my skin echoed throughout the room. Instead of knocking me over, the bag had been stopped in its tracks. It suddenly swayed down and resumed its original position. I uncrossed my forearms and examined them in the wall mirror behind us. The point of contact revealed small metallic indents on my forearms. These tiny indents in my forearms appeared to shine with the same pigmentation as Grandpa's fist.

"It's a gift, one to help you protect. It's a start," Grandpa whispered.

Later that day I began reviewing more of the animal anthology. I whirled through page after page searching for animals that could potentially stop a grizzly bear. The more time that passed from that encounter allowed me to think. I needed to cultivate a plan of action about how I would defend myself from Fedrov and his grizzly bear Magnum. From what first started as fear, slowly grew into the opportunity I needed. I spent my entire life comparing myself to my father and now my grandfather. Both were respected and recognized individuals in society as leaders and powerful trainers. I'd give anything to receive the same level of respect and love from my community. I'd do anything. With my newfound power, I could challenge and defeat Fedrov for good! He's eluded being captured for so long, and if I were the one to stop him, I would be recognized as one of Ignacia's top trainers. I'd gain the same level of respect and support from Ignacia that my father and grandfather have obtained after years of service. It would be difficult, of course, but I have to get strong enough to complete my goals and become the new captain of the Hero Regime.

The list of animals that could face off against Fedrov's grizzly was surprisingly long. Some I didn't even think of, such as rhinos, elephants, hippos, bison and even moose. All of those animals supposedly had the natural ability to stop a grizzly in its tracks. However, this was not the animal Fedrov had in his possession: Magnum was a monster. I was going to need a powerful predator in order to defend myself from this high-level threat. My fear of Fedrov and Magnum became the driving force for me to continue to study.

Grandpa and Dad both reminded me that I was safe and that nobody was going to get through them. Between the application exam, dinner last night, and the Dark Trainer after me, I always had something to fear.

After my father left the house with Shadow last night, Rus, Roxanne, Grandpa, and I helped clean up what was left of the dining room. We swept up the pieces of shattered glass from the table, trashed the major broken items, and let Dusty and Diego eat some of the food off the floor.

Once the larger items were discarded I decided to walk my friends out. The two made their way to the front door while I walked behind them. On my way out of the kitchen, I noticed my father's present sitting on the kitchen counter. I picked up the gift and the last trash bag from the kitchen. Rus opened the front door as they both waited for me on Grandpa's porch. I hugged them both again but noticed the two of them walked away arm in arm on the way to Rus's car.

Seeing the two back together gave me a weird feeling in the pit of my stomach. It wasn't anger; it wasn't sadness per se. It was the rotten love child of jealousy and envy, a begrudging sense of resentment that left me sourer than before. I walked to the edge of the driveway and pressed the "open" button on the side of the trash transporter. It transported trash through a variety of underground tunnels directly to the dump located on the outskirts of The Capital. There the trash was sorted, reduced, and recycled into everyday household items or compost. The transporter lid lifted upward, and I placed the last trash bag into it.

My fingertips remained pressed together and would not release my father's gift into the bin. Feelings of momentary frustration left me upset with Dad for what he'd done, and I blamed him for ruining my birthday dinner. After unwrapping his present and opening the box, a tiny smile started to grow across my face.

Inside sat his old red hat with the word "Ignacia" on the front. It's the hat that he wore throughout his Cultivation Squad training days. Eventually, Noah and Shadow became the best Hunters the Cultivation Squad and Ignacia had ever seen.

"I can't."

I carefully pulled the hat out and dropped the box into the trash alongside the mailbox. My father had a habit of saving old items that were meaningful to him. Recently within the past two years he'd made it a mission to share those items, memories, and experiences with me. I was grateful for each gift that he'd shared with me, but my own zomorodi would be nice, too. A slight smile grew on my face as I looked at the red hat.

After a long day of training and a nice hot shower, I plopped down at my desk and attempted to study more before dinner. I looked over to the corner of my room and admired the set of wooden shelves I'd built with Grandpa many years ago. On top of the shelf sat my father's gloves alongside the new edition, his old training hat. These were two items I would be sure to take with me wherever I was assigned. I had become fond of his gifts over the years because he found himself while he was wearing these articles of clothing. If they helped him that much in the process, I'd hoped they would serve a similar purpose for me. My father found these items important, and they were very dear to him. I grew jealous of the items and hoped that he would be proud of the trainer I'd become. Regardless of the flashiness and pomp, I didn't care what people said: I was proud to be a Steele. I remembered my ancestor, Geo Steele, and his story. The story alone became another source of motivation, one which would continue to grow and define me as a person. I wanted to be the strongest trainer in all of Ignacia in order to protect the lives of people and animals alike. I decided then and there I would do my best to accomplish my goal regardless of the outcome. I would take on and supersede any obstacles that stood in my way.

Grandpa called me downstairs for dinner a few minutes later. He decided to keep the meal simple with his famous chili, a hot dish served best after a long day of pushing your body to the limit. It was filled with a happy mix of spices, beef, beans, and chopped onions. Served alongside it was some fresh grated cheese, sour cream, and sweet cornbread.

We kicked off dinner just like every meal that we shared. We ate our food quietly as Grandpa's cool collection of jazz music played in the background. Grandpa found the soothing sounds of jazz calming and relaxing. After spending years of his life constantly thinking, running, and moving, he's had a difficult time slowing down. Stress became one of his greatest enemies; music was his solution.

"You know I'm gonna miss your home-cooked meals when I'm shipped off," I muttered.

"You haven't been accepted into the program yet, and you're already saying goodbye?"

I was taken aback by Grandpa's comment. I'd spent years training, researching, and studying for this monumental event. I'd already started packing my bags. "I'm ready. You said it yourself."

Grandpa placed his spoon down in his bowl. "Justin, there is nothing anyone can say or teach to prepare you for this world. You've been taught and mentored by two of the top trainers in Ignacia, but tomorrow will be the first time you are immersed into our world."

"Are you joking? What about yesterday? And the night before? Grandpa, I've seen what this world is like, and I am not afraid."

Grandpa took a deep breath and strictly addressed me in a low volume. "You won't know anything until you have a partner of your own. The bond you two will share, it will shape how you see the world. Tomorrow you will face your worst fears, and if you succumb to them, you will fail. But if you overcome them and succeed, you will receive the greatest reward there is." Grandpa looked down as his right hand began to shake. His body was trembling.

"Grandpa, are you okay?"

The shaking in Grandpa's arm subsided as he placed his left hand over it to steady himself.

"Yes, yes, I'm fine. Just tired after all the training today. Be sure to do some more studying tonight. We'll have to have you there by seven tomorrow morning to begin the application exam. Let's leave here by six forty."

I hugged Grandpa good night and hopped up the staircase like a jack rabbit on a mission. I checked the clock in my room. It read "7:30 p.m." Once I sat down at my desk, I reached down to my left-hand dresser drawer to pull out my Pre-Application Examination Booklet. The book had been in my possession for the past year. I'd run through each page at least ten times to ensure nothing would surprise me. I started at page one and steadily made my way through the four different sections: Psychology, Mathematics, Geography, and a Written Prompt.

Each section had been designed to directly correlate to each dimension of the program. Every question indirectly focused on an animal, a place, and a response to a multitude of scenarios. I was aware of what the Animal Bridging Council was looking for with each applicant and that, realistically, perfection was unachievable. After a few hours, I decided to head to bed and get some shut eye.

I took out my phone and sent a message to Roxanne. "Hope you had a great day! Can't wait to tell you how it goes tomorrow. Wish me luck!" I sat awake in bed awaiting a response while I slowly drifted into darkness. I lay there waiting, struggling as I stared at the ceiling of my room. I couldn't tell where the darkness started or where it ended. My eyes held out for another ten minutes before dozing off. Sadly, I had refused to rest in attempts to receive a response that I would eventually find out, never came.

The alarm on my phone went off and woke me up early, much earlier than I preferred waking up. I detested the sound of blaring crows screeching out at one another. However, it proved to be a very useful sound to scare me awake each morning. I turned over in bed and reached for my nightstand to silence it. I read the time on my phone's screen, 5:30 a.m., with no new messages. Disappointed, I refused to let it get me down. My day had finally arrived. I leaped out of bed and knocked out forty pushups to help my body wake up. I stretched my limbs and jumped in the shower. I pondered what kind of animal I would be assigned. "A white tiger would be cool," I whispered aloud in the shower.

A ferocious white tiger, one of the rarest species of big cat due to its recessive mutation in gene color. It would be appropriate and represent me very well. I'd never seen one up close or in the WT before. It'd be something different that would help me stand out as a Hunter. An unlikely circumstance, I'm sure, but it was worth hoping for, nevertheless. I finished showering and changed into my applicant shirt.

All applicants received a specified, gray-colored t-shirt in the mail after they had submitted their request for an application exam for the WT program. Grandpa brought my shirt home from work with him exactly one month ago today. The gray shirt featured two blank openings designed to be filled and customized, one larger circle located in the center of the shirt and another on the right shoulder sleeve.

Once applicants successfully completed their tests and were admitted into the program, the Animal Bridging Council presented each trainer with two modules and had them placed on the new trainer's shirt. The modules revealed the division placement on the right sleeve while the center module expanded and revealed an enlarged silhouette of the animal that the trainer was assigned to.

All committee members cast their votes after viewing the applicant's abilities and progress throughout the three portions of the application. Once a decision was made, the trainers would be given an animal partner, they would then meet, and moments later they would be connected through partner patches. Once the two were successfully in sync, they would receive their orders of where their division would like them to report. Swimmers with the Exploration Squad would report to North Ignacia. Flyers with the Transferal Squad would report to East Ignacia. Builders with the Construction Squad reported to West Ignacia, while Hunters and Farmers with the Cultivation Squad reported to South Ignacia.

I grabbed my black and red backpack from my room before I headed downstairs. I stopped in the kitchen and saw Grandpa had been up and moving. He was wearing his favorite, gray-striped suit, white button-down shirt, and sported the burgundy tie I bought him for his birthday last year.

"Looking sharp, Grandpa."

Grandpa chuckled as he continued filling his thermos with coffee. "Well, I have to impress my grandson today and make sure he doesn't make a fool of himself."

I nervously laughed as I filled my black water bottle with water from the fridge. I collected some snacks from the pantry: two protein bars, an apple, and a banana. I safely stored them all in my backpack. Double-checking, Grandpa asked if I had my ID.

Yawning, I said, "Yep."

"Snacks? Bandages? Towels? Water?"

Yawning again, I added, "Yep, all set."

Grandpa had accepted his desk job with the Council of Animal Bridging for the WT almost twenty years ago. He humbly accepted the new position and quickly became acting president for the council. He rubbed the top of my head, messing up my hair that I had just spent ten minutes on. We walked out the door together and got into Grandpa's zomorodi. I pulled down the mirror from the passenger's side.

"Come on, Grandpa, not the hair."

"You need to focus on things other than your hair."

My fingers fished my phone out of my pocket as I examined the bright screen, and noticed it was already 6:45 a.m. We steadily drove into the city as we dodged the oncoming traffic and arrived at the courthouse with five minutes to spare.

Grandpa paused and looked over to me, "Please, just do your best. Remember your training, okay? I'll make sure you're taken care of."

An uneasy doubt hid beneath Grandpa's words. We parked the vehicle, and I stepped out, practicing what I would say. Dusty followed behind Grandpa as I approached him on the steps, "Whatever happens, let it be fair. No funny business. Place me where I'm meant to go."

Grandpa paused, turned back to face me, smiled, and nodded accordingly.

We entered through the clean, courthouse revolving door, a special place I'd only visited a handful of times on grade school field trips, but a part of me always felt as if I were entering the building for the first time. My breath was heavy, my hands were clammy, and I was becoming more and more nervous at the thought of failure. Inside sat a metal detector with multiple security guards posted on both sides of the entrance. We put our bags through security and had the guards check our items. I presented my driver's license while Grandpa presented his employee ID badge from the council. Dusty strolled by the security guards as he monitored the lobby for any potential threats. The guards politely greeted us and admitted access.

The courthouse chamber was gigantic. I immediately looked up and gazed at the ceiling. It was a glorious sight filled with artistic murals of animals working alongside people to build Ignacia. In the large portrait, there was a Latin sigil circling the epicenter of what appeared to be an outline of the continent of Ignacia: "Gaudebimus una ope animalium." I looked over to Grandpa. He'd caught me looking at the sigil, leaned over, and softly whispered, "We will rejoice together with the help of animals."

It was a beautiful piece that took over a year to design and five more to paint. However, the left corner of the piece had a small area that appeared to be etched away and was not recognizable. I was confused as to why such a masterpiece had been so crudely violated. The team's original artists must've believed, whatever it was, was important. I never got around to asking about it.

Grandpa hugged me one last time. "Remember what I taught you," he whispered before walking toward the black wooden stage which sat at the center of the lobby.

Grandpa and Dusty ascended the side staircase of the counsel's tall, golden desk, which had been conveniently placed behind the stage. Each of the four spaces on the desk were placed specifically for each member of the Animal Bridging Council. The spectacle continued to play an important role in the ceremony which would occur after a day of blood, sweat, and tears. I could see more applicants standing inside a large circle on the floor in the center of the chamber. The circle featured four different walk-ways which lead from the entrance to three different doors.

Once I reached the outskirts of the circle, I saw Rus introducing himself to the other applicants. My stomach sank.

I fearfully asked, "Rus! Wait, what're you doing here?"

Rus laughed. "Now, I know what you're thinking. I'm supposed to be here tomorrow, but they canceled tomorrow's application day! So, they said I could come in a day early! Isn't that great?"

"Yeah, it's something." I nervously half smiled.

I looked around and watched the other applicants in the room. I counted eight individuals total, four young men, including Rus and myself, and four young women. The girls seemed to find company among themselves as three of them chatted about school, animals, and whatnot. One girl seemed to stand out since she kept to herself. She was taller than the others and had dark hair and bewitchingly pale skin. She had a creative design of a white dove tattoo on the back of her neck. The young woman seemed uninterested in the people around her as she continued staring up into the mural and was lost in her own world.

An alarm sounded and the lights began to dim. A spotlight appeared on stage as a young woman wearing a long, silver dress, black gloves, silver hood, and a black mask stood in the center. The mask seemed to envelope her face. I couldn't make out her eyes, her mouth, or any recognizable features. She introduced herself to the group with a distorted voice.

"Welcome, new applicants. Come, gather around, everyone please stand together here in the center so we may begin. We have a long day ahead of us, and we need everyone's full attention. The time is 7 a.m. on July 10, 3045. All applicants present are accepted from the fourteenth and the fifteenth of July. You all have been accepted to apply for the Wildlife Training Program. Every applicant must complete and pass each trial in order to receive a placement into a specific division and then be awarded their own partner. Failure to pass a selected area will result in immediate termination from the program. Unless permitted otherwise, you will not be offered another chance to reapply for the program."

My heart was pounding so loud I thought it was going to burst. I could feel my body tightening as I clenched my fists. Suddenly, the color of my fists began to change. I peered down and saw the metallic color spread over the top of my knuckles. I was shocked by the sudden change and the amount of power that came over me. I was excited, scared, but most of all I was afraid of being discovered. I nervously tucked my hands into my pockets and began taking deep breaths. I had felt the urgency sink in and knew that I had to calm down. I thought that if I relaxed the power would settle, and I could try my best to control it.

"The first portion of this process will feature an aptitude examination, ensuring all applicants have the proper mindset of an animal trainer; it is designed to test the boundaries of your education. Once you successfully pass the written exam you will receive a brief break before moving on to the combat portion. Once you progress through the physical portion, you will receive your last break. Those who pass will go to the hero portion. Only completion of each of the three courses will conclude with a decision from the Animal Bridging Council."

I looked around the circle again, studying my group analytically. Some were taller, maybe stronger, and with Rus being smarter, at first glance I did not stand out more than anyone else. Each applicant carried their own backpack. Everyone in our group seemed completely fixated on the Masked

Woman on stage. All, that is, but the girl with the dove tattoo. She seemed to be counting the applicants silently on her fingers. Our eyes met for a brief second, but we both turned away. I had to stay focused on the job at hand. The severity of the upcoming events had been on my mind for the past eighteen years. The fear of failure lingered over me. I knew that the actions I performed that day would dictate how I'd spend the remainder of my life.

"I must remind you all that these tasks are designed to push each applicant past his or her limit. Not everyone is meant to be an animal trainer or a part of this program. If that is the case, you may still have a future working with, for, or alongside different divisions if you so choose. We appreciate your understanding and wish you all the best of luck. Please come up to the stage to collect your application number and continue on through the first door on your left to begin the aptitude exam. All phones must be turned off and turned in upon entry. Let your hearts be true and ring in the name of Ignacia."

Each applicant walked anxiously toward the small black staircase to the right of the stage. We slowly moved across the small dark space in front of the golden desk where my Grandpa sat alone at the desk with Dusty behind him. I somehow found myself closer to the middle of the line while Rus was amped up and ready to go as he bounced in place at the front of the line. He proudly moved across the stage with a determined look on his face as he claimed the title of applicant number one.

When it was my time to walk across, I buried my hands deeper into my pockets and received the number five module. The woman placed a module inside the right sleeve of my applicant shirt. The shirt instantly displayed the number five in the center as well as the right sleeve. I descended the staircase and examined my updated shirt. I pulled my hands out of my pockets and noticed they had finally returned to normal. I continued to examine the new changes made to my shirt through a large mirror carefully positioned at the front of the lobby. I was in awe.

Once each person received their assigned number, a door suddenly opened in the left corner of the lobby. We moved as one as we all hesitantly walked toward the door. I turned back and noticed Grandpa watching me as I walked away. We made brief eye contact. He studied me plain faced as I noticed his thumb rise above his computer.

As inconspicuous as possible, I half nodded back and attempted to hide my smile while also trying to both conceal and overcome my fear and anxiety. I moved forward with determination as I entered the brightly lit testing room. A large, militarized man stood at the front of the classroom carrying a big bowl that had the sign "CELLPHONES HERE" written above it in red.

The frightening military man loudly commanded, "Sit down and shut up. I don't need to know your name, and you don't need to know mine. There will be no talking, no whispering, and no communication between any applicants while inside this room. Once your test is complete, and you click 'send,' you will turn in your computer, and I will happily inform you if you passed or failed in front of the other applicants. That's right, one way or another each and every person in this room will know if you passed or you failed. It's that simple. After you have received this information, leave the room, and you will be directed to either the break room or the exit. A visit to the restroom will be offered during the break and only during the break."

The tall, militarized man didn't seem to care about any applicants who entered his room. He was rude, loud, and blatantly disrespectful to each applicant he came across. The testing supervisor had bright white hair and a deep scar along his neck, but it was strange because he had no animal partner nearby. Once the man collected our phones he placed the bowl on his desk and passed out compact, foldable computers, branded "WT" on the top of each monitor. I looked over at Rus who didn't seem to have a care in the world. He was daydreaming and getting lost in the overhead lights of the barren, pale classroom.

"You will have two hours to complete this fifty-question aptitude exam, including the following sections: psychology, mathematics, geography, and an essay at the end," the military man barked. "You may go back and review your answers in different sections as you please. And as the saying goes, 'Let your hearts ring true in the name of Ignacia.' Your time starts now."

I pulled out some scratch paper and a pen as I flipped open my computer to read the first section of the exam. The entire first page solely asked for personal information, name, date, and time. The following page consisted of psychology which was both interesting and enjoyable. Each question requested short answers and required a fill-in-the-blank response. Some of my favorite questions were as follows:

"You arrive at a public location with your wolf, and there is a trainer nearby with her jack rabbit. You have no choice but to be in close proximity to the prey of your animal. What do you do?"

> **Response: "I will keep my wolf's focus on a task and goal that takes its attention away from the rabbit. I will command its attention elsewhere with either primary or secondary reinforcement."**

"You and your Panamanian White-faced Capuchin are tasked with moving large books to an elevated shelf. You have no ladder, just a ceiling fan which is a foot from the high shelf. What would you do?"

> **Response: "I would have my Capuchin hold onto the fan with its tail, and I would pass each of the books up to it to be placed on the shelf accordingly. Knowing such a task, I would factor in periodic breaks so as not to over-exert it."**

Lastly, "Name factors beyond training that can play into your animal's behavior in the field."

I considered many options and attempted to list each one that came to mind.

> **Response: "Such factors might include social dynamics with different animals regardless of the species, environmental factors like weather, physical status of the animal, and amount of hunger."**

After I carefully answered each question in the psychology section, I flew through the following mathematics and geography questions with ease. I remembered the many hours studying with Rus during the past school year. I glanced up before I began the written portion and noticed the military man. He glanced down at his desk and pressed a red button. A wall monitor appeared on the board behind him. The timer began at "30:00" and the countdown for the remaining time was displayed.

I saw Rus stand first, proudly turning in his computer. The man looked to his own computer monitor and began reviewing Rus's answers. He examined each section of the test while reading and re-reading Rus's responses.

I began to read the prompt for the Essay Response question: "You have made it. Well done. You have successfully achieved placement into the division of your choice. Now that you are here, what are you going to contribute to this program? Explain your personal selection of this particular field, why you should be placed in it, and if you were not chosen for your preferential faction, what would be your second choice?"

After five minutes of brainstorming, I looked back to the front of the room and noticed the military man reach out and shake Rus's hand. "Congratulations, Applicant Number One, you've passed the first portion of the application process. Please proceed to the break room just outside the testing room door and continue on with your journey to joining the WT. Well done." The military man handed Rus his phone back, while Rus graciously accepted and glanced back at me. He smiled at me and laughed before exiting the room.

I continued to write, "I believe I would be best suited for the Cultivation Squad because I possess the agility, stability, and adaptive mindset to overcome any and all obstacles. I have what it takes to hunt, grow, and protect any and all members with whom I am assigned to work. The Cultivation Squad is dedicated to helping everyone, whether it's growing crops, hunting down criminals, or becoming one with your partner. Farmers and Hunters are the ones with the drive to protect and allow other divisions to safely grow. I have sculpted my abilities, my work ethic and personal sense of belonging into the same squad that has helped raise me for the past eighteen years."

Another applicant hesitantly rose from his seat and collected his things. He was shorter and much heavier than me. The young man appeared to be slightly older, as if he were there to retry the application. He handed his computer over to the large military man at the front of the room. The testing monitor collected his computer, reviewed his personal computer for the applicant's answers and began reading.

After just three minutes he announced, "FAILURE. Applicant Number Six, please gather your things and make your way toward the exit." He stripped the module off the sleeve of Applicant Six and tossed his phone back to him. Applicant Six was shocked and disappointed. He walked toward the door, each step looking more and more painful, as he slowly left embarrassment consumed him. I was surprised at how offensive and cruel the instructor was, but I suppose it made sense. They want to push our buttons to see if we could handle the stress.

"If I had to make a secondary decision–"

I remembered my mother and what my father said about her wanting to try. Maybe the Exploration Squad would be a good fit. But what about Roxanne? What about Rus? What about our plan to work together? All of our plans for the future would have been for nothing, or maybe for the first time, I'd have a mom. I thought that was something worth fighting for.

I continued to write, "If I had to make a secondary decision on what group would be best suited for me, then I would suggest the Exploration Squad. The division expresses similar philosophies when it comes to a sense of growth, freedom, and protecting one another in the depths of the unknown. If given the chance to represent the WT, I would be honored and best suited to be in either one of the following divisions. I know what it takes to aid and teach those who seek guidance and security. Let me be the guiding hand that not only helps my team but also carry the beacon of safety and security for each citizen of Ignacia."

I peered up from my piece and noticed the applicant in front of me had finished her test. The applicant collected her things and stood up to turn in her computer. She was a short young girl with blonde hair and blue eyes. She confidently smiled and delivered her test to the military man. I rose from my seat and gathered my things. I cautiously glanced across the room one last time and noticed the same brunette girl from before finished with her exam. Her computer sat closed as she watched the remaining applicants in the room.

I began to walk across the classroom toward the desk and awkwardly stood behind the short young woman.

After about five minutes the instructor stated, "Applicant Number Eight. No ma'am, not today. Applicant Number Eight has failed. Please collect your belongings and make your way to the exit."

He gently took the module off her sleeve and handed the girl her phone as she turned and quickly walked out of the room. She was breathing rapidly on the verge of tears before she dramatically closed the door behind her. I stood tall and accepted my fate. I nodded respectfully to the instructor and handed him my computer. He quickly reached over his desk and grabbed the device out of my hand. The man opened my computer and looked back at his own. He then smiled maniacally. The man seemed to know exactly who I was, but I was not certain if this would help me or hurt me depending on how my family had previously treated the supervisor.

The next seven minutes felt like the longest seven minutes of my life, the fear, the rush, and the anticipation began to rise within me as if someone had frantically shaken me like a bottle of soda, filling my body with pressure. I felt as though my head had turned into a giant red balloon and was going to pop! The blood vessels in my face started to thicken as the red pigmentation highlighted my sweaty complexion.

The man muttered, "Applicant Number Five. You know, I didn't think I'd get to meet another Steele. I was wrong. Luckily, you weren't. Congratulations, Applicant Number Five, you've passed. Proceed through the break room door on the left just outside the door and continue on with your journey to joining the WT."

I smiled and carefully collected my phone from the bowl. I whispered, "Thank you, sir."

The man muttered to himself as he continued to watch me depart from the room. "Justin Steele. An unfair threat that must be neutralized."

I paused for a moment as the comment made under the man's breath resonated in the air. My eyes grew with fear as I attempted to decipher what he'd meant by that or why someone in his position would make such a comment toward me. Things were just heating up and I knew I wasn't safe. I continued forward and pretended that I didn't hear the man's intimidating threat. I was elated to be free of that room and even more so from the military man. I exited the room with a deep sigh of relief as I carefully walked toward the breakroom.

My problems were just beginning.

CHAPTER 4

Pushing Through

I was taken aback and robbed of my joy as the military man's comment lingered in my head. I tried to smile and celebrate my accomplishment in the short time I fast walked to the break room door for my own protection. My left palm pushed open the large white door and led me to several large circular cafeteria tables. Rus sat on the middle table munching on a protein bar. He sat there as if he were the coolest guy in Ignacia. His orange and blue running shoes propped on the actual seat while he sat on the table. The room was similar to the classroom, both bright and desolate aside from the restrooms and soda machines.

Rus laughed, "See! Nothing to it. I knew we'd be the first ones done!"

I sighed. "I, unfortunately, was not the second one to finish. We lost six and eight."

"Huh...Interesting. Well, wasn't meant to be then."

The two of us reached out for one another as our hands collided in a loud handshake. The sound of pride and gratitude echoed across the room as

Rus proudly reclaimed his position atop the table. I hesitantly sat at the table in a nearby chair.

We held no doubt in our minds that we would succeed in this joint venture. I was surprised to see him but also slightly relieved. I didn't feel alone knowing Rus had my back. One by one we noticed the remaining applicants enter the break room.

With two failed applicants that left six potential applicants with the opportunity to be admitted into the program. I began to chow down on a protein bar and apple when I calmly whispered to Rus, "You were introducing yourself to everyone when I arrived, right? Can you tell me, who all is left?"

Rus smiled and cracked his knuckles. Rus had a way of learning names much quicker than I ever could. It was a business tactic his parents instilled in him when he was younger. Rus sank down from the table into a regular seat alongside me. "Aside from you and me being the only hunter and Flyer backgrounds in the room, we have Fay, Applicant Number Two, the strong, red-haired girl over there in the corner. She's a Builder, must be from out west."

"What about Number Three, the dark-haired girl with the dove tattoo?"

The mysterious girl sat alone in the corner eating her lunch, content with her peanut butter sandwich and reading on her tablet. I quickly examined the tattoo more intently and noticed the back of her neck, neatly done, a dove spreading its wings as if in flight.

"I don't really know," Rus whispered. "All she said was that her name is Lyza. She didn't say where she was from or what she's pursuing. But that big guy at the soda machine, Number Seven, that's Wyatt. He's a Builder with a working background from West Ignacia. Supposedly, his dad helped design some of the larger buildings in The Capital. Potentially, somebody to worry about."

"How would you even fight a guy like that?" I stuttered. "He has no weak points."

"Yeah, dude is as solid as a stone wall. But everyone has a weak spot."

"Yeah, I suppose you're right. Would yours be Roxanne?" I smiled hesitantly.

He looked back at me almost offended. "That's bold. What do you mean by that?"

"Nothing! It's just the other night, at dinner, seemed like you guys were getting pretty close."

"I mean, yeah it's complicated, but who knows what might happen. Why do you care?"

"You both are my best friends, shouldn't I?"

Rus gave me a subtle look and noticed the small amount of perspiration forming on my forehead. Had he known how I felt about Roxanne? Was he genuinely concerned? Was he doubting our friendship? My mind began digging deeper and deeper assuming the worst of the situation based upon one stupid comment I had no place in saying. I knew how Rus was in relationships, and I didn't want him to take advantage of Roxanne's feelings for him.

Little by little, I felt his demeanor change toward me. I had to think of something quick in order to steer the conversation back on track. I muttered, "Well, she's lucky to have you. How do you think the next challenge will go?"

"It's the combat portion. I'm sure Herschel gave you all the ins and outs on these challenges."

I took a deep breath, thankful to avoid the topic of Roxanne. Why did I bring her up in the first place? I had to get all that out of my head for now.

As for the next challenge, the last words Grandpa muttered to me continued ringing in my ear: "Remember what I taught you." The nerves were beginning to return to my body, crawling up my spine like a Cellar spider stalking its prey. Each step on a different vertebra, enveloping more of my body with hesitation and doubt. The fabric that paved the path to my future relied on the combat portion. I had to succeed, whatever it took. I vowed to myself that I would not lose.

A few moments later the same military man opened the door and announced, "Justin Steele, you're needed in the hallway for a moment."

The eyes of the remaining members in the room shot over to me. I nervously looked to Rus with heightened concern while sitting still. Fear came over my friend's eyes as if they had called his own name. My heart sank as my mind began to think of the worst possible scenarios. I hesitantly stood and nodded in understanding. I left my bag with Rus on the table and approached the military man. We exited the room as I calmly followed behind and tried to swallow my fear. This was it. All of my many hours spent studying and training would amount to nothing.

The military man walked me down a hallway and through a set of automatic doors. We turned left and then right. The many hallways painted white featured the occasional framed photo of a WT trainer and their partner. We finally reached a room on the corner of the hallway. The military man reached into his pocket and pulled out a key card. He swiped the key card and opened the door. Once we entered the room there were two armed guards standing alongside an elevated medical chair. I became concerned and fearful for what may happen next. Who was this man and what was he trying to do?

"What are we doing here?" I asked. "I'm Herschel Steele's grandson."

The military man answered calmly, "Justin, my name is Jung-lee, as you know I am the instructor assigned to lead the first portion of the WT application. Come in and have a seat."

I slowly moved to the medical chair and stared at each armed guard before I sat in the chair.

Jung-lee continued, "It's come to the Animal Bridging Council's attention that you are in fact the blood relative of our president, Herschel Steele. That being said, I have to ask, how alike are you?"

"How alike are we?" I nervously responded.

"Do you share the same abilities?"

"Umm..." I looked down at my hands unsure and unaware how to answer.

"Justin, let me remind you. You are under oath and any breach of trust or lying of any sort will lead you to disqualification."

"I am," I hesitated nervously.

"You are what?"

"W-we have the same power. I guess you could say, we share the same gift."

"I see. I appreciate your honesty. But just in case you want to use that ability of yours." Jung-lee motioned to the two guards. The two men grabbed each of my arms and strapped my arms to the chair. My fight or flight mode had been activated and my first reaction was to pull away aggressively. I clenched my fist attempting to activate my power.

"Come on. Come on!"

My emotions began running rampant and I was unable to regain control. My blood pressure was rising as I forcefully tried to pull away. The men refused to give an inch and successfully strapped my arms to the chair. I sat in the chair and continued struggling to pull my arms free from the straps. Jung-lee brought out a sharp metallic tool from a medical stand near my chair.

"We will now plant this inhibitor chip in your spine. Please note it will be a little uncomfortable at first, but it's just a safety precaution to protect the other applicants. This should even you out. If you try to remove this before you complete your application, you will be disqualified."

Suddenly Grandpa burst through the door with Dusty by his side, "WHAT IS THE MEANING OF THIS?"

"Grandpa!" I yelled.

"Mr. President, we are following the protocol and procedures by planting an inhibitor chip."

"The hell you are. Did you receive clearance for this? Who authorized this?"

"Madam Yue personally sent me down here after learning that your grandson was applying today. The council voted before you arrived this morning."

"Take your hands off my grandson."

The two-armed soldiers stood still and looked back at Jung-lee.

"NOW." Grandpa sternly stated.

The men quickly released me and left the room while Jung-lee slowly followed after them.

"Of course, Mr. President," Jung-lee muttered. "Two minutes. But if he doesn't comply, he will be disqualified."

Jung-lee closed the door behind him, and Grandpa looked back at me. Grandpa walked over and kneeled down in front of my chair.

"I'm sorry. This is my fault."

"After everything you've taught me, you couldn't have said, 'Hey, by the way, since you take after me, they're going to drill a chip into your spine!'" I said sarcastically.

Grandpa exhaled deeply, "It's more complicated than that. They're afraid of us. Of you and of me. We're different Justin. We have this power that is unlike anything this world has ever seen. I wanted to be compliant and inform them more about this gift, so that they wouldn't be afraid of me. But now, they know how it works and how to diminish our ability. They know how to stabilize us."

"I understand. I hate needles, but it makes sense. It has to be fair for the other applicants."

"If you want a career in the WT, to join me and your father in this organization, then yes. It sucks, it's not fair and it shouldn't be you, but it is."

I exhaled deeply and wiped my face. "Grandpa, it's all right. I promise, let's get this over with."

Grandpa stood and placed his hands on my shoulders.

"I'll be right here, and I'll make sure nothing bad happens to you. Remember your training and do not be afraid. This power does not define who you are. You do."

Grandpa leaned in and hugged me tight.

"You can still fight. The gift is inside you," he whispered.

Jung-lee busted through the door. "Time is up, Mr. President. Has Justin agreed to doing this or not?"

Grandpa glared back at Jung-lee then looked back at me. He smiled, nodded, and patted my back.

"Yes he has. Justin here is prepared to move forward with the inhibitor chip. Of course, your armed guards will no longer be necessary. I myself will remain for the procedure."

Jung-lee sighed. "Sir, I believe you would be much more comfortable—"

"By my grandson's side."

"Of course, as you wish. Let us begin the procedure."

I nodded and trusted Grandpa with the procedure. The fear of feeling sharp tools drilled into my spine made me worried about how it would affect my ability to move freely. But I knew the procedure was the right thing to do.

After five minutes of installing the device successfully in my back, I was able to walk away with little to no pain. The inhibitor chip had been successfully sewn in and sat just above my shoulder blades. The numbing feeling kept me from achieving my maximum strength. A flash of anger raced down my spine as I clenched my fist. The feeling left my muscles aching from the device. Grandpa and I left the room as he led me back to the waiting area.

"Remember, you are not allowed to remove it. Follow the rules and you will be all right."

"Yes, sir."

"I'll see you soon. Keep fighting."

I stood in the doorway of the waiting area as everyone turned around and faced me.

Rus walked up to me and handed me my bag, "Are you all right? I thought you were gone for sure."

"Yeah, I'm all right."

"What happened?"

"It's a long story. That testing supervisor, Jung-lee, is not as nice as he looks."

"I believe that."

An announcement came over the intercom. The speakers inside were booming with the same voice we had heard on stage. The Masked Woman spoke: "Congratulations to all our soon-to-be Wildlife Trainers! You have passed the aptitude exam with ease, but that does not mean you are a part of the program just yet. Next, we will move into our combat portion. Please exit the break room and report to the main hall again for further instructions. Applicant Number One, Applicant Number Two, Applicant Number Three, Applicant Number Four, Applicant Number Five and Applicant Number Seven, I will see you all shortly in the main lobby."

Rus didn't waste a second and began walking out the door. He didn't look back to see if I was following or if I remained close by. His gesture made me realize that I had to stand up for myself. I walked forward with pride, tightening my fists through the numbness, and was ready to fight any and all challengers that stood in my way. I had to make it a priority to look out for myself.

The Masked Woman appeared on stage, waiting until we all returned to the center circle of the room as we did prior. "Thank you for continuing this process. Before we press on, I must legally remind you all of the following safety precautions. Do any applicants have any heart, lung, kidney, or other health conditions we should know before continuing the next part of the exam? Each of you visited a doctor and received a physical examination in preparation for this application. You all received promising reports with no problems; however, this next section will test physical strength, stamina, and determination. Speak now or forever suffer the consequences that may follow."

My lungs experienced trauma at a young age which caused them not to develop properly. Multiple asthma attacks at the age of two made breathing a challenge. However, Grandpa never wanted the condition to limit or stop me from enjoying the day-to-day living. I had been spoon fed the idea that I grew out of it.

One day I pushed myself too far past my limit, and my lungs seemed to operate sporadically. They would not communicate with the body as they should. One of my lungs collapsed which required me to stay in bed for three days until it was safe to walk again. From that day on I learned the value of each breath that I took.

For safekeeping, I started carrying a highly concentrated inhaler, labeled "Unibort," on my person at all times. I remained silent, for the sanctity of my future.

The Masked Woman continued, "Good, as your files state, you are all happy and healthy applicants who can take devastating blows to your internal organs. I just wanted to make sure. Upon entry into the next room, the door closest to the stage on your right, we will begin our hand-to-hand combat portion. Please keep in mind your goal is simple. Take down each opponent who is positioned against you. One applicant will begin as the defender, one will begin as the attacker. When you are tasked as the defender, you will not receive any padding or protection. You must disarm and strike down your opponent using your body and defensive abilities. Everyone must be a defender and surpass at least four rounds. If you are able to defend yourself and surpass those four rounds, you will successfully move to the final portion. As a defender, if you are knocked off your feet and disarmed before the end of the fourth round, you will be asked to leave. Attackers, you will be knocked down and out of bounds, but you will remain; however, if you are knocked unconscious, you too will be asked to leave.

"Oh, I almost forgot! As a defender, you may also ask for more opponents after you clear four rounds and will still move forward to the hero portion. The more opponents you disarm, the better off you will be for the animal selection process."

I whispered to myself, "The punching bags, clever old man."

"Now then, we will begin the process in numerical order. Applicant One, will begin the combat portion and will defend himself against Applicant Two. Once he succeeds, the next round he will continue against Applicant Two and Applicant Three and so on and so forth. You must defeat at least four applicants in the fourth round to move forward. Once inside, each attacker will be placed in body armor to give each of you an advantage over the defender. Your speed will be limited, but you will carry more protection with you and will be able to last longer for the future rounds. We have armored staff on standby who may jump in if a defender proceeds beyond expectations."

Rus yelled out, "I have a question!"

The Masked Woman answered, "Yes, Applicant One?"

Rus confidently asked, "What's the record? Better yet, how many rounds will it take to beat the record?"

The Masked Women chuckled. "Well, that would be quite ambitious, but I'll entertain the thought. The highest recorded number of rounds completed by someone before retiring was fifty. And yes, I mean five-zero. I implore you all not to strive for the record. The applicant who succeeded this had little to no energy left for the hero portion. Play smarter, not harder. Now then, listen well over the intercom for instructions in between rounds as well as who will be next to step up."

The door to the right of us opened automatically. I looked back at Grandpa again just as I did before. He nodded at me with determination and understanding. I nodded back and made my way through the doorway of the next challenge.

Inside was a dimly lit room with a large indoor matted ring. The wide, rectangular, padded, burgundy room featured a wall full of safety equipment intended to be handed out and utilized by us. All of the elected applicants were to become attackers, everyone except Rus.

Once the lights came on completely, there were two short, older, male instructors, two men wearing and showcasing the same safety armor. They called themselves the Bonsai brothers. The black-haired brother stepped up, "I'm Bon." The blonde-haired brother stepped up. "I'm Sai."

The two spoke and moved in sync, "And we are the Bonsai brothers! Do not be afraid. We are twins!"

"Welcome to the combat portion," Bon said.

"Applicant One, please place your belongings down and stand in the center of the fighting arena," Sai said.

"Remember, your objective is to knock each attacker down or out of the ring," the two said in sync.

Rus moved to the left corner of the room and placed his belongings down. He knelt next to his bag and took off his shirt. Rus looked at his shirt and smiled before placing it inside his pack and stepping into the middle of the ring. The Bonsai brothers helped gather burgundy foam safety armor for

Applicant Number Two to wear. Each attacking applicant was armed with a head piece, elbow protectors, a chest piece, gloves, and a mouth guard. However, the defender was given nothing. Applicant Number Two was the tall red-haired girl who seemed very strong. She had the physique of a bodybuilder, but Rus was no pushover. He was tough, had a leaner muscle build, and he was fast. Her fighting stance was grounded, slow, and centered. She entered the ring and watched Rus like a red-tailed hawk admiring her prey from above.

"Round one, Applicant One and Applicant Two. Fight!" Bon announced.

Rus wasted no time and immediately launched himself toward the red-haired applicant. He ran at her with the intention to bulldoze her over. With his combined speed and stamina, I could tell he was ready to fight with every ounce of his being.

Instead of launching a full-blown attack, he maneuvered left and stepped right in order to sweep the woman's leg. Applicant Two jumped up and punched Rus directly in the face as he was returning to his stance. Rus turned back immediately and grappled his arms around the girl's neck. He locked his right forearm around her neck and kicked the inside of her right knee. Suddenly the woman dropped to the floor as Rus remained standing.

Sai announced, "End of round one. Applicant One remains!"

Applicant Two spoke to Rus as she raised her fist toward him. "Nice move, too bad it won't work a second time."

Rus raised his fist and politely fist bumped with her glove. "We'll see about that."

"The name's Fay, by the way," Applicant Two remarked.

"I remember. I'm Rus," he smiled.

I began clapping awkwardly, reluctantly finding myself the only one applauding Rus in the room. Rus looked over at me with a bruised cheek and nodded to me while smiling. A silent "thank you" was received. Rus was a fighter. He'd trained with his father who was trained by his father, the alleged last known living crystal claw trainer. Mr. Zhang would train Rus for hours on end; however, he and I had never sparred against one another. I realized that I would now have to forgo fear and pain and even friendship, knowing the inevitability of having to go against Rus so that he could continue his journey into the WT. I would be his last opponent of the combat portion. I swallowed deeply and cleared my throat as I mentally prepared for a fight I believed I would lose.

"Round two, Applicant One versus Applicant Two and Applicant Three. Fight!" Bon announced.

Rus was now fighting Fay and the dark-haired, young woman, Lyza. The two women slowly began to circle Rus as he stood watching both. He tightened his fists and breathed easy, as he detected Fay's attack just moments before she launched herself at him. He simply dodged to the right while he extended his left leg behind. He brought his left leg inward to trip Fay as he forced his right palm into her spine in one fluid motion, causing her to fall to the floor.

Lyza wasted little to no time moving in on Rus while he was dealing with Fay. She raised her right leg attempting to roundhouse Rus once he connected his right palm to Fay's back. Rus quickly raised his left hand as he turned to Lyza and blocked her kick. He brought his right arm underneath Lyza's leg and forcefully punched her leg. Lyza flew backward but somehow remained on her feet. With quick thinking, she was able to change her fall into a backflip.

Rus got into his fighting stance. His legs lay stacked diagonally shoulder-length apart, hands up while he continued to bounce, a method similar to the one my grandfather had taught me. Lyza stood still and took a deep breath as she took her stance. Her legs bent and spread far apart while her body moved closer to the ground. Lyza covered more surface area with her legs and afforded less breathing room for Rus with her left arm out and her right arm close to her body. Rus ran at her and jumped while raising his right fist. Lyza stood her ground and raised her forearms. With the combined effort of gravity, the strength of his punch and his body weight, Rus successfully landed on Lyza and knocked her to the floor.

"Round two complete, Applicant One remains," Sai announced. "Next up is Applicant Two, Applicant Three, and Applicant Four. Applicant Five you are on deck. Please hurry and collect your armor!"

I maneuvered through the applicants and quickly made my way to the right side of the room. I examined the different colors and sizes of padded armor that covered the wall. There were several colors ranging from burgundy, to green, and blue. They all seemed to be extremely worn down and often used all except for the black safety armor in the top right-hand corner.

"What's the black armor for?" I asked Sai.

Sai smiled and snickered. "That's only for the elite members to enter the ring. That's who we must resort to if they last for too many rounds."

I imagined Grandpa as if he'd put on the black armor and slammed his fist into opponents. I'm sure he'd absolutely obliterate them all.

"Round three, Applicant One versus Applicant Two, Applicant Three and Applicant Four. Fight!" Bon yelled.

I lost track of time and quickly started throwing my safety armor on. I carefully positioned the burgundy body armor over the inhibitor chip. First was the snug, stinky head piece, then the oversized chest piece, followed by the sweaty, used arm protectors, and finally, some warm mixed martial arts grappling gloves. I felt like a discarded gym sock. I was covered in sweat that was not my own and was unsure how well I'd be able to fight in the padding. Regardless, I closed my eyes and inhaled through my nose and out my mouth. I reminded myself to watch my breath and to try my best. Everyone was watching. I glanced up and noticed four different cameras carefully placed on the ceiling in each corner of the room. The cameras didn't miss a single strike, dodge or maneuver that occurred on the floor.

Suddenly I heard Sai announce:

"Round three complete, Applicant One remains. Next up is Applicant Two, Applicant Three, Applicant Four and Applicant Five."

I peered over to see three girls rise from the mat as Rus stood in the middle of the floor dripping sweat from his body and blood from his nose. He was calm and content. He understood the job at hand. Fay stepped away to drink some water she had stored in her pack. She appeared to be more tired than Rus. Lyza removed her head piece and wiped the sweat from her forehead as she continued to stretch. Applicant Four was still trying to stand up. The thought dawned on me that Rus may not be backing down or taking it as easy on these girls. He's going up against me and three other applicants. I felt torn because it was my duty to fight him as hard as I could, but a part of me still wanted him to pass. If he didn't pass, he wouldn't be with me and Roxanne in the Cultivation Squad. Of course, I realized that I could not allow myself to think that way, not about my best friend. I had to focus on myself the same way Rus had to. All I could do was hope for the best.

"Round four is about to begin, Applicant One versus, Applicant Two, Applicant Three, Applicant Four and Applicant Five. Ready? Fight!" Bon announced.

I stood my ground ready in my fighting stance, my legs shoulder length apart as I held my hands up ready to block whatever hits may come my way. I clenched my fists as they rubbed alongside the soft interior of the gloves. Rus immediately sprinted toward each of the girls one by one and attempted to force them out of bounds. Once he knocked Fay out of bounds, Lyza saw his approach and decided to go after Rus directly. Applicant Four started to back up and accidentally stepped out of bounds. Lyza and I were all that stood in the way of Rus moving forward to the hero portion of the exam. Rus yelled out, "Two to go! Come on, Justin!" I ran after Rus as he lifted up his fists. I remembered each moment he stole with Roxanne in front of me and a part of me became angry. Rus threw a right-hand punch at my face, but I forced my left hand out to block and change course with my right hand. I brought my right fist up into Rus's stomach.

Rus effortlessly blocked my uppercut by cupping his hands together over my fist and head-butted my face. I stumbled backward attempting to keep my balance. Rus had hit me so hard that my head piece became lodged over my eyes. I lifted the head piece up and witnessed Lyza throwing jabs at Rus. However, he was struggling to block each one. Which is when he brought back his fist once more and made contact with Lyza's face. I heard a slight yell of pain escape Lyza's body as his fist made direct contact with her cheek. I was enraged when he struck her down. My eyes grew large in shock and in anger. I took a deep breath and concentrated my attack on Rus. I could feel a heat stirring inside me like a blacksmith's forge. As if the inhibitor chip and my gift were having an internal battle within my body. I ripped off my right glove and tightened my fist. The weight in my hand began to grow but the color of my fist remained the same.

Rus quickly raised his left fist and swung at me with full force. I watched Rus try to steer his punch to the middle of my face. My rage began to stir as my blood began to boil. My aggression took me to a place that made me forget where I was. That was when our fists collided. I delivered my punch directly into Rus's right-hand. Our fists clashed for a moment until I pushed through Rus's fingers. I felt Rus's fingers fracture inside Rus's hand. I fell forward and somersaulted out of bounds. My hand felt as if it had been run over by a truck. Rus remained standing, unphased, in the center of the mat with a fractured hand. He had little to no strength left, was covered in sweat, but still remained standing. In the end, he pushed through the pain.

CHAPTER 5

Hero Work

I looked up from my bowl of chili at Grandpa as we sat at the dinner table.

I hesitantly asked, "What activates it? I mean, how do I control it?"

Grandpa smiled and placed his spoon down as he swallowed his current bite.

"You have to direct it at something. Think of it as if you have a job at hand, one that needs to be completed. You either attack or defend. When you figure out how to complete the task, your body will do the rest."

"What if I lose control?"

"Our gift requires constant focus. Now if you lose that focus while activating it, your body will lock up. Your muscles will meld together and leave you defenseless. The effect is temporary, but you have to use it carefully."

"Will I be allowed to use it in the combat portion?"

"No, no you won't."

"Round four is complete!" Sai loudly announced. "A warning to applicant Number Five: if you remove your safety armor again before your turn, you will be disqualified. Applicant One remains. Applicant One will be moving on to the hero portion!"

"Do you wish to continue?" the Bonsai brothers asked simultaneously.

I looked down and noticed my fist had been badly bruised and bloodied. The inhibitor chip was nullifying my gift which caused the skin to split in between my fingers. I witnessed Rus hobble over to the Bonsai brothers and outside of the arena, displaying his own injuries with fractured bones and split skin on his left hand. Rus's eyes found me from across the room. He looked at me with heavy eyes drenched with pain and disappointment. He quickly looked away, wiped the sweat from his eyes and forced out a stubborn remark.

"I'll stay put. One. More. Round!" Rus announced.

The Bonsai brothers cheered and reached for their individual sets of bongo drums placed next to the safety armor. Both brothers howled with excitement as they slammed onto their drums. I knew Rus was past his limit and needed to retire, but he wanted to look as desirable as possible for the best partner and the best division. He had his heart set on something else, something I wouldn't have ever found without his friendship. Pride. Rus took some medical supplies out of his pack along with a bottle of water. He drank half the bottle and poured the other half on his head.

I took out medical supplies from my bag to tend to my fist. Afterward I put my glove back on and walked over to him.

"Are you all right?"

Rus pulled out a cement bandage, a gray, quickly solidifying fabric; unfolded, it can be molded into any position the user wishes. The bandage remains intact regardless of any hit, liquid, or heat. The wrap hardens, essentially making the wearer stuck with a healing cement-like block on their wound. It's designed for emergency purposes only. Rus carefully wrapped it around his left hand.

"You know, I expected something like this would happen. To be pushed, I just never expected it would come from you. What the hell was that?"

"Rus, I'm sorry. The way you hit Lyza—"

"Because she's my opponent! This is what we are asked to do, Justin!"

"You're going into the next round one-handed. You won't be allowed to swing that bandage at anyone, and if you do, you'll be disqualified. They'll call it a weapon. Come on, man, I didn't mean to break your hand!"

Frustrated, confused, and shaking his head in disbelief, Rus walked off.

Lyza wiped the blood away from her lip and glared at Rus. She had the look of someone who had killed before, one that was both enticing and frightening at the same time.

Rus tied the fabric along the inside of his hand in an attempt to guide his bones. He carefully molded his hand into a fist and locked it into place. Once the band secured his hand, he cautiously walked back to the mat.

"Just tap out and retire now!" I yelled. "Save your strength for the hero portion!" Rus smirked and lifted his left hand enclosed now in the heavy compress. "Why don't you make me?"

Rus walked backward onto the mat while he continued to make eye contact with me. He accidentally backed into Applicant Number Seven, Wyatt. He was the largest applicant applying for the WT. He was 6'8, three hundred pounds of muscles and had the ability to break Rus in half. I was thankful I did not have to face him this round, but a part of me was worried for Rus. Wyatt had a dark aura about him as he examined Rus up and down before forcefully shoving Rus away from the center of the mat. Rus was exhausted and in pain from the round prior. He was in no shape to face off against a room full of opponents, let alone Wyatt.

Wyatt muttered, "This will be fun. I wonder if it's possible to remove you from the competition myself."

"Let's see how hard you can hit, big man." Rus glared up at him.

"Round five is about to begin, Applicant One versus Applicant Two, Applicant Three, Applicant Four, Applicant Five and Applicant Seven. A win from this round will provide a better standing in the animal selection process." Bon announced.

"Rus, please. This man will kill you," I whispered.

"FIGHT!" Bon yelled out.

Without hesitation, Wyatt ran directly at Rus. Wyatt picked up speed and faced Rus with his right fist raised. Rus began to dance around the mat, dodging just underneath Wyatt's fist. Rus rose from the other side and faced me alongside the other applicants in the ring in our fighting stances. Rus studied the room and moved toward Fay once again. He pulled back his right leg going for another ankle sweep. He released his right leg back to swing at Fay's left ankle.

Wyatt continued after Rus and spat out, "Come here!"

Rus ducked down before he could follow through Fay's ankle while Wyatt threw a deadly punch with his right hand. Rus successfully dodged to the right just as Wyatt connected his punch to Fay's face. She was launched about ten feet, knocking her out of bounds and unconscious. I looked around and noticed the Bonsai brothers were not reprimanding Wyatt for causing harm to a teammate. It was a clear violation of the exercise to harm another armored applicant. Instead, they rushed to Fay's side and made sure she was okay to continue. Fay still needed to succeed as a defender if she was going to be admitted into the hero portion. Her face appeared red and swollen as she remained motionless on the ground.

Bon exited the room hurriedly to retrieve ice and a medic bot while Sai continued to keep watch. Grandpa never told me about this part of the process. I looked over to Lyza as she stood tall in her fighting stance. She noticed me looking at her and annoyingly looked back at Rus.

Before I knew it, Rus was moving in on Lyza again and attempted a roundhouse kick with his right leg. As Rus lifted his leg and began swinging at Lyza, she dodged by crouching low and connecting her right fist to the inside of his left knee. Rus became unbalanced and wobbled backward to get away and catch his balance.

Wyatt grinned from ear to ear, a sinister look of evil engulfed his eyes as he rushed at Rus. Wyatt lifted both his fists attempting to punch Rus into oblivion. He pulled back both of his arms attempting to slam into Rus's back. Just moments before he made contact, I managed to jump in front of Rus and held up my forearms. I closed my eyes and mentally prepared to embrace the heavy hit from Wyatt. When I closed my eyes, I remembered the first time I met Rus. I was unsure if I could access enough power to defend myself from such a powerful blow. I remembered the friend that I made, how he made me feel whole, and not alone. I clenched my fists tight ready to embrace the full force of the blow.

I heard a slight "tink" sound before opening my eyes. I opened my eyes to see Wyatt's gloves had been stopped by my forearms. The gift had been nullified but I was still strong enough to stop Wyatt's punch.

"That's some high-quality protective gear," I announced awkwardly.

Until I glanced down and noticed part of my safety armor had ripped. The severe force of the impact caused the fabric of the gear to tear. The pain came shortly after the point of contact. Wyatt wasted no time trying to force his way through me.

I was amazed I had stopped Wyatt in his tracks without any of my power. I looked back at Rus as his mouth dropped. Before anyone was able to utter another word or throw another punch, Rus kneeled down, reached out with his good hand, and tapped on the mat twice.

"Applicant One has chosen to retire," Sai announced. "Congratulations, you will be moving forward to the hero portion of the application! Applicant Number Two, will be next... Umm, hopefully."

As the day continued, Rus was exempt from having to take part in the combat portion as an attacker. What the Bonsai brothers did not mention was that once you complete and pass this part of the course, you no longer have to continue as an attacker. Rus was, once again, the first to make it back to the break room that had been transformed into an infirmary. Rus received medical treatment on his left hand. A multitude of small medical bots worked carefully to remove his cement band aid. The medic bots realigned and fixed each of Rus's fingers as if they were brand new. The amount of technology the courthouse staff had at their disposal was unheard of. After Rus left, they filled in his role with a bonsai bot.

Bonsai bots were automated artificial intelligence bots that embodied the same characteristics of the fighter that it was designed to study. The bonsai bot learned and absorbed all of Rus's moves and resembled Rus in size, weight, and facial expression. Essentially, it became a robotic Rus. Each bot was designed with built-in pain receptors and acted very similarly to the fighter it learned from. Grandpa told me that the bots sometimes even picked up catch phrases during a fight. Each bot was equipped with different levels of difficulty and continued to get harder after each round.

Fay was unable to continue because of the concussion she received from Wyatt. She was knocked out of bounds but more importantly she had been knocked unconscious. Therefore, Fay was unable to move forward in the WT application process. The Animal Bridging Council had to vote to see if she would be invited back to compete in the WT again. If the vote was unanimous, Fay would be allowed to return another day and retry the program. Wyatt truly did a number on her. It was a depressing site as Bon removed her Applicant Number Two module. Fay was taken out on a stretcher and replaced by a Bonsai bot.

During the next few rounds Lyza was able to successfully knock out both bots. She playfully pushed me out of bounds and slammed Wyatt's face into a wall. It was all very satisfying to watch. After she surpassed the fourth round, she tapped out and moved on to the hero portion. Once Lyza left and made her way back to the break room. She was replaced by another bot. Applicant Number Four could not defeat all three bots in the third round. She was pinned to the floor by Lyza's bot and was disqualified.

Finally, there we were, just Wyatt and me, surrounded by a roomful of AI units. I removed my gloves, my shoes, my socks, my head piece, and my applicant shirt, revealing my sore, skinny muscles and exposed inhibitor chip lodged into my spine.

"This is the future, huh? Pfft, pathetic," Wyatt muttered.

"Artificial intelligence?" I asked.

Wyatt laughed. "No, fake opponents. What is that sticking out of your back?"

I stood up straight. "It's nothing."

"Wait, I know you. It's Steele, right? That's your name, isn't it?"

"Do I know you?"

"I saw you walk in with Herschel Steele. Of course, you're related."

"It doesn't matter who I am. Right now, what matters is what we do on the mat. That's it."

"You don't get it do you? You're not getting to the hero portion.

"Umm, why not?" I was startled by his comment.

"The way I see it, your dad destroyed countless buildings fighting members of the AFA. That destruction bankrupted my parents."

"Didn't your family have insurance on the buildings?"

"We couldn't afford it! Builders always had a bad rap. Being paid less than any other part of the country. When we do the most work. You dealt my family a deadly blow. Now, I'm going to return the favor."

"I am not my father, and I'm sorry about your family. If you have a problem, find me on the mat. Until then, leave me alone."

Wyatt grunted and walked back to the right side of the room alongside the Bonsai brothers.

We'd been inside the room for two hours straight. I sipped a little water and took a puff from my inhaler. I wanted to be in that break room with Rus and Lyza. To hear their side, to apologize and make sure we were all okay. But first, I had a job to do, and I wasn't going anywhere until I disposed of these bots. Within the first three rounds, I did not attempt to access my internal armor. I had no choice but to remember my Grandfather's training, which allowed me to dodge each one of the bot's attacks. I'd block, punch, and kick each one of the bots out of my way until each one fell to the floor. It was only when I made my way to round four that things really started heating up.

Bon announced, "Round four, Applicant Number Five versus bot one, bot two, bot three, and Applicant Number Seven. Remember, after you surpass this round you will be admitted into the hero portion. Ready? FIGHT!"

Finally, the moment that I had been waiting for arrived. I wiped the sweat from my brow and got into my stance. The same stance my grandfather taught me to get my blood pumping and move faster than my opponent. I looked down at my fists and noticed how bruised they'd gotten from defeating the previous bots. My breath was beginning to thin, and I could hear a small wheeze from my chest. I couldn't allow myself to think about my lungs. Now was no time to harp on weakness. I breathed in deeply and saw Wyatt raging straight toward me.

"Come on, Steele, let's get to it!"

I dove after Rus's bot and wrapped both of my arms around its head into a grappling hold. I pinned the bot's arms in the air around its head. Rus's bot slid its right leg behind me and attempted to kick the inside of my right knee. I quickly turned with the bot's head in my left hand. I lifted my right leg and blocked the bot's low kick. I kicked the bot off balance and slammed the bot's head to the ground.

Once Wyatt reached me, he launched his notorious right hook. I quickly dodged to the left while struggling to stay in bounds. He opened his left hand and reached out to grab my throat. I knew this man was trying to do more than knock me out of bounds. I saw fit to treat the situation as if he were a villain. I grabbed his left hand with both of my hands wrapping it behind his back into an arm bar. I lodged my right hand down on Wyatt's shoulder blade and jammed his wrist upward. I attempted to dislocate his arm entirely.

Wyatt pulled his body forward and turned left into me, knocking me off his arm. He began wailing high velocity hammer fists at my head, attempting to take me out. I carefully dodged each hit by imagining they were punching bags, while I remained standing.

After about six swings, Wyatt stopped to catch his breath. I turned to see the other two bots rush toward me. I reached down for Fay's bot's left ankle, since she was smaller and lighter I had the best chance of being able to lift it. I quickly grabbed the ankle and slung the bot into Lyza's bot. Lyza's bot fell out of bounds as I turned around and continued, slinging the bot into Wyatt.

Wyatt turned just as the bot made direct contact with his face. He grabbed the bot from me and threw it out of bounds. He paced backward, blinking rapidly as if he could not see properly. It appeared as if he were cautiously wobbling around, waiting for his vision to return or for me to make the next move.

He laughed. "Ha, nice throw Steele. You know this won't stop me!"

Wyatt began swinging his arms with his full force behind each swing. I was able to dodge the first haymaker to the left, the second punch to the right, even the third swing by jumping upward. However, the fourth haymaker was much faster than the others, and I had no time to respond. Wyatt put all of his body weight into his fist and powerfully punched me backward. I was forced backward, but luckily remained on my feet. I looked around surprised and questioned how I was still standing. Drops of blood began to seep from my lip. I licked my lips and wiped my face. The man hit much harder than the punching bags, that much was certain. I shook my head and remained focused, as I watched Wyatt catch his breath and regain his sight.

I silenced my mind and attempted to access my gift and tried to go on the offensive. The weight from my metallic strength remained within, yet I could not fully access it. I was not getting anywhere with Wyatt, and I was running out of options.

I remembered one of my grandfather's teachings on pressure points, recalling the exact location on the body in order to immobilize your opponent. I began to carefully study Wyatt's body as he slowly approached me. I slowed my breathing down and searched for small areas of his massive body that revealed a nerve that lay close to its surface, where the only support the nerve had was bone or had little to no muscle mass to protect it. He had minor openings on his face that were not protected by muscle. I had to stick and move.

My feet slowly circled Wyatt just as Grandpa circled me during our training sessions.

Prowling about the mat, stalking my opponent, I said, "You know you remind me of someone."

"Oh yeah? Who's that?" Wyatt asked.

"A bully. Someone I faced just a few days ago. Someone who's in jail," I snarled.

"You and I both know there's only room for one of us to move forward, and it's going to be me," Wyatt barked back.

I should've just knocked him out of bounds and been done with him. But even if I had knocked him out, he would've torn those bots apart and rejoined us in the hero portion. What if he did the same thing to Lyza and Rus? I knew Wyatt had to be stopped. No one should've been that cruel to their potential team members. I decided I'd stop him there and then without a second thought.

My feet dug into the mat as I leapt toward my opponent with quick precise movements. Sweat ran down my heavy fists as I launched them in-between Wyatt's thighs and knees. I continued sprinting around Wyatt delivering minor blows to his knees.

Wyatt backed away and began slowly learning my movements and fight patterns. He waited until I got close for him to make his move. I approached his right knee for a heavy blow when I noticed Wyatt's left fist approaching my face. I quickly dodged out of the way and redirected Wyatt's punch by slamming my fist into Wyatt's unpadded wrist. His wrist went limp and that was when I knew my plan was working.

"AGH! Come here!" Wyatt cried out in pain.

He reached out his right hand and swiped at my shoulder. Thankfully I was able to leap over his arm before I latched onto the back of Wyatt's neck. My forearms constricted around the giant's throat and rigorously tightened around his airway. The blunt point of my wrist successfully lodged into his trachea as I placed my left hand under my right and enhanced my hold.

Wyatt struggled to breathe and attempted to reach behind to try and pull me off. Lucky for me he was not able to reach me due to the thickness of the padding. The pads limited his flexibility and that's when I learned that he could not stop me. The giant applicant backed up and was attempting to take both of us out of bounds. I released my left hand and began punching Wyatt's neck as hard as I could.

Suddenly Wyatt fell to the floor struggling to breathe. I landed gracefully back on the mat while Wyatt started to flip and flail on the mat. He resembled a fish out of water. I brought back my right leg and followed through with a powerful roundhouse kick. Wyatt's body flew backward and crashed into the padded floor. He lost consciousness as blood dripped from his nose.

"Applicant Number Five has completed the fourth round, which means he will be moving onto the hero portion! Do you wish to continue?" Sai yelled out.

I looked around the room and examined the sweat and blood accumulated on the mat during my four rounds. At that point, I had an important decision to make. Continue on and destroy some bots or move forward and go to the break room? The opportunity was there, and I knew how I wanted to spend my time.

Blood continued down the corner of my mouth, "I'm pretty tired. I think I'll head to the break room."

"Excellent decision," the Bonsai brothers announced. "Applicant Five has chosen to retire and will be moving on to the hero portion!"

Bon moved toward Wyatt who was still out cold on the floor. "Can we get a medic bot for Applicant Number Seven? Medic!"

"Applicant Five, please gather your belongings and head back to the break room. A medic bot will be there to assist you," Sai said.

I placed my hands together and gestured toward Sai, "Thank you."

My lungs continued to struggle as I left the matted floor and retrieved my backpack. I nervously took out my shoes and socks and began getting dressed. The soft socks and inside of my shoes hugged my feet like an old friend as I pulled my Applicant Number Five shirt over my head. My fingers clasped around my backpack strap as I slung the bag over my right arm and departed. As I opened the door, I was met by a school field trip that appeared to be in the middle of a guided tour of the courthouse.

Young smiling faces all circled the lobby mindlessly examining the mural. I continued to walk by the class as a young boy glanced down from the mural and noticed me. The smeared sweat and blood on my face was not a pretty sight. The boy stared at me as if I were a rock star. I was familiar with the look. I had admired Dad and Grandpa in a similar fashion since I was little.

"Hello!" The boy waved.

I waved back and smiled. "Hey there."

"Are you taking the WT application?!"

I nodded. "Yep, I've completed the written exam and the combat portion. All that's left is—"

"The hero portion!" The boy continued.

I laughed. "Yeah that's right." A slight awkward lull occurred as the boy continued staring. I wiped my face and responded.

"Uh, yeah, I'm going to go get cleaned up, all right?"

The boy nodded. "Okay, good luck!"

A subtle smile grew across my face as I noticed Grandpa working steadily on his computer. I could tell he was emailing back and forth with his other three council members regarding the current standings of our group of applicants. They verbally could not speak out about the applicants in public. However, they could review the combat portion on their computer monitors. Grandpa had stopped for a brief moment and flared his nostrils. It seemed he wasn't overly happy that I punched Rus so hard. Grandpa continued typing on his computer and peered up at me. He nodded, smiled, and walked away from his desk into a nearby hallway. I nodded in understanding and headed toward the break room.

When I opened the door, I felt a slight jolt of pain in my left hand. The fist-to-fist encounter with Rus was catching up to me as my adrenaline subsided. I looked up and was overcome with a tidal wave of tension. The air in the room was incredibly thick, and it affected all who entered. Lyza sat on the far-left side of the room alone, drinking water and lying on a hospital bed. Rus sat alone on the far-right side of the room while two small medic bots continued working on Rus's hand. Rus and Lyza both glared back and forth at one another blaming the other for their current predicament. Both turned and glanced up at me from their beds when I entered. Lyza quickly looked away while Rus smiled and waved with his good hand.

There was a hospital bed assigned for me in the middle of the room. A small piece of paper sat folded on the bed with my name: "Justin Steele, multiple hairline fractures in numerous fingers, possible concussion, possible broken ribs, laceration on the lip, and possible broken nose."

A small medic bot spoke to me as I approached the bed. "Applicant Five, Justin Steele, is there anything I can get you? Ice? Pain medication? Bone regenerator additive? Bottle of water?"

I placed my bag alongside the bed and deeply exhaled. "That all sounds amazing. Yes, please."

The bot opened up and dispensed a small plastic cup with pills, pain medication, a bottle of water, and flew over to the mini fridge in the room. The bot flew back to my bed and placed all the items on the bed. The medic bot quickly x-rayed my body.

"No immediate or permanent damage to bones and or vital organs. Is there anything else I may assist you with? Bandages?"

I swallowed the meds and drank the water, "Nope, all good. Thanks."

The bot retreated upward toward what seemed to be a ventilation shaft, suddenly the shaft opened as the bot carefully flew through. I drank all the water and placed my bag on my bed. I unzipped the middle compartment from my gray and red backpack and pulled out my Unibort inhaler. My lungs were undergoing too much pressure in my chest. After I inhaled two puffs, the pressure instantly lifted. My body was beginning to go past its limit. I had to pace myself in the upcoming hero portion.

Lyza spoke calmly, "I see you were able to stop that jerk, Applicant Seven."

I carefully looked over toward the freckled, dark-haired young woman. She had a charming, foreign accent when she spoke. I began getting lost in the deep pools of brown in her eyes. Lyza delivered her words with such grace that any listener would enjoy a conversation with her.

My head turned back around and realized I hadn't responded to her comment. I glanced to my right and repositioned my body to face her. "I'm sorry, are...you...talking to me?"

"You were the only other person in here to take down the big guy, so yes I think so."

I laughed. "Oh, okay yeah. Sorry I just- Yeah. He was a piece of work. How did you know that?" I moved my bag and turned the bed toward her.

Lyza pointed behind me at the three TV monitors mounted on the wall above the doorway. She was resting in the hospital bed as she removed an ice pack from her right cheek, revealing where Rus had hit her. She still managed to have a sense of humor throughout the application. She laughed. "That guy was an ass. They show combat portions in here. How did you feel going against all the bots?"

I laughed. "Well, yours wasn't as tough as you, surprisingly."

"Just goes to show there is only one of me. I am Lyza."

"I know." I stuttered and corrected myself. "I m-mean I know you have a name. Yeah, sorry I- I'm Justin."

"I know. Justin Steele. You fight well. I think you will do well in Cultivation."

"That's certainly the goal. Where do you want to go?"

"Anywhere but here. I think any division will do. Just want to get away."

My eyes continued to study Lyza as she stared into the distance longingly. A mysterious energy seemed to linger beneath her skin. There was something different about her. A part of me was intrigued by her and wanted to know more. On the opposite side of the room a medic bot was finishing up on Rus. My friend sat still, staring at the monitor mounted on the wall. I stood and walked over to him, hoping to mend the fractured feelings of our friendship. In the background of the room, the Bonsai brothers were attempting to nurse Wyatt back to health. He was not waking up.

"Hey, man, how're you doing?" I hesitantly asked.

"Shh. Look." He pointed up at the television.

Bon approached the cameras mounted in the combat room. "Due to technical knockout, Applicant Number Seven cannot continue. Applicant Seven is disqualified as well and will not be invited back for unruly and disrespectful behavior. The remaining applicants are Applicant One, Applicant Three, and Applicant Five."

"Thank you for your hard work, and we wish you the best of luck with your application process into the WT," Sai announced.

The Bonsai brothers simultaneously yelled out, "Let your hearts be true and ring in the name of Ignacia!" The brothers bowed and waved to the cameras before they were shut off.

"How'd you do that?" Rus asked.

I peered down at my left fist and placed my ice pack over it, "Grandpa trained me."

Rus stared at my fists. "Guess you ended up finding Wyatt's weakness."

"He was his own weakness. Wyatt was mad and blamed me for his parent's financial situation. He was arrogant, but I had to pinpoint my attacks carefully."

"Exposing the smallest pressure points. I suppose your way was successful."

I glanced down at my fist, embarrassed. "I guess you can't always punch your way out of everything."

Rus raised his newly cast left arm and lifted a black permanent marker in his right hand.

"Tell that to my hand. You want to sign my cast?"

"Rus, I'm so sorry. I got carried away."

I signed my name on his sturdy blue cast which protected his forearm, wrist, and entire hand. "Sorry for breaking your hand. Much love, -Justin." I felt Lyza's negativity radiate toward Rus. Rus looked back at her and stared. I glanced back over at Lyza to see her glaring at Rus. I could tell Rus felt bad, but I was confused why he hadn't yet apologized or why he hadn't said anything to Lyza since I got there. I wanted her to know she wasn't alone in this and that she was no longer an enemy but our ally and maybe even a friend.

"He's sorry for hitting you! Aren't you, Rus?" I yelled as I nudged his left shoulder.

Rus turned toward me annoyed and glanced back at Lyza. "Yeah. I'm sorry about that."

Lyza leaned up in her bed and removed her ice pack. Her cheek was not as swollen as before, and the ice had helped nullify the redness in her face. She began to laugh loudly. Lyza's humor baffled me as I peered back at Rus confused and slightly concerned.

Lyza laughed. "It was part of exercise. No need. We are good. But try that again, and I will break your other hand."

After a second to meditate on her response, Rus laughed and then realized the gravity of her words. I became concerned for my own feelings toward this girl. I felt protective and grew angry at the thought of anyone harming her. Even the way she threatened my best friend was exhilarating. However, I was not off the hook just yet.

The next portion was going to push us to the next level. I remembered the layout of the course Grandpa had drawn up for me. I had to remember to stay focused at all costs. The possibilities were endless.

The Masked Woman suddenly entered the room with Jung-lee on her right and the Bonsai Brothers on the left. I returned to my empty hospital bed and turned it back around to face them.

"Applicants, the time has come," the Masked Woman announced. "Congratulations to all of you for making it this far and passing the first two portions of the Wildlife Trainer Application. The three of you have exemplified the definition of what it means to be a Wildlife Trainer. However, this portion will be extraordinarily difficult. The hero portion is housed in a giant stadium connected to the Courthouse. It is designed to feature obstacles that will present multiple opportunities to test your reaction time, your understanding of animals, and your problem-solving abilities. The hero portion has three parts. The first is called 'Mammal in a Maze.' Each of you have been randomly selected and assigned a specific mammal you must locate in the maze. Each mammal has a key tied around it. The objective: enter the maze, locate your assigned mammal, and remove the key safely in order to move to the next step. You must not and cannot physically harm your mammal. Failure to retrieve your key or mistreating your assigned mammal will result in disqualification."

Suddenly, the large screens showed three, red animal silhouettes on the screen. It took us little to no time to identify each animal. There was a canine of some sort, a kangaroo, and a rabbit.

The woman held up a small white cue card to read off the mammals assigned to each of us. She paused for a moment before examining Rus. "Applicant One. Your mammal will be a wild dog."

Rus nodded as she turned her attention to me and prepared to read her cue card. She said very plainly, "Applicant Five, you will receive a Ja–" Jung-lee suddenly stepped forward and whispered in The Masked Woman's ear. She looked at Jung-lee and then again back at her cue card. She continued, "My mistake, Applicant Five you will receive a grey kangaroo."

My brain began to scramble. I knew everything there was to know about a grey kangaroo. It was one of the largest kangaroos in existence; it could jump up to nine meters with each leap. It somehow used less energy the quicker it moved. These kangaroos were notoriously large, quick, and powerful. I was in trouble.

The Masked Woman continued on with Lyza, "That just leaves Applicant Three, the last available mammal for you to retrieve a key from will be a jack rabbit."

I couldn't help but question the situation. It appeared that the Masked Woman was originally going to announce the jack rabbit for me, but Jung-lee changed it. Why was he actively trying to make life more difficult? I was confused but even more annoyed.

"Retired military armed forces admiral, Jung-lee, please continue with the second part," the Masked Woman continued.

The rude and ruthless Jung-lee stepped forward with another cue card in his hand.

"We call this one, 'Search and Secure.' Once you have your key, you must exit the maze immediately. Do not waste time, or the hostage you are sent to save will perish. You each will have to venture into one of three locations. You must find a way to push through your location, rescue your captive, and guide them out safely. Remember to go through the location. If you retreat, you will not locate the exit. The Bonsai brothers will explain the third part after I announce the randomly selected locations for you three."

Jung-lee looked at his cue card and smiled before looking at me. "Applicant Five, you will penetrate the factory for your hostage."

Jung-lee continued as he glanced at Lyza. "Applicant Three, you will dive down to the submarine for yours."

Lastly, Jung-lee looked to Rus. "And Applicant One, you will climb up the treehouse to rescue yours."

"Excellent work to all of you," Bon spoke immediately.

"You have done very well," Sai continued.

"Here we hold the final part."

"The last obstacle before you join our organization."

Bon and Sai spoke simultaneously, "The Apex Predator."

Suddenly three more animal silhouettes appeared on the three screens. It wasn't until after I identified each one that I knew in my gut which animal I was bound to receive.

"You have been randomly selected to face one apex predator as your opponent," Bon continued.

"The objective is not to physically harm your opposition," Sai followed up.

"You must disarm them and neutralize the threat," Bon and Sai said simultaneously.

"Once the threat is neutralized and both you and your hostage are safe, you must cross the finish line with your captive unharmed," Bon stated.

"If you and your hostage cannot cross the finish line..." Sai followed up.

"You will be disqualified. Everything you have accomplished will be for nothing," Bon and Sai said simultaneously.

"Now, Sai will announce the apex predators that each of you must face," Bon stated.

Sai placed his cue card directly in front of his face so he could read it. Sai yelled out, "The Spotted Hyena will face applicant Number One."

Sai focused on Lyza. "The Saltwater Crocodile will encounter Applicant Number Three."

Sai arrived and examined my bed with worried eyes as his eyes eventually found mine. I felt his sympathy from across the room. I mumbled the animal under my breath just a moment before he declared my fate.

"Jaguar," I whispered.

"Lastly, the Jaguar will face off against Applicant Number Five," Sai proclaimed.

"You will have twenty minutes to complete all three obstacles," the Masked Woman declared. "You have approximately five minutes to report to the third and final door on the right-hand side of the lobby. It will take you to the hero portion starting line inside the stadium. At the sound of the buzzer, you will rush into the maze and begin the process simultaneously. Once this portion is successfully completed, we will announce your division and partner at the Animal Pairing Ceremony. Good luck to each of you and remember—" All of the WT application supervisors spoke simultaneously, "Let your hearts be true and ring in the name of Ignacia!"

I instinctively reached for my pack for the remaining protein bar and apple. I pocketed both in case I needed them during the last trial. I looked over and watched Rus slowly stand from his bed, exhaling deeply. He was trying to push his body forward to continue. Lyza and I both stood by the door waiting for him.

Without turning to me, Lyza asked, "Will he be all right against an apex?"

"He has to be," I sighed.

Rus made his way across the room and reached us near the door. "Well, come on, we only have a couple of minutes before we start!" He hid his pain behind his positivity, attempting to show no fear. In that moment, it appeared to us he may not have wanted us to see him afraid. I knew the act was not for us. It was for himself.

Trying to smile, I joked, "You're going to get a tortoise if you move any slower!"

Collectively, the three of us walked through the lobby carrying our backpacks. Three of the four overseers of the Animal Bridging Council all stood and watched us from atop their golden desk as we prepared to begin our final challenge. I couldn't find Grandpa, he wasn't at his desk, and it was unlike him not to be there for me. The three of us arrived at the doorway and entered one by one. First, Rus walked through confidently. Lyza followed shortly after, and then I stepped into the doorway. I was prepared to face off against some big-time animals. Before I entered, I looked back at Grandpa's empty desk. I exhaled deeply and stepped through the large doorway.

The doorway led us to a large stadium decked out with bright lights. The space had been upgraded with specialized appliances which made each applicant believe they had entered into a very different environment. We followed the bright yellow walkway down to the entrance of the maze. The first obstacle was nearby. The maze's heavy cemented walls sat twenty-five feet high in front of a bright yellow starting line. None of us were able to see past the giant cement walls that sat inside the stadium. We placed our bags down in the corner of the room next to the door we had entered. The large door we walked through suddenly closed, and the sound echoed across the space. A giant sports clock sat in the top left-hand corner of the stadium; an old relic left behind from hundreds of years ago. The timer on the scoreboard displayed "1:57" and was counting down the remaining time we had left. I spent the last two minutes stretching and peering into the maze attempting to locate any animal inside.

Thirty seconds remained as the Masked Woman announced, "Now, applicants, please select one of the three starting positions."

Three empty spots remained in front of us leading down three different entryways to the maze. Suddenly, I saw a giant silhouette hopping alongside the third entryway. I quickly walked toward the far-right racing position. Lyza stepped in the middle entryway while Rus hesitantly walked toward the remaining spot. The three of us looked at each other. Lyza seemed calm and calculative. She began pinpointing her path into the maze. Rus looked over at me and smiled before facing forward. I turned my body toward the maze, and there stood a giant, male, Eastern gray kangaroo. The marsupial stopped and stood tall. It appeared to be about eight feet tall. With giant legs like that, he could easily move up to forty miles per hour and average six feet per leap. I momentarily lost faith.

The giant digital buzzer rang, and we all began running toward the maze. The three of us entered and separated into our pathways. I saw the male kangaroo waiting for me. The closer I got, the stiller he became. I could see the shimmering key resting on his neck, hanging from a thick black lanyard. I was nervous because of the potential backlash alpha males release upon other kangaroos. Usually, male kangaroos are the ones who fight for territory and potential mates. I stopped about ten feet in front of the kangaroo and jumped to my left side, attempting to take the key by surprise. However, the kangaroo simply turned toward me, placed his tail back on the ground and launched his two studded feet into my mid-section.

I fell back instantly, slamming into the floor. The piercing blow to my mid-section was explosive. I felt the years of fighting, training, and the past victories he won over previous competitors; the many challenges he must have overcome in order to be the best in his mob of kangaroos. The kick took the breath out of me, and I struggled to stand and get my lungs back on track. I coughed repeatedly as I stood. The alpha kangaroo quickly bolted, making his way into the maze. I pulled my inhaler out of my pocket and took a big puff. I felt my lungs return to their intended state. I began sprinting after the giant marsupial as he romped down the maze's cemented hallways. He bounced with massive leaps, defying the laws of gravity. Down each hallway, he forked right, then left, and I struggled to maintain the pace needed to catch him. The kangaroo eventually disappeared from my line of vision. From behind I heard the approaching sound of a key jingling. I quickly turned to face my opponent only to find a small jack rabbit racing by me with a string trailing behind it.

Lyza was right on the rabbit's heels. She must've set a trap and found a way to slow it down using some baited string. The small mammal was losing its momentum as Lyza leaped toward the rabbit and landed on the string wrapped around its ankle. The rabbit was stopped instantly. It struggled to break away as Lyza calmly slid the black strap off the rabbit's back. After she collected her key, she removed the string and released the rabbit, allowing it to scurry away.

Lyza winked at me. "See you at the finish line, Justin Steele." She ran away with her key in hand. Every sore bone in my body became jealous of her timing. Lyza was unstoppable. The sports clock continued to run: 15:21. Just a little over fifteen minutes left until my AI hostage would bite the bullet. Suddenly, something ricocheted off the walls and shot into the air. The massive kangaroo had somehow found a way to climb the maze walls. He was leaping around the maze as he pleased. If I was going to have a chance to catch him, I had to scale the maze wall myself and use the wall-to-wall jump Grandpa taught me. The hallways appeared just narrow enough to scale.

I clenched my fists and began running alongside the maze wall. I confidently jumped upward, allowing both of my feet to land on the side of the maze wall. I applied the full force of my hamstrings into the wall which launched me to the other side of the maze wall. I jumped again and applied the same force into the wall with my right leg. I too wished to defy the full force of gravity. I pushed my foot into the wall and was lucky enough to launch myself upward. I rose high enough to land on top of the maze wall. The kangaroo stood atop the wall facing me, ready for another challenge.

"All right. I'll be taking that key now."

The kangaroo sneezed and wiped his nose.

"And now I'm talking to a kangaroo."

The kangaroo crouched down and sprung toward me. Each leap was made with more tenacity and speed than the last. I was nervous, but I hadn't come this far to be knocked down by a kangaroo, no matter what size. I remembered my dream and the teachings Grandpa had taught me. My body stood still as I placed my forearms out in front of me. I clenched my fists and prepared to embrace a hit from my opponent. I did not wish to cause any harm to the kangaroo: The priority was to defend myself from any further potential injury. I had to time it out right, and it had to be done quickly. This was my only chance to grab the key. I'd absorb the hit and jump toward the kangaroo to grab the key. I knew the possible peril of crashing onto the cement below, but it was a risk I had to take.

The kangaroo was just a couple of feet away from me when he stopped, placed his tail down again and lifted himself up in the air. I carefully positioned my forearms up to block the hard-studded feet of this alpha male, grey kangaroo. He connected both feet with his muscular legs into my forearms. I crouched and pushed forward and somehow successfully absorbed the blow which knocked the kangaroo off balance. The kangaroo began to slip and fall off of the wall. I quickly reached out for the key, barely grasping it with my right hand and reacting quickly enough to jump after the kangaroo. I grabbed his muscular left arm with my left hand. We were both hanging from the top of the maze wall by the strength of my right hand. The kangaroo began biting at my hand. I slowly eased him down before he kicked off the wall in a similar style I'd used to scale it.

The kangaroo paused, looked back at me for a moment and then leapt away. I pulled myself back up on the maze wall. I regained my balance and stood back up as I examined the old brass key. It was a massive key that was probably for a very large lock. I pocketed it and noticed the clock counting down: 10:12. With a little more than ten minutes remaining, there was no time to lose. I had to locate and get through the factory. I could see white smoke plumes in the distance alongside a giant treehouse. "That's got to be it."

I cautiously jogged atop the four-foot-wide wall that stood between me and a twenty-five-foot drop. A treehouse stood high in the distance on the far left of the stadium wall while a body of water appeared alongside it. A dense factory stood on the right side of the stadium surrounded by a body of water. I continued jogging forward. I even saw Rus in the distance desperately trying to catch his assigned wild dog. Rus was quick and was gaining on the dog's trail. It wasn't until he pulled out a protein bar and threw it in front of the dog that he was able to snag the key off before the dog aggressively bit back. The dog paused while Rus continued forward through the maze. I was relieved that he was able to carry on.

As I got closer, my eyes fixated on the factory entrance. It was a large, cement building with a wooden drawbridge and green ooze dripping down the outside of its walls. I made it to the last wall of the maze in the distance. I had no choice but to improvise and slide down the wall in order to save time. About halfway down I pushed off of it entirely and rolled sideways. I landed safely back down and pushed myself off the ground with haste. I noticed a restless pool of deep water lay between the treehouse and the factory. I was somehow comforted to know that we all weren't far from one another. My legs moved faster into the dark entrance of the factory.

"Where are you?" My voice echoed through the hallways.

I heard a muffled mumble in the distance. The interior was infested with rats, chemicals, rocks, eroding cement, and ancient lockers. The factory resembled an old employee lounge, one that had experienced some kind of chemical reaction that'd gone horribly wrong. I opened the lockers, I rolled massive rocks out of the way and attempted to listen more intently. I wasn't able to hear anything from anyone.

"WHERE ARE YOU?" I shouted with desperation.

Another small murmur carried across the factory walls. The sound came from a faintly closer source. A large doorway that stood alongside the lockers on the right side of the factory. After a hard shove the old door collapsed and crumbled. Inside were two steaming chemical reactors, both oozing with more green chemicals than I had ever seen.

The screens alongside the reactors stated "OVERLOAD". The chemicals were starting to spread throughout the room. Across the large room I could see someone's arms and legs were wrapped in chains, head covered with a white pillowcase. The person's mouth must've been taped shut because I was not receiving any kind of verbal response.

Leaping across the room, I dodged the chemicals and tore off the bag triumphantly. Only to find Grandpa with tape plastered across his mouth. He had been restrained with four locks, two on his wrists and two on his legs.

A nervous smile grew across my face as I ripped the tape off. "Well, this is a new look for you."

"Don't lose focus. Concentrate on the task at hand."

Fishing out the key from my pocket I began working each lock one by one. "Is everyone required to experience this sort of thing?"

"It's different with each applicant," Grandpa winced.

The first two unlocked with ease but I paused and asked, "I'm curious. Are applicants allowed to help other applicants?"

Grandpa sighed. "It depends on the circumstances, but I wouldn't recommend it. It's a gray area, which is why you should focus on your own path. Remember, after this we face off against a jaguar. What's your plan?"

The remaining two locks dropped to the floor as I hugged him. "Of course, a little heads up about this portion would've been nice."

"That's seriously where your head is? Come on son, hurry up and escort me out of here safely."

"Jung-lee said we have to push through."

Once I scanned the room I noticed the green ooze was beginning to block the exit and cover the majority of the floor. Behind us was a large window, I noticed the old rusty white latches and pushed both to the left. The ancient window latch instantly fell off. My tired hands pulled the window up, and caused the glass to fall out and into the water that surrounded the factory.

"Hmm, that'll work," Grandpa shrugged.

I forced myself through the broken window. "Mind the broken glass."

Grandpa cautiously climbed through. "Well, I'm not going to ignore it."

We both stood cautiously alongside the backside of the factory as we held onto the wall tightly. There was about a foot of grass between the factory and the body of water behind us. We used the grassy trail to shimmy alongside the factory wall until we were clear.

In the distance, I could see a small wooden bridge that led to the finish line. Lyza immediately rose from the water, breathing deeply, gasping for air. She swam alongside an older woman with similar facial features. Without warning, I heard a small splash as something had entered the water near the finish line. Vibrations pulsated across the surface of the water as a shadowy figure swam toward her. The three animals originally stood alongside the finish line. The apex predators.

Two predators, the spotted hyena and black jaguar, stood alongside the finish line, which meant the crocodile was already on the move. A hyena bolted over to the treehouse as if it had been unleashed to attack Rus. The crocodile was in the water and after Lyza. The jaguar sat waiting at the bridge walkway. I knew it was waiting for me.

My eyes grew big, "Oh no."

"You're telling me," Grandpa agreed.

We finished moving alongside the factory and stood directly in front of the bridge walkway.

"LYZA! LYZA!" I screamed.

Lyza suddenly stopped swimming and turned to face me. She was completely unaware of the predator swimming toward her. "What?"

"The crocodile!"

Lyza turned around but was suddenly pulled under. Her hostage became scared and frantically swam toward us.

"Come this way! Hurry and get out of the water!" I turned to face Grandpa, "Do I need to stay by your side in order to pass?"

Grandpa thought for a moment. "No, but I can't be harmed."

"Then stay here, stay with Lyza's hostage, and do not move unless you're threatened. If your safety is at risk, yell for me."

Grandpa Herschel nodded. "Don't do anything you'll regret."

5:29 remained on the ancient score clock as I fearfully glanced up before diving headfirst after Lyza.

"I won't." I dove deep into the water and swam as fast as I could. Deep down in the water I saw a large submarine sinking into the bottom of the tank. The crocodile had pulled Lyza down deeper by her ankle and was trying to drown her.

She was frantically trying to pry the crocodile's mouth open but had no luck going against the second strongest jaws in all of the animal kingdom. The deeper I swam the more pressure poked at my lungs, but I had to rescue Lyza. My arms and legs propelled my body forward through the water until Lyza was just an arm's length away from me. The saltwater started to sting my eyes causing my vision to blur. My body could only take so much, but I was running out of options. After blindly searching around the water, I'd located the croc. The crocodile soon released Lyza once I forced my right fist inside its mouth.

The crocodile's bite pressure started to squeeze each immersed bone and muscle in my right arm. One thought alone enveloped my mind as I attempted to twist my elbow and extend my forearm. Pain. The saltwater crocodile bit down harder and harder as Lyza returned and punched the massive reptile in the eyes. The croc quickly released me and allowed me to follow Lyza to the surface. I'd forgotten the gargantuan reptile's eyes were the only weakness on the exterior of its body.

We quickly swam toward the bridge walkway. I emerged successfully and star-fished onto the walkway. Lyza and I lay gasping for air as the same circuit board of lights sat directly above us. I slowly forced myself up into a crouching position on the ground as Lyza did the same.

Lyza faced me. "Thank you." Her lips found my cheek, and I tried not to smile.

The older woman ran toward Lyza with open arms, "Lyza! You are okay, yes?"

Lyza nodded, examined the time that remained, grabbed the woman's hand, as the two bolted across the bridge. Straight above me lay the deciding factor between becoming a suit or joining the WT. Without hesitation, I grabbed Grandpa's arm and ran after Lyza. Once the end of the bridge was in sight, the black jaguar stood guard, baring its teeth, and waited for me. Lyza and her captive hesitantly walked around the jaguar. Each step was fearful but precise. Crouched, the dark jaguar seemed focused on me and each of my movements. I was twenty feet behind Lyza as the jaguar snarled and jumped between the bridge and Lyza.

Once Lyza crossed, Grandpa whispered, "Justin, we have fifteen seconds. It's now or never." My hands fished out the apple and protein bar out of my pockets. "I'll draw it out. Run." My eyes faced forward focused on the big cat's movements. Grandpa nervously replied, "But you have to be there!" Fear and angst continued to stir under my skin. "I will be. NOW MOVE."

There was no other way out, I had to push through, so I ran at the jaguar head on. I closed my eyes and remembered everything I'd experienced today. The hardships, the laughs, and the fights. Was this where my journey ended? Had it all really been for nothing? No, it was for Rus and Lyza. They would move on and become full-fledged WT members.

I felt as if time had slowed down. Each step I took felt like five minutes. I saw Lyza exhausted and holding her rescued hostage; Rus stood alongside Roxanne. They were all cheering for me, clapping, screaming, and trying to throw the jaguar off. I threw both the apple and the protein bar in the water at arm's length of the jaguar. At first his eyes followed the snacks; however, he quickly redirected his vision back on me. I tried to divert the animal's point of focus, but at my speed, I posed too much of a threat. The jaguar's pupils dilated as he decided to pursue me, I suddenly jumped to the right. The jaguar had entered fight or flight mode and aggressively opened its mouth as it lunged for me. It pounced toward me, prepared to kill. I closed my eyes and lifted up my forearms. With no time to focus or respond, I couldn't utilize my gift. Suddenly, without warning, the same giant, male, Eastern grey kangaroo jumped in front of me and slammed the jaguar into the water with his studded, muscular legs. I looked up to see just five seconds remaining on the clock. I sprinted through the finish line just half a second before the alarm rang.

BIINNNNNNNGGGGGG

The Masked Woman's voice came over the loudspeaker, "Congratulations, to our new Wildlife Training Members! You have successfully passed the hero portion."

I grabbed Grandpa and pulled him in for a hug. I was overwhelmed. Lyza held the woman she rescued tight while Rus and Roxanne embraced one another. We all began smiling and hugging one another. We had finally done it and we were over the moon excited to receive our partners.

The Masked Woman continued, "We now invite you to prepare for the Pairing Ceremony led by the Animal Bridging Council. Please follow Jung-lee, who will return your backpacks, along with a new change of clothes and restroom supplies so you may shower and prepare to look your best for the ceremony. Jung-lee will then lead each of you back to the main lobby. The ceremony will occur in one hour in the lobby. The members of the Animal Bridging Council must report to the meeting space to make their final selections. Medic bots will remain on standby to help tend to any wounds accrued during your time with us today."

I glanced back and caught a glimpse of the kangaroo staring at me. It sneezed, wiped its nose, and hopped back across the bridge. I stood there surprised, thankful, and relieved.

Jung-lee entered from a large white door with a warm towel for each of us. Grandpa grabbed one for me and walked back toward me. He placed the towel around the back of my neck.

"You know, I've never seen Hank do that," Grandpa exhaled.

I pointed at the kangaroo, "Hank? You mean the kangaroo?"

Grandpa smiled and nodded, "You must've done a number on him if he was willing to jump in like that."

I could feel my eyes watering. "No. I was lucky. I almost died back there."

Grandpa patted me on the back, "You displayed true courage! I'm proud of you, Justin. Welcome to the WT. Now your real journey begins. I'll see you at the ceremony."

I wiped my face as Grandpa departed from the stadium and ventured past Jung-lee to meet with the other council members. I continued forward and saw Jung-lee waiting for me. Lyza walked side by side with her captive while Rus leaned on Roxanne each step of the way. Jung-lee led us through the same white doorway. He led us past what appeared to be gray office cubicles. Each cubicle included an analyst reviewing footage of us from throughout the day.

Roxanne turned around while she was escorting Rus and waved at me. I hesitantly waved back and noticed Lyza witnessing our awkward exchange. I walked alongside Lyza. She was limping where the croc had gripped her ankle. I wanted to make sure she was okay. I wanted to know what Lyza was thinking throughout this process and how she was feeling. Her hostage slowly walked ahead of her. I wanted to speak with her, but I didn't want to sound overbearing or over-interested. What if she were angry that I interfered with her apex predator? At this point, we'd come this far, and we were all exhausted from the day we'd survived together. I made it a mission to talk to her before we all left to prepare for the ceremony.

"Are you, all right?" I asked Lyza.

"I will live. Would you believe me if I said I had been through worse?"

"I don't know. Today was pretty heavy, but I guess it's possible. Listen, I'm sorry if..."

"Do not do that."

"Do what?"

"Apologize for saving me. You did well, Justin Steele. Just leave it at that."

"I don't think you understand—"

"No, you don't understand. You don't know me, or my life, or what I am trying to do. Just do your thing, and I'll do mine. One more thing—"

"Yes? And what do you want—"

Lyza grabbed my face with her right hand and pulled it into hers. Our lips met as if they were two long lost lovers. The embrace illuminated the hallway and I felt like I was walking on the sun. It was a legendary warmth, one that I wouldn't dare open my eyes to see. I was afraid to face the solar flares.

CHAPTER 6

A Coata-what?

Lyza pulled away from me abruptly, our glittering encounter faded away. She continued on, casually walking behind Rus and Roxanne. I stood as still as stone, ensuring I was awake and that the kiss had actually happened. My smile quickly faded as I faced forward and caught sight of Roxanne staring back at me. She seemed slightly disturbed at the sight of Lyza and I sharing a kiss. As she stood in place, Rus whispered something to her with a concerned look on his face. He seemed oblivious to why she had stopped in the hallway. Lyza cautiously passed Roxanne and Rus as she walked arm and arm with her rescued captive. I froze when my eyes met Roxanne's, a shared line of vision that lasted for just a moment too long. She quickly turned back around and walked arm in arm with Rus.

The following hour seemed to race by faster than a roadrunner running from a coyote. Jung-lee escorted me and Rus to the men's locker room on the other side of the rows of cubicles. Jung-lee gave each of us bathroom bags full of single use products, new uniforms, and even took our order for dinner. The Animal Bridging Council provided dinner for all newly appointed members into the WT. We were given a choice of salmon, cod, or a fried fish Po' boy. I couldn't remember the last time I had fried fish, so I trusted my gut and ordered the sandwich.

Jung-lee looked at Rus, annoyed, "I'll be back with your two fish Po' boys soon. Be ready in fifteen minutes gentlemen. Mr. Steele, I'll need you for five minutes. Please follow me." I nodded in understanding and followed Jung-lee out of the locker-room. Rus watched with concern and curiosity as I exited the room.

We walked down the hallway and returned back to the previous room. Inside there were no armed guards nor Grandpa.

"Now let's get this over with and remove that inhibitor chip," Jung-lee said.

I nervously sat back down in the chair and exhaled deeply before Jung-lee removed the chip. It was surprisingly a lot faster than when he originally implanted it. Once the chip was successfully severed, I could feel my gift slowly returning to my body. The weight intensified as I flexed my muscles and clenched my fists. I exited the room without muttering a word and made my way back to Rus in the men's locker room. I removed my dirty clothes and threw them in the trash then showered, got dressed, and put on my new uniform. By the time I was out of the shower Jung-lee had re-entered with freshly cooked sandwiches. Rus stood in a towel and was changing when Jung-lee entered.

"Goodness gracious, soldier! Put some britches on before someone sees you!" Jung-lee yelled.

Rus threw his towel back over his body and laughed, "Britches? What are britches?"

Jung-lee looked away awkwardly as he tucked his shirt in and adjusted his collar, "Now, I have your food."

Rus opened the box, "Oh, I ... I actually ordered the cod?"

Jung-lee seemed unamused and left the food on the locker-room bench. He made it a mission to leave before Rus could make him feel more uncomfortable.

The newly provided uniforms looked very similar to the ones we wore that morning. However, the left side of each of our shirts read "Wildlife Trainer." I was excited to get back to the lobby and receive the long-awaited opportunity of a lifetime.

Rus and I quickly started getting dressed while we ate.

"Now are you going to tell me what's been going on? What was that about?" Rus asked.

"They had to remove my inhibitor chip." I threw my new shirt over my head.

"What! An inhibitor chip? Why did you have to wear one?"

I laughed. "It wasn't my choice. I have a gift or special power like my grandpa."

Rus started to comb his hair. "What can you control like gators or something?"

"Um, no. It's like armor of some sort, they thought I would be cheating if I was able to use it."

I clenched my muscles and squeezed my fists. My eyes peered down as I focused my energy on my hands. A small bit of metallic coloration appeared just on the edges of my knuckles.

Rus looked in awe. "Yeah that definitely would've made things easier."

After a moment, I lost focus and the metallic color quickly faded from my fists.

I took a bite of my sandwich. "I don't even know how to use it."

Rus continued fixing his hair. "Could be worse. They could've just cut off your hands, that would've been fair."

I threw my towel at Rus's head. We quickly finished our sandwiches while we walked to the ceremony. We placed our personal belongings on the side of the stage and were directed to our seats. The next thirty minutes went by quickly. Rus, Lyza, and I were placed upon the stage in the lobby. We sat atop the small, black stage on three black stools. It was the same stage where the Masked Woman had awarded us our applicant numbers just hours prior.

Over time, the Animal Pairing Ceremony had become more of a press spectacle. It happened almost every day at the same time and in the same place.

We all watched as energized reporters, press hungry photographers, and determined journalists from across Ignacia entered the lobby. These daily additions to the ceremony were responsible for keeping society in the loop. Each individual played his or her role in adding to the daily gossip.

Day-to-day lifestyles all changed in the blink of an eye during these ceremonies, sometimes for the better and sometimes for the worse.

Interlocking my fingers, I nervously sat on the left side of the stage. Strategically, my chair had been carefully placed underneath my grandfather's seat at their shared golden desk. I wasn't sure if the seating arrangements were predetermined or just a lucky coincidence. I looked at the grand golden clock in the corner: 6:30 p.m. Reporters brought in luminescent light fixtures, which lit up our faces for the duration of the ceremony. Only close family and friends were the other people able to attend the ceremony personally.

I remembered the exact moment when Rus's mom and dad entered and sat in the third row with their birds carefully perched on the back of their chairs. Both of his parents had become Flyers at an early age, but the two didn't meet until they were stationed to the same commanding staff years later. Rus's father generated and oversaw the national business side of Ignacia with his golden eagle. Rus's mother oversaw transit and travel for all major flight companies with her California condor always close by. The two met at a Transferal Squad corporate meeting, and the rest was history. Rus had spent the majority of his life surrounded by birds and expected to receive nothing less. However, the application exam did not base one's selection upon those provided for other family members.

The couple wore their Transferal Squad uniforms. Both wore white button-down shirts that pictured their animal as well as their division on each fold of their formal collars. All Flyers received perch add-ons to assist with their bird seating within social events. Both parents smiled with untiring pride as they waved toward Rus and me. I hesitantly waved with a slight wince of shame in my eyes. I hadn't spoken to them since before I quit the IPS. I knew I would need to explain what happened after the ceremony. Sitting alongside them was Roxanne.

Rus was immensely happy and dumbfounded by the luminous distractions. You'd never guess that the guy fractured his hand just hours before. The pain he'd experienced had vanished and was overshadowed with hope. I'd never seen him smile so much. He appeared untouchable, as if he were on top of the world. Rus absorbed each ray of light that shined upon stage as if he were a sunflower. I was happy for him. I quickly scanned the crowd with no luck in locating my parents. There was not even a hint of my father let alone my mother. There were two seats in the front row marked "Reserved." I wasn't sure who the seats were for or why they were there, but it gave me hope.

The Masked Woman approached the freshly waxed, redwood podium.

"Good afternoon, Ignacia, as you all are aware, this year we are celebrating fifty-nine years of successful animal training within the Wildlife Training Program. Our program was originally created by the Arc Task Force in 2986 with the sole intent of protecting and treating animals. As time progressed, however, the founders voted on a more beneficial solution for both animals and humans. Animals were paired with members of our program, and endangered wildlife were able to re-enter society safely alongside the protection of a trainer. Today the WT promotes three new members into different occupational divisions of Ignacia. Each animal is assigned to a WT member best suited for their distinct skill set. The applicants you see today have each passed three difficult trials and will now receive their divisions, their partners, and assignments. Each animal has been hand-selected and approved by our Animal Bridging Council."

The Masked Woman turned her head and surveyed the lobby. "Our Animal Bridging Council is composed of some of the best trainers, directors and people Ignacia has been fortunate enough to have represent us. I now have the privilege of introducing each member. Beginning with our president, Mr. Herschel Steele, and his partner, the American alligator, Dusty! Herschel has been a part of the WT for fifty-three years. He was the director for the Hero Regime for thirty years before joining the committee for almost twenty years."

My grandfather entered the lobby from the back office and suavely walked across to his spot on the golden desk atop the stage. I looked up at him as he waved to the cameras and mustered a smile. He peered down at me as we all applauded him and winked. He reached his desk and remained standing while Dusty followed behind and leaped onto a platform behind his desk.

The Masked Woman announced, “Next, we have our Vice President, Emmeline Carmichael, and her partner, the Galapagos sea lion, Sandy. She has been a part of the WT for about thirty-eight years and served as director for the Exploration Squad for twenty years before joining the committee for the past thirteen years.”

Grandpa never once spoke about his coworkers. A small, middle-aged, woman with gray hair and glasses briskly emerged from the hidden hallway. I assumed they were departing from their meeting with newfound decisions from their conference room. She had a stern posture and business-centered energy while her sea lion, Sandy, energetically followed, casually plopping her flippers behind her. Emmeline Carmichael was a powerful leader who did very well in the program. She’d spent years battling the AFA as well as researching the ocean floor. The VP brought newfound discoveries to light and shared them with Ignacia. Emmeline stood behind her desk next to Grandpa. Sandy jumped onto another small black platform behind her desk.

The Masked Woman continued, “Following Emmeline, we have Demetrius Fowley, and his partner, the mountain gorilla, Ukuri. Demetrius has been a part of the WT for forty-three years. He served as the director for the Construction Squad for twenty-five years before joining the Animal Bridging Council for the past fifteen years.”

Out walked a strapping bald man with a lighter complexion. He was older, mid-fifties, tall, lean but full of muscle. I could tell the man had done years of physical labor due to his stern posture. He had muscles bursting through his apricot-colored, button-down shirt. Behind Demetrius walked his giant partner, Ukuri. This gorilla was a colossal tank of brawn, standing about six feet tall. Ukuri used to be the strongest member of the Construction Squad. He could lift bulldozers, cranes, and had the skillset to create buildings up to forty stories high throughout Ignacia. As Demetrius made his way to stand behind his seat, he made eye contact with Grandpa. The council members smiled as both Emmeline and Grandpa saluted him. Ukuri hopped up to the platform behind his portion of the desk. His gorilla sat patiently and closed his eyes, while the crowd began to wonder if the ape was meditating, but we realized the gorilla had fallen asleep once he started to snore.

The Masked Woman excitedly proclaimed, "Last but certainly not least, we have our most loyal WT and committee member, the world-renowned author, Madame Yue and her partner Rong, the Cassowary! Madame Yue has been a part of the WT for fifty-five years. She served as the director for the Transferal Squad for thirty-two years and has been a member of this council for the past twenty-two years."

The older woman struggled to use her cane as she hobbled the short distance from the doorway to her desk. All of the committee members applauded her as she entered. The audience rejoiced in her attendance with a standing ovation. Madam Yue stopped at her desk and waved to the crowd while Rong, her Cassowary, slowly made her way to the allotted platform area located behind her desk. Madam Yue's platform was designed differently than the others. It was soft and padded so Rong could sit and patiently look out to examine the crowd. Madam Yue was a living legend. She single-handedly created the IPS postal unit brand from the ground up. Her organization had delivered jobs and opportunities to all Flyers admitted into her division. She wrote the book, *Patches,* skillfully explaining her invention of the partner patch. Though Madame Yue seemed old and feeble on the outside, something about her exuded an unusual dynamic quality. Her demeanor seemed to reflect an energy and aura that could subtly stop everyone in this room. She had a background in the ancient and mystical arts. I could feel there was something stirring underneath the surface between her and Rong. Collectively, all council members looked to each other and simultaneously sat in their chairs.

Grandpa had made it a mission never to bring his work home with him. Sometimes the office encountered heartfelt days where people were touched by an animal's love, a great reminder of why they did what they did. On off days, others detested the animals they were awarded and elected to leave the program altogether. This decision left the animal alone and companionless in the courthouse. When this occurred, the animal was returned behind closed doors and remained in the lab until another contender arrived, possibly the day after, and was awarded a second chance. If the animal were rejected again, it was deemed unfit to pair and remained in the lab instead of returning to society.

The Masked Woman continued, "Now that we have our committee leaders present, let the animal pairing process begin! Each partner awarded today is best suited for that particular trainer's unique skills, and together they will work to represent their divisions to the best of their abilities. New WT members, if there are discrepancies, disagreements, or refusals, please let it be known immediately. We will direct you to meet with us accordingly after the ceremony to discuss your alternatives."

There weren't any alternatives. Either the newly admitted trainer would keep the partner they were awarded, or they'd choose to leave the program altogether. I knew for a fact if they stuck me with any animal, there was zero chance of me leaving the program. I was confused by how someone was so incredibly cold-hearted that they'd say no. I couldn't jeopardize the future of an animal raised under professional care. I couldn't withhold the opportunity for an animal to leave the lab and go out to face the trials of society with a trusted protector. Though in the back of my mind I could feel my body was beginning to catch up with me. My mind was strong but my body was beginning to shut down. Even after a hot shower and a warm meal, I was physically exhausted. My hands were sweating, my forearm had some bite marks from the croc, my muscles were aching, and a part of me just wanted to go home and sleep. However, I was fully aware I would not get much sleep tonight. There would be a new animal, no, partner that I would be responsible for. The missing piece I'd been endlessly searching for my entire life. They would be my partner, a reliable animal that I'd spend every moment with and work to better our relationship to the best of my ability.

The Masked Woman began the assignments. "We will start in applicant order. Russell Zhang, grandson of Jericho Zhang. Demetrius, has the committee reached a verdict?"

The crowd began to murmur among themselves. "Zhang?" "Zhang? Is that Jericho's grandson?"

Demetrius rose from his desk. He lifted his written report and announced loudly, "As Secretary for the Animal Bridging Council, it is my responsibility to convey the decision we came to as a group for each newly approved WT member. Russel Zhang, please step forward."

Rus stood from his chair as he clenched his right fist. He inhaled deeply through his nose and slowly out his mouth. Sweat began to trickle down his forehead.

Demetrius continued, "For the written portion, you performed exquisitely. You passed your written exam with a perfect score and truly embodied the role of number one in the beginning stage. During the combat portion, you chose to continue past the recommended checkpoint to test your ability, even after your hand had been fractured. This behavior was deemed reckless and self-sacrificing. It wasn't until an attacker stepped in to protect you from further harm that you recognized there was no dishonor in retiring. The final portion, even after you sustained quite a few injuries in the combat portion, you were able to perform to the standard of a hero. You caught your key, you freed your hostage, and you successfully deterred the apex predator."

Demetrius nodded to the Masked Woman, and she stepped forward with a small gray box.

Demetrius read on, "For your courage to push through challenges and willingness to enter the unknown, it only seems fit we grant you a role into... the Exploration Squad."

Members of the audience started to applaud. The Masked Woman placed a blue module onto Rus's right shirt sleeve. Suddenly the shirt changed color to a bright royal blue. My closest friend was in shock by this announcement. His eyes enlarged as his eyelids disappeared. However, Rus's face did not show excitement or joy. A seed of worry had been planted, and it couldn't help but bloom into fear. I saw his anxiety begin to chip away at him. His eyes remained forward and fixed on the lights, the audience, and the cameras. Rus stood nervously but came to terms with the announcement and accepted the decision. Reporters muttered to themselves aloud, speaking into their microphones and recording devices.

Again, low murmuring followed in the audience. "Exploration Squad?" "Shouldn't he be in the Transferal Squad?" "Why would they do this?"

Demetrius continued, "Order please! Order. As a new addition to the Exploration Squad, you will be gifted an animal that will guide you through the depths of the unexplored ocean. You will work alongside team members who are just as fearless and strong-willed as you. To someone who is gifted academically and physically, we must provide you with a partner who embodies the same abilities. An apex predator. Gentlemen, please escort out his partner."

Suddenly a hidden doorway rose from the right side of the courthouse lobby. Out came a giant hovering carrier filled with water, about fifteen feet wide and ten feet high featured an opening on top maneuvered out by six men. The floating carrier was draped by a thick brown tarp. As it hovered into the audience's view, everyone could hear breathing from inside the unit.

"A blowhole? Is that a cetacean?" Rus whispered under his breath.

It had to be a marine mammal based upon the breath sounds and use of the blow hole on top of the enclosure. Demetrius motioned for the six men to remove the tarp and turned to the Masked Woman and nodded. The Masked Woman picked up the second module and placed it in the center of Russel's shirt.

Demetrius spoke, "Gentleman, if you would please. Russel Zhang, your WT partner will be a killer whale, also commonly known as an orca. He is the fourth calf we've initiated into the program. All facts on the animal will be presented to you after the ceremony. Congratulations. Stand by as we apply the partner patches. Please take this time now and allow your partner to share his name with you."

Suddenly, the news crew members of the crowd stood with exhilaration and spoke into their cameras sporadically.

"THIS JUST IN!"

"Russel Zhang, alleged grandson of Jericho Zhang."

"Will be the first Zhang to be admitted into the Exploration Squad!"

"He will be the fourth in the program to partner with a killer whale!"

The crowd seemed concerned, and unapologetically enlightened. The module opened in the center of Russel's shirt revealing the silhouette of a killer whale. Flashes of photos were taken throughout the lobby of Rus and his face of astonishment.

Rus's right sleeve read, "Exploration Squad" and "ORCA" was stitched above the whale silhouette. Rus mustered up a smile, waved to the crowd, and cautiously watched the hovering container. He slowly walked toward the young Orca and placed his left hand on the glass. Rus breathed in nervously and looked deeply into the eyes of the calf.

Suddenly, without hesitation, two men clamped partner patches onto both the calf and Rus. Rus felt the patch harshly clamp into his skin on his right upper arm below his shoulder. The Orca calf's patch was placed just above the dorsal fin behind his blowhole. Both partner patches synchronized as the two became connected emotionally, physically, and mentally.

The first fifteen seconds were said to be ferociously painful, but afterward you would feel better and would then be able to transmit all forms of communication with your animal.

Rus looked down at his newly equipped patch and looked back at his newly appointed partner. The two stared at each other for a moment before Rus nodded and smiled. It seemed as if he had an internal conversation with the whale. People talked among themselves, and reporters continued with their news stories.

Demetrius' voice rose, "Order, people. ORDER."

The crowd quickly quieted down, and the reporters returned to their seats.

Demetrius reluctantly continued, "Finally, Mr. Zhang, now that you have taken the time to greet your animal. What name would your partner like to be called?"

Rus glanced from the glass and back to Demetrius, "His name is Kanoa."

Demetrius smiled and nodded in understanding, "Very well, your orders will be given to you shortly after the ceremony. It is your job to learn and master your partner patch. Learn it, study it, and always keep your papers with you. May you and Kanoa travel, learn, and grow together in order to face the tasks ahead. Congratulations."

"Thank you." Rus bowed in gratitude.

Rus placed his hand on the glass once more before returning to his seat on stage. The six men maneuvered Kanoa's hovering carrier to the far-right side of the lobby to ensure he was still within Rus's sight. I saw his parents mustering a smile and whispering among themselves. I thought Rus was unsteady, lost, and unable to grasp the decision made, but once the partner patches connected the two, he seemed content and even comfortable with his partner. His smile reappeared though it still carried the weight of uncertainty, which created an even heavier look than before.

The Masked Woman announced, "Applicant Number Three, Lyza Rybakova, daughter of Mila Rybakova. Demetrius, what has the committee decided?"

Demetrius looked over to Emmeline as she passed a large manila folder to him.

Demetrius opened the file and began listing off Lyza's report, "Lyza Rybakova, please step forward. After reviewing all of your hard work today, we will break down each part of the application. You completed the written portion with an above average score. However, your talents tended to shine in the second and third trials. In the combat portion, you held your own and refused to stay down going against your fellow applicants. You retained focus on your objective and saw to it that your enemies could not knock you down. You took down your fellow applicants even after surviving four rounds as an attacker. You also received assistance from an ally throughout the third requirement of the hero portion. This does not, however, break any rules, providing or receiving assistance from a fellow applicant.

"That being said, you successfully completed and defeated each enemy that came your way. You have an intensity in each action that you put your mind to. You are resourceful and reliable in a fight whether it's on land or in the water."

Demetrius nodded to the Masked Woman as she stepped up with a small blue box.

"For your courage to push through challenges and seeker into the unknown depths below the surface, it only seems fit that we grant you, too, a role into the Exploration Squad."

The crowd started to applaud once more. The Masked Woman placed her blue module onto Lyza's right shirt sleeve. The shirt changed color to a bright royal blue. Lyza continued to stand in place. She appeared relaxed and showed little to no concern by the announcement. Again, flashes from cameras filled the room across the lobby. Lyza stepped forward, waved, and mustered a smile. She displayed no signs of grief, pain, or remorse, only contentment. Her eyes remained forward fixed on the bright light from the audience and cameras. Reporters muttered among themselves, speaking into their microphones, and recording devices. "Lyza Rybakova is marked as the second newest member of the Exploration Squad!"

She glanced down into the first row of the whispering audience and found the woman she had rescued from the hero portion. The older woman was sitting in the front row, delighted with Lyza, and started waving excitedly to her. Lyza smiled and waved back.

"Now, Lyza Rybakova, as a new member of the Exploration Squad, you will be gifted an animal that will guide you into the depths of the unexplored ocean. You will work alongside fellow team members who are just as fearless and strong-willed as you. Lyza, we have entrusted you to define the new age of the Exploration Squad and to find the answers some seemed to miss. Whether it is alone or working alongside your team members. We're counting on you. Gentleman, please bring out her partner."

The same set of six gentlemen walked out the secret doorway and returned, as they moved another hovering glass carrier full of water. The tank seemed to be half the width of Kanoa's carrier. However, the container stood the standard ten feet tall and was covered with a similar brown tarp. The container was maneuvered closer. The audience heard loud breathing and clicking coming from the top of the carrier. It resembled the sound of Kanoa's blow hole and seemed to be another marine mammal.

Demetrius motioned for the six men to remove the tarp. He then turned to the Masked Woman and nodded to her. The Masked Woman removed the second module from the blue bag and placed it in the center of Lyza's shirt. The shadowed silhouette of the animal opened and revealed a rough-toothed dolphin. Lyza's right-hand sleeve displayed, "Exploration Squad" and above the silhouette "DOLPHIN" was stitched.

"Gentleman, if you would please. Lyza Rybakova, your Wildlife Trainer Program partner will be a rough-toothed dolphin! It, also, is a member of the cetacean family. He is the first rough-toothed calf we've admitted into the program. All facts on the animal will be presented to you after the ceremony. Congratulations. Please stand by as we apply the partner patches. Please take this time now and allow your partner to share his name with you."

Lyza looked adoringly at the dark gray calf that moved in the carrier. The dolphin examined Lyza as she stood alongside the glass. She began playing at the glass with the animal attempting to grasp his attention. She was jumping up and down, moving side to side as the dolphin instinctively responded and followed her movements. Both were very curious about one another, but they moved together as a unit. It was as if the bond was there instantly and instinctively. I could tell by the glimmer in Lyza's eyes that she was truly happy. Both men moved in and clamped patches down on Lyza's arm and the dolphin's dorsal fin.

"Ouch! Watch it! A little warning or something, eh?" Lyza yelled. Moments passed before she looked intently back at the carrier. It was as if the rough toothed dolphin was speaking with Lyza telepathically.

Demetrius loudly asked, "Lyza, if you please. What is his name?"

Lyza grinned and looked up at Demetrius, "Ivan. His name is Ivan."

Demetrius smiled and nodded in understanding, "Very well, your orders will be given to you shortly after the ceremony. May you and Ivan travel, learn, and grow together in order to face the tasks ahead. Congratulations."

Lyza and Ivan continued looking at one another intently through the glass. Ivan inched his body up to the glass and gently pressed his melon into the carrier where Lyza had placed her hand.

Lyza rubbed her hand on the glass in place and whispered, "I'll be right back. I promise."

Lyza kissed her hand and pressed it alongside the glass where Ivan's melon remained. She returned to her seat with her newly presented partner patch. Both she and Rus had glistening new shirts and patches. Both technological pieces shined with five different buttons all brightly lit.

I acknowledged their partner patches, and asked "Man, how are we going to sleep in those things?"

Lyza shrugged her shoulders, "We have to read directions on it or something."

Rus whispered, "Yeah. Isn't there like a sleep mode in chapter two—"

The Masked Woman spoke abruptly, "Applicant Number Five, Justin Steele. Son of Noah and Teresa Steele, captain of the Hero Regime. Grandson of President Herschel Steele. This is our final new member for the day. Demetrius, when you're ready."

Demetrius looked over to Grandpa, he took out a bright green folder from his side of the desk and passed it down to him. Demetrius nodded in understanding.

Demetrius hesitantly announced, "Now, ladies and gentlemen, this will be our final pairing for the night. However, I must share, this has been one of our more difficult decisions as a committee. We reviewed the events from today and argued on a clear division for this applicant, but we have finally come to a conclusion. Let us begin. Step forward Justin Steele."

I exhaled deeply and stood from my chair and crossed to the center of the stage. Demetrius continued, "Justin Steele, you performed above average with your written test results. Each answer recorded was thoughtfully considered, heartfelt, and accepted. However, there were a few circumstances that could have been handled differently. All in all, you passed the written portion by reaching the approved score.

"During the combat portion, you violated one of the regulations early on against Applicant One. You removed your safety gear in order to cause more harm to an applicant. If you reviewed your handbook on this section of the application process, you'd notice in Chapter Two, sub section E, it clearly states –"

I interrupted, "Each attacker must include all layers of padding. Failure to abide by this will result in point deductions… I understand that, but my emotions got the better of me–"

Demetrius interjected, "Excuse me, Mr. Steele. I haven't finished."

"Forgive me, sir. He hit Lyza and I lost my temper."

Demetrius exhaled and continued, "It will be noted that you apologized for the events that affected Applicant One in his performance. It is also recorded that you protected him in the following round from a much stronger opponent. We all believe he may have sustained more injuries against that opponent if it had not been for your safeguard. Justin Steele, it recently came to this council's attention that you are not like the other applicants. You carry a gift. Handed down from our president, Herschel Steele. You also have a big heart for others. If somebody gets in your way, you step up and face the challenger head on, with or without your gift. Just as you did against Applicant Seven, who was disqualified because he could not continue."

I could hear the low murmurs and comments being shared in the audience of the lobby. The feeling in the air changed from celebratory to concern. "Justin Steele has a gift?" "Was he docked points?" "How will this impact their decision?"

Demetrius cleared his throat abruptly and continued, "As for the third and final part, the hero portion. You befriended the mammal you came in contact with, Hank, our kangaroo. He is one of our oldest animals that has served the WT application process for a long time. Hank has been with us for thirty years, and he has never followed anyone the way he did you after you saved him. You expressed care and heart toward an animal attempting to harm you. You successfully saved your hostage, protected Applicant Number One from Applicant Number Seven, saved Applicant Number Three, and were able to finish without a second to spare."

Demetrius nodded to the Masked Woman as she stepped up with a small red box.

"For your warm-hearted empathy and undying determination, it only seems fit we grant you a role into... the Cultivation Squad."

The audience began to applaud. The Masked Woman placed a green module onto the right sleeve of my shirt. Suddenly, the color of my shirt changed into a rich shamrock green. I stood in place, vibrating with overflowing joy. I continued to stand, attempting to hold back tears. I lifted both hands into the air with relief. Reporters muttered among themselves again and spoke into their microphones and recording devices. "Justin Steele will be, in fact, entering the Cultivation Squad!" "He will be following the Steele family legacy!" "He takes after his father and grandfather!"

My eyes peered down to the first row where the empty chairs sat. I imagined what my father and mother were doing at that very moment. I'd hoped they were watching from afar. A small tear slowly descended down my cheek. I glanced back at Grandpa who smiled proudly and applauded me from atop the tall golden desk. I checked back to see Lyza and Rus, both smiling and clapping for me. At that moment, the light fixtures shined bright in my eyes. I felt the crowd beaming at me with more applause than I could have imagined. The feeling was unlike anything I'd ever experienced, all for me, all for a single moment of recognition. It all brought me great joy and happiness. I'd never been prouder to be a Steele.

Demetrius continued, "Justin Steele. As a new member of the Cultivation Squad, you will be gifted an animal that will assist you in mastering the ways of the land. You will work alongside fellow team members who are just as hardworking and headstrong as you. You are the new age of team members to help lead the Cultivation Squad. The bond you create with your partner will redefine animal bonds made within the WT. It is your job to find the answers you need in order to grow with the earth and face your enemies. Some will attempt to put you down, and others will tell you that you cannot accomplish something. I challenge you: do not take no for an answer. Ladies, please present him with his partner."

This was the final step in the application process. Something I'd waited for years to be gifted. Two women walked out escorting an adolescent beast, an animal that would help me tackle the Hunters Camp within the Cultivation Squad just as my father did and his father before him. I was ready to train and surpass any obstacle.

Suddenly two women came out from the hidden door carrying a giant, dark gray blanket. The two of them carefully hid what lay inside. Both stood grinning and showcasing their courthouse uniforms. The two stood directly right of the stage in front of both Kanoa's and Ivan's habitats.

Demetrius motioned for the two ladies to approach me and unveil the blanket. He turned to the Masked Woman and nodded to her. She removed the second module from a red box and placed it in the center of my green shirt.

"Ladies, if you would please. Justin, your Wildlife Trainer Program partner will be a coatimundi!"

My face changed from excitement to confusion. I felt as though a giant question mark had been stamped on my face. Of all the animals I'd grown up with, studying, learning, this was not an animal in my father's animal encyclopedia. I was confused and a bit bewildered. What was this animal? I was dumbfounded.

"A coati...mundi?"

The two women slowly unwrapped a small blanket. Inside sat a small, tan ball of fur who appeared very comfortable wrapped up in her blanket. She wasn't afraid or struggling to get up and run away. No, she was sleeping and enjoying the softness of the blanket. The endearing kit had a long-striped ring tail and resembled a raccoon. It was strange, she had a small snout that seemed similar to an anteater. The fur ball slowly wiped her eyes and looked up at me with confusion. She was extremely fluffy with small black whiskers poking out on both sides of her face. She twitched her small, round ears which poked out the top of her head. The longer I looked at her, the more adorable she became.

A brief moment of disappointment quickly came and went. After shedding the discontent, I opened up my heart, and that small coati filled me to the brim with warmth and love.

I was caught off guard by her face. The coati's cuteness drew me in and was unlike anything I'd ever experienced before. I hesitantly continued petting her belly with my right index finger when her nose shot up. The small creature started to sniff every inch of my hand. She gently placed her tiny hands over my finger, and carefully studied the different scents. Both women started to push her toward me and into my arms. Before I knew it, I was cradling one of the most precious animals I'd ever seen. Her long and sharp fingernails pressed into my skin as she began to climb up my forearm. It was slightly painful, but I didn't mind. She was curious and wanted to investigate. The Masked Woman gently pressed the new module into my right sleeve and a coati silhouette appeared on my shirt. Curiosity continued to overcome the small mammal's senses as she looked out at the audience and quickly hid from the bright lights. I pulled her close and carefully looked back in her eyes.

Demetrius announced, "She is a member of the Procyonidae family, and the first coatimundi we've introduced in the program. All facts on the animal will be presented to you after the ceremony. Congratulations. Please stand by as we apply the partner patches. Please take this time to tell us the name she gives you."

Suddenly, the two women standing by pulled the coatimundi away from me and moved in to apply her partner patch to the top of her right arm. I heard a loud squeal come from the small coati and my fight or flight response was activated. She was afraid and was frantically trying to pull away from the two women.

I lunged forward and pulled my right arm away from the Masked Woman. My eyes remained on the two women as they failed to attach the partner patch to the coati's arm. I looked down as my fists began to change color. The same metallic coloration started to fluctuate over my hands. The Masked Woman reached out again for my right shoulder and grabbed my arm.

"DON'T HURT HER!" I yelled in anger, yanking my arm away again, as I shifted my focus on the women trying to clip the partner patch on the coati. A scowl of disapproval radiated from my face as I glared at the two women attempting to harm the small creature.

At that point the metallic color completely enveloped both of my hands. My breathing became heavy as my emotions were getting the better of me. The anger that flowed through my veins was overpowering my sense of logic. So much so that the only thing I cared about was removing my partner from the clutches of both caretakers.

The two women took one look at me and became instantly terrified. They abruptly released the coati and allowed her to fearfully run back to me. She climbed up my leg until she reached my left arm where she lounged comfortably and continued to pant in tiny, short bursts.

My blood was boiling after seeing her so scared, but it only intensified once the small coati cried out in fear. Somehow my emotions had gotten the better of me and I had succumbed to them yet again. A deep root of anger rose within me as the metallic coloration remained over my hands. The gift had been activated solely from my anger. I peered up at Grandpa as he stood from his chair and shook his head in embarrassment.

The Masked Woman stared up at Demetrius as she awaited his response to my actions. He grimaced and glared down at me with disappointment. I examined the room as scared, and concerned newscasters, animals, and families all watched me to see what I would do next. Photographers and news reporters continued taking photos as I relaxed my hands which allowed my palms and fingers to return back to normal.

Struck with disapproval and disbelief, Demetrius questioned, "Mr. Steele, if you decline the partner patch, you will not be permitted to continue within the WT."

I pulled the young coati close into both arms. She was finally starting to relax as she curled into a ball secured. My lungs expanded as I attempted to take a deep breath. It was my lack of self-control that caused me to lash out and potentially harm two caretakers. I slowly walked back over to the Masked Woman with my head down in embarrassment. As my body and mind started to let go and relax, the metallic coloration dissipated completely. I hesitantly raised my right arm for the Masked Woman to apply the partner patch.

"Please. Just don't hurt her," I said nervously. The Masked Woman looked up to Demetrius, he nodded, and she stuck me with the partner patch.

The pain I felt was as if a boiling pot of grease was poured onto my right arm. On the outside, I sat as still as a frozen pond in the middle of winter. On the inside, however, I was on my knees slamming my fists into the ground, attempting to cause pain elsewhere to alleviate the pain of the patch. It became a necessary pain, one I felt I deserved from my previous actions. My body welcomed the burning sensation as anxiety surrounded me. The two caretakers who had recently appeared cheerfully just moments earlier, approached me with caution and fear.

I faced forward and cradled the young coatimundi in my left forearm. She sat calmly while sniffing and licking the sweat from my arms. I continued breathing heavily as more sweat accumulated on my forehead.

"Do it. Hurry." I whispered to the caretakers.

The two women hesitantly nodded and carefully connected the partner patch to the small coati's right arm. She immediately started biting and clawing at the two women once they connected the patch. The small fur ball jumped off my left arm and leaped to the floor as if she was going to attack them. After that moment everything became very quiet.

I could see and hear everything from everyone around us but a sudden silence filled my mind. The silence overcame the nervous reporters speaking into their cameras. My ears refused to open or listen to Demetrius's instructions. All I could hear was a looming pause as if I'd lost my hearing all together. Suddenly, a small whisper started to form inside my head. My mind felt the presence of someone else. It was strange how quickly I picked up the fear, agitation, and aggression from someone else. That was when I peered down and turned my attention back to the small coati.

"Hello? Can you hear me?" I whispered.

The small coati turned around and re-directed her focus back to me.

"Are you okay?"

The whisper began to grow, and I could almost understand it. "Co...Co."

"What's that? Coco? Is that your name?"

"Coco."

I nodded in understanding and knelt to the floor and placed my hand on my chest, "Justin, you can call me Justin. I'm going to be your partner."

I waited for a response as if I anticipated the animal could speak English. Instead, another long pause continued. She looked at me, tilted her head to the right and started to scamper toward me. She wasn't fearful, she wasn't aggressive, she was curious, and I could feel everything she felt in that moment. When she arrived at my feet, she looked up at my face and looked me in the eyes. I felt her soft heartbeat. Her whiskers brushed up against my cheeks as she sniffed my nose.

I pressed my forehead into hers, "I'll protect you, Coco. I promise."

Coco climbed back up my left leg to my shoulders. I picked up her blanket off the ground and threw it over my right shoulder as she maneuvered to my left. In the midst of the wave of silence that overcame the room, I remembered my outburst and indecent act of aggression. I had to apologize quickly so we could continue with the ceremony and complete the onboarding process.

My focus returned to the golden desk. "Demetrius, forgive me for my outburst. As for her name, her name is Coco."

Demetrius glimpsed over at Grandpa before he channeled his disapproval at me. "Very well. Know this, Justin Steele, we have no tolerance for emotional imbalances. Control yourself in the line of duty or suffer the consequences. Now, your orders will be given to you shortly after the ceremony. May you and Coco, travel, learn, and grow together in order to face the tasks ahead. Congratulations. Congratulations to you all."

The remainder of the ceremony felt like a blur. Once Coco and I were connected through our partner patches, I focused on her and stared at her lovingly, learning where each strand of fur lived. She studied me, sniffed, and memorized my scent. I felt her heartbeat, her breath, and each of her emotions. After a while she looked out at the audience from my shoulder. I could feel the curiosity she felt as I hoped she could feel my amazement. I knew there was nothing more on this earth I could love more. Our bond was almost overwhelming.

Once the ceremony ended, Rus, Lyza, and I were all awarded giant "WT" backpacks. Each pack included all of the information we needed to know about our animal and about each division we were in. The pack also included a thick book inside, *Patches* by Madame Yue. The same book that taught each new WT trainer how to utilize their partner patches. Inside my pack I found a file on Coco, specific books, and files on "The Cultivation Squad," one on farming and one on hunting. My hand fished out an adjustable red harness and short leash for Coco to wear. I immediately placed her blanket inside the pack and her small body into the harness. My goal was to familiarize her with the harness as early as possible. I clamped the black leash to the harness and carried Coco on my shoulders.

The members of the Animal Bridging Council left their desks one by one as they gathered their partners from their respected platforms and retreated the way they came. Grandpa descended from his seat and walked toward me for a big embrace.

"Congratulations, son. You protected everyone, and it got you where you needed to go," Grandpa Hershel whispered.

I smiled and responded thankfully, "I'm sorry about the outburst. I don't know what happened. Maybe I'm just exhausted? This patch is killing me. Can we go home now?"

"It's all right, you'll get used to it. You have to be more vigilant and remember where you are. I've got to finish up some paperwork in the back and get everything else you need. I'll be out in thirty then we'll go home."

I nodded while scratching Coco's chin, "All right, we'll be here."

Grandpa smiled, "I know you will."

Grandpa quickly climbed back up the stairs to his desk and collected Dusty from his platform as the two walked back through the door.

My eyes peered over to the other side of the room and caught Lyza standing next to Ivan's carrier. I decided to try my best to walk over with Coco on my shoulder. I began moving with no problem while Coco remained steadily mounted upon my left shoulder. As we approached, we noticed Lyza, moving alongside the habitat in order to retain Ivan's attention.

"He's a cute one."

Lyza jumped in fear.

"Sorry! I was just going to say I think you guys will make a good combo."

Coco became curious at the smell of saltwater and began climbing down my left arm and approached the glass. I raised my left arm and allowed her easier access to learn the new scent. Once she reached the hovering carrier she carefully sniffed around the condensed habitat. Her tail was in the air helping her control her balance. She sniffed the glass with urgency, wanting to see if what lay inside was friend or foe.

Lyza kept her eyes and energy focused on Ivan. "I think so too. He is so curious about everything."

I laughed while Coco continued sniffing the glass. Ivan noticed Coco and inched up toward her. Coco scratched at the glass, attempting to climb into the habitat, but with no luck.

"Ha yeah, I can relate. So, do you have your orders?"

"They are in my pack somewhere. Right now, I am just enjoying my time with him. I want to focus on Ivan and learn what makes him happy."

We watched the two as they played alongside the see-through glass. I began to pet Coco and pulled her back into my arms. She climbed up my chest and sniffed around my mouth. I whispered to her as she pulled down my bottom lip with her small hands. She too wished to know what made me tick.

"Ah, first base already? I did not know you were so easy, Justin Steele."

I slowly maneuvered Coco away from my mouth and tried to act cool. "Well, there's a lot you don't know about me. I'd like to tell you more, but I'm not sure when I'll see you again."

"Ah, you are funny. I like you. We will be at The Docks tomorrow. Come see us then."

"Okay, yeah, we'll be sure to stop by. Can I get your number?"

"Unfortunately, I am not that easy. I will see you tomorrow, Justin Steele."

The older woman from the front row ran up to Lyza. She joyfully hugged Lyza with a loving embrace. Lyza pulled her toward the habitat and introduced her to Ivan.

"Fair enough," I whispered.

My phone buzzed in my pocket. Coco noticed the buzzing and began to crawl down to investigate. She inserted her small head inside my pocket, hoping to find something new. I carefully pulled her head out and fished my phone out after.

"1 new message from Dad." I hesitantly opened the notification on my phone.

Hey, son, it's Dad. Got caught up today on the North Ignacia pier. Malcolm and his gang were up to no good. They were attempting to infiltrate one of the Exploration Squad headquarters. Your mom and I were able to team up to try to apprehend them. However, they escaped in a nearby sub. Your mother's partner, Shelly, is in pretty bad shape. We've notified the Exploration Squad, so Malcolm will be pursued and stopped. Sorry we weren't able to make it there today. I turned on the live stream to watch just as you named your coati! How exciting, first one in the program! I hope that partner patch didn't hurt too bad. Haha. Proud of you. I am excited to see what you two accomplish.

We'll catch up soon!

Love you. -Dad

My world began to sink as the longing to see my father returned. There wasn't anything I could do to change the situation but exhale deeply and close my phone.

Rus stood nervously alongside his habitat with his parents close by. His mom and dad both stood by and waved at the orca calf. Surprisingly Roxanne was nowhere to be found, and I couldn't tell if Rus was aware of her absence or not.

I unapologetically announced myself and offered my right hand, "Good job today, Rus."

Rus noticed me with Coco atop my shoulder. He turned to face me. "Yeah. Good job, man."

He casually shook my hand using his freshly cast hand.

"Congratulations, Justin! You did so well!" Mrs. Zhang yelled out.

Mr. and Mrs. Zhang stood closely by with their birds perched on their backpacks. Mr. Zhang's Golden Eagle and Mrs. Zhang's California Condor both sat and stared at Coco. I felt Coco's fear and anxiety rise. She dug her claws into my shoulder in attempts to jump off and run. However, I grabbed her the moment after she leaped off. I pulled her close as she buried herself in my arms.

Mr. Zhang nodded his head. "A fair exchange of strength and knowledge was shared today. Well done to you both."

"Justin, we heard you quit IPS drone delivery? Why? What happened?" Mrs. Zhang asked.

I winced and attempted to find the words. "It's sort of a long story, but the drone was on sight when Laura Dean was hit. Then it was destroyed by the AFA. It was a rough night, and I didn't know how to move on from there. So, I quit."

Coco could feel my embarrassment. She lifted her head and nestled into my chest.

"Justin, you did nothing wrong," Mr. Zhang interjected. "The program is designed to deliver mail, not criminals. If you ever want to work again, let me know."

"Thank you, Mr. Zhang. I'll keep that in mind, but I think I may have my hands full with this one."

Rus peered down at Coco and smiled, "She seems sweet. I think you two will work really well together."

I thought for a moment, "Yeah, I hope so. We have a lot of work to do."

"I mean I'm sure you guys will be successful as Farmers in the Cultivation Squad. She's not a predator or anything, but I'm sure you both will do just fine," Rus commented with a belittling tone.

My smile changed and turned into a frown, "The division allows any omnivore the chance to challenge a Hunter for a spot in the Hunter's Camp. Correct?"

"Is that right?" Rus scoffed. "Huh. Well, I wish you both luck, man."

"Come on, Rus. Don't be jealous because I'll be on land while you'll be in the depths of the ocean. Look at Kanoa. You have a powerhouse of a partner. I mean is it Roxanne that's–"

"Justin, you don't get it. You clearly don't know what you're talking about. I mean look at this orca. He's huge! I have no idea how I'm going to take care of him. I think I have enough to worry about right now."

Mrs. Zhang grabbed Rus's shoulder, "Sweetheart, this is all a part of the process. You can do this. Just listen to your partner."

Rus's father looked through the new paperwork inside Rus's pack, "Aren't you going to The Docks? It says here the WT provides you with a free habitat and meal plan for you both. That'll be a great place to start."

Rus looked back at the glass and back at his dad, "Of course, I should've remembered that. Then that's where we'll go."

"Rus, I'm sorry I didn't mean to–" I said, ready to offer an apology.

"Yeah, you didn't. Did you? I think you've done enough for today. We ship out Monday. Same as you and Lyza. Then you'll never see me again. I have to go."

"Rus, please. Come on, you're my friend. I'm really sorry for what happened today. Maybe we can stop by tomorrow."

"All right, we'll see you then. Dad, can you guys help me get Kanoa to The Docks?"

"Already on it, son. I was contacted earlier this afternoon and the trucks are outside standing by for transport. One for you and even one for your new friend Lyza."

"See, you got this! One thing at a time, Rus. I'll catch up with you later."

"Yeah. Later," Rus nodded.

I reached my hand out to perform our handshake. However, he offered me his fractured hand again and pounded his hand into mine. I pulled my hand back with concern. Rus began to walk away as the cameras, flashing lights and microphones pressed into our faces.

"Justin! Justin Steele!" reporters yelled.

"Justin, how do you feel about your new partner?"

"Justin, how do you like your new division?"

"Justin, how will you follow in your father's footsteps without a predator?"

"Justin, how will you spend your time in the Cultivation Squad? Farming?"

"Justin, how do you think this affects your chances with the Hero Regime?"

Suddenly Grandpa Herschel swooped in, pulled me away from the cameras and out of the lobby. Coco clung to my arm attempting to hide from the flashing lights and loud noises. Dusty followed, shaking his tail behind him to keep any and all reporters from following us. We successfully dodged the news crew and made our way to Grandpa's zomorodi. We got inside as Dusty climbed into the back seat.

Coco saw Dusty enter the vehicle and began freaking out. Coco was squeaking loudly, jumping up and away from Dusty at all costs. She was trying to get away from what appeared to be a giant predator. This amount of fear toward a potential predator is normal. However, Dusty showed no interest in her. Still, I was frightened for Coco. Her fear was overwhelming.

I began petting her softly and whispering to her, "Coco. Breathe. It's okay, I promise. Look at me." Her fight or flight mode was activated, and I could tell she felt trapped. I carefully placed my pointer and index finger under her narrow mouth and raised her head up to look at my eyes.

"Dusty is a friend," I continued. "He's Grandpa's partner. I promise they are not going to hurt you. You're going to be okay. I'll protect you, remember? Take it easy, Coco."

Coco's demeanor quickly began to change. She exhaled deeply and began to relax as she sat calmly in my lap. She nestled into a little ball once again as I slowly rubbed her head with my hand. The little fur ball was scared, and I understood she was in a new place with new people and potentially new predators. She just needed to spend more time with all of us. I was amazed at how quickly her emotions changed based on what I said. I knew she felt my concern, warmth, and love as a sort of reassurance. It was almost as if she could understand me. I pulled Coco's file from my bag. It appeared to be a bright shamrock folder that matched my shirt.

"Birthdate: May 12th, 3045. 2 months old.

Breed: Coatimundi. South American Coatimundi.

Scientific Name: Nasua Nasua.

Habitat: Primarily used to forested areas; cloud forests; however, due to human influence coatis prefer secondary forest edges.

Food: Coatimundis are omnivores, those who may survive on both plants and animals.

Biology: They have long tails that are used for balance. They are very flexible and have strong claws for climbing and foraging. They have the special ability to reverse their joints in their ankle bones to descend trees headfirst.

Lifespan: Before WT, a lifespan of up to eighteen years, with the WT lifespan, coatis may live up to seventy years.

Known predators: Birds of prey, snakes, jaguars, mountain lions, ocelots, and jaguarundis.

Fun facts about your partner: She is immensely playful, kind, scent oriented, overly cognitive, and aware of her surroundings. She is more than capable of learning. She enjoys climbing, digging, and shiny objects.

Bad habits: Fearful and overly cautious of her surroundings."

"Oh, well, that makes sense. We'll have to work on that."

My fingers grazed the top of her head and down her back. She was afraid because everything she'd experienced that day had been incredibly new and stressful. It was going to take some time for her to become a hundred percent comfortable.

Before I knew it, Grandpa pulled into our driveway.

I was unsure where to begin, "So, are you going to tell me what all the 'arguing' was about today between you and the council?"

"I don't know what you're talking about," Grandpa hesitated.

"The discussion of my placement? Did it have anything to do with Coco?"

Grandpa Herschel turned off his vehicle and stepped out of his zomorodi, "Justin, you did well and got into the Cultivation Squad. Let's leave it at that. All right?"

Coco casually climbed onto my right shoulder as I placed the large WT backpack on my left shoulder and got out of the car. "I just want to know what really happened."

Grandpa locked the zomorodi and turned to face me. "You still hungry? Let me make something, and then we'll talk."

Over the years, I learned to be blunt and more direct like Grandpa. Seeing him like this and deterring certain questions or key topics was very new and almost worrisome. What wasn't he telling me?

For the next hour and a half, I provided Coco with a tour of the downstairs. I then let her off her harness and allowed her to explore freely. She joyfully climbed the furniture, attempted to climb the curtains but ripped through them with her sharp nails. She pooped in Dusty's corner, and he retaliated by chasing her around the living room. It wasn't until I cleaned up the poop and rescued her from Dusty that Grandpa had finished our dinner.

"Soup's on!" Grandpa Herschel yelled. As I sat down at the table, he asked, "Shouldn't you start packing?"

I shrugged. "I've got the weekend to prepare. Tonight, I want to make it about Coco. I want to see to it that she's comfortable."

Grandpa scoffed at how I carried Coco on my shoulder. I felt whole and happy that I finally had someone, something that made me feel not only responsible but also full. I was bursting with joy and pride. But I was also somewhat hesitant about The Cultivation Squad and the fact that Coco was not a predator.

As an omnivore, it would take some special training to defeat someone from the Hunter's Camp and become a Hunter. Regardless, tonight was not the time to overthink my position. Tonight was about relationship-building.

All it took was but a few moments for me to fall in love with Coco. Grandpa had concocted another marvelously flavorful meal for the umpteenth time. His leftovers had been carefully cooked, braised, and minced into a masterful array of chicken, squash, Brussel sprouts, topped with bacon, and mashed potatoes.

Grandpa presented everything on the newly delivered, redwood dining room table he had just purchased. Coco descended from my shoulder and attempted to sit on my lap as I ate. I began cutting my food until Coco reached onto my plate with her little claws, scratching the plate's surface. I carefully guided her claws away until she decided that sticking her nose on my plate was a better option.

"No, no. I suppose you'll have to start eating separately from me."

"May not be a bad idea. But be careful and make sure she doesn't become aggressive!" Grandpa Herschel exclaimed.

"I'll look for early signs of food aggression."

After visiting the kitchen to retrieve a small side plate, I wasted very little time loading it up with a small portion of each entree. Coco's diet was a healthy mix of vegetables and proteins. Being an omnivore gave her the ability to eat both meat and vegetables whenever she preferred. She leaped for her small plate after it was carefully placed in the chair alongside me.

"Make sure that chair doesn't end up like my curtains, please."

"She'll be fine. I promise. And I'll buy you a new set of curtains tomorrow."

"No, no you save that money. You'll need it for tomorrow. You need to shop for everything you'll need at camp. Clothes, gloves, hats—"

"You know I still haven't forgotten. I want to know, Grandpa. What were you and the council fighting about?"

"Fine," he appeared a little vexed with my question, but he exhaled a heavy breath, "Now that you're in the WT, I suppose I can share some of this with you. It was either you get Coco, or you go to the Exploration Squad." Grandpa looked down at his food and took a large bite of Brussel sprouts with bacon.

"What do you mean by that?"

"You succeeded during in-water combat, better than anyone else there. Emmeline has been on my ass lately about Exploration Squad members disappearing, so they need more recruits."

"Disappearing?" I asked, concerned. "So, are you sending people to-? Does Dad know? Does Mom–"

"Yes. He knows, she knows, we're investigating this quietly," Grandpa muttered. "The Exploration Squad is one of the most important divisions. They are the sole explorers of the ocean that are actually mapping the ocean floor. They have seen and experienced things that you could never imagine. That's why the new additions have such high-powered animals. They're strong, agile, and resilient by nature. Not to mention the ability to withstand the dynamic levels of pressure while also fending off any potential predators."

My mind began to race at the thought of WT members getting lost at sea or facing off against potential undersea animals. What else was down there? I returned to reality after a brief moment and remembered the people who were not there today at the ceremony.

"Grandpa, where were they today? My parents–" I hesitantly asked.

Grandpa placed his silverware down, "I'm sure they have a good reason for not being there. Didn't your father message you?"

Suddenly, Grandpa's phone rang once, notifying him that he'd received a message. Grandpa wiped his mouth, stood from his chair, and walked back to the kitchen where he'd left his phone. Brief whispers echoed from the kitchen as he read the message to himself. After a moment he visited the living room, grabbed for the remote, and turned on the television.

A newscaster reported, "Today on the scene, this past afternoon at The County Pier, Noah Steele and several members of the Hero Regime chased down a culprit by the name 'Malcolm.' The culprit was attempting to pry partner patches off Exploration Squad members. Chuck Daily is on the scene. Chuck, we're going to you live."

A mugshot of a man with glasses appeared on screen. He was broadcasting his report from the County Pier. Next to the gentleman stood my father.

"That's right, Alexandria. Malcolm, the leader of this unidentified group of terrorists was seen stopping people at gunpoint, forcing them beneath the pier and stripping them of their partner patches. Noah Steele, can you please tell us more?"

My father spoke, "That's correct. This man who has decided to move against the WT is forcing the unthinkable onto innocent participants in the WT, attempting to steer people away from their partners and disposing of their partner patches. We tracked him to this pier and attempted to pursue him; however, we received reports that he'd escaped in a miniature submarine before we arrived. Three victims were rescued and received replacement patches for themselves as well as their partners."

A picture of the culprit suddenly appeared on screen.

My father continued, "Subject is a 26-year-old man. Dark hair. Traveling alongside a red maned wolf. If anyone sees or hears anything, please contact the local authorities immediately, and we will be right behind them. Thank you."

Grandpa muted the television. "Justin, have you ever heard of this man?"

"No. No I haven't. Why?"

"This man is strong, cunning, and has no sympathy for others. He must be stopped."

"Grandpa, I'll be fine. I finally got my partner, and we're not afraid. I mean what is it going to take to show you I am ready? What am I supposed to do?"

"Nothing. You continue on your journey to protect this country. Just call me or your dad if you see this man. Your father will run the Hero Regime, and your mom will continue on with the Exploration Squad. I suppose we all have a part to play in this."

"You made the right call. Putting me and Coco together, I mean. So, thank you."

Grandpa took another bite and pointed at me with his spoon. "I know I did. But you two have to learn to fight. Coco has claws, and she needs to use them. They will be her most powerful weapon until her fangs come in."

"She'll get fangs too? That's awesome!"

"Justin, after dinner, please go learn everything there is to know about your animal, and don't come out until you know everything about coatimundis."

I ate my dinner, taking big bites of chicken as Coco dipped her nose in her potatoes. After dinner, I placed the harness back on Coco and took her outside to use the bathroom once more before bed. After she completed her business, I grabbed our new WT backpack and led her upstairs to my room. She hopped up each stair with more enthusiasm than the last. I flipped the light switch on and illuminated the room. Coco immediately ran to the bed and jumped on top of it. I sat at my desk while Coco inspected the room, staking her claim to it, too. She began to climb the shelves in the corner. She sniffed, scratched, and played with the different items my father had gifted me.

Coco grabbed the red hat with peculiar intent and brought it down from the shelf. She buried herself in the hat on top of my bed. There was something confusing about the hat she didn't understand. She loved the scent so much she wished to smell like the hat, so she continued to roll all around and enveloped herself in it. I walked over to the bed, picked up the hat and placed it on my head. She began climbing my arm up to my head where she attempted to dig her elongated nose underneath the side panels of the hat. I rubbed her back as she sat atop my shoulder sniffing the hat. I knew from then on that I needed to bring the hat with me for secondary reinforcement. It would be a means of motivation to keep her absorbed and focused upon completing a task. I could use it as a tentative reward.

I spent the remainder of the evening learning all I could about South American Coatis on the web. Several online articles taught me what they eat, how they mate, their gestation period, their aggression, along with their average size and weight. I felt much more confident about working alongside an intelligent animal that was both aware and cognizant of her surroundings. After I completed studying, I found Coco fast asleep on my pillow. I decided to place the hat next to her while she slept. I knew this was a great opportunity to shower.

I pulled out Madam Yue's book, *Patches* and opened it up to the table of contents: Chapter Six: Bathing. I skimmed it quickly and learned that if I pressed the blue button, it became waterproof. The wearer would be secure of any potential damage to the partner patch to the person. I took off my dirty clothes and jumped in the shower. I was nervous because I knew Coco was asleep and unwatched. I needed to be quick and would quickly return to check on her. I became nervous about being nervous because I knew Coco would feel my nerves and be tempted to wake up. It was the most stressful shower I'd ever experienced. I quickly got out, dried off and found Coco exactly where I had left her.

I turned the desk light off and carefully maneuvered my way into bed without waking her, or so I thought. I saw her left eye slowly open as she stretched her arms out in front of me. I kissed the top of her head and whispered, "I love you, Coco. Now get some rest." I reached over to my right shoulder and entered the sleep code onto the partner patch. As the light on both of our patches began to dim, the heavier my eyelids became. I wanted to continue to watch her to make sure she slept well, but the weight became too much. I took one last yawn before tapping out and giving into the night.

CHAPTER 7

The Docks of Exploration

The following morning arrived in the blink of an eye. A sound night of deep, rejuvenating sleep highlighted a tight soreness that enveloped my arms, legs, and mid-section. With the WT application behind me, I reflected on everything I'd put my body through in order to pass the challenges. I slowly wiped the sleep out of my eyes before placing my left hand down in a steamy pile of coati poop.

"Ah, shit."

I knew I should've woken up earlier. I rushed to the bathroom to wash my hands and noticed my partner patch in the reflection of the bathroom mirror. The patch itself had not lit back up. I looked back at *Patches* and began reviewing the table of contents and found "Chapter 2: Waking Up."

The chapter stated, "Each night the partner patch gathers energy from your body while you sleep in order to function properly the following day. You must carefully select the three main buttons to restart the patch daily so it may resync to your partner. You must click the following button on your patch: first orange, green, and blue. Once your patch begins blinking enter the same sequence into your partner's patch. The two will then turn green simultaneously, reestablishing the connection."

I quickly pressed the three buttons in the correct order according to the book. Once it began blinking, I turned around to locate Coco and saw that she was not in my bedroom or bathroom. I opened my door completely and yelled down the staircase.

I called out, "Coco? Coco?"

"She's down here in the dining room, waiting for breakfast."

I hurried down the staircase and found her standing in the same chair with her two front hands on the table as if she were waiting for her breakfast to be served to her.

I walked over to her and pressed the orange, green and blue buttons in the same order. Suddenly I reconnected to Coco's energy, her feelings, her hunger, everything had returned.

"And we do this every morning? That's crazy," I muttered.

Grandpa brought over two plates of bacon and eggs to the table and responded, "Partner patches? Yeah you'll get used to them. Not the most relaxing device to deal with. Can be a bit of a nuisance really... Well, look at that, she really likes your father's hat."

I looked down and noticed she had dragged the red hat my father had given me, all the way down the stairs to breakfast. I decided to reach down and pick it up and put it on my head. Coco immediately started to climb my arm, digging her sharp, little claws into my skin, each scratch hurting a little more than the last.

She got to my shoulders and stood tall to continue sniffing the hat. I could feel she was understanding what the article of clothing was designed for. She looked down at Grandpa and back at the food. Coco climbed back down to the chair, but before she began to eat off my plate, I rationed my plate and took a fourth of my eggs and bacon onto another side plate for her to enjoy.

I could feel through the patch that Coco was becoming more comfortable with each meal she shared in the dining room. This was her primary reinforcement. This would provide for a morning meal to afford her enough energy to follow more instruction as the day went on. Living the past two months in a lab could not have been fun or enjoyable. I wanted to do everything I could so that she would forget those negative memories and replace them with positive ones.

Grandpa brewed a pot of coffee and brought it over to the table. We enjoyed our cups of coffee as we spoke about our weekend goals and decided to plan another training session for early Sunday, tomorrow, morning. Grandpa wanted me to practice some potential combos with Coco so we would be prepared to face off against a hunter in the Cultivation Squad. I knew we had to get to The Docks today if we were going to have a chance to see Lyza and Rus before we all departed. Their large marine animals had limited their ability to travel.

"Can I borrow the zomorodi? We need to head to The Docks to see Lyza and Rus before they ship out."

"That depends. Am I going to find something inside it later that will make me regret this decision?"

"Um, have I ever left anything behind before?" I responded hesitantly.

Grandpa smirked, "No, but you never had a coati alone in it before. Just be sure to get it back in one piece. You need to pick up supplies today as well. Go by Barney's in the Cultivation section. There's a kit suitable for Farmers and one for Hunters. Grab both."

"Why do I need to grab a Farmer's kit? We're going to become Hunters!"

"Son, you don't know that for sure. You and Coco will be responsible for completing and passing your first challenge. And there's nothing wrong with being a Farmer for a little while. You learn the lay of the land. You work more with your hands and learn an invaluable set of skills."

"You sound like you would know all about it."

"It's my job to know these things. You on the other hand need to be better prepared."

I bowed and nodded sarcastically. "How would Madam Yue respond to that? 'It will be done.' I gotta go get dressed. Oh, and I need to wash my sheets!" I began walking backward towards the stairs, trying hard not to smile.

"Poop in the bed?" Grandpa called out.

"Poop in the bed." I smiled and then laughed.

"Poop in the bed! Ugh. Speaking of green and brown, that reminds me: your uniforms came in. Feel free to test them out today. Package is over by the door."

I bolted to the front door. Coco came running right behind me. She felt the excitement inside me grow and a burst of genuine curiosity overcame us both. I pulled the heavy box open and found twelve shamrock green shirts similar to the one I received yesterday, six short sleeves and six long sleeves. The design featured the species name of my partner, the division name, and a shadow silhouette of a coati in the middle. Included also were six pairs of blue jeans, six pairs of cargo pants, and two pairs of brown working boots.

"Hmm interesting, for today, I think we may need to alter our wardrobe a bit. What do you think Coco?" The clueless coati paused and leaned her head to the side.

Grandpa countered from the dining room, "Do not alter too much. You're representing the WT and the Cultivation Squad now."

"Of course, yeah I understand." A sneaky smile spread across my face as we dragged the heavy box up the stairs.

Once we closed the door, our energy and excitement spiked to an all-time high. She and I made quick use of the cardboard. I pulled out all of the WT apparel seconds before Coco viciously dug her nails in and pulled the box apart. The adventure to customize my outfit began as the sounds of heavy rock and roll played in the background. The sense of pride that overcame me as I put on the Cultivation Squad shirt was overwhelming.

My stereo volume had originally been turned up as high as it could go, but once I turned the music on, Coco started screeching and pulling up the carpet. Unfortunately, I could no longer blast music in my room without stressing out my partner. The coati silhouette featured a vivid orange circular background as if it were in front of the sun. It was an amazing uniform that I was proud to wear, however, the blue jeans were a little too blue for me. The uniform they sent me was the original requirement to be worn by all Cultivation Squad members of the WT. However, my start date was still a few days out, and that provided me an opportunity to slightly customize my appearance. Instead of the required blue jeans, I decided to add my own personal flare of black into the mix. I was sporting my standard Cultivation Squad shirt but with my torn, black skinny jeans and black shoes.

From that day on I was physically representing the Cultivation Squad and in essence the WT as the latest member of the Cultivation Squad. It was about seventy degrees out and cloudy with high winds which made wearing black jeans bearable. The lion clock in my room read 11:15 a.m. I harnessed Coco, attached the black leash, grabbed the keys from Grandpa and jumped in the zomorodi. Coco sat next to me in the front as she began bathing herself.

I'd never been to The Docks before, but I assumed it was due northeast Ignacia about a mile or so away from the County Pier, somewhere between the Flyers and Swimmers. Nevertheless, I launched my GPS system on my phone to help guide us there.

At first glance, I saw the outstanding size of the stadium-like structure. I could tell the WT had invested an immense amount of money into the facility. I was blown away by the size of the set up. The glass facility was built four-stories tall. Beautiful greenery with interconnecting stone paths surrounded it. From the top, a couple of window washers were at work cleaning all that glass.

Each habitat was equipped with four inches of carbon fiber glass strong enough to stop an ion beam, the newly improved bullet proof status. The WT spared no expense designing this place to be hospitable, colorful, and accessible for Swimmers and partners in the Exploration Squad. It appeared to be a multitude of tunnels, resembling the multi-pathways created by hamsters in design. Each tunnel was 80% filled with water and 20% of controlled air circulating each waterway. The tunnels went up, down, and sideways ranging in a variety of setups depending on the animal. We parked the zomorodi just outside The Docks near the newly painted parking lot.

The yellow and white lines highlighted the bland and empty land just alongside the large stadium. Each set of lines provided a warning for parked vehicles to be vigilant and aware of the ongoing renovations that were occurring to expand the facility. There was a stretch zomorodi that covered most of the first floor of the parking lot. I'd never seen a vehicle so large up close.

I stepped out of Grandpa's zomorodi with Coco carefully secured atop my shoulder. I was leaving the parking lot when I saw a figure surrounded by four muscular bodyguards all in black suits and black sunglasses. He was an older gentleman in his mid to late fifties. The suit wore expensive sunglasses, a large gold watch, a gray jacket with a sky-blue button-down shirt and a matching navy-blue bow tie. I was walking toward the entrance when the bodyguards forced us off the sidewalk.

"Seriously? We're just walking by," I scoffed.

The older man stopped in his tracks and lifted two fingers from his left hand. He took off his shades and glimpsed down on me and Coco.

The man in the suit grinned. "Well now. Who do we have here? A young member of the Cultivation Squad?"

I examined the brute strength of the group of bodyguards as they glared at me aggressively. "Uh, yes sir. We just received our orders yesterday."

The old man pondered, "Yesterday? Ahh yes that's right. And a coati for a partner? Hmmm, why, you must be Justin Steele."

I swallowed nervously. "Yes sir, who are you?"

The man laughed and pulled out a business card. He offered it to me with the same two fingers he'd originally signaled his guards with. I hesitantly grabbed the card and pulled it back close to me. I flipped it upward and read the name.

The man placed his sunglasses back on, "Vladimir Mathias. But you can call me Vlad. If there's anything you need, all you need to do is ask, Mr. Steele." The man signaled his guards and waved goodbye as they began walking toward the stretch zomorodi.

I placed the business card in my pocket and continued on through the front door. Once Coco and I waited in line and passed through security, we were questioned by a desk clerk. She was a large, older woman with a sour exterior hidden behind a thick pair of black glasses. The desk clerk spoke with a defeated, negative tone.

"Welcome to The Docks. What is the intent of your visit today?"

"Hi, umm visiting friends."

"What are the trainers' names?"

"Russel Zhang and Lyza Ry—uhh... Hmm it's a long last name. Uhh baka. No, no. Rybakova! They're both expecting me."

"Do you have identification?"

"Yeah, I have it right here, my driver's license." I handed her my driver's license from my wallet.

She read it aloud, "Any relation to Teresa Steele?"

"Umm, yeah, she's my mother actually."

"Your mother? She was my mentor, back in the day. Strange, she never mentioned having any children."

"Ha, yeah small world... I'm going to go now—"

"Please do not touch, hit, or harm any of the habitats during your time here. If you can abide by this, you are good to go. You'll be visiting Rybakova in Block B and Zhang in Block C. Enjoy your time."

I nodded and walked in through a set of revolving doors. The entire facility looked more like a giant aquarium instead of a dock. The floor was wood colored and rustic as if we were on a boat sailing across the ocean with modern technology instilled in the glass surrounding the infrastructure.

Bright lights flickered from above, highlighting different animals in different habitats. Some habitats had trainers in the deep water with their animals working different behaviors. Coco and I were both amazed by the setup. Trainers seemed really in sync with their partners, and this was a great beginning point before getting sent off to the Exploration Squad.

They had a rehabilitation wing and assigned daily classes to assist with newly assigned trainers. All new trainers were provided with an instructor to help familiarize themselves with their animals. We saw a man introducing learning behaviors to his tiger shark, a woman attempting to reprimand her giant octopus, and a woman consistently flipping with her manta-ray. Each trainer and partner pair were at different points of their animal training process.

We made our way to Block B first to locate Lyza and see how she and Ivan were getting along. The interior of the facility was dark but well-protected and very clean. Small lights shone from the roof, the floor, and even in the water.

We walked alongside several habitats with no sign of Lyza. It wasn't until we surveyed the third glass habitat and caught a glimpse of a young woman in the water hugging her dolphin. A tall, slender man in a wetsuit was leaving the habitat. The man looked at me rudely as he passed by.

A jealous voice whispered inside my brain. "Who the heck was that guy? Was he her boyfriend? He seemed pretty strong."

Coco scratched my arm with concern as she silenced the jealous commentary, but somehow I replaced them with nervous thoughts. The man laughed and continued to walk away. A toxic exchange with the man left me feeling inferior. My hands found the door handle as I stood in the hallway confused, concerned, and then I realized I was unable to open the door altogether.

When I looked inside the glass door, there stood Lyza holding her dolphin Ivan in what looked like a hug. The two seemed to have become more comfortable and aware of one another. Knowing that my knock on this habitat door would interrupt the powerful and intimate moment, made me regret coming to see her first. The physical trust that was shared in the water between the two was beyond visual: it was spiritual. She was like an angel, floating in the water serving her part as a newly devoted guardian.

I hesitantly knocked on the glass door. The young woman raised her head suddenly and looked up to see someone waiting at her door. She slowly pulled away from her adolescent dolphin and got out of the water. She was wearing her new uniform, a tight black wetsuit with a blue rough-toothed dolphin silhouette on the front.

At first, she appeared neutral and emotionless, but as she got out of the water, I knew she was irritated at anyone who would interrupt her training session. However, once she discovered it was me, her frown seemed to turn into a soft smile. It was a subtle grin that wanted you to know that she recognized your existence. She reached in her bucket next to the door, tossed Ivan a fish, and then opened the glass door to her habitat.

A bright smile illuminated her face in the dark hallway. "No, thank you. We did not order any pizza. Did you, Ivan?" Ivan squeaked in the background, as he manipulated the air sacs in his blowhole.

"Did you order a Coati? Because she's our last one." Coco jumped off my shoulder and landed at Lyza's feet.

"Hello, little one. Oh, my goodness, you are adorable, Coco. Come in, come in."

The air in the room was mixed well by the ceiling fan blending the sweet smell of frozen herring and saltwater. It was a cozy, dark room with romantic light fixtures carefully placed in the water. A waterbed designed for a king, a sofa for the trainer to relax on with a built-in, waterproof heater, a waterproof chair and a thirty-by-thirty pool of water for Ivan to swim in. This room allowed the trainer to be close to his or her partner at all times. The Docks had a food court and shower center for trainers to use during their stay. Both were just a short walk away from Block B. I knew she was able to break away and eat, but it appeared to be a very demanding location.

I knelt down next to the pool of water looking for Ivan, "Hello, Ivan! Where are you, bud?"

Ivan's head popped up out of the water and planted his mouth directly in front of me. I was startled by his quickness and closeness in the sudden encounter. Lyza tossed another fish in his mouth from a giant silver bucket. Ivan suddenly dipped the front of his mouth or rostrum down into the water and jerked his head upward to splash me. He splashed water out of his mouth and up into my general direction. Coco was able to evade the water by fleeing to the nearby sofa. However, I was directly in the line of fire and absorbed each ounce of water that was forcefully ejected.

Lyza laughed hysterically and snorted, "Did you not think you would get wet coming here?"

I spat water out of my mouth. "I guess I should've seen that coming. Still worth it!"

I slowly began to stand and waddled over to a waterproof chair. Lyza walked over to the towel rack next to her bed and grabbed two towels. She threw a towel at me while she wiped her face with the other before putting it on the sofa to sit. Coco moved from her original spot on the couch and snuggled up next to Lyza. My tired partner seized the opportunity to take a quick nap.

Lyza gently glided her hand over Coco's fur. "How was your first night with this one?"

I hesitantly laughed, "Well, it started out nice, once we figured out the sleep mode of the partner patch. Then I discovered the present she left for me when I woke up."

"These things happen. It was your first night together, and she was in unfamiliar territory."

"I wish she'd familiarize one of the litter boxes I left out for her."

"Maybe it is something the two of you can work on. What is she like?"

"She loves to eat. Once she learned where we eat meals, that's the only place she wants to be."

"A girl who knows what she wants. I admire that. A great opportunity to reward her behaviors with primary reinforcement. She seems to like you."

I smiled. "Yeah and I'm obsessed with her. It's crazy, all it took was a few hours with her, and now I can't imagine my life without her."

"I know how you are feeling. Maybe this is why we are in the program."

"What do you mean?"

Lyza carefully removed her leg from under Coco. She stood, grabbed her bucket of herring, and sat alongside the habitat to feed Ivan. "I mean people feel lost, unfulfilled, and useless all the time. If we took that time and gave it to an animal, it would make us feel better. No?"

"Of course, that's like the fundamentals of why the program was created. It gives us the opportunity to care for animals and ensure they have longer, happier lives."

"Yes, but we also do it for ourselves. We are selfish."

"I suppose everyone is a part of this program for a different reason. Why are you here?"

"To fulfill a purpose and learn everything I can about how to be a better person. Why are you here?"

"Wow. That's such a better answer than mine."

Lyza laughed. "Wow, you suck, Justin Steele."

I rose from the chair and moved over to Coco on the couch, "I know, I know. But honestly, I don't know any more. I was here to follow in my father's footsteps. But now, I'm here for her. To learn everything about her and one day, be the best leader in the WT."

"Power, power, it gets old. You are here to be like your father?"

I scratched Coco's head and faced Lyza, "Can't it be both? I mean yeah he's the strongest trainer in Ignacia. And yes, I hope to be one day as well. What's the phrase? Like father, like son?"

Lyza placed the bucket down. "Not always. People do not always end up like their fathers."

"What about your father?"

Her tone suddenly changed. "I do not want to talk about him."

"All right, then what would you like to talk about?"

"I got my orders."

"That's exciting! Where are you going?"

"The Two Hundredth Division at Exploration Squad headquarters. Aboard the ES Sandpiper. We will be at the bottom of the ocean, but that is not the lightest conversation topic either."

"Who was that woman you saved?"

"My mother. Well, she is not really my mother. She is my godmother, Emma. But I just call her my mom."

"I always wished I knew my mom. I feel like we'd be friends, she, and I."

"Life does not pull many punches, but I am sorry."

I rubbed my neck and nervously stood, "Yeah. I am too."

A momentary pause multiplied in size and overwhelmed the room. Jolly hymns with sounds of the sea embellished the minds of hopeful trainers working throughout the habitats of Block B. A hidden intensity lay restless underneath the surface of my skin. My core began to twist and turn with unspoken thoughts and urges. The desire to tell Lyza the truth of my feelings sat trapped in my mind. The fear of rejection ignited an inner struggle. One feud between my mind and my heart. I wanted to tell her the truth, but some part of me would not allow it.

"Listen, I want–Agh."

Lyza turned and asked, "What is it?"

All I had to do was tell her how I felt about her. It was as if an invisible, sound-proof wall came down and sat between us. I couldn't say or do anything for her to get my message across.

"I think."

"You think? What, Justin Steele?"

"I think... You'll be great. In the Exploration Squad."

"Oh, yes. Thank you. Well, the Cultivation Squad will be lucky to have you."

"Thanks. I wish things could've turned out different."

Lyza stood. "No. This was the way it was supposed to be. You go your way and I go mine."

"Right. Maybe, I'll see you again. I'll save you from your next crocodile encounter."

"I think you will be the one who needs saving."

The two of us laughed and looked at one another. We allowed the unspoken words to diminish and burn out. The unknown embers that lay within would remain intact, safely locked away, waiting for the opportune moment.

"Write to me," Lyza mumbled.

"Write to you? What... like ... a letter?"

"I want to hear about the adventures you go on with Coco."

"Okay. Where will I send them?"

Lyza walked over to her waterbed and pulled out her backpack hidden beneath the bed. Inside she pulled out a royal blue manila folder. She opened the folder and brought it over to me.

"Here."

She pointed to the address on file underneath a large picture of a submarine. The vessel was just one of the few submarine living-quarters where the Exploration Squad resided. Certain students were sent to distinct vessels depending on their job. I pulled out my phone and typed the address.

"I will. Be safe, Lyza. Please."

"I will see you again, Justin. Count on it."

Lyza raised her arms and walked into me for a hug. I pulled Lyza close, my right-hand found its way behind her neck. Cradling her and gently holding her head on my shoulder. Fireworks erupted in my mind as goosebumps scattered across my forearms. I allowed time to stop. We stood frozen in that moment. It was one embrace I would never forget. I was fearful it would be our last.

While Lyza and I embraced, Coco climbed up my leg and found her way to my shoulder. She began sniffing Lyza's face. Lyza pulled back laughing but kissed Coco goodbye with a polite peck on her forehead. I rubbed Coco's chin as she stood on my shoulder.

We turned and tried to leave Lyza's habitat without glancing back. My body couldn't help but shake the eerie thought that I had more that I needed to say before she shipped off. I reached for the door but slowly turned around before opening it. I turned around to face Lyza once more as our eyes connected for a single moment before she turned and dove into the habitat with Ivan.

My feelings would have to wait, and I knew we both had more important things to worry about. Lyza was fearless and ready for what came next. I looked forward to the possibilities of what lay ahead for her and me.

Coco and I made our departure from Block B with a new feeling of warmth and fulfillment. I had found another reason to be hopeful, the thought of holding Lyza again was something worth fighting for.

CHAPTER 8

A Furious Feud

The bioluminescent invertebrates from the surrounding habitats in the hallway illuminated the walkway to Block C. The glossy glass reflected off the lights and created euphoric romantic clouds. The remnants of Lyza's fishy scent lingered on the tips of my nostrils, allowing me to relive the moment of our embrace once more. The same overwhelming warmth enveloped my every move. A pole stood in the middle of the hallway, one that I spontaneously whisked my body around. Coco held onto my shoulder tightly, digging her claws into me. I couldn't help but relish the thought of seeing Lyza again. The unspoken feelings shared between her and me became a new driving force for me. I felt as if I'd leapt onto a staircase of clouds and had to find my way to the top to reach Lyza.

I knew the feelings I felt were consuming my thought process, but I enjoyed the idea of rejoining Lyza and tackling the world together. I pulled Coco down from my shoulder, wincing a little in the process, and into my arms.

I held her right claw in my left hand and rocked her from side to side as if we were ballroom dancing.

Of course, I had little to no dancing experience, so the sight was a pretty unusual thing to behold. I didn't care. It was a silly spectacle that caused multiple trainers and coordinators to laugh as we moseyed through the hallway together.

We made a small pit stop at the food court and noticed there were only three vendors to choose from. Each vendor included a diverse selection of seafood. However, each featured a certain item that was correlated to members of the Exploration Squad. The choices were as follows: *The Fisherman's Wife*, *Octopus Inn* and *Fishtails*.

Each food stand sounded less appetizing than the next. We found the first option to be the most reasonable and noticed they offered fish and chips as one of their entrees. I decided to order a platter: it was a reliable go-to meal option that seemed fitting for the occasion. We later discovered *Octopus Inn* offered sushi, and *Fishtails* had freshly cut salmon, cod, and herring. *Fishtails* featured options that could be served fried, grilled, or raw. This vendor was intended for a variety of WT partners.

I decided to pay for a raw slice of salmon and give it to Coco. It was unsafe for her to be eating something fried and processed. We quickly scarfed down our food as if we hadn't eaten in years. After we finished our brief time in the food court, we continued our journey to find Rus and ventured into a hallway on the other side of the food court.

We entered through the following hallway marked "Block C." Coco and I approached the first enclosure. We noticed the habitats were much larger than those in Block B. Lyza's habitat was large, but these spaces were fully developed stadiums. One hundred yards long and full of thousands of gallons of ocean water; each one provided the best learning environment for the larger additions to the Exploration Squad. The first habitat on our left featured a stadium-style habitat space. It was an entertainment area, fully lined with metal benches and chairs. A small female trainer stood on the middle platform facing the water. She had five large buckets of what I assumed to be the shark's food source, also the primary reinforcement. A twenty-five-foot-long whale shark with a very wide head rose to the surface and moved toward his trainer. The small trainer grabbed one of the large buckets of small invertebrates and emptied it into her partner's mouth. At first glance the food in the buckets appeared to be spaghetti, but as we looked closer, it was small shrimp and krill. We continued on past the large windows of the habitat and located the next enclosure down the hallway. The glass was tinted and dark so all who walked by could not look inside the habitat. We looked to the right of the viewing window and noticed a door. I decided to take the chance to find out if Rus was inside.

A sign hung on the door. "Warning: Training in Progress! Do not disturb!" I knew the risk of being yelled at or even thrown out of The Docks was a possibility if it were the wrong habitat. But it was a risk I was willing to take.

I slowly cracked the door open and glanced through the small opening. Inside there were two men in wetsuits. One was in the water while one was on the platform facing the habitat. The two men stood about thirty-five yards away and were difficult to identify.

Suddenly, we witnessed Kanoa briefly leap out of the water and dive back down into the depths of the habitat. The high energy behavior created a massive splash and soaked the man on the platform. I opened the door more and hesitantly stepped inside with Coco on my shoulder. The man from the platform waved and that was when I knew it was Rus. It looked like the man in the water with Kanoa was providing a training session to assist Rus.

The area was very large and similar to the whale shark's habitat. The entertainment area included a very different layout in relation to Lyza's. The majority of the room was also a stadium style full of metal chairs and benches. Rus's habitat was designed for a multitude of viewers, trainers, and coordinators to meet, watch, and discuss training methods for select WT trainers.

We walked down the staircase into the audience area. We crisscrossed, jumping through a variety of benches and chairs in order to shorten the walk. As we made our way closer to the platform, I noticed Rus watching the man work alongside Kanoa.

"How'd you manage to pull this off? This place is huge! How are you, man?"

"I know, right? VIP status! Nah, but we're good. Just trying to learn more and more about Kanoa. He's fast."

The man in the water began riding Kanoa on the surface of the water as Kanoa raced around the habitat.

"Wow, that's awesome!"

Things had been a bit jaded between Rus and me since we spoke yesterday after the Animal Pairing Ceremony concluded. I was a bit apprehensive, and I wanted to make sure we were able to repair any damage that may have affected our friendship.

"How was your first night with your new orca?"

"Kanoa finally simmered down around 12 a.m. I could tell he felt lonely. Of course, he never fully goes to sleep. Only a portion of his brain shuts down. With unihemispheric slow-wave sleep, a part of his brain never turns off. He's confused about everything right now, and with so much movement it's been difficult for him to get comfortable."

"I get that. Once I figured out the partner patch code, it practically forced Coco's eyes shut."

"There's a partner patch sleeping code?"

"Haven't you been reading *Patches*?"

"When would I have time to do that?"

The other man riding Kanoa was led back to the platform, he leaped off of Kanoa's back with ease and approached me, "This is a closed training session. You're not supposed to be here."

"Can we take like a five-minute break? We'll be ready to go again," Rus asked.

The man exhaled and sighed, "Fine. But be ready. You're riding Kanoa next."

The muscular man in the wetsuit nudged me out of the way. I looked at him closely as he looked back and grimaced. A faint memory of the man lingered as I attempted to study his face. He was the same trainer that had left

Lyza's habitat just moments before I arrived. I looked back at Rus, "What's up with him?"

"He's a bit uptight, but no worries. Come on! Follow me. Let me show you around."

Rus ran toward a spiral staircase on the left side of his habitat. We jumped down from the center platform and followed him up the staircase. Rus moved without a moment to lose, and we followed with haste and didn't want to waste a moment of the excitement he had to share. We reached the top and found a hidden loft apartment space. Rus had been given a similar living space as Lyza. His loft was equipped with a large waterbed, a kitchen table, a nightstand, a bathroom, a heated sofa, a mirror, and a miniature fridge! It was no secret with the Exploration Squad, the larger the partner you received, the larger your living quarters were at The Docks. Rus had certainly reaped the benefits of having one of the largest marine mammals in the program.

Rus stood proudly. "Well, what do you think?"

I was blown away. "I think it's an amazing space."

"The habitat is amazing, and I'm extremely close to Kanoa. Just a quick dive bomb away. The instructor says it's the best way to begin each morning. To jump in the water with Kanoa at the start of each day. It builds trust."

Rus opened the door on the south side of the room. Outside sat a diving board just twenty feet over Kanoa's habitat. I took a seat on the heated sofa and placed Coco down to relax. Rus walked over to the mini-fridge, pulled out a soda, tossed me one, and grabbed one for himself.

I popped open the cap and took a sip. "Thanks. Sorry for interrupting your training. The instructor seemed very uh, concerned about you and Kanoa."

"The guy is good. We've been working with him on trying to teach more learning behaviors and get things done, but not much has changed since you and I last spoke. Half the time I feel like I have no idea what I'm doing."

"That's not true. We're learning everything we need to about our partners for the first time. It's all about relationship building. I'm sure Kanoa is learning just as much about you as you are about him."

Kanoa squealed from his habitat. Rus peered out over the diving board and gestured to Kanoa.

Suddenly, Kanoa jumped out of the water, posed in the air, and crashed back into the water.

"Wow! That was great!"

Rus grabbed a bucket of herring from his living room and tossed several fish down to Kanoa.

"He wishes I swam with him 24/7. He loves food, back rubs, and swimming very deep. That's about all I've learned so far."

I noticed Rus's WT backpack on the other side of the sofa. The zipper sat open, and inside I could make out Kanoa's file. I reached over and pulled it out to review. "You read his file?"

"Of course. He's almost two years old, he's intelligent, loyal, friendly, and very curious about everything around him. Prefers primary over secondary reinforcement."

"That's a good start."

"Yeah. Don't get me wrong, I'm thankful. He's great, Kanoa is strong and I know we'll do well under water. But Roxanne."

I sighed. "Have you spoken to her since the ceremony?"

"Haven't heard back from her. Nothing. I'm starting to think we've reached the end of our time together."

"No, it's a lot to process for both of you. If it helps, I think I know how you feel."

"How?"

"I stopped at Lyza's habitat before I came here. It was nice. We talked, we laughed... But—"

"But?"

"But we knew that distance would be too much. So, we're going to stay in touch and see what happens."

"How? We're going to be at the bottom of the ocean?"

"I'm gonna write to her."

"Write to her? Hah, okay."

"I'm not giving up. Lyza is different, man. She's worth the wait."

"Remember that day you asked me to come over? It was the morning you'd just broken up with Carrie."

I scoffed. "Carrie? Carrie Macintosh?"

"Yes, and when I pulled in and got out of my car, you were in shambles."

"My first breakup. But you told me, 'It's the right thing to do. Move on and move forward.'"

"I'm starting to think I should take my own advice. Next time you see Roxanne, can you ask her to call me?"

"Why can't you call her?"

"I don't want to scare her off, Justin."

"But you just...Sure. I'll bring your name up."

"Thanks, man. I'm not sure what's happening. All I know is that Kanoa is in the center of it. I'm just going to have to trust him. How're those new superpowers of yours?"

"I don't know. I haven't tried it out much since I brought Coco home."

"You should! If I was you I wouldn't rest until I had it under control."

"Maybe you're right. I'll need to get the hang of it eventually."

"You wanna listen to this new song that just dropped?"

"Of course, but isn't your trainer coming back?"

"Just one song, come on! I've been listening to it since the ceremony."

"What's it called?"

"'Rogue Wave' by Lil lion Man. I'll play it throughout the habitat. Watch this!"

Suddenly Rus linked his phone up to the sound system in the stadium. The song began playing, and it was heard clearly even from Rus's loft. We were bobbing our heads and enjoying the music until we heard Kanoa squealing again.

"Is Kanoa going to be okay with the music?"

Rus yelled back, "Yeah, he's fine. It's averaging at ten hertz. Anything above fifteen hertz could hurt him. But he's fine. He's just hungry. He's always hungry."

Rus continued to feed Kanoa from his diving board until the song ended. I placed Kanoa's file back in Rus's WT backpack. At the bottom of the bag, I found *Patches.* The book appeared untouched and unused. Once the song came to a close, my mind began to wonder. I remembered the last conversation Rus and I had after the Animal Pairing Ceremony. Some part of me couldn't help but worry about our friendship. It was stupid to have doubts after one argument, but I couldn't rest until I knew we were in a better place.

"Rus, I know last time we spoke things were a bit rough between us. I just wanted to say I'm sorry."

"For what? Don't sweat it, Justin. Everything's good on my end. Just a lot going on."

He'd brushed my comment off as if he'd rehearsed it. He didn't think twice about what had happened after the ceremony. He had much more to worry about. Hell, we both did.

The only thing I could think of to deflect the subject was, "You ready for Monday?"

"No doubt. They'll escort us to their secret location for training. Then they'll pick up the new recruits in one submarine and another sub to help gather and safely store each animal."

"How will they move Kanoa?"

"There's an entrance to the ocean at the bottom of this habitat. That's how they were able to get him in here. They have a whole loading and docking team onsite. It's pretty cool, and I won't have to do much."

"Sounds efficient. I'm excited for you, man. I know I'm ready to hit the ground running."

"You sure you two are ready to be Hunters? The predators, the bounties, and the challenges you two will have to face?"

"We have to be. I mean, it's going to take some time for sure. She's a bit timid right now, but we're gonna work through it and get some combinations in."

"Well, I think you'll surprise some people. Can't remember the last time a coati became a hunter."

"We will be the first, you wait... What was up with your coordinator though? Especially that attitude of his?"

"He said he was new and really excited to work with Kanoa. He didn't seem to talk about anything else. Gosh what was his name? I think it's Mel or Mal, I know it starts with an *M.*"

My eyes grew big as I realized, "Wait... Was it Malcolm?"

Suddenly an explosion occurred at the entrance of the stadium causing the sound system to go silent. The tinted glass windows surrounding the habitat shattered and fell to the floor. Smoke filled the doorway when two figures appeared in the thick gray smoke ready to unleash havoc.

The same man that was riding Kanoa just minutes before emerged with a red maned wolf. He had changed out of his wetsuit and stood smiling with his arms crossed. The criminal had long brown hair that came down over his face and covered his left eye. Malcolm wore a darkened gray and purple shirt with black pants and black gloves. He carefully held an ion beam in his left hand. Ion beams were notorious for their power and ability to melt objects on impact. They were far deadlier than any gun with bullets.

An emergency alarm started blaring which triggered the emergency doors to close down the entrance door. Thick metal bars came down over the windows and doorway. The emergency procedures were designed to keep all ocean life secured and weed out any separate entities. We were locked in with Malcolm Ula, the same man my father was trying so desperately to put away. We both moved closer and tried to get a better look. I cautiously poked my head out from the spiral staircase as Coco jumped onto my shoulder. Rus opened his living room door and looked out from his diving board.

I was shocked. "Rus, that guy does not work here. That's Malcolm Ula. The guy from the news."

Rus's eyes got big as he looked down at Kanoa. Kanoa squealed and swam over toward Rus's loft.

"Well, well... Now this is a surprise. I came for Mr. Zhang's prize possession, but I suppose I could take a side of Steele," Malcolm proudly announced.

"Rus, we have to get out of here," I whispered.

"No, I won't let him take Kanoa."

"Rus, Malcolm is heavily armed with a strong partner. He has an ion beam."

Rus stared down at Kanoa, "I don't care, I have to protect him."

"We should face him together then. It'll be better that way."

"I'm gonna check on Kanoa first, I'll meet you outside of the habitat."

I started moving slowly down the spiral staircase, distancing myself from Rus. Rus immediately dove into the water and frantically swam over to Kanoa. Once we reached the floor I placed Coco on the ground. I unhooked her small black leash and hid her behind some of the nearby metal chairs.

"Stay hidden," I whispered to Coco and then I turned my attention to Malcolm. "What do you want, Malcolm?"

The criminal laughed. "Were you not listening? I'm here for the whale!"

"NO! I won't let you take him." Rus yelled out.

Malcolm pointed his ion beam at Rus. "Ah, ah, ah. That's enough out of you two. Time is of the essence, and we have places to be."

Malcolm brought out a small remote device with a bright red button on it. He aimed the remote at Rus and pressed the button. Suddenly Kanoa pulled away from Rus and began flailing around in the water. He cried out in pain from his blowhole as if he were being attacked.

"Kanoa! What's wrong? STOP IT!" Rus yelled.

Pained by the sight, I demanded loudly, "What are you doing?"

Malcolm sneered. "I'm returning Kanoa to his natural state. In essence, I'm increasing his testosterone and making him more aggressive toward Mr. Zhang. It's a little painful at first, but it'll be over soon. Once Mr. Zhang is gone, then the whale will be a free agent."

I tightened my fist and turned back and faced Rus struggling to help Kanoa. "Rus! He's using a chemical incision. He must've placed one on Kanoa somewhere. You have to find it and remove it!"

Rus began examining Kanoa as he continued to flail in the water. He nodded in understanding, "I'll find it! Justin, get out of here!"

"Not yet!" I glared back at Malcolm, "He's mine."

Rus dove deep down into the water and desperately swam after Kanoa.

"Why do you want Kanoa?" I demanded.

Malcolm pointed the gun over at me and laughed. "What is with all these questions? Fine. If you must know, he's the key. The missing piece in locating the Exploration Squad. Think of the technology, the discoveries, the advancements. It will all belong to me. And rightfully so. You two bore me and have no say in the matter. Let's wrap this up. Roy, dinner time! Nothing like coati for dinner huh, Justin, my boy?"

The man smirked with amusement, making me sick. Anger and fear began to stir inside me. If this man did defeat me, he'd feed Coco to his maned wolf, steal Kanoa, and have the address Lyza gave me from my phone. I would not let that happen. I clenched my fists when suddenly a metallic shine grew and covered my hands. The gift had been activated by my anger and my fear. I had to use this power while I still had a chance.

I picked up one of the bulky metal chairs in front of me with ease. I pin-pointed my target and threw it toward Malcolm. He stood fifteen yards away which made it a very low possibility of actually making contact. I missed my mark miserably, but I had to do something to get the situation under control. My powers couldn't deflect an ion beam. I hurled another chair with more force, closing the distance to Malcolm, but he preemptively blasted the chair before it could make contact. The chair melted down onto the stadium floor. I had to distract him and get close enough to cause some damage. I needed to stall and provide enough time for Coco to get away. I grew angrier and threw more chairs toward him and at his maned wolf Roy.

Malcolm's maned wolf stood tall, one of the tallest dogs in the animal kingdom. They were known for their amazing sense of smell and hearing, and they were just one of the natural predators for coatimundis. I knew he was going to be difficult to stop. Roy paused and fixed his ears on the metal chairs and benches. Luckily the noise from Kanoa's splashing along with the melting metallic chairs clashing against other benches made it difficult for Roy to zone in on Coco's location. Coco had never been in a fight, nor had we experienced any real combat together. I was worried for Rus and Kanoa but most of all Coco. I had to stop Malcolm before Kanoa attacked Rus otherwise their connection would be destroyed. Malcolm was right about one thing: time was of the essence.

I decided to go on the offensive and get closer to Malcolm to make my move. My legs moved with speed and intensity up the stadium stairs. The ion beam had a delay. The beam had to charge for a second before Malcolm could fire a shot. I was able to anticipate when the beam would fire which allowed me time to plan and dodge accordingly. I continued up the staircase jumping around in order to evade each blast from the ion beam. I started jumping from row to row of metal chairs and benches as I pursued my target. I balanced on one of the elongated metal benches and sprinted straight toward Malcolm. As I quickly approached my target, Roy suddenly leaped over me. The long lengthy legs jumped over three rows and landed two rows down. However, I couldn't afford to be distracted by his partner just yet. The room was too full of misty moisture, salt, and cleaning chemicals for Roy to acquire Coco's scent. She had successfully avoided him up until that point.

I swiftly climbed up to where Roy came from and landed between the chairs and benches. I peered forward and saw the criminal standing just twenty feet before me. My partner patch started blinking as my heart rate began to rise. I bolted after Malcolm as he continued to open fire on me. I was able to carry two stacked metal chairs from a nearby row and continued toward Malcolm. I cautiously hid behind the chairs as I ran. The ion beam made contact with the chairs, causing them to melt in my hands, leaving me with only fragments.

As I closed in, I chucked the smaller chair fragments at Malcolm. I'd specifically aimed for his face and his gun. Malcolm stood his ground and continued firing his weapon. I dove and slid on the wet floor until an opening revealed itself. I successfully landed behind Malcolm. Only a two to three second window would decide how successful my attack would be and I needed to respond accordingly. I located my target, remained focused on my opponent, clenched my right fist, took a deep breath, and unleashed a heavy blow.

"STOP IT!" I screamed.

I made contact instantly with Malcolm's back. The point of contact caused him to launch ten yards forward; however, he seemed unaffected by the hit. I pulled back my hand and examined the metallic coloration covering my hand. He exhibited no sign of pain. The criminal turned around in an instant and moved in on my position. I launched another punch with my right hand as he successfully dodged and grabbed me by my face with his left hand. Malcolm wore a special pair of carbon fiber gloves with small holes revealing the palm of his hand. The AFA member had so much power and muscle that he was able to lift me by my skull. I felt like a stuffed animal caught by an old arcade crane machine. Malcolm lifted me up and turned to face Kanoa and Rus in their habitat. I desperately held on trying to pry his hand off my face.

Malcolm laughed and pulled me in closer. "I suppose you haven't heard about me. You see, I specialize in shock absorption. My armor and gloves are specifically designed for dealing with someone like you. They not only protect my body, but they suck up the strength from those trying to harm me, which allows me to give it all right back."

I was in a very tight spot but had little time to react. My metallic hands grabbed onto his left wrist and began squeezing for my life. I successfully pried my fingers in between his glove to protect my face. Malcolm quickly pulled back his right fist in a similar fashion to my punch and released a powerful hit directly into my stomach.

My body was in shock, my vision was blurred, and I became as limp as a lifeless corpse. The impact of the punch sent me flying over fifteen rows of benches. Finally, I collided with several metallic chairs on a lower row. I rolled over attempting to catch my breath, but I could barely breathe. The blunt trauma took the air out of my lungs and had caused, I was sure, severe damage to my ribs.

I looked over in a daze and saw the maned wolf land on a metal bench just left of my collapsed body. I miraculously flung my body over and onto Roy as anger engulfed me. I forced myself to calm down, to purposefully breathe in through my nose and out of my mouth. I looked down and noticed my gift was still activated. The metallic shine spread over my hands and wrists.

Roy managed to break away from me but only for a brief second. I reached out for his tail and pulled him back in with my right hand. He growled and turned around to bite into my right wrist. I felt little pain as I jammed my right wrist farther back into his mouth and scooped up his body with my left arm. Roy began clawing and attempting to pull away from me at all costs. I slowly pulled the heavy predator around and faced Malcolm.

Malcolm dropped his gun and calmly spoke, "What a turn of events! Such an interesting power. You feel no pain, do you? As if you yourself have become hard as steel. Like your grandfather I presume. No. No that can be, you're not nearly as strong. You're running out of steam aren't you?"

"Is that something you're willing to gamble?" I tightened my grip on Roy.

Malcolm sighed deeply. "Fine, Justin, you win. Release Roy and I will remove the device pulsating through Kanoa's bloodstream."

I spat blood on the floor. "I'll believe it when I see it."

The two of us locked eyes as he pointed his black remote back at the struggling killer whale and pressed the red button. Suddenly Kanoa stopped struggling. Rus was able to successfully climb on top of him. After a few moments, Rus discovered a flashing green light attached to Kanoa's dorsal fin. The incision had been manually placed next to Kanoa's partner patch. Rus meticulously pulled the device off Kanoa and threw it out of the habitat. It landed at Malcolm's feet.

"Justin, we're good. I got it!"

I continued glaring at Malcolm while Rus rubbed the top of Kanoa and rode him back to the platform in front of the habitat.

Malcolm reached into his pocket and pulled out another remote, "Remember, you wanted this."

Malcolm pressed down on the green button which caused the habitat's doorway to the ocean to open. Kanoa wasted no time and seized the opportunity to escape. With Rus on top of Kanoa, the two were out of the picture. It was just Malcolm and I left at a standoff.

Malcolm slowly walked down the stairs closer to me and opened his arms. "Your friend will be greeted by my underwater counterparts. My friends will succeed in attaining the asset. Always. Have. A. Failsafe. Face it, kid. You've lost."

I was struggling frantically to think of ideas of how to stop him. I was anxious, worried, and did not know how I would beat him. Malcolm cautiously walked down the staircase looking at the floor every other step. It wasn't until he reached the bottom level that Malcolm reached down on the floor and yanked Coco up by the tail.

My anger intensified, causing me to tighten my grip on Roy and pull him closer.

"Let her go!"

Malcolm tightened his grip on Coco's tail.

"I said, let her go. RIGHT NOW." I forced my wrist in between Roy's jaws. I could feel the pain intensifying on Coco's tail as she whimpered.

Malcolm smiled and yelled back, "They say with partner patches, you can feel everything the other feels? Is that right? Why don't we test that theory? Huh? Like I said, you have overplayed your hand. It seems you can't protect anyone, Justin. Can you?" He laughed maniacally.

Malcolm squeezed her tail, and it felt as if my spine were being torn apart. The pain was excruciating, but it was nothing compared to watching Malcolm harm Coco. I couldn't allow him to hurt her.

Every fiber of my body tightened. "Fine. Fine."

Once my left arm relaxed and pulled away from Roy's mid-section, I whispered, "Man, I hope this works."

The only option that remained was one that I hadn't yet experienced. It wasn't until that specific moment that I realized I had to transfer my power to Coco. My left hand pressed down on my right shoulder and activated my partner patch. The large red button in the center of the device activated the transfer as every ounce of energy left my body. The overwhelming amount of energy and power inside my body transferred directly to my partner.

Coco immediately rolled upward and raised her right claw as her body and size continued to grow. Her entire right hand and elongated fingernails changed into the same metallic color of my fists. She slashed through Malcolm's left cheek and dragged her nails down his face. Malcolm screamed in pain, dropped to the ground, and released his grip on Coco.

She quickly hopped from chair to chair as she set her course for Roy. I released my right forearm from Roy's mouth and dropped to the floor. I had little energy left in my body. I felt like a sponge that had been rung out to dry. The maned wolf ran at Coco and leaped into the air.

Roy bared his teeth and opened with his mouth wide to land on Coco. Coco's eyes changed color to the same bright metallic silver. She had incredible speed which allowed her to dodge the wolf with ease. She proceeded to jump on top of Roy and began scratching and tearing at his fur. Coco leaped off of him, and the maned wolf began to whine as it retreated back to Malcolm.

The criminal started to bleed as he covered the left side of his face and attempted to stand. He tried to hobble back up the staircase to his ion beam. Roy slowly followed Malcolm up the stairs. However, within arm's reach of his ion beam, Malcolm tripped on the final step. He reached out and grabbed the gun. Before he could stand, my father Noah and his partner Shadow stealthily entered the scene.

Shadow immediately pounced onto Roy and pinned the wolf down to the floor. My father placed his right foot on top of Malcolm's wrist.

"That's enough, Malcolm. You've done enough."

Malcolm reached over to try to remove Noah's foot. My father responded by kicking him in the face.

Rus and Kanoa suddenly resurfaced in their habitat as Rus came up gasping for air. Kanoa spat two scuba divers out of the water and onto the platform. The two were armed with spear guns and appeared critically injured. I exhaled deeply before closing my eyes and passing out.

CHAPTER 9

Uncovering New Enemies

I woke up in a daze with Coco licking my face. The scent of Coco's fur, wet metal, and chlorine filled my nostrils. My father had subdued Malcolm, his maned wolf, and Malcolm's men all to a nearby bench. It wasn't long before the police entered the habitat and took custody of the attackers. The police first approached and questioned Rus concerning what all had happened while my father questioned me.

"What were you thinking? This is the second time you've been caught up in dealing with crooks. You could've been killed!"

I rubbed the top of Coco's head as she nestled into my shoulder.

"Dad, this is what I signed up for. This right here. Malcolm was trying to remove Rus and take Kanoa! He was making Kanoa attack Rus and wanted to use him to infiltrate the Exploration Squad."

"Why would he do that? Did he say anything?"

"Malcolm mentioned the Exploration Squad. About taking control. I thought you and Mom were already on this?"

"He escaped in a submarine before, but this is different. We found his submarine located along the south side of The Docks. We knew it was only a matter of time before he ended up here."

"What do you mean? How did you get in here if we were on lockdown?"

"I broke the bars."

"How?"

"That's not really important at this point in time. This is Hero Regime business. Right now, we need to focus on the job at hand."

"That may be. But I'm a part of the Cultivation Squad, which allows me the privilege of knowing potential threats to the inhabitants as well as any potential predators against Ignacia."

I could see both annoyance and pride in his eyes as he looked at me. "Justin, this is not your jurisdiction but it appears that Malcolm has found a way to infiltrate the Exploration Squad."

"Isn't it just a bunch of different submarines?"

"It's one of the world's most hidden facilities. Even if he had a submarine, he couldn't just dive into the ocean and find it. Unless, he already has. There is a small ventilation shaft for the Exploration Squad hidden in the depths of the Pacific Ocean. One that someone could, hypothetically, swim up through. Someone or some mammal, such as Kanoa, could potentially fit inside and swim through."

"How would Malcolm know that?"

"There must be a viper in our midst."

The police captain walked over to speak with my father. "We've gathered the culprits and placed them all in custody. We'll see what they know. From what I heard, Russel Zhang did very well in fighting off Ula and his men. You should consider yourself lucky."

My father and I looked at the policeman puzzled. "Except he didn't fight off Malcolm. We did, my partner Coco and me. Check the left side of his face: those are coati claw marks. All Rus did was take off the signal jammer and fled out the door from his habitat."

"That's not the report we received."

The police captain awkwardly looked back at Rus as he sat up on his platform next to Kanoa. Rus sat feeding Kanoa as if nothing had happened.

I hopped up to the middle platform and stood behind Rus. I asked concerned, "Hey, why did you say that you stopped Malcolm?"

Rus continued looking at Kanoa, "I didn't. We stopped him and his men. After Kanoa made a break for it, I tried to get him to turn around, but once we were out of the habitat, those two men were down there waiting for us. They ambushed us! One launched a harpoon at me while the other threw a net over us. Kanoa swam after them, grabbed them, and held them in his mouth. After that, we swam right back to the habitat. You and I both stopped Malcolm."

Rus turned around and passed Kanoa a large fish.

I was surprised by his response. "I guess you're right, in a way, but I fought him. You saw me fight Malcolm."

"Justin, you defeated Malcolm, and I took out his men. That's it. It's not a big deal."

"Yes, but who got him to disengage the device? Who held his partner captive? As he attempted to bite my arm off?"

"I didn't see that."

"How can you say that?"

"Justin, I was a little busy with Kanoa."

"Justin," my father called out.

My father shook his head back and forth telling me to calm down in the presence of the law. I could feel my anger begin to boil inside me. I glanced over at Coco and reminded myself how exhausted we'd become, and that it was time to go home. I exhaled deeply.

"You're right. You know what? It's not a big deal. I'm sorry. Nice work today."

"You, too." Rus turned around and sat on the platform alongside Kanoa. He began feeding Kanoa and working multiple learning behaviors with him. No handshake, no hug, and no kind of sympathetic goodbye. It was cold and bitter, like the lingering saltwater taste on my tongue.

Was this going to be our friendship? Consistently taking advantage of one another's kindness and apologizing for it after? How could we continue on like this? I shook my head in frustration and decided to ignore the worrisome signs of toxicity. I nodded in understanding and exhaled the frustration that was building up within.

"Out of sight, out of mind," I whispered.

I stopped walking for a moment, and a part of me grew sad. I wished that I could have simply walked away and never looked back without saying a word. Instead, I muttered, "Thank you for your help. I'll never forget it. Be safe."

Rus remained seated, he petted Kanoa, and remained silent.

Coco sniffed around my face and caught a teardrop that fell down my right cheek. Her nose quickly absorbed the wetness as she nestled into me. I hopped off the platform and back toward my father. I walked past him, the police captain, and started up the staircase of the stadium. I looked down for the duration of my walk out of The Docks. It allowed me to disconnect momentarily from my surroundings.

I continued walking out of the habitat and continued thinking of all the different things Rus had done for me. He helped me grow, he taught me incredible music, Rus made me try new things, and we had a bunch of adventures together. But now I had to do my own thing. I was sorry it all led to us going our own separate ways. I wished him the best of luck with all his future endeavors.

My father caught up to me and escorted me out of the building with Shadow following behind us. Many people saw my father and attempted to approach him. Some wanted photos, others wanted autographs. I walked back to grandpa's zomorodi, safely parked outside The Docks. I carefully placed Coco down in a nearby patch of grass to use the restroom before we departed.

My father caught up to me. "Justin, talk to me. What'd Rus say?"

"Nothing. Just the way he saw things. Our time as friends has come to an end. He's heading north and I'm heading south. It's better this way."

"Now hang on just a minute. This is the second time you were able to step up, challenge someone in an entirely different league and stop them in their tracks. You have what it takes for the Hero Regime, and you know it. Rus does not have that opportunity. Maybe he is more upset by that than you know. Malcolm is notorious for destroying relationships among trainers and animals. Don't let him destroy your friendship. You can never have too many friends, Justin. Remember that."

I safely secured Coco in the passenger seat. She sat comfortably as she bathed herself. I hugged my father and thanked him. I turned on the zomorodi and played some of grandpa's favorite music that he'd saved on his hard drive. The soothing touch of smooth jazz music brought me back to my senses. The music allowed me to relive some of the good times Rus and I had spent together. Coco eventually became annoyed with the seat belt and attempted to pull herself out of it. By the time we pulled back into our driveway, she had successfully maneuvered her way out of the seat belt.

It wasn't until I returned home that the damage my body had taken finally caught up with me. My adrenaline had finally run out. I was punched with more force to my mid-section than I had ever taken. My core began to burn as I slowly walked inside. I leaned on the wall as I slowly battled each step on the staircase. Grandpa saw me painfully walking.

"Justin are you all right?! What happened?!"

"Malcolm Ula. He was at The Docks."

"Are you hurt?"

"No. No. I just think he may have broken a rib or two."

"Oh, then you're fine? Come on, you need to rest. Let's get you up to bed."

Grandpa hurried up the stairs and placed my right arm over his right shoulder. He carefully assisted me up the stairs, into my room, and placed me on my bed. The business card Vladimir Mathias had given to me fell out of my pocket. We finally made it back to my bed. I leaned forward to take my shoes off when the level of pain began to intensify.

"I'll call for a medic bot and get you some medicine. It'll be here in no time."

When he walked out of my room he found the business card on the floor. About five minutes later he returned with two large tablets in his hand and a glass of water.

"I know it hurts. The more you move the more pain you'll be in. Take these with water."

I quickly took the pills and drank the water. "What was that?" I asked.

"Supplemental bone growth. Should have you up and running again by tomorrow morning. Just in time for training. I'll make some soup."

"Can you prepare some food for Coco please?"

"You bet. What does she like?"

"Chicken, veggies, and fruit. Please."

"I'll get right on it. But before I forget, who gave this card to you?"

I winced in pain and looked over and saw him holding the business card.

"Yeah, some old suit with bodyguards. Seemed pretty high end. He was just leaving The Docks when I walked in. Why?"

"Son, that's Vlad. Vladimir Mathias is the CEO of the suits. He's incredibly cunning and border line diabolical. When he wants something, he will do whatever to whoever in order to get it. If you see this man again you run and you call me. Do you understand?"

I nodded my head. "All right, all right. I wasn't going to call him."

"Promise me."

"I promise I won't associate with him."

Grandpa crumbled up the business card and threw it into the trash can alongside my bed. He walked out of the room and started making dinner. I slowly looked over and saw the card sitting in the empty trash can and decided to leave it be. At least until I gained the strength to lean over and pick it up.

Coco began climbing around my room again while I lay in bed. She would sniff, snort, and scamper about on the carpeted floor. She found my father's old hat once again and began playing with it. She brought the hat onto the bed and stepped on top of me. I winced in pain as Coco immediately jumped off me. After twenty minutes of re-familiarizing herself with the territory, she eventually jumped back on the bed and lay next to me. She detected my pain emotionally and physically and decided to nestle into my right hip. I had reached my limit for the day, and knew I needed rest.

The afternoon quickly turned to evening. The medic bot arrived soon after from the courthouse and x-rayed my mid-section. Two broken ribs and two dislocated fingers. The bot safely wrapped my midsection and prescribed pain medication. It supplied grandpa with more bone growth medication to speed up the healing process. After grandpa escorted the bot out the front door, he returned an hour later and woke me up with a large bowl of soup along with a small, assorted plate of food for Coco. I was lucky to have something in my stomach after a day of craziness. Grandpa grabbed my desk chair and sat alongside my bed to feed me soup so I didn't have to move. After grandpa brought up ice packs, pain medication and made sure I was set up to heal correctly, he sat down while Dusty slowly made his way into my room. The three of us had not been in my room together for a very long time. As he spoon-fed me tomato soup, I told him about all of the events that transpired with Rus, Lyza, and Malcolm.

"So, what's next?" Grandpa asked.

"What do you mean what's next? I'll write her a letter and we'll be—"

"Pen pals."

"What're pen pals?"

"It's an old saying for those who keep in touch by writing letters back and forth."

"Oh. Well, I don't want to be her pal. I want to be her pen boyfriend."

"I think that may be something to discuss with her. Patience, Justin. All good things will come in time."

"I think you'd like her."

"I already do. I saw that peck she gave you on the bridge. And she's strong. But that business with Malcolm and with Rus. Why did you get so fired up?"

"I don't know, I guess I felt like I was being used. Like, Rus wanted the recognition. He wanted to enter the Exploration Squad with a win under his belt."

"Justin, come on now. You two have been through a lot together."

"Maybe it's meant to be."

"You two just need to grow on your own for right now. Maybe one day you'll see each other again."

"We'll see. I'm gonna get some sleep."

"Of course, remember training in the morning. We have a lot to cover."

"Even with the broken ribs?"

"It's just two of them, and besides the bot says you'll be good to go by tomorrow."

"They better be. Thanks Grandpa, we're looking forward to it."

"You want a pen and paper?" Grandpa asked hesitantly.

"Yes please," I fearfully admitted.

Grandpa brought in a small foldable bed table for me with a pen, paper, and an envelope. He carefully placed it over my lap before he left. After he closed my bedroom door, I hesitantly attempted to stand and slowly walked to the bathroom before getting ready for bed. My legs had fallen asleep which made my feet feel like two limp bricks. I grabbed my animal anthology and brought it over to my bed. I lay down comfortably and positioned the book on top of a pillow. I searched for the entry on maned wolves.

"*Chrysocyon brachyurus*:

- Maned wolves have the diet of an omnivore, allowing the animal to survive on small mammals, fish, birds, eggs, insects, fruit, and vegetation.
- The average height of a maned wolf is between two and three feet.
- The largest maned wolves are known for their leggy stature and can reach up to fifty pounds in weight.
- Despite the name, the animal is not a wolf nor a fox but relates to the extinct Falkland Island wolf.
- Adult maned wolves can run up to a maximum speed of forty-seven miles per hour.

- Maned wolves used to only live up to thirteen years in the wild."

Coco used one of her litter boxes and leaped back into my lap in bed. I slowly closed the anthology and placed it on the floor close by. I embraced Coco and brought her into my arms. A feeling of trust and warmth overcame me. I was thankful to have her back with me, and I was excited to sleep the pain away. I reached for my pen and wrote to Lyza. I was nervous and a bit scared as my anxiety reminded me of the importance of my first letter. It had to be perfect, not too long, or too short. My confidence quickly began to dwindle and drown in the presence of my nerves. Coco started scratching at my arm as if she were attempting to remove the nerves that had sunk into my body. I took a deep breath as I pressed the pen into the paper.

All of my nerves suddenly left my body as I thought of nothing but her smile. I turned red, and in an instant, everything seemed weightless. I wrote about the many difficult interactions that occurred briefly after she and I said goodbye. How a day of furious feuds left me beaten, bullied, and broken. Memories of what I'd gained and what was lost started to linger in my mind. I assured her my training had paid off. I left a warm remark, "Good night, Lyza." It was that simple, alluring comment that allowed me to sleep soundly and not question the letter I had just written. I checked my backpack and found my file where it included all of the information on my orders. Inside was the address of the camp where I would be training. "19340 Savannah Lane, South Ignacia, 81532."

I folded the letter carefully and placed it on the foldable desk. Grandpa had placed an envelope and stamp at the ready. I leaned back in bed and looked over at Coco. She was nestled into a ball as she cuddled with my father's red hat.

I may have lost someone dear to me today, but I had gained a supportive counterpart. I entered in our partner patch sleep code and drifted off into the depths of midnight's darkness.

"You must channel your energy to one another, effortlessly," Grandpa announced. "Focus only on your partner. Let her hear your voice, smell your scent, and memorize your movements. In grave situations, you will only have each other to get yourself out of them. You must learn to move as one. Once you've mastered that, combat will seem effortless."

I knelt on a padded mat and faced Coco, sitting across from me on the wooden dojo floor. Coco's eyes remained on mine while she plopped on the floor until she lost focus and began grooming herself. Dusty sat in the corner and carefully watched us work while Grandpa slowly circled us. Grandpa maneuvered alongside us as if he were a shark capturing the full image of his potential prey.

"Observe."

Grandpa raised his right hand and signaled for Dusty to approach. Dusty quickly waddled across the floor until he was four feet in front of Grandpa. Grandpa slowly leaned to the left and raised his right hand as Dusty leaned his body to the right and attempted to raise his left leg and five toes off the ground. Grandpa leaned to his right side and raised his left hand; Dusty continued to mirror Grandpa's actions, leaning his body to the left and raising his right leg and five toes off the ground.

"Allow Coco the opportunity to mirror you. You both need to physically see how the other moves."

I stood on the mat as my toes pressed into the freshly sprayed surface. My lungs expanded as I took a deep breath, closed my eyes, and opened them. Coco looked up from grooming herself and stood as well. I slowly placed my right hand on my hip and then slowly raised my hand high. Coco saw this and watched me accordingly. She was confused by the exercise and thought my arm was an invitation. The small coati scampered across the floor and climbed up my arm to my shoulder.

I calmly removed her from my shoulder and placed her four feet away from me. My eyes focused on her with determination and the desire for us to complete this exercise right. I stared into her eyes and thought to myself, "Okay, you can do this, girl. Just raise your left hand when I raise my right. You can do this."

"Now, Justin, let's try again. Begin to stretch your body and ask Coco to follow your lead."

I nodded in understanding. "Coco, come on, Coco, do what I do."

My body crouched down lower and raised my right hand upward without breaking eye contact with Coco. Coco took a moment to examine her left hand with her small claws extended. She suddenly crouched lower and raised her left hand upward.

I was ecstatic that she heard me! I was amazed how she could follow my lead even after such a short period of time together. I smiled big and walked over to her, picked her up, and provided loving affection for her reinforcement. Since we had eaten just an hour beforehand, I knew the use of food would not be the best way to reward her. Grandpa chuckled and stopped walking. I could tell he was somewhat surprised at how receptive she was to my commands.

"How about that? An excellent start. Now you follow her."

I placed Coco down and backed up four feet once more. I continued to watch her movements and imitated each one. Coco continued looking back at me while making small squeaks and squawks from her elongated snout. She tilted her head to the left, and I tilted my head to the right. Coco became overjoyed and ran up to me and hugged my leg. It was as if she were rewarding me with the same reinforcement. She hugged my leg and began sniffing my foot. I looked back at Grandpa confused.

"She's praising you as you praised her. Who would've thought? That's one smart coati. Let's continue and utilize this ability in combat. Let's practice scratching your opponent."

Finally, the moment to practice real combat with my partner had arrived and I was ecstatic. My head bobbed forward in understanding as I picked Coco up for a reset and placed her hands and feet in front of me once again. I closed my eyes and took a deep breath. I lunged forward, extended my right arm with flexed fingers, and quickly scratched at the air with all my strength. Coco witnessed my movement, studied her left paw again, sniffed it, and raised it in the air.

A laugh started to grow in the pit of my stomach as I admired Coco's cuteness. However, in order to grow with my partner, I knew I couldn't laugh, smile, or show her any sort of praise. If I wanted her to learn, she'd have to comprehend what I'm asking of her. "No, lady, scratch at the air, just as you did yesterday. You can do it."

My muscles tightened as I assumed the position and performed the act again, slashing at the air with my right hand. Coco studied my movements again and then examined her left hand once more. Suddenly she raised her left hand and brought it down as she attempted to mimic me and scratch at the air. The strike to the air was not quick, not angry, nor did it have any power behind it.

Grandpa continued to circle us. "Hmm we're on the right path. Let's take a look at the partner patch. Do you have Madam Yue's manual, *Patches*?

After opening the closet door alongside the dojo wall, I pulled out the stool with a towel, a bottle of water, a bowl of water and the book carefully placed on top. I took the manual out from underneath the items and flipped open to the table of contents.

"What chapter?"

"Chapter Seven: Power Transfer." Grandpa continued to pace and examine Coco from a distance.

After flipping through the book, I located the untouched crisp page of Chapter Seven. The hardback book was known nationwide for its clarity: its ability to ease trainers across Ignacia in assisting with forming complete trusting relationships with new partners.

I read the beginning of the chapter aloud, "The partner patch is not just about being connected with your partner but also transferring the strength of one partner to the other in order to escape difficult encounters. Trainers will utilize this feature to either help their animal reach their maximum potential in a fight or borrow their partner's strength in order to face off against potential enemies."

Grandpa nodded. "Mhm, now put the book down. It's one thing to read it and another thing to learn it."

A deep breath exited my mouth as I dropped the book alongside the wall and dragged my feet across the wooden floor to rejoin Grandpa and Coco in the middle of the dojo.

"It is a great read, and I implore you to finish the book before you arrive at camp. Better yet, finish it tonight or tomorrow on the way to South Ignacia. You barely survived against Malcolm yesterday, there's no way around it. You managed to give Coco all of your strength by sheer luck. Look over in the mirror and look at your partner patch. It's a part of you now, and you need to know how every inch of it works."

I walked over to Coco's side of the dojo and rolled my shirt sleeve up and over my shoulder to examine the partner patch.

"The largest button on the patch is the transfer button. It's what you pressed yesterday though you had not selected the necessary settings to guarantee one hundred percent success. The first setting you should know is the smaller knob located directly above the start button. This smaller knob is where you can select the level of power you wish to transfer or have transferred to you. The smallest button on the patch is below the power switch. The switch only has two options: one on *Animal* and one on *Trainer*. This is where you initiate who receives the other's power depending on the situation."

"There are three sidebar buttons, and each has a different function and serves different purposes: The top left one is the button that initiates sleep, which is why it's listed as 'S.'

"The middle sidebar button has a giant "A" on it because it provides a hit of adrenaline to be shot directly into the bloodstream. Sometimes that one final push is what is needed in order to achieve victory.

"Finally, the last sidebar button beneath adrenaline is the button stating 'SH'. This is the *Shadow* option. If the shadow option is pressed while selecting a trainer, then the animal will shadow the trainer's movements in any and all instances. This can be useful when trainers are responsible for leading their animal through a fight."

I exhaled deeply. "Yeah, I need to finish the book. Sooner rather than later."

"The sooner you have the partner patch mastered, the better your combinations will be in a fight. Let's work some potential trials with Coco. I'll get the punching bags."

A couple of hours later we broke for lunch. Grandpa whipped up some club sandwiches and Coco and Dusty were delighted to have the excess chicken, ham, and turkey plated for them. The thought of leaving tomorrow had not fully hit me yet. I was apprehensive about leaving Grandpa and Dusty by themselves, but I also couldn't be more excited to embark on my journey with Coco. I had already started packing. Since I forgot to pick up the supplies Grandpa entrusted me to collect yesterday, he had our groceries and my supplies shipped to our front door.

Grandpa arrived at the dining room table and passed out the plates to Dusty, Coco, me and finally for himself. He sat down, placed his napkin on his lap and dove into his sandwich. I glanced over at the clock and noticed it was already 1:00 p.m.

"Is it already one? That's insane!"

"That's what happens when you train hard. Don't fill up too much. We have a lot more work."

Coco plopped down in her chair and picked each piece of meat up with her tiny claws and began chewing with her small teeth while Dusty enjoyed chomping into large pieces of chicken. The four of us ate quickly but enjoyed the meal with the sound of soothing jazz playing in the background.

"Are you sure we can go up against the larger predators? They're going to take one look at Coco and do everything they can to eat her."

"Exciting, isn't it? It will be your job to be brave enough for the both of you."

"Just be brave? That's how I'll beat them?"

"Bravery will stop fear in its tracks and allow you to think more clearly to locate a solution."

"Grandpa, I've learned that fighting is more like a game of chess, not checkers. You can't just think for yourself, you must try to anticipate your opponent's moves."

"That's the spirit."

"But Zeus and Malcolm. They didn't fight like anyone in the WT. Did they?"

Grandpa swallowed the last remaining bite of sandwich. He wiped his mouth and carefully thought about his response. "They fought with the intent to kill, not the intent to subdue. They simply trust their animal to complete that goal if they cannot."

"But they can't speak or know how their animal is feeling. How are they considered partners if they aren't connected?"

"Sometimes there are those who see that as a distraction. There are many out there who do not treat animals with the same kindness that we do, Justin."

"What about Geo Steele? What did he do?"

"That was a long time ago. Before partner patches were even thought of. But there was a time when Geo had to work together with Cici in order to protect his family."

"What happened?"

"I'll tell you."

Geo went on to have a beautiful family. A loving wife, young son, and beautiful daughter. The two parents raised their children on the farm in South Ignacia together. When Geo brought Cici home, she was immediately a part of the family and was around for the birth of both of his children. At first, the nearby community was apprehensive of Cici due to their appearance. Once Cici learned how to change their form into different animals, the nearby townspeople grew to love them, and started to build relationships with the alien life form. Cici would follow Geo around everywhere he went. They would help out around the house, assist around the farm, and work with many of the animals on the farm. It wasn't until about ten years after living together, that something happened to Geo's family.

His family was visited by a criminal, a man who had been sentenced to death. The convict was originally locked away for murdering his brother. Of course, the man who was slayed happened to be Geo's neighbor. One day Geo was coming by to ask for some of his tools back and found the man in an altercation with his brother. The criminal was placed in jail by Geo and Cici who had assisted with his arrest and brought him to justice. However, the criminal escaped his prison by digging underground, but when he surfaced from the earth, he found himself just a few miles away from Geo's farm.

The criminal had a past relationship training, breeding, and raising a pack of coyotes. He studied them, fed them, and quickly became their true alpha. When the man started with just two coyotes he raised them to become the alpha pair to mate and grow their pack. Over time the pack grew significantly in size over the years up to one hundred coyotes. After being locked away, his coyotes tracked down his scent and remained in the woods close to the jail. The alpha pair kept the group close by as they all patiently waited for the day their true alpha would return. After he escaped, he returned to the outer lands of the jail where he was welcomed back into the pack. The man waited until nightfall in order to enact his revenge.

That late afternoon, Geo and Cici had run to the store together to pick up some items for dinner. When they returned from the store, they witnessed the unthinkable. The criminal had not only surrounded the house with coyotes. He had Geo's family in the dirt outside their home. Each of them was gagged and kneeling in the dirt. The criminal stood next to Geo's wife, laughing as Geo got out of his truck. Emotions were high, Geo was terrified, and he needed help.

'You cost me my family. Now I'm going to take yours! Come closer so we can make this quick,' The criminal said.

'They did nothing wrong, nothing at all. It was me. I put you away, not them. They are innocent!' Geo yelled back.

'Geo, this man will not spare your family's life. He will take their lives. He will kill you. The only way to free them is to fight,' Cici said.

'How? Cici, I don't know how to fight.'

'No, but you know how to protect. Get out there and protect your family.'

'What about the pack of coyotes?'

'I'll remove them from your path.'

'Be careful. Cici.'

'Always.'

Geo became angry and walked out from behind his truck. He closed his eyes and breathed in, remembering his family's happy, smiling faces. He opened his eyes and was enraged. He clenched his fists and walked directly toward the criminal.

The criminal blew his whistle and signaled to his coyotes, "Get rid of him!"

The coyotes growled and crouched down into attack position. Suddenly, Cici ran past Geo at the group of coyotes. Their body started to grow rapidly in size as their skeleton morphed and four legs sprouted from their body. They took the form of a giant white wolf. Cici began attacking the coyotes and ripping each of them apart. Fifteen coyotes began to strike and swarm the wolf. Geo was shocked by the sight of Cici but saw that they had killed each coyote they came in contact with.

'Cici? How?' Geo thought to his partner.

'Get moving, Geo!' Cici responded mentally.

The criminal started firing his gun at Cici. They growled as the bullets approached their body and bounced off with no damage. Cici grew angrier and continued tearing coyotes apart left and right. It wasn't until only three remained that Cici howled into the sky. In return, the three coyotes turned tail and fled in fear. Cici then turned their attention to the criminal while Geo focused on his family and saw his wife in tears. His anger enveloped him. Geo's power was so strong that his armor grew rapidly and covered his entire body. It was a legendary level of power that I have never successfully achieved. The criminal saw this and became afraid. He aimed his gun at Geo as our ancestor continued walking quickly toward him. The criminal fired at Geo who raised his right forearm and deflected the bullets. The felon continued firing multiple shots at him until Geo was within arm's reach. Geo grabbed the gun in the criminal's hand, bent it in half, and knocked it out of the criminal's hand. Geo picked the man up with one hand.

Geo had every intent of killing him. But Geo peered over and saw his children watching him intently. He didn't want his family to think he was a monster. Geo's rage began to fade as he tossed the man down. The criminal paused and began to laugh at Geo's mercy. He clapped, 'Wow. I'm surprised. But will remain forever thankful-'

Suddenly, Geo punched the man directly in the stomach. The farmer hit the criminal so hard that he flew back thirty yards. He broke six of his ribs and sent the man to the hospital for a month before he was sent back to prison. Geo's family was saved and would grow to love and appreciate Cici even more.

"So that was the first time the two of them fought alongside each other?" I asked hesitantly.

Grandpa nodded. "It was the first time they had to. Cici transformed into different animals in order to protect Geo and his family. The two of them learned how to protect each other."

"What happened to the criminal? Did he die? Was he executed by lethal injection?"

"He escaped again, evaded the law, got out of town, and started a new family. The tarnished coyote trainer tried to move past the event, but he became obsessed with Cici. He told his grandchildren bedtime stories about Cici. That was when the criminal made it a lifelong mission to obtain Cici for himself and his family."

"The criminal, what was his name?"

"He changed his name a few times in order to avoid being captured, again. But the last one became one I'd never forget. The last name that he went by was Zhang. Tung Zhang."

CHAPTER 10

New Beginnings

My mouth dropped. "The criminal's name was Tung Zhang. Does that mean, Rus, he wouldn't have any connection to this criminal? Would he?"

Grandpa sighed. "Tung was Jericho's grandfather. The criminal is Rus's ancestor."

I couldn't wrap my mind around the thought of Rus's family coming from criminal beginnings. Or the fact that Rus's grandfather was the last recorded crystal claw trainer. How could he have been?

I swallowed my last bite of sandwich. "But wasn't Jericho Zhang the last trainer to have a crystal claw partner?

"Yes. He was given a baby flamingo after he completed his WT application. He reported the baby's name was Cyan. However, contacts and relationships had been made beforehand behind closed doors. Jericho knew Cyan was rescued from the ARC project, and since Jericho was one of the first trainers with the best results in the WT application history, he was entrusted with Cyan."

"What made Jericho so special? What was his combat portion record?"

"Are you asking how many rounds Jericho was able to complete?

"Mhm."

"Fifty rounds."

"FIFTY? Just as the Masked Woman said."

"The kid was unstoppable. Jericho was obsessed with our family's legacy. I've worked every day attempting to restore our family name and make peace with the demons of our past."

"What about Cici? Where do they fit into all of this?"

"Cici left the family under Geo's final wish. His son Edmond wanted to step up and claim Cici as his own partner, but Geo wouldn't allow it. His dying wish was to allow Cici to go, to set out into the world and create a home for themselves."

"And Cyan? What happened to the last crystal claw?"

Grandpa deeply sighed. "Jericho was a leader, a man that everyone in Ignacia looked up to. Despite our differences, he was my brother and my friend. We tracked down the Dark Trainer together, and we were closing in fast. But Jericho got too close and was found dead two days later. We found him in his bed. The Dark Trainer was responsible."

My eyes grew big. "What? How did you know it was him? Why wasn't this on the news?"

"We found his calling card on Jericho's bedside table. A white business card with a black skull in the middle, it was a small card he always left behind as we followed his trail of breadcrumbs. The Hero Regime arrived the following morning, and we were all heartbroken when we found him. Cyan was nowhere to be found. We attempted to continue to track down the Dark Trainer, but we were never able to locate him. It's so easy to lose track of what's important in this world." Grandpa wiped his face with his napkin.

"Grandpa, I want to do this right. I want to represent our family the best I can. Show me how."

"Let's get back to training. There's something I want to try."

We made our way back to the dojo carefully following behind Grandpa. It was strange. I felt as if there was a motivating intensity that lingered in each breath I took. I carried Coco on my shoulder and placed her down next to me on the mats. Grandpa wheeled out the newly repaired punching bags. My stomach sank at the sight of them. I was worried about Coco being hit by one of the heavy punching bags.

Grandpa stood on the opposite side of the room with Dusty behind him. He pulled back his sleeve revealing his partner patch. He adjusted it accordingly and looked back at me and Coco.

"This is what I do. Adjust the power level to nine. Never go to ten. Let's give the power to the animal first so switch the option up to 'Animal' and press transfer!"

Suddenly Grandpa closed his eyes and pressed down on his partner patch. Dusty's body began to double in size. The amount of strength and power Grandpa possessed had been transferred into Dusty. Dusty opened his mouth and appeared to have the same metallic shine on each of his teeth as Grandpa's fists.

"The armor? He transferred the gift!" I whispered to myself.

Grandpa remained standing in place. He looked back at his partner patch and readjusted the settings and pressed down on the transfer button once more. Dusty slowly returned to his original size. The older alligator remained frozen in his same position as his strength began to flow into Grandpa's body whose muscles began to intensify, his veins began to bulge, and his body resembled one that was strong enough to wrestle a gorilla. "You may use their strength as your own in order to defend yourself against enemies."

The retired leader of the Hero Regime continued to surprise me with his strength. He clenched his right fist as he activated the same powerful gift. Grandpa's fist shined with a bright metallic pigmentation. The master of the protector's armor smiled almost as if he was surprised, he could still activate his gift. After a moment or two, the smile vanished as his hand began to shake. Sweat started to cover Grandpa's forehead as his breathing intensified. The legendary gift that Herschel Steele once used to protect millions slowly started to fade. Grandpa's body began to lock up which caused him to struggle to move. The transfer of power from Dusty's body had become too much power for his body to carry. Herschel carefully reached for his right shoulder with no luck. With his arms locked up and muscles too tight, Grandpa's body was in trouble. I saw what was happening and immediately rushed to his side. The palm of my hand slammed on the large middle transfer button as Dusty's original strength slowly returned to his body. Grandpa dropped to his knees, breathing heavily.

"Grandpa? Grandpa, are you all right?!"

He laughed in pain. "Ha, it never gets old. I'm not as young as I used to be, son."

"No, no, you're not. Don't overdo it, old man."

"It takes a toll after a certain amount of time, so whatever you have to do to subdue your opponent, do it fast."

"You transferred your gift to Dusty?"

"Just as you transferred your gift to Coco to stop Malcolm."

"We got lucky. I don't remember much."

"Based on what your father told me, Coco used your gift to scratch up Malcolm and his partner."

I looked over to Coco who sat patiently on the mat and tilted her head to the side.

"She has what it takes, and I think we can achieve great things together."

"First we're going to master that transfer to make it as effective as possible."

"Sounds good, Grandpa. Where do we start?"

"It's your turn. Grab me a chair and take your positions on the mat."

Grandpa spent the remainder of the day working alongside Coco and me. I was able to practice utilizing my gift more along with multiple fighting techniques with Coco that would prove useful for the trials ahead. That night, we showered after a long day of training before dinner. Grandpa needed the time for his body to rest, so instead of cooking as he always did, we had pizza delivered.

I completed the meal prep for Dusty and Coco while Grandpa took some medicine to relax his muscles while he lay on the living room sofa. I could tell he was physically exhausted from training. He turned on the television while I delivered the food to Coco and Dusty. Coco began nibbling at the chicken and fruit on her plate while Dusty devoured a half rack of ribs. I came back to the living room to find Grandpa watching home videos of him and me. The video was filmed a long time ago. It featured me when I was four years old and sitting at the old dining room table. I was coloring while I was eating.

In the video, Grandpa asked, "What're you coloring there?"

"Animals!" I muttered under my breath.

"Oh, yeah? That's pretty good. Who's that?"

"Dusty. He's swimming in the pool."

"Wow, that's very nice."

"Thanks!"

Grandpa whispered, "I knew you were special from the moment I held you. You had an energy about you that I couldn't describe."

I remained silent, unsure of what to say to such a kind remark. I felt as though I didn't deserve it. After a few moments, I found the words.

"You taught me everything I needed to know. I wouldn't be who I am without you."

Grandpa looked up at me from the sofa, "You're going to do amazing things, kiddo. And I'm going to be there by your side, every step of the way."

Suddenly, the doorbell rang, and I made my way to the door. I opened it up and found a Pizza-Bot 3000 from Argyle's Pizza House.

"Argyle's Pizza House! We have one Hawaiian pie for Herschel Steele?" The pizza drone pilot announced.

"You got it."

"Wait, aren't you Justin Steele?"

"Uh, yeah, I'm Herschel's grandson. Why?"

"No way, this is awesome! I'm like your number one fan. Can you sign my receipt?"

"Uh... yeah sure, but don't I have to sign it anyway?"

"You got me there! But yeah, I guess you're right! Well, here's your pizza and have a spectacular night."

The pizza drone's oven door opened as I grabbed the piping hot pizza box out of the drone's heating storage unit and signed the receipt pad on the drone's extension arm.

"Yeah, thanks. You, too."

It was incredibly strange that the pizza delivery carrier recognized me. After placing the pizza on the counter and plating two slices I decided to check my phone. My social accounts must've been booming with notifications. But when I selected the newsfeed on one of my platforms, there was a video mashup that had been titled "Justin Steele". The video itself featured me fighting in the WT combat portion, fighting against Zeus in the street and fighting against Malcolm in Rus's habitat.

Someone had gathered security footage of me and put it together into one video. It was posted, shared, and trending. There were millions upon millions of views of the video mashup. At one point the video stopped and focused on me when I got my partner patch and how aggressive I became when they took Coco from my arms. I watched and became embarrassed and ashamed of my behavior. The video ended with me holding Coco next to Rus's habitat. I was unaware how or why this video was created. After watching it, I plated pizza for me and Grandpa and took my phone into the living room.

I handed Grandpa his plate, and I sat on the sofa chair adjacent to the couch.

"Did you see this video of me floating around?" I questioned.

"This video?" Grandpa asked, pointing at the TV.

"No, there's a video online. There's edited footage of me fighting Zeus, Malcolm, and even Wyatt from the WT application?"

"Why would someone make that?" Grandpa asked in an innocent tone.

"The pizza carrier recognized me and said he was my 'biggest fan.'"

"Interesting. Well, your skills are all online now then?"

"Everything I've done so far. But how does someone go about doing that? Why would somebody make that?"

Grandpa pulled his glasses out of his pocket. "Let me watch it."

I pulled my phone out and showed him the video and explained when each encounter occurred. After the video ended, Grandpa took a bite of pizza.

"Hmm, you look good. People are going to hate you."

"What? Why?"

"They'll be jealous of your minute of fame. Don't let it affect your ego."

"No, Grandpa, you don't understand. Somebody had to hack into public records, traffic cameras, WT cameras..." I looked at him, concerned and paused. "Grandpa, please tell me you didn't have anything to do with this."

"I didn't have anything to do with this."

"Ok."

"Your father did."

"What? Why would he do this?"

"He just wants the world to see you and how strong you are. Noah probably thinks it will help get you into the Hunter's Camp faster and away from the Farmer's Camp."

"How does he think this is helping? Did you know about this? Why didn't you stop him?"

"You think that man would listen to me about anything anymore? When Noah wants to do something for someone, he does not rest until the job is done."

My headspace was clouded with angst and subjected to scrutiny topped with a dash of fear. The thought of not being able to please others sent me into a cold sweat. The few victories I did achieve were purely due to luck. Yes, I had combat training from Grandpa. But it was not the primary factor contributing to my success. I had my gifts, my hope, and an unrelenting inner strength. These were the driving factors that allowed me to step up and face any combatant who tried to cause harm to me, my friends, or my family.

I collapsed onto my bed later that night once my bags were packed, my copy of *Patches* in hand, and a phone full of notifications from people I didn't know. I put my phone charging on the floor. Everything Coco and I had experienced that afternoon had been draining for both of our mental and physical states. She curled up next to me, exhausted after a full day of training and a full belly from dinner. Tomorrow was the opportunity to start over and begin our journey into the Cultivation Squad.

I knew individuals would have preconceived notions of who I was or what I was capable of. They'd take one look at that video and start ripping me apart before taking the time to get to know me. I was going to have to learn to ignore those people and do my best. Of course, that's easier said than done. My phone continued vibrating on the carpeted floor. I finally looked up from bed and saw someone was calling me. It was difficult for me to read the name of the caller from the bed.

"Uh, hello?"

"Hey, Justin?"

"Oh... hey, Roxanne. What's going on?"

"Nothing much. Just finishing up some packing. Are you excited for tomorrow?"

"Oh no doubt. It's going to be fun. Definitely a lot to learn and a lot of new people."

"Yeah, well at least we know each other! So, we won't be completely alone."

"Fair point. It'll be nice sharing a camp together."

"Yeah. Hopefully you two will be in the Hunter's Camp with Diego and me, but I suppose we'll see."

"Yeah, there's like a trial or something."

"I know first-day omnivores are sorted based on combat ability alone. Will you two be ready?"

"We're going to do our best! First coati in the program after all, so I like our odds."

"I saw your video."

I swallowed nervously. "Oh, yeah, not really crazy about it, honestly. I'm surprised it's still up."

"What do you not like about it? You fought very well."

"Thanks, we didn't really have much choice. We just got lucky."

"No, you two are great fighters. Don't sell yourself short."

I calmly exhaled as a sense of relief overcame my headspace. I was thankful to receive such thoughtful words. Roxanne had simply called to check up on me. I was lucky to have a friend going to camp with me. I remembered Rus's comment about wanting me to ask her about him. Instead of ignoring the subject completely, I decided to inform her of the full story of what occurred between Rus and me.

"That last fight in the video, the one with Malcolm Ula? That was not the only fight that occurred at The Docks."

"It was Russel's habitat, wasn't it?"

"Yes."

"He means well, Justin. You two have been friends forever."

"Just a couple years before we met you."

"We'll be in the Cultivation Squad. He'll be in the Exploration Squad. There's not much we can do..."

Almost without thought I blurted out, "You love him, don't you?"

"What?"

"You love Rus. It's plain as day!"

"Why are you asking?"

"Because you both have had this thing where you're together, you're not together, you want to be together, but you aren't really together. It's just confusing. And as someone who cares about both of you, it's a little difficult to keep track." I laughed nervously. There was a moment of silence on the phone.

"I don't," Roxanne hesitantly answered.

I sighed. "He has a lot on his plate. About two tons worth if it's any consolation. According to my grandpa, we all have some growing to do."

"My father and I will be at orientation just before 10 a.m. tomorrow morning. Maybe we could wait for you and Herschel at the orientation booth?"

"Yeah, yeah. That'd be nice. I'll be exhausted. But yes, we'll meet you guys there."

"Great, well, I'm gonna get some shut eye. See you tomorrow!"

"See you then!"

"Bye."

"Bye."

I placed my phone back on the ground as Coco glanced at me from the bed. She was falling asleep with her eyes half open.

"Everything is okay, Coco. At least we'll have one friend who's excited to see us tomorrow," I whispered.

Coco buried her head underneath a pillow and fell asleep. I crawled back over to the bed and climbed back up onto my soft mattress. My eyes stared up at the ceiling as I imagined the different outcomes of tomorrow. I knew there was great opportunity on the table that Coco and I needed to seize for ourselves.

We couldn't just sit around and wait for the division leaders to place us into the Hunter's or Farmer's Camp. We needed to make it abundantly clear that we belonged with the Hunters. I thought of Lyza and Ivan. I hoped tomorrow was a painless transition for them. I'd drop my letter in the mailbox tomorrow morning so that she'd receive it on her first day. I reached over and entered in the partner patch code as the two of us willingly fell into a deep sleep.

Grandpa greeted us at 5:00 a.m. with a full hot breakfast. We quickly ate, packed up the zomorodi with my belongings, I showered, brushed my teeth, and changed. I put on one of my new shamrock green Coati Cultivation Squad shirts, my father's red hat, some blue jeans, and a new pair of brown cleats.

I dropped my letter for Lyza into the mailbox, and we hit the road all by 6:30 a.m. Since we had a three-hour ride in the zomorodi, I knew I would have enough time to catch up on sleep. Grandpa was kind enough to take time off to drive me to South Ignacia for Cultivation Squad orientation. He began berating me with questions, asking me detailed questions about *Patches*. I told him I was on the last chapter. It was then that I realized I would have little to no luck with him allowing me to sleep.

"Gramps, it's the last chapter. I'll read it later on tonight before I go to bed."

"No, you and Coco will be too busy meeting people and making friends. It's a beautiful site located right in the midst of nature. Several different ecosystems all under the careful watch and care of the Hunter's Camp."

"All right, all right, fine. I'll finish it now."

I flipped open the manual to the last chapter titled "Maintenance."

"Maintenance? What kind of maintenance?"

"If something ever happens to your patch, each division has a patch specialist to help refill and repair your device depending on the situation."

"Hmm, definitely will have to remember that."

"Oh, you will. They do monthly checkups on everyone's partner patch to ensure the maximum protection and coverage for each pairing. Dusty and I got checked just last week. Isn't that right, Dusty?"

Dusty remained sleeping in the back of the zomorodi in his own row of the vehicle while Coco and I sat together in the front with Grandpa. I decided to heed Grandpa's advice and finish the book. I remembered that I would be seeing Roxanne throughout the camp. She would have already completed the manual and would want to compare notes regarding the subject. I couldn't do that if I wasn't finished. The remainder of the trip included smooth jazz and many meticulously placed words to inspire all thinkers to want to learn more about his or her partner patch. Just as I finished the last page, I looked up and noticed the wide landscape of the Cultivation Squad campsite.

I attached Coco to her leash and slowly opened the passenger door. We immediately stepped out of the vehicle and stretched our bodies from the three-hour road trip. Coco started pooping as soon as I put her down. Grandpa laughed as he popped open the trunk of the zomorodi. There were a handful of other zomorodis parked outside of the camp entrance filled with proud parents and newly admitted members of the Cultivation Squad. Applicants who had completed the application and received their orders for the following Monday, which means six days of newly awarded trainers and partners arrived each Monday morning.

Grandpa looked around at the surrounding zomorodis and recognized each of the newly admitted trainers. Multiple parents started to approach Grandpa, they all thanked him repeatedly and wanted a picture with him, that is, until Dusty waddled over and scared them off. Grandpa blamed Dusty when in reality he knew Dusty was his own private security guard. They utilized this tactic quite often when the two of them were out in public. Grandpa carried my large, black suitcase while I carried my WT backpack and duffle bag full of supplies for Coco.

On the outskirts of the parking lot stood a large green tent with the sign "CHECK - IN HERE". A shot of fear slowly slithered down my spine as I approached what felt like another test. Doubt began to set in, and that was when I mentally began a customary refrain, "You will never be good enough to appease your father or grandfather." I slowed down my pace while self-doubt enveloped my body.

Grandpa looked back at me. "Hey, you got this. You can use your power here. No more inhibitor chips. You're going to have a great time and make a lot of friends."

"Okay. I suppose it'll give me a leg up with the competition."

Grandpa looked up at the check-in sign. "Just don't get cocky."

I looked up as we approached the sign-in desk. A giant platypus sat on the table alongside a middle-aged woman who sat on a foldable chair with a giant gray computer in front of her. The woman wore a lime green shirt with a black silhouette of a platypus in the middle of it.

"Good morning, Mr. Steele, and welcome back."

Grandpa politely smiled back and nodded. "Good morning, thank you, Mrs. Peterson. Lovely to see you again."

"And who do we have with us today?"

I cleared my throat. "Justin, ma'am, Justin Steele."

"Well, welcome to the Cultivation Squad and congratulations! Let me just find you on our registration list."

I nodded and nervously glanced over at Grandpa. He nudged me in the arm attempting to remind me to relax.

She examined the list of names from her computer and typed loudly. "Uh-huh, it says here you have an omnivore and will be competing in a challenge today?"

"Yes, ma'am. Coco and I will do our best to try and join the Hunter's Camp."

"A coati? Wow, we have coatis around camp. You'll find a few of them in one of our surrounding ecosystems just east of the Hunter's Camp. We've never seen one with a trainer though. This will be a treat."

"Yes, ma'am."

"Let's go ahead and get you signed in. I'll hold onto your luggage here in the meantime. We have to do that until you're placed. Once you've been given a camp, we will deliver your luggage to your sleeping quarters."

She pulled a tablet out from under her desk and handed it over to me with a stylus pen to sign. "First, we'll need a signature on your waiver."

"Is this another safety waiver?"

Miss Peterson smiled. "In case you die, this indicates we aren't legally responsible."

My mouth dropped as I searched for Grandpa's disapproval.

Grandpa laughed. "Man, some things never change. You'll be fine! Don't lose your head."

I exhaled deeply. "Yeah, literally." I signed on the electronic pad with the stylus.

"Okay, now swipe to the left and give the following information: birthdate, any allergies, emergency contact, and such."

I added all of my personal information on the device and handed the tablet back to the woman. Grandpa and I carefully set down my luggage in the far corner of the tent just as the rain began. I pulled out my black umbrella and placed Coco back on my shoulder. We hesitantly exited the tent and passed through the tall wooden gate. As we crossed the ancient arch in the center, I immediately spotted Roxanne jumping into puddles with Diego, accompanied by her father. Roxanne was wearing black rain boots and jumping into a nearby puddle while Diego was attempting to pounce onto the puddle.

"Justin, over here!" Roxanne waved and yelled.

Grandpa and I walked over to Roxanne and her father, Calvin Reeves, Mayor of Ignacia. His partner Phillip, a small black rat, sat on his shoulder. I slowly brought Coco off my shoulder and cradled her in my arms in case she became afraid of Diego. As we got closer Roxanne muttered something to Diego. Suddenly Diego sat upright with his paws on the ground in front of him. He appeared calm, gentle, and approachable. Diego appeared to be a completely different jaguar in comparison to the one I met just a few days prior. Grandpa and Mayor Reeves made small talk while Roxanne, and I introduced our partners.

"See, Coco, he's a nice big cat. We like Diego."

Coco immediately started sniffing the air as we approached Diego. However, little rain drops seemed to dampen Diego's scent. Once we were within three feet of the big cat Coco became frightened of the potential predator. She began clawing up my chest and digging her nails into my uniform. She stood on the back of my neck and rested on top of my hat.

I sighed. "Give her some time, she'll come around."

Roxanne smiled. "I know she will. Isn't this great? We finally made it! Even in the rain, everything is so green and beautiful!"

I examined the two divided camps closely. On our right was the entrance to the Farmer's Camp which had a bright massive field of crops that included a variety of fruits, vegetables, and medicinal herbs. Behind the croplands stood a large wooden building that resembled a greenhouse.

On our left, we saw the entrance to the Hunter's Camp where the challenge field sat waiting. The field itself was sand-based and a bit rocky. The rain caused it to turn muddy and almost flooded. It was solely designed for trainers to challenge one another with their partners in order to climb the ranks in camp. I was yearning for the opportunity to be on that field and test our abilities.

"Yeah, it's really something," I whispered to myself.

The Cultivation Squad camp was old and looked as if it could definitely use an upgrade. The building structures seemed to be hundreds of years old. A large brick dining hall with a clock tower stood in the middle of the two camps. A small podium was set up outside the large brick building.

Soon five more new pairs of trainers and partners joined us. Roxanne immediately started introducing herself to everyone. I stood by closely as she introduced me to everyone she met. I was thankful to have such an outgoing friend to help ease the tension.

We met Luke and his new partner "Harry," an aardvark; Kevin and his new partner "Fang," a grey fox; Davis and his new partner "Sam," a British Saddleback pig; Jake and his new partner "Wally," a capybara; then the last trainer was Sammy and her new partner "Ruby," the Holstein Friesian cow. All of the trainers had been given specific instructions on which camp they were joining. Kevin and Roxanne had both been selected as Hunters while Luke, Jake, Davis, and Sammy were all designated Farmers. Everyone had an assigned placement, everyone but Coco and me.

The same lady from the check-in booth stood on the small podium with an umbrella in one hand and her platypus in the other. "Good morning, everyone. I see you took the liberty of introducing yourselves. It's a great exercise for focusing on social skills with your new partners. My name is Julie Peterson, but everyone just calls me Miss Peterson. This is my partner Fran. I'm the Orientation Manager here at the Cultivation Squad. I also teach botany in the Farmer's Camp. Now it's my job to ensure each of you know where everything is when you are here. We want you to be both comfortable and confident during your time here with us. Now we have a couple of items in store for you. We will be providing a brief tour to showcase the entirety of our facility. We'll meet for lunch in the dining hall. Then we have a few challenges happening later today that we will all get to watch. Two trainers on site will be competing against one another in attempts to rise in the ranks, but we'll explain that here in a bit. Any questions before we start?"

"Yeah, where are the bathrooms?" Davis asked.

Miss Peterson smiled. "I'm glad you asked. The closest one is located inside the dining hall on the left. I insist everyone who needs to go, do it now."

"Good thinking," Grandpa muttered under his breath.

Before I knew it, the entire group followed behind Davis into the dining hall and to the restrooms.

The hall was full of fresh scents of breakfast, freshly squeezed orange juice, crispy hashbrowns, and mountains of scrambled eggs. There were hundreds of tables and benches filled with trainers both young and old. Trainers were quickly coming and going freely throughout the space. Some collected their meals and grabbed a seat while others threw their trash away and departed. It resembled an ongoing ecosystem in the sense that there was an unspoken food chain, and the head of the hierarchy were the top trainers in the Hunter's Camp.

You had your stereotypical manual laborers as members from the Farmer's Camp coexisted alongside the predatory minds of the Hunters. I could see there was a thick unspoken line between the two camps, and according to Grandpa, there always had been. Regardless of the towering wooden fence that bordered the two camps, the only common areas that were shared amongst both sides were the dining hall and bath houses.

I hated how separated the camps were. It was hard to believe the Cultivation Squad was one whole division when in reality it seemed as though the two camps were almost completely disconnected.

"This is the Zhang Dining Hall and Clock Tower," Miss Peterson announced. "The structure was renamed in honor of Jericho Zhang. He was the last recorded crystal claw trainer, top trainer of the Cultivation Squad and, of course, leader of the Hero Regime. Jericho believed in bridging the two camps together and highlighting the importance of both sets of animals in order to survive. He believed that limited technology was the best way to ensure natural growth to help recreate and preserve ecosystems. We renamed this structure shortly after he died. We have his painting here to remind us all not to fear change and to push back valiantly against the AFA."

"Yeah, something like that," Grandpa whispered to me condescendingly.

I covered my mouth and attempted to hide my laughter. Miss Peterson was as sharp as a tack and saw my smile from a mile away.

"Now it's come to my attention we also have a celebrity in our midst. Mr. Zhang's right-hand man, and current president of the Animal Bridging

Council, Herschel Steele." The parents of the group slowly applauded while trainers at surrounding dining tables began to look from afar.

"So, tell us all what brings you here today, Mr. Steele?"

The parents and newly admitted students started whispering amongst themselves. Grandpa waved and smiled. He then exhaled deeply and placed his hands on my shoulders.

"My grandson, Justin, is here to walk in my footsteps. He'll be following the family legacy. The Cultivation Squad is the first step in the right direction."

"Yes, well thank you both for being here. May I also remind you kindly not to talk while I am speaking. It's quite rude. Thank you."

Grandpa's smile faded. "Yes, ma'am, understood. We do apologize."

I'd never seen or heard anyone speak to Grandpa like that, except maybe my father. Grandpa was an icon in the public eye, but it was clear Miss Peterson did not care one bit. She didn't hesitate to shut him down in his tracks. I felt a bit of tension in the air after that between the two of them. As we continued the tour throughout the facility, we saw the interior of the giant greenhouse. It had some of the latest technology to study plant life. We weaved through both housing units for each camp.

The Hunter's Camp's housing was updated apartment-style living quarters, king-sized beds, and great views of the camp. The Farmer's camp only had Spartan safari-style tents, simply four walls and a queen bed, individually designed and assigned to Farmers. I had to become a Hunter. I'd spent years training for this moment. However, it was the Farmers that supplied the Cultivation Squad with their food. They provided working relationships with members of the Transferal Squad. Together the two squads had the power to supply fresh produce around the country. The Cultivation Squad was incredible. We slowly made our way back to the front of the Hunter's camp. The rain suddenly cleared up as more members from both camps approached the challenge field. Some sat while others stood as close as possible to find a great view of the challenge field.

"Oh goody, we're just in time. We have two separate challenges today." Miss Peterson pulled out her electronic pad from her purse. "Up first we have Cameron, one of our newer members from the Farmer's Camp, facing off against Jackson, a member from the Hunter's Camp who has just completed his first year. Cameron's partner is Rudolph, an adolescent white-tailed buck. Jackson's partner is Legend, the eastern, white-bearded wildebeest."

"Why are they challenging one another?" Davis asked.

"It's a challenge to move camps. If Cameron and Rudolph win this challenge, they will be welcomed into the camp as honorary Hunters."

"What happens if they lose?" Sammy asked.

Miss Peterson paused. "Then he will remain a Farmer and must wait another six months if they wish to try again."

"And if Jackson wins, what does he get out of it?" Kevin asked.

"He will receive a rise in rank. You'll learn that different colored patches depicting the ranking of each member of the Cultivation Squad. Better start keeping an eye out for those. The higher your ranking, the more payment you receive."

Sweat filled my palms as anxious thoughts of failure began to cloud my judgment. Grandpa saw the fear latch on to me and placed his hand on my shoulder to shake it off. I looked up to him as he smiled and nodded at me with nonverbal reassurance. My fists tightened as I nodded in understanding.

"Come on, Justin, let's get a closer look!" Roxanne exclaimed. She grabbed my hand and started dragging me closer to the viewing area.

Cameron and Jackson stood facing each other. The clouds dispersed as if they had been told to do so. Not a single cloud in the sky threatened to cast a shadow on the challenge the two trainers had agreed to. The mud had started to dry up but seemed prominent enough to slow down challengers, slick and slippery enough to cause someone to fall.

Cameron was a larger, out of shape, Farmer of the Cultivation Squad. He stood nervous and intimidated by the confident hunter in front of him. Each trainer displayed his ranking patch proudly on the left sleeve of his uniform. Both partners stood tall, focused, and intently set on causing harm to the other animal in front of them. They each stood just ten yards away from one another. A stout, gray-haired referee stood between the four of them. He wore large reflective sunglasses as he examined both trainers and partners. He had a bright red patch on his left sleeve. The referee mumbled something to each trainer, each one nodded and the ref dropped two red flags between them. The two creatures instantly lunged at one another, fearless, brutal as the two animals clashed. Both sets of horns and antlers pushed against the other as hard as they could while hoping not to disappoint their trainers. The two collided and were locked in a battle of resistance and stamina. Each strenuously attempted to bulldoze the other but was unable to do so.

Roxanne and I moved closer and watched the challenge from about fifteen yards away from the action on a small cement bench shaded by a wooden gazebo. We were close enough to feel the sandy residue linger in the air and blow into our mouths. Diego sat at Roxanne's feet while Coco hesitantly sat on my right shoulder. I scratched the top of her head to reassure her that she was safe.

Both trainers left their previous positions and ran toward the other. Jackson was first to make contact by throwing rapid punches at Cameron's body. Cameron jumped back and dodged before he reached for his partner patch. I could see he pressed the lowest button on his partner patch which activated his adrenaline. Cameron clenched his fists and ran after Jackson.

Coco scratched at my shoulder. "Hey, it's okay, girl," I muttered to Coco.

"JUSTIN, WATCH OUT!" Roxanne screamed.

My eyes shot up to see the same wildebeest fling the young buck at the bench that we sat on. With little time to react, I pushed Coco safely out of the way with my right hand and stood in front of her. My fists clenched as I activated my ability, ready to open my palms to try and catch Rudolph's body as it hurtled toward me. I inhaled deeply and focused on the large animal. My hands hardened as the steel pigmentation grew over each finger. I closed my eyes, stepped forward at the last moment, and when I opened my eyes, somehow, I had safely caught that one-hundred-and-fifty-pound buck with my bare hands. I carefully placed him down and looked back at Roxanne. She looked confused and bewildered.

The referee blew a loud whistle. "Penalty! No other trainer interaction is permitted during a challenge. We'll have to reset the fight."

"That won't be necessary, Mr. Rigby," Jackson stated confidently.

The referee then noticed Cameron had been knocked out and lay still on the rocky field. "That decides it. Jackson is our winner! He moves up to level thirty."

The referee glanced back at me with annoyance. He examined me closer and saw my hands. He ripped off his sunglasses and blew his whistle once again. "It's Justine Steele. Isn't it?"

"Umm yes sir?"

"You have a challenge today. To see if you have what it takes to join the Hunter's Camp."

"I think so."

"Oh, I know so. Come on out here."

I looked back and held my arm out for Coco before she scurried across and up my shoulder.

Roxanne and Diego followed me down to the field. The look of confusion and concern had not left her eyes. I slowly walked down a small flight of wooden stairs and entered the challenge field. The sun became so bright and hot that the moisture in the field had completely dried up. It felt like rocky cement with a beachy sandy feeling. I approached the referee slowly and watched as he took his sunglasses off and reached out to shake my hand.

"John Rigby. I'm the director of the Hunter's Camp," the referee said. "Behind me are just a few of my top trainers. For this challenge, you won't be battling them. I'm going to give you a chance. You may select any Hunter, old or new, on this campsite. But choose wisely, once you've made your decision you must honor it."

I started searching the outskirts of the challenge field. I saw a tiger, a wolf, a fox, even an ocelot, but I noticed a figure in the distance behind me standing outside the circle. The figure stood lingering in the shadows. It didn't take me long to recognize the face of my soon-to-be opponent. The guy leaned against the side wall of the dining hall clock tower. He wore the same black beanie on his head and was smoking a cigarette. He didn't seem to have a care in the world while his partner stood behind him and chewed on his boots.

I pointed my finger at the figure and looked back at John. "I challenge you, Todd Ramos."

My high school enemy lifted his head up as his eyes met mine. A sinister smile enveloped his face. He spat out his cigarette and pushed himself off the nearby wall while his crocodile Al followed behind him.

"All right, Steele. Let's see what you've got."

CHAPTER 11

Refusing Defeat

Todd and Al casually crossed the circle of sweaty trainers. Farmers who had been outside all morning planting, pulling, found time to cross over to the Hunter's Camp in order to witness another daily challenge. One by one those who saw Todd approach, quickly backed away and cleared a path. Todd and Al stood but five feet away from me and Coco. Moments passed while more members of the Cultivation Squad stopped what they were doing in order to find a seat to watch another challenge. Al began to hiss and inch forward while Coco sniffed the air to familiarize herself with their scents. She could sense my growing frustration with Todd. She tilted her head to the side as I glared at Todd. We had to win.

I clenched my right fist as visions of high school attacked my brain. The amount of ridicule and embarrassment Todd caused me was frustrating. My eyes fell into the dark depths of Todd's eyes. The more I looked, the more I began to notice subtle changes about the two. Todd's hands had roughed up and his uniform appeared unclean, covered in dirt. My challenger had small bags under his eyes as if he were exhausted. Al had grown in size in just a matter of days and had gained a few new scars. It quickly became apparent that Al was also no longer wearing a harness. He could've attacked me and Coco right then and there, and nobody would've stopped him. It was strange. They held themselves with a different energy, and that was when I began to worry.

Mr. Rigby stepped between us. "Back it up, you two. Todd, you know how this works. The challenge won't begin until directed to do so." The four of us backed up another couple of feet.

I scoffed. "How does he know how this works? He just got here!"

"Todd here has been challenged twice this past week alone."

"Come on, Rigby. Let's get this over with," Todd muttered.

"If you're in such a rush to lose, there's the door. Save us the trouble and forfeit." My eyes were like daggers attempting to pierce through the smug smoker.

I was trying to be strong for Coco, to inspire her to be brave and step outside of her comfort zone. If we could get on the same page mentally and emotionally, we could do anything. A small tingling sensation vibrated on the back of my neck. I could feel my anxious partner shaking. She was nervous with so many unknown people and predators surrounding her. My right hand rubbed along her back as I dug my fingers through her fur. I was attempting to calm her down so that we could challenge Todd properly. However, the shaking did not stop. She was worried about facing off against Todd and his adolescent croc.

The slender Hunter stepped forward. "You have no idea who you're messing with."

"I've got a pretty good idea." I was all bark and no bite. With Coco shaking in fear, I would have to defend her against both of them. I needed her to be brave and find the inner strength to defend herself.

Todd smirked. "You know I've seen your video. And I've gotta say, I'm not impressed."

Rigby raised his hands and gestured to everyone to vacate the challenge field. Members from both camps backed away and Roxanne exited the field with Diego right behind her. The director brought out his two, red flags. He spoke plainly to me and Rus. "There are only three rules to remember: One. Only the challengers and their partners are permitted to face off on the field. If you leave the field you are disqualified. Two. You cannot kill the other challenger or their partner. Three. If you or your partner cannot carry on, you will be asked to forfeit. There is no dishonor in knowing your limit. Are we clear?"

"Yes," Todd sighed.

I unclipped Coco's leash and tossed it to Roxanne. "Let's do this."

Mr. Rigby waved his red flags between us. "BEGIN!"

Todd took four small pellets out of his pocket and held them between his fingers. He and Al both split up in opposite directions as they circled me and Coco. They moved with amazing speed and tenacity. It was difficult to maintain focus on them. Todd dropped each pellet carefully behind him and unleashed a variety of smoke bombs. The smoke grew rapidly and fully engulfed the field. I decided to escape the smoke by sprinting to the outskirts of the field. I secured Coco by grabbing her and placing her on my shoulder, holding her in place. I turned my head to make sure she was okay. She was still shaking from the mysterious predators that lingered in the smoke.

"It's okay, Coco. We can do this. We have to be brave."

I faced forward and found Todd's shoe directly in front of my face. My nose caught the brunt of the kick which slowed down Todd, but the full force of the kick knocked me to the ground, causing my back to slam against the rocky challenge field. I quickly maneuvered Coco around my neck and onto my chest before I struck the ground.

My dad's hat fell off at the point of contact. I brought my hand up to my nose and saw the blood start to trickle down. Smoke continued to shield Todd and Al from any head on attack. The concern I had for my well-being quickly dissipated as my anger started to grow. A small feeling of darkness began to slither throughout my body like a rosy boa digging underground. My eyes began to water. I exhaled deeply and forced myself off the ground to my knees.

I placed Coco on the ground and pushed myself up. "Come on, Coco. Get ready!"

Coco leapt off and stood battle ready. She started sniffing the surrounding air, searching for our opponents. My small partner remembered their scent and knew where they were. Coco squealed with excitement as if she'd located them through the smoke. That was, however, until I heard Todd drop more smoke bombs. His smoke veil was the perfect place to hide, to hit, and run repeatedly.

My frustration caused my anger to multiply the more I squeezed my fists. The metallic shine grew over my palms, fingers, wrists, and forearms. The angrier I got; the more power became accessible. I was beginning to feel more comfortable after my training sessions with Grandpa. It was as if I could access more of my gift. Coco's protection became my priority so I knew that if I had more armor to use, I'd have more to send to Coco.

I nodded to Coco. "Now is the time. Let's share this power."

My left hand reached over my right shoulder as I adjusted my partner patch to a "*5*" for fifty percent power transfer. Selected *ANIMAL* to receive the power and pressed down on the red transfer button in the middle. My body began to weaken as my metallic shine condensed back to only cover my knuckles, and fingers. The strength from my body had been absorbed, but the pain seemed bearable. Coco continued to grow in size as the same metallic shine covered both of her hands and sharp nails. She was the size of a fully-grown capybara with metallic talons stronger than an eagle. My anger intensified as Todd continued to sprint laps around us. We didn't stand a chance if we couldn't hit him.

"COME OUT TODD. FACE US."

I pulled my arms back and tightened all of the muscles in my shoulders, arms, and hands. My hands forcefully collided, producing a metallic clap that reverberated with such force it sent out a powerful wave of air. The collision of my hands was strong enough to push away the majority of the smoke.

A metallic sound echoed through the field at the point of contact. Todd's smoke veil had been pierced and the openness revealed Todd's location just as he moved in to punch me. He stood just a few feet away from me with his fist raised, closing in on my face again.

Todd was ridiculously quick with his attacks, so much so that I had no time to react or block his punch. His heavy hand rammed my face to the ground. The blunt trauma to my face caused my nose to pop. It felt as though someone had torn it off my face completely. I assumed that he'd broken it.

More blood flowed out of my nose and into my mouth. The rich iron consumed my taste buds as I collapsed to the ground again. My eyes tried to glance around, but my vision was blurred from tears. I continued blinking and prayed my eyes wouldn't give out on me. The sound of quick breaths and small squeals whispered into my ear as Coco was running in fear. I raised my head and peered behind me as Al sprinted after Coco.

"COCO! Side swipe left!"

Al had cornered Coco on the far-left side of the battlefield. He lunged at her with his jaws open, ready to bite. Coco quickly dodged to her left and scratched Al's right eye. The young croc let out a whimpering roar in pain. Todd refused to allow Coco to continue to harm Al and moved in on her.

Somehow I was able to force myself up and jog after Todd. My heart rate started to climb as the thought of Todd harming Coco shook me to my core. The harder I ran, the more my body gravitated toward the ground. Each step I took into the field made me feel heavier. A massive presence intensified in my body, trying to get out as I moved after Todd.

Todd made it to Coco just moments before me and pulled his leg back as he attempted to deliver a heavy kick. Coco's combined strength enabled her to move faster than Todd, which allowed her to effortlessly dodge each kick. She screeched and raised her left hand full of sharp nails and attempted to scratch Todd.

The slender challenger instinctively leaped backward to avoid Coco's strike just as I had caught up to him. He stood facing Coco with his arms to his sides. Dragging the rocky terrain beneath my feet, I threw my arms over his shoulders and squeezed as tightly as possible. The bear hug tightened around his narrow frame and slender figure until his body started to crack.

Todd was like a mealworm being consumed as he squirmed and grunted in pain. I lifted his body higher and slammed him into the ground. Al lunged at me from behind as his teeth connected with my right leg moments after Todd's face collided with the field. This allowed Coco time to retreat to the other side of the field where it was safe. Al began biting deeper into my leg and sank his sharp teeth into my right calf. I curled my metallic fingers into a fist and punched him in the eyes repeatedly until he let go.

My right leg felt as if it were on fire, burning with remnants of flesh hanging off the sides. I hobbled back to Coco on the other side of the field, but Todd started to stand up. He cleared the rubble from his face, his arms weakened as he struggled to adjust his partner patch. I heard him successfully slam down on his transfer button. I started to hobble faster and moved closer to Coco.

"Coco, on me! Hurry!"

Coco moved like lightning and was getting closer to me. My breath was heavy, I stood and held out my left hand for her to jump. Time slowed down as fear and anxiety began to stir into a chemical mixture set for disaster. She was just a few feet away from me when I felt a sudden gust of wind blow by me. Out of the corner of my eye I saw Al leaping after Coco. He'd become even larger and much faster because of Todd's transfer. My partner jumped to my arm but was intercepted by Al's massive jaws.

With the help of the power transfer from Todd's partner patch, Al had become the size of Dusty! Al's massive jaws clamped down onto Coco she let out a yelping cry.

Fear and anger wrestled within my mind like two serpents which made me want to push my body harder. Al slid by me with Coco's body locked between his jaws. I reached out instantly and grabbed Al by the tail. I aggressively pulled his body closer to me.

"Let her go!" I barked at the young croc.

The dense weight of his body alone was unbearable. My adrenaline was pumping, and my heart rate was climbing as I saw Coco struggling to break out. My vision had become the color of my flashing partner patch, red. Once I pulled Al's body close enough, I slammed both of my fists into his back, causing his jaws to release Coco. Al let out a massive roar in pain.

Al immediately changed his focus back to me. He quickly turned around with his jaws open and lunged at my right forearm. I was able to block his jaws with my left forearm. His strength and size were beginning to overpower me. I began breathing harder and allowed my anger to take over. More of my blood spilled, and a certain darkness persistently continued to expect more out of my body. I felt each of his teeth digging into my metallic skin. Al's transferred strength was able to penetrate my armor. I raised my right fist and punched him in his scratched left eye. The damage alone was thankfully enough for him to release me.

The croc quickly retreated to the other side of the field. I stood bleeding from my left forearm, my nose, and my left calf. I was losing a lot of blood as Coco limped back over to me. My body dropped as I fell to my knees and reached out for her. She limped over to me and crawled into my arms. I held Coco close as she returned to her normal size, which allowed my strength to return as well. There was no doubt that we had been beaten, and I knew at that point there was nothing more I could do.

"I'm sorry, Coco. I'm so sorry," I whispered as I forced my right hand onto the ground and tapped on the field to indicate our forfeit.

John Rigby waved his red hand flags. "Winner! Todd Ramos and his partner Al! The two have now been promoted to level three in the Hunter's Camp!"

John Rigby walked over to Todd and placed a level three patch on his uniform. The members of the Cultivation Squad applauded as Grandpa rushed to the field. He grabbed a first aid kit from one of the medics and rushed to my side. He quickly applied bandages and gauze to my open wounds.

"Keep pressure on that and wait until you're alone to cry. It's okay. You are going to be okay."

I struggled to breathe and coughed excessively but motioned for Coco. "I'm fine. Just help her!"

Grandpa began cleaning Coco's wounds and applying bandages to her. Medics rushed in shortly after to tend to Todd and Al as well as me and Coco. Todd acted as if he weren't hurt even though I nearly broke him in half. Dusty crawled up behind Grandpa and stood in front of me and Coco as he faced Al and Todd.

Dusty let out a giant roar while Todd and Al fearfully stepped back. Todd's medics jumped back in terror until John Rigby stepped in between us with his partner Raven at his side. Raven was a large grey wolf with beautiful black fur that glared at Dusty as she bared her teeth. She growled and stood in a pouncing position with the intent to kill.

"Dusty, leave them be. Sorry, John, old habits die hard."

"Keep that gator in check, Herschel. There are no sore losers here."

Grandpa nodded. "You know that Raven really has grown up, hasn't she? She was just a pup the last time I saw you two together."

Rigby walked up to Raven and patted the top of her head. "She's a killer and always takes care of her pack. The Hunters are nothing less than her family."

Grandpa smirked. "Good to see you too, John."

Members of the Hunter's Camp rejoined the field and ran to Todd's side. Dusty backed off and placed his jaws on my lap. I could feel his sadness and concern just as I felt Grandpa's. People continued to applaud Todd's victory with back pats, various handshakes, and friendly smiles.

It was a feeling I yearned for. The feeling of acceptance and warmth, it isn't something one could buy. A reassurance that everyone around you likes you and supports you is something you have to earn.

That night I knew he would celebrate just as he did after his prior two victories. Food, drinks, heroic stories of the battlefield about how he defeated us. From that day on, I vowed that I wouldn't stop until I beat Todd. I remembered a time when he was my friend, and now he was the most respected new edition in the Hunter's Camp. I had so much to prove and such little time to waste.

Two muscular men in white medical uniforms came and carefully lifted us up and gently placed us down on a hover stretcher. They walked alongside us and directed the stretcher back to the Zhang Dining Hall. Before we departed the field, Todd's eyes met mine as a sinister sneer covered his face. I glared back and held Coco close. I wouldn't allow him to hurt us again. Grandpa walked alongside us followed by Dusty, Roxanne, Diego, and Mayor Reeves.

Roxanne peered over the challenge field and found a sliver of my red hat stuck out from underneath the rocky terrain. She and Diego made their way back on the field to retrieve it for us. After crossing through the main hall, we soon found ourselves awkwardly waiting inside an elevator which took us to the third-floor infirmary.

Inside was a full hospital setup where eight other members sat resting in large hospital beds, their animal partners alongside them.

I found the previous challenger, Cameron, asleep in a bed alongside his healthy partner, the white-tailed buck named Rudolph. A team of nurses and medic bots all circled the room as they tended to each trainer and partner.

Rudolph sat patiently waiting for his trainer to wake up. The men placed us down in the next bed over from Cameron. Roxanne, Diego, and her father arrived shortly after and sat close by in the waiting area. They waited patiently to hear updates about both me and Coco. Roxanne rubbed Diego on the head while her father took a phone call and nervously paced around the room. Coco remained in my arms, lying still. Her eyes were closed, and it was scary how little her body moved. The small coati felt weak, and her breathing was labored.

"Can we get a nurse or a medic over here?" Grandpa asked loudly.

"Please someone! She needs help!" I yelled.

A nurse and medic bot quickly came over and examined me and Coco. They performed numerous tests, took x-rays, patched up my nose, took blood samples and diagnosed Coco with multiple broken bones.

"She has two broken ribs, a fractured hand, and a broken leg. We'll need to fix her and hold you both up here for two maybe three days before you can return to camp. For now, we'll need to repair and realign her broken bones."

The nurse gently picked up Coco from my lap and placed her on a small hover stretcher.

The medic bot finished installing a hyper healing cast on my nose after popping it back into place. My cast made it nearly impossible to breathe out of my nose. Once the procedure was completed I sounded as though I had a heavy cold and a lot of built-up congestion. As if things couldn't be any more embarrassing.

My stubbornness allowed me to lean up in my hospital bed and counter. "Three days! We have to get back out there and train!"

I clenched my fists and tried to access my armor, tossing, and turning. Grandpa clenched his fists and activated his metallic armor.

He pushed me down onto the bed. "Justin, stop. This is embarrassing!"

I stopped moving and was shocked by Grandpa's remark. The impact from his hands landed directly on my abs. I'd never heard Grandpa raise his voice and speak so harshly to me.

The nurse spoke sternly, "Do we need to bind you to the bed? You aren't going anywhere! Between the number of stitches you'll need, your fractured leg, broken nose, and fractured arm, you're lucky you aren't bleeding out."

"You don't understand. I have to get back out there." I calmly spoke.

"And you will, but now you rest. Just be glad your opponent didn't bite into any major arteries."

I lay down silently and stared up at the poorly painted ceiling. It had shades of beige and white paint. Small fragments were deteriorating and trickling down one after the other and exposed the older layers. Grandpa and Dusty walked away shortly after he raised his voice.

He spoke with Roxanne's dad before he went to find Miss Peterson. I'd be assigned to a safari-style tent equipped with plumbing and electricity.

Before they left, Roxanne and her father walked over to my bed.

"Are you okay?" Roxanne kindly asked.

"No. Nothing about this is okay. Coco is hurt, I'm stuck in bed, and to top it off, I'm becoming a Farmer."

"I'm sorry, Justin. Give it time, it won't be forever. I have to go, but I'll come back and visit soon. I promise." Roxanne placed my father's hat back on my head.

Feeling shame and embarrassment, the only safe space I had was under the bill of my hat. I pulled it over my eyes. "Thanks, Roxanne."

"You did a fine job today, Justin. A fine job. Get better soon," Mayor Reeves said.

"Thank you."

The two of them walked away as I reclined my head back and concealed my face.

A hospital bed was not the place to be after losing a fight. I replayed the challenge over and over again, pondering how I could've done more and how I should've done more.

Three hours later the day had quickly turned to night. That evening a nurse returned Coco to me enveloped in casts and bandages. She was sleeping soundly and heavily sedated from the procedures they'd performed to restore her health. The nurse later brought us hot food from downstairs, but I wasn't hungry.

The food ran cold and sat on my bedside table. Coco's body was covered in wounds from just one bite from Al. My fingers grazed her bandaged bites and all I wanted to do was cry. It wasn't until I heard a voice that scared me back to reality.

"Umm, excuse me?"

My head turned instinctively to the left and noticed Cameron had finally woken up.

I coughed. "Uh, mhm... hey. Yeah, what's up?"

"Are you, all right?" Cameron asked.

"Am I all right? What do you think?"

"Looks to me like you got beaten as well."

"Yeah. I bet you know all about that." I examined his bloody lip and black eye.

"That I do. But you're Justin Steele. Right?"

"How do you know me?"

"I saw your video. Actually, everyone here did."

"So I heard, I mean... I didn't make it. It's not mine."

"You didn't? Well, I thought it was pretty cool how you knocked out like three bad guys!"

"Two. One of them was just the combat portion."

He turned, adjusting his body to face me, "Yeah but nobody here had to face someone that big in the combat portion. It was like David and Goliath."

"I got lucky."

"What happened today? Who beat you?"

I sighed deeply. "Todd Ramos."

"Oh, yeah. He's a tough one. A pair of newbies but he and that crocodile are deadly. Why would you choose him?

"I guess, I don't know. I wanted to prove that I could finally beat him. We went to school together."

"Oh-ho there's your problem right there! You were thinking with your heart and not with your head."

I scoffed. "Well, then why'd you lose?"

"I'm different. I just suck. No offense, Rudolph." Rudolph dropped his head and turned away.

I laughed as the pain started sinking in. My body began to ache from being beaten so badly.

"I'm Cameron, and this is Rudolph."

"I know. Miss Peterson wouldn't stop talking about you guys."

"Heck of a first day, huh?"

"You're telling me. Having to spend the first three days in the infirmary is not what I had in mind."

"We all have to start somewhere."

"Why'd you want to be in the Hunter's Camp by the way? Rudolph isn't a predator," I asked hesitantly.

"Well, technically you don't have to be a predator. You just have to know how to fight.

"Hmm, I didn't know that."

"Plus, they have the best apartments and the best parties. You wait, the Farmer's Camp is not all it's cracked up to be."

"Weren't you assigned to the Farmer's Camp though?"

"Yeah, but that won't stop me from trying. I've been here for a year now, and we've challenged two Hunters so far."

"Why not just give up?"

"Because nothing good in this life comes easy. Even if that means we have to work harder, then so be it. That's what we'll do."

I resumed my previous position and glanced back up at the poorly painted ceiling. I sat in silence as his words resonated with me. Coco was out like a light, and I felt her breathing return to normal. I was embarrassed because of my defeat today, but maybe Cameron had a point. This was no time to give up. If Cameron was going to continue to fight, then so was I.

"Let's do it together," Cameron whispered.

"What do you mean?"

Cameron leaned forward to face me. "Join the Hunters Camp! That's what we're here to do, right?"

"Right."

"So, swear to it."

I sighed. "I swear."

"I can't hear you!"

"I swear!"

"Shut up! We're trying to sleep here," a frustrated random sleeping trainer complained.

"Sorry!" Cameron reclined in his hospital bed. "Just a few days here and then we'll be back out at the Farmer's Camp."

Grandpa and Dusty quietly entered the room and examined the sleeping trainers and partners. Cameron sat up in his bed, brushing Rudolph. Grandpa and Dusty made their way over to our beds and noticed my demeanor had changed.

"Justin, how are you? Have you eaten?" He studied the untouched dinner tray on my side table.

"I'm all right, Grandpa."

Cameron stood from his bed. "Wow, Herschel Steele. And his legendary partner Dusty!"

Grandpa pulled up a chair and sat close by. "I see you've made a friend."

"Grandpa, this is Cameron and his partner Rudolph."

"Hello, Cameron, you and Rudolph sure gave that Hunter a run for his money."

"Cameron is going to join the Hunter's Camp. We both are, and in six months we'll challenge them again!"

He shook Cameron's hand and faced me. "That's the spirit. Well, I certainly wish you both luck."

"I'm gonna run to the bathroom. Do you need anything, Justin?" Cameron awkwardly muttered.

"No, I'm good. Thanks."

Cameron nodded. "Nice to meet you, Mr. Steele. Come on, Rudolph."

Grandpa smiled and waved as the two exited the room.

Grandpa patted me on the shoulder. "You're all unpacked and set up in your safari-style quarters."

"You mean my tent?"

"Justin, it's like camping with style. I promise you'll be fine. I'm afraid it's time for us to go."

"No, can't you stay the night?"

"I have work in the morning, son. Many more kids out there that need partners. And partners that need new trainers. Keep an eye out for the next batch next week."

"Grandpa, thank you for being here."

Grandpa sat on my hospital bed and rubbed Coco's body. He looked at me and then rubbed my head.

"I'll always be here for you. You take care. Continue to train, and we'll be back to visit. I promise. Isn't that right, Dusty?"

Dusty started to climb the hospital bed in an attempt to see me. He lifted his jaws on the bed as I rubbed the top of his mouth. I was sad because I knew I would miss them fiercely.

"Don't waste a second, Justin . If you're able to train, then you're able to win."

He hugged me before leaving the room. I knew the feeling of sadness wouldn't last, but the fear of losing Grandpa left me vulnerable. Grandpa was my biggest fan, my number one supporter, and he had always been my protector. I lost the privilege of seeing him every day. In more ways than one, my way of living was about to change forever.

But from that moment on we weren't alone, and we never would be again.

The next few days passed at a rate similar to the speed of a red footed tortoise. Dull, motionless, and incredibly slow. So much so that I was quickly losing my patience. It wasn't long before I started to eat more to regain my strength. I continued to balance on the side of our bed and forced myself to complete multiple rounds of double crunches. I'd complete a set of one hundred, all before any nurse could catch me. I tried my best to take advantage of my current placement. The infirmary had a large glass window which allowed everyone on the third floor to stare down at other members of the Cultivation Squad.

Me and Cameron gazed out the window for hours watching as I started to learn more about each camp. The entrance to both Farmer's and Hunter's Camps sat directly in front of us. Each camp was responsible for completing a variety of daily tasks. They were all like little worker ants in a giant colony. Some Farmers were stockpiling food for the winter, while Hunters were out tracking down AFA members and collecting their bounties.

Farmers would plant, water, and weed out the crops in the front of their camp. While Hunters were in charge of protecting and rejuvenating nearby ecosystems. Coco and I learned the infirmary was a happening spot for many Hunters. Those who lost challenges and some even if they'd won would still sustain enough injuries that required medical attention.

We had our partner patches checked and updated by the onsite repairman. It made sense having a Patch Repairman located on the third floor. It was a requirement of both camps to ensure trainers and partners were happy and healthy. The nurse came by and removed the hyper cast from my nose. I would never take breathing from my nose for granted again. Roxanne came by and visited the following day. She and Diego brought us plates of dessert from downstairs. Chocolate mousse cake with a large scoop of vanilla ice cream.

I introduced her to Cameron and Rudolph as we hesitantly shared our dessert with Cameron. Rudolph took one look at Diego and became very anxious. The young buck started breathing heavily and quickly backed away. Cameron called Rudolph back as his white-tailed partner tip toed closer to the bed. He and Diego locked eyes as the thought of fight or flight created tension in the room. Coco slowly limped over to the edge of my bed and started sniffing at Diego. Diego recognized Coco and walked closer to her. I placed my hand up in front of Coco and gently scratched Diego's head.

"Diego is a good jaguar. See, Rudolph, he's very nice," I whispered to the young buck.

"Back, Diego. Be nice," Roxanne snapped.

The buck returned to the bed alongside Cameron. Both Diego and Rudolph sniffed each other and stood more calmly and peacefully. Diego exhibited no signs of negative or aggressive behavior. Roxanne was able to relax as she shared her first-day experience along with all of the different classes she attended. The six of us shared a few laughable moments of small talk. Everyone was having a great time until Roxanne had to break away and report for patrol.

Late night patrols were a requirement for all new additions to the Hunter's Camp. Their job was to patrol the outskirts of camp and protect the surrounding ecosystems for their first few months. Once John Rigby deemed you trustworthy, he entrusted members of the Hunter's Camp with assignments.

Sometimes this included tracking down classified individuals and bringing them to justice. There were a wide variety of criminals on the WT's radar who had managed to escape confinement and needed to report for their crimes against Ignacia. That's where Hunters came in. The camp was well-known around the country. Roxanne revealed they had a certain saying, even though it was more of a pledge.

"Hunters will be fearless until there is no need. Hunters will fight until there is no need. Hunters will protect, always, and forever."

Todd and Al suddenly entered the infirmary. "How sweet is this? A den full of dorks."

I stood from my bed and glared at him from across the room.

Todd smirked. "Ah, Justin, how's the arm?"

I walked out from my hospital bed and up to Todd. "It's actually coming along nicely, but these stitches I'm not a fan of. In fact, maybe I should go ahead and break some?"

Al began to hiss as I slowly approached him and Todd.

"Now, Justin, we mustn't make a mess. Then you'd live in here permanently. Hmm on second thought—"

"What is it, Todd?" Roxanne loudly interjected.

"You're wanted for patrol, and Rigby wants you on Squad Five. Of course, that's tough work for a newbie. You think you can handle it?"

"Todd, aren't you on Squad Five?"

Todd smirked. "Yep, lucky you. You kids have fun playing doctor. We'll be out protecting the world."

Todd turned to leave just as I grabbed him by the arm. Coco climbed to the top of our hospital bed and watched from afar. She could sense my anger rising within my body.

"Look at my partner over there." I whispered as I slowly began to squeeze his arm. "Go ahead. Look at what you did to her. If you ever hurt her again, I will break you. And I'll be sure you don't make it back up here." My skin started to shine as the metallic color enveloped my hands. I felt my fingers squeezing Todd's blood through the layers of muscles and tendons.

He glared back at me. "Take your hand off me."

I steadily lowered my hand, exhaled deeply, and quickly launched my left hand at his throat and pinned him to the ground. My right-hand launched up in the air as I anticipated his partner's attack. Al quickly launched himself at me. I intercepted the croc's attack with my right hand and squeezed his jaws shut. Todd brought both of his hands to my forearm and attempted to break free; however, his strength was no match for my metallic armor. He struggled to breathe as his throat sat exposed in my hand while Al attempted to barrel roll to break free, but I was not giving an inch.

"Justin. What are you doing?" Roxanne yelled.

Forcing myself, I muttered, "I'll see you in six months. Until then. Stay away from my friends."

I released both of them as Todd coughed and struggled to breathe and Al awaited orders to attack. I calmly stood and returned to my bed moments before the nurses returned. Coco remained at the top of our bed and watched as Todd and Al glared back at us.

The head nurse strutted in. "What is going on here?"

"I... uh... slipped. Yeah. We're just here for Roxanne. It's time for patrol."

Roxanne stood and slowly crossed the room, looking back at me and Cameron, ashamed. I wasn't proud of my actions, but a line needed to be drawn. I wasn't going to allow Todd to vindicate my time in The Cultivation Squad. This was a new playing field, and I had no problem reminding him of the damage Coco and I could cause.

Coco and I remained in bed restless. She had a bad habit of climbing the metal pole which held my medical IV drip. As each day passed, more of Coco's casts and bandages were removed. I was still bruised a little internally and my stitches were still fresh. The stitches on my right arm popped open and were bleeding slightly as a result of my actions the night prior. When a nurse asked how it happened, I was forced to lie. "I fell going to the bathroom."

Our time spent in the third-floor infirmary allowed me to get to know Cameron and Rudolph very well since we resided less than seven feet away from one another. Rudolph and Cameron both snored and had gas problems. Coco, on the other hand, dug into her sheets while she slept. Between the three of them, I found it difficult to sleep.

At one point, I forced myself to use my headphones if I was going to get any sleep. Fortunately, I was able to doze off to the sound of smooth jazz. I understood why Grandpa enjoyed it so much. We became comfortable in the infirmary and I remembered how nice it was to have friends.

On the morning of the third day, we were released and allowed to return to the Farmer's Camp. I was happy to watch the remainder of Coco's bandages and casts come off. The medication along with the quick work of the medic bots fixed us both up nicely. Coco had a couple of scars from Al's bite that circled her body. Collectively they all looked like little tattoos. Coco began walking and moving on her own but was recommended to take it easy for at least a week. I took a nice hot shower that morning in the infirmary and changed into one of my Cultivation Squad uniforms. I placed Coco back on my shoulder to ensure her protection.

We finally departed the infirmary and entered the dining hall around 8:00 a.m. We'd long awaited the chance to partake in their legendary breakfast firsthand. In the infirmary, they pre-made a sort of cold breakfast, but you could have anything you wanted downstairs in the dining hall. Fruit, toast, hash browns, omelets, everything was completely included when you're a member of the Cultivation Squad. I made a well-balanced plate for me and one for Coco. The four of us sat down and ate quietly until we were joined by Davis and his Saddleback pig, Sam.

Davis walked up to our table. "Justin, hey, how are you?"

"Oh, hey, we're good. Just a couple of days in the infirmary, and we're good to go."

"Nice. I'm sorry about what happened. If it's any consolation, we like the Farmer's Camp, and I think you will, too."

"Thanks, Davis. Glad you and Sam are having a good time. Do you know Cameron?"

"No, not yet. Hey there, I'm Davis, and this is my partner Sam." Davis smiled and offered his hand to Cameron.

Cameron shook his hand respectfully and smiled back. "Cameron, and this is Rudolph."

Sam moved closer to Rudolph and began to sniff and snort at him. Coco left my shoulder and crawled across the table to sniff Sam. It was a triangle of sniffing and familiarizing themselves with one another. We all ate breakfast together and departed the dining hall after being confined to that one building for two and a half days.

"You may wanna touch base with Herbert in the Green house. That's where his office is," Davis advised.

"Who's Herbert?"

"He's head of the Famers' Camp. Don't worry, he's cool. I'll introduce you," Cameron chimed in.

We walked through the bright field of crops and past the rows of safari-style tents until we reached The Greenhouse. Inside we found a small office located behind the computer lab portion of the plant conservatory. Cameron, Rudolph, Coco, and I hesitantly walked through the door.

Cameron entered the office first and called out, "Hello? Herbert?"

Suddenly the lights turned on, and in front of us stood a tall, slender man wearing blue overalls, a white button-down shirt, brown boots, with short brown hair slicked to the side. He wore thick brown glasses that covered most of his face.

"Good morning, you guys! Ah, Cameron, welcome back to the Farmer's Camp. I'm sorry about your loss yesterday, but I'm sure you'll be victorious next time. Don't you worry."

Cameron stepped aside and motioned to me. "Justin, this is Herb. Herb, this is Justin."

Herb approached me. "Welcome to the Farmer's Camp!" He shook my hand, his palms covered in dirt with soil lodged under his fingertips.

"Herbert Sanders at your service. I'm the director of the Farmer's Camp. This is my partner Neville. Oh, please mind the mess. We were just differentiating levels of soil and sedimentation."

He fished into his middle pocket of his overalls and brought out a large mole. The mole slowly opened his small freckle sized eyes and sniffed around my face. Coco leaned forward from my shoulder and attempted to sniff him. Neville heard her sniffs and fearfully began to squirm.

"Okay, okay. I'll put you back in," Herbert mumbled to Neville. He placed Neville back in his middle pocket. Herbert then grabbed a handful of soil from his desk and placed it inside the pocket and sprinkled it over him. I looked at Cameron confused and slightly concerned.

"Is that a European Mole by chance? They're very rare. I didn't think there were any in Ignacia?"

"Ah, you have a good eye. Correct. Neville is one of the only European Moles in all of Ignacia. He's the best at what he does."

"Which is what?" I asked.

"He removes unwanted critters from our crops. I was just about to unleash him for the day. You guys can come with us. I'll have your day-to-day assignments for you as well. Cameron, if you and Rudolph please rejoin Squad One in the wheat and corn fields behind the Green House."

Cameron sighed deeply. "Yes, sir."

My friend patted me on the shoulder and departed from the Greenhouse. "See you out there!"

Herbert glanced at me with a perplexed look. "Justin. That's right, I read your file. Justin Steele."

"Yes sir."

"And this must be your partner Coco. What a beautiful little coati. You know we have a few of them around camp. Hi, little one. You have some great fingernails for digging!"

"There are other trainers with coatis?"

"I'm afraid not, but there is a small band of coatimundis that roam the outskirts of both camps. They are involved in one of the many ecosystem projects. They are safely monitored by the Hunter's Camp."

"I'll definitely keep an eye out for them. Did you know we were coming?"

Herb began measuring the volume of piles of soil. "Of course, well technically I only remember because I spoke with your grandpa before he left."

"Really?"

"You know Herschel was the one who placed me with Neville. But we've got your game plan all mapped out. We have you in the fields working in the front with crops in Squad Three for the first few days so you two can heal up properly. Once you're fully recovered we'll place you in the fields with Cameron and Squad One. Sound good?"

"Sure. Umm, that works I guess," I answered unenthusiastically.

"What's wrong?"

"Sir, you need to know that I have every intention of becoming a Hunter. My father did it, my grandfather did it, and in six months I'll have my chance for a rematch."

"Of course, I completely understand."

"You do?"

"Justin, this camp isn't designed for everyone. If you're a hunter at heart, who am I to stand in your way?"

"So, can I just transfer?"

"I'm afraid not, we have to get you strong enough for your rematch. That's just the way things are around here. Until then, start small. We'll add to your workload each day. You'll be the strongest Farmer in no time!"

"All right, Mr. Sanders, thank you."

"Not a problem, Justin. Oh, and call me Herb. Have you gotten settled in yet? Let me check the roster."

Herb pulled out a large wooden clipboard and flipped through pages of dirty papers until he landed on a long list of names and numbers.

"Since you are one of our latest additions, we have you in housing unit number 314. It's located on the east side of the housing units not too far from the out houses. Remember, your key is under the mat. Go ahead and get situated. Be sure you leave your cell phone in your room and personal belongings inside your new space. Meet me at the front of the camp in thirty. We'll explain more about what you'll be doing each day."

"Yes, sir, sounds good, Herb."

Coco and I exited the Green House and scanned the hundreds of safari-style tents. We walked about fifty yards east and found unit number 314. It stood about fifteen feet high, had two small windows at ground level and a wooden door in between. I grabbed the key under the mat and made my way inside. The welcome mat sat just in front of the door and read, "Wipe your feet on me!". I carefully wiped my shoes before entering the new space.

Once inside I saw my bedroom was in the same room as the front door. The floor was sleek brown and wooden as if it had been renovated and cleaned. The AC was pumping nice cool air into the tent. It was similar to the rooms that Lyza and Rus had at The Docks. A bed, a chair, a desk, a marble countertop, closet space, and a dresser to put clothes in.

"Grandpa was right. Camping in style," I whispered happily,

My luggage had been sensibly organized and placed next to my bed. A letter had been carefully placed on top of it. I cautiously looked at the return address on top of the envelope:

Lyza Rybakova.

CHAPTER 12

Digging for the Truth

Time seemed to pause as a warm feeling glazed over the surface of my skin. The thought of Lyza taking the time to write me this letter filled me to the brim with smiles. I carefully placed Coco down on our new bed. My thumb slid down the special blue lining etched into the edges of the letter. I knew I was needed at the front of the camp. A part of me would not allow myself to leave my tent without reading what Lyza wrote. I jumped on the new queen bed and held the letter in the air as I read it.

Hello, Justin Steele,

I am glad you survived the attack at The Docks. Had I known you were going to find trouble, I would've at least joined you. Then again, it seems you have a knack for finding trouble. Another reason why you will be the perfect addition for the Hunter's Camp. We just moved into our new room when I found your letter. It was a sweet letter, but I think you need more practice. Luckily, I am patient enough to show you how it is done. Ivan is very happy that his habitat is connected to my room. One side faces my room while the other leads to ocean access. Honestly, it all looks very expensive. The Exploration Squad is a mysterious place. It's always very dark outside of the Sandpiper submarine. People are usually nice, but not everyone. I am sorry about you and your friend. I saw Rus and his partner Kanoa. They moved in down the hall from us, he did not seem like himself.

Tell me everything about the Cultivation Squad! What is it like? Are you a Hunter yet?

I will patiently wait for your next letter.

Sincerely,

Lyza Rybakova

My heart melted as I brought the letter down on my chest. I remembered our last embrace, that timid feeling which kept me from opening up and saying more. It was a daunting feeling, one that haunted me daily. I reminded myself that the next time I saw her, I'd tell her how I felt. Coco walked across the bed and stood on my stomach on top of the letter. I scratched her head and kissed her forehead before moving her off to prepare for farm work.

I put sunscreen on my face, my neck and behind my ears. I prepared for a multitude of sweaty and tiresome tasks that would leave my body in grave need of a shower. With Lyza and Ivan on my mind, I wanted to succeed in everything I did. They inspired me to do and be more. I grabbed a new set of gardening gloves out of my Farmer's Camp kit. I put my new tool belt on around my waist. The belt came equipped with a wide array of tools: cutting pruners, a trowel, bamboo gloves, a foldable rake, a cultivator, and a transplanter. All were mandatory tools each Farmer was required to have on hand.

As I continued getting ready, I started to think how I would respond to Lyza's letter. I wanted to impress her with stories of excitement and not reveal my failure in the Cultivation Squad. I reached my arm down to the bed and signaled for Coco to jump up my arm. She quickly scampered across the bed with a few excited pants. She made her way over my covered arm as I threw on my red hat. Coco proudly stood on top of my head and continued to take in the new scents and sensations our safari tent provided from a new height.

I attached Coco's leash to her harness as she casually sat on my shoulder. We walked out the door of our new safari tent and locked it up behind us. I pocketed my new key, and we made our way to the front of camp.

Coco felt slightly heavier as she sat on my neck. I could tell she was growing and slowly putting on more weight.

After being in the hospital the past few days, she seemed chipper and excited to be back outside. We passed many trainers and partners alike. I was excited to meet new people and try to reshape my image in the eyes of both camps. I didn't want them to know me as the son of Noah Steele or the grandson of Herschel Steele.

Each Farmer we saw waved to us, so we politely waved back. It wasn't until we reached the front of the camp that I heard snickers from a few Hunters pointing at us from the neighboring camp.

"Just ignore them. They'll get over themselves." I heard a familiar voice from behind that almost startled me,

A shorter girl was working on the ground next to a gardening cart. She was picking weeds out of a variety of different plants. Behind the girl stood a black and white spotted Holstein Friesian cow. I quickly recognized the girl as someone Roxanne and I met on the first day. Looking up, she smiled. "How are you feeling?"

I remained quiet. I was embarrassed by how badly we lost to Todd but also at the fact that I couldn't remember this kind girl's name. My thoughts raced as I searched for a remnant of her name. No luck. I would simply have to ask.

"We're feeling much better, thanks... What was your name again? I'm sorry."

"No, that's okay. There was a lot happening that day. Hi, I'm Sammy."

"Nice to re-meet you. I'm Justin. This is Coco, and this must be your partner?" I asked, pointing to the cow standing behind her.

Sammy stood up and rubbed the top of the cow's head. "This is Ruby! She's my perfect, big-headed tank." The cow stood lazily chewing and eating grass. She suddenly stopped chewing, pooped, and went back to eating.

"Wow. She... uhm, seems very healthy." Coco leaned over my shoulder and sniffed the scent of the nearby cow and her droppings.

Sammy laughed. "She's fertilizing the plants, oh...which reminds me. Herb mentioned you're up here in Squad 3 today, right?"

Sweat seeped into my eye. "Yeah. Apparently for the first few days. But I was supposed to meet him up here—"

"He was here a few minutes ago. He just released Neville."

"He's a cute mole isn't he?"

Sammy laughed. "Herb loves his little mole. Neville is currently underground removing little insects, parasites, and other pests. It's our job to do the same above the ground. I guess Herb left you with me. Let me show you what we do each day."

"All right, where do we start?"

Sammy and Ruby walked us through a multitude of tasks from planting to watering, weeding, digging, and harvesting. She had a vast knowledge of fruits, vegetables, and a variety of medicinal herbs. Sammy's knowledge, however, was not due to any class or training she'd received within her first few days. Sammy knew the information because she grew up on a farm in South Ignacia. Her father owned and operated one of Ignacia's finest dairy companies, so it was no surprise she ended up with a cow.

Coco was able to assist me with digging up crops like potatoes and onions. Sammy showed me what tool did what. It was like a gardening course on steroids. During each harvest, I had to practice at least twice before I was able to perform the simplest tasks successfully. It was pretty obvious I was not used to manual labor.

We worked through miles of cropland plantations, performing these tasks over and over. Sammy appeared to be a natural at this type of work. It didn't take me long to realize how invaluable of a person she was to know here. She was kind, funny and generous to everyone around her.

Sammy's alarm on her watch sounded. "Oh, it's 12 p.m., time for our lunch!"

I peeled my sweaty gloves off my hands and panted. "Thank the Lord."

After three hours of manual labor, my shirt was drenched, my hat was soaked in sweat and Coco was panting hard. The two of us were wiped out, and the day was just getting started. I pulled out my water bottle and began guzzling. I had a foldable bowl that I pulled out of my belt and quickly filled with water for Coco. She sipped the water quickly and eventually jumped into the bowl to cool her body temperature. After she left the bowl, she climbed back on my shoulder. The water from her body fell off her fur and blended in with the sweat stains on my shirt.

Sammy carried herself well and seemed generally unaffected by the difficulty of manual labor. We followed her and Ruby back to Zhang Dining Hall. We walked into the air-conditioned space to find hundreds of sweaty and smelly members of the Farmer's Camp. I was amazed to see how many Farmers there were. Davis and Cameron stood alongside each other in line on the other side of the dining hall. Sammy and I patiently waited in line together with our partners.

After a few minutes we eventually selected our food from the menu items once we reached the front of the line. We all walked over and joined Cameron and Davis at one of the long wooden tables. The four of us complained about the heat, talked about our partners, and compared different behaviors we were working on with them. It had to have been one of the best lunches I'd ever had.

It reminded me of the lunches I used to share with Rus and Roxanne. The past lunches were spent wondering, hoping, and praying to become something more. As the still frame of my friends lingered in the back of my mind, a part of me started to miss them.

My eyes blinked as I snapped out of it and remembered where I was. I knew I wanted to spend more time with Sammy, Cameron, and Davis. They were all incredibly accepting and very supportive. We were all in a new place just trying to learn what we needed to do in order to rise in the ranks. I knew at that moment I was exactly where I was supposed to be. A buzzer went off in the Zhang dining hall which informed the members of the Farmer's Camp that lunch break was over. It was time to begin our classroom session for the day. Once Farmer's Camp finished their lunch at 1 p.m., the cleanup crew of three janitorial staff members wiped down tables as their three Billy goat partners ate the droppings off the floor. After the cleanup crew finished their round, the Hunter's Camp kicked off their lunch period.

As we departed the dining hall, I glanced back in time to catch a glimpse of Roxanne walking into the dining hall. She was smiling and laughing as she walked with other girls I didn't recognize. I stopped in my tracks and attempted to wave. However, she was too invested in the conversation with her new friends. She was happy though, and that was all that mattered.

Coco and I re-joined our lunch mates and walked out of the dining hall and made our way over to the Green House. Coco wanted to walk on the ground alongside Davis's partner, Sam. The two continued to sniff each other as they walked in front of their trainers. We entered the towering old structure to find the lights on and creaky wooden ceiling fans moving around the humid air.

The building itself needed some technological modifications. The room was covered with outdated floor tiles that appeared weathered and cracked. Piles of dirt and soil sat scattered in the corners of the room. An old projector stood in the middle of the class and projected a large photo of our country, Ignacia, onto a thick white scrim. The layout of the classroom included numerous desks and computers scattered throughout the room. I felt as if I were in an under-funded high school from the stone age.

I took a seat alongside Cameron. Coco quickly leaped onto my lap and started to fall asleep. There were about twenty-five members in the class. The class included the first three weeks' worth of Farmers who were required to report to Herb. I saw a variety of animals and members I had not yet met. There was a chipmunk, a squirrel, a raccoon, a opossum, a porcupine, a snapping turtle, and other small mammals. Herb entered from his office. He stood proudly and waited until the room quieted down.

"I hope everyone had a productive morning and enjoyed their lunches. Today we will be reviewing some history in preparation for more agriculture-based studies. Our job is to build, create, and excel. If we can continue to plant, grow, and harvest, we will do what Ignacia needs in order to blossom. Everybody with me?"

The class nodded and remained focused on Herb as Coco climbed up onto my shoulder.

"Now then, can anyone tell me about the Dutch Elm Crisis?"

Davis hesitantly raised his hand. "It happened in 2980 up in Northern Ignacia."

"That is correct, uh, what was your name?"

"Davis Graham, sir."

"Thank you, Mr. Graham. Class, what else can you tell me? Anyone? Come on, please. Don't be hesitant or bashful."

Multiple members raised their hands in a flash. They all wished to be recognized and answer Herb's question.

Herb called on a student in the back row of the Green House. "Yes, ma'am, Miss Bates."

"Genocide on a global scale. Hundreds of thousands of deaths."

Herb winced. "A bit dark but, yes, you are correct, Miss Bates. People! What we are looking for is historically accurate information. Raw, valid, facts, guys. We want the story and learn how the WT came to be. We don't want to miss a beat. So that's what we'll do. Let's review that story, shall we? Every nook and cranny of it."

Herb crossed the room and slowly walked through the rows of students. "Almost a century ago, Ignacia was a booming country. Built by money-hungry suits with corporations funding every bad decision made. So much so that we had several corporate districts located in the northwestern region. Thousands of people spent day after day fixated on turning a profit. The nation had lost sight of its natural resources. One of these corporations was called Energy Biochemical Specialists LLC or EBS. I'm sure you've heard of them."

Sammy, Davis, Cameron along with the majority of the room nodded their heads. Herb changed the slide on the projector. It showed the EBS towering structure that sat next to a deep forest.

Herb sighed. "One day, EBS was experimenting with a vaccine in order to expand the lifespans of different germs to fight bacteria. They were going to make millions and become the front runners in the world of medicine. They decided to test their man-made vaccine on a very powerful virus: Ophiostoma Ulmi. This virus was powerful and, more importantly, incurable. Now the scientists at EBS were up for the challenge. They placed their compounds against the bacteria but continued to fail miserably. A year passed and the scientists became exhausted. They could not create a vaccine strong enough to combat the virus. They decided to safely discard their experiment by burning all evidence in a furnace. However, the janitorial staff of the building claimed that it was taken out mistakenly and placed in the garbage. A multitude of health cases started breaking out in the nearby environment shortly after.

"The virus found a way to adapt and mutate based on the chemical reaction from the man-made vaccine. It infected beetles, bugs, and all sorts of insects! The birds started to eat the infected insects, while the nearby predators ate the birds.

"This virus continued to change and grow until it destroyed its host completely. It became a plague that continued to destroy everything in its path. The amount of loss shook our country to its core and caused ecosystems in North Ignacia to collapse. The climate change that occurred in Ignacia was overwhelming.

"Hundreds of species of animals began dying out from this virus alone. Human beings suffered with thousands of casualties. Food shortages began erupting throughout the country. Scientists begged the government for change and to invest in the environment in order to protect our patrons, our animals, our natural resources and to stop funding major corporations. Six years later, in 2986, the Arc Project was created."

I couldn't help but remember Grandpa's story. Of how he and Uncle Fred sat in a storage unit for days until they were rescued while their parents became infected and suffered. Herb highlighted the amount of death and environmental ruin the country experienced. The slides depicted full hospital beds, full veterinary offices, and my mouth dropped.

Herb continued, "Those earlier members of the task force were responsible for collecting, protecting, treating, and reengineering animal DNA. Scientists knew if they studied each individual mutated virus, they could formulate a vaccine to help cure each animal, and they could protect certain species from dying out. Once all the non-affected animals were successfully collected, they destroyed the infected forestation the only way they know how."

Herb changed the slide to a photo of people with gas masks burning down trees with flamethrowers. Herb pulled out his lighter and ignited a small flame, "They burned it to the ground."

We all sat filled with discomfort in the awkward space that Herb managed to create. He released his lighter, diffusing the flame. I placed my hand on Coco in fear of losing her to such a wicked fate.

Herb sneezed abruptly and awkwardly wiped his nose with his forearm. He continued, "Where was I? Yes, as I was saying, scientists knew that if animals died out and we were left without any primary resources, then humanity would soon follow. They expressed their concerns to the big-headed suits who controlled the country. Somehow, someone convinced them to provide financial assistance and fund their animal rehabilitation project. Henceforth, The Arc Task Force was enacted in 2986, and the rest is history."

The class continued on and broke the new members into different squads of their camp. It seemed like a relatively familiar exercise where Herb pointed at someone and told him or her which squad they would go to. He carefully read down the list of his new members on his dirty clipboard. When he got to me, however, he said, "Justin Steele. Floater."

I was very confused on where I was to report and what I was supposed to do. The last time I spoke with Herb we clearly discussed staying with Sammy in Squad 3 for a few days. Herb looked up from his clipboard and saw the look of confusion on my face. He pressed the bridge of his glasses up his nose.

"Mr. Steele, you are a floater, someone who goes to a different group every day. Today you were with Squad Three in the croplands. Seeing how well you did there, I'm moving you to Squad Two tomorrow. You'll be here in the Green House."

Davis leaned forward, looked at me. "Nice. I'll be in here, too!" He smiled and gave me a thumbs up.

I smiled and did the same. I was relieved that at least I would continue to have a friendly face in each new space.

Later I learned about the different jobs that occurred in Squad Two; however, they were not the jobs that I needed in order to get my body where it needed to be. During the rest of our time in the Green House, Herb classified the newer group of members and explained the importance of each job.

"Now I don't want anyone confused about the different groups or system of labor here. What's Squad One?"

The class yelled back in unison, "Plowing fields!"

Herb raised two fingers, "Excellent, what about Squad Two?"

The class shouted, "Making Medicine!"

Herb laughed and raised a third finger. "That's right, and finally, Squad Three?"

"Harvesting!" The class screamed.

Herb wiped the sweat from his brow, "And what did the duck say to the Farmer after he ate the Farmer's crops?"

The class looked at one another, searching for someone who knew the answer.

Herb smiled. "Put it on my bill!"

The room was split in two amongst students who indulged Herb's sense of humor and those who were unaffected by the joke. After three hours of reviewing jobs, daily tasks, and Herb's comical dad jokes to the group, we were released from the Green House and returned to our original posts.

Coco and I rejoined Sammy and Ruby in the croplands. We continued our work by picking, snipping, digging, plucking, and gardening hundreds of fruits and vegetables. After someone collected a bounty of crops, he or she was supposed to deliver their collection to the loading dock located on the backside of the dining hall. There the produce was cleaned, prepped, and 75% of the crops were shipped off to the different areas of Ignacia. The other 25% was kept and stored at The Cultivation Squad to provide team member meals. After we completed our drop at the loading dock, Miss Peterson appeared out of nowhere."

"Mr. Steele, may I borrow you for a moment?"

I looked over to Sammy, "We'll catch up with you guys in a bit."

Sammy smiled. "Take your time. We'll see you later!" She continued rolling the cart back over to the crop lands with Ruby by her side.

I walked over to Miss Peterson on the loading dock and followed her inside the dining hall. Inside stood twenty to thirty people separating, cleaning, cutting, and preparing fruits and vegetables on a moving assembly line. Each person had a small bird that resided on each of their shoulders as if they were members of the Transferal Squad. Sammy told me later that the Cultivation Squad had an arrangement with the Transferal Squad. Flyers sent their people to clean, prep, and ship out products to the market, and the Farmers would share a portion of the profits. I stopped momentarily to observe, but Miss Peterson did not stop walking. My eyes peered up and noticed she was on the other side of the room. I quickly followed after her while Coco remained on my shoulder.

After we left the separating room, I followed her down a tall hallway. Four distinct framed timber doorways appeared leading to four different offices. The doorways had been carefully designed, sculpted, and sanded. The hallway alone could've passed as a museum. We continued down the hallway until we arrived at the last office on the left. Miss Peterson pulled out one of her keys and opened the large door. While she fished for her keys, an office door opened on the opposite end of the hall. It was the same older gentleman I'd run into at The Docks. Vladimir Mathias.

The older man wore a two-piece, navy-blue suit, gray fedora, black leather gloves, with a grey overcoat and the same navy-blue bow tie. Vlad exited his office door but had no guards with him. He chuckled when he turned around and saw me.

Mathias laughed and raised his hat, "Ha-ho! Good to see you Mr. Steele."

I remembered Grandpa's words and how I was supposed to run away from him if I was to ever see him again. I slowly backed away and attempted to walk into Miss Peterson's office.

Vlad continued, "I never did hear back from you. If you need anything, don't hesitate to call. I suppose you know where to find me now, don't you?" He laughed to himself and walked down the hallway toward the exit.

I fearfully entered the office and hid away from the leader of the suits. I closed the door behind me as my head began to fill with questions. I voiced my concern to Miss Peterson, "What's that man doing here? He's not in the Cultivation Squad."

Miss Peterson approached me confused, "Mr. Mathias? Oh, he's one of the largest donors for our division. Naturally we decided to award him an office to come and go as he pleases. You'll see him here from time to time. Are you all right?"

I asked myself internally, "Were the suits more involved with the WT than we knew? What was their goal? What did Vlad want?"

"I'm fine, thanks." I knew that Miss Peterson would not give me the honest answers for the questions I had.

The office was decadent and included an immensely high ceiling. The gold painted structure included a lovely chandelier with a mixture of glass and crystals hanging from it. She had a brown, waxed, desk that looked as if it had been hand-crafted from a freshly chopped down tree. Housed in the corner in a small area of the room was a small pond surrounded by soil. Inside the water resided her large male platypus.

"Please take a seat, Mr. Steele, so we can go ahead and get started."

I wiped the sweat coming down my face and sat down in a soft furnished chair, fearing my shirt might leave sweat stains. Coco tried to climb up my arm back to my shoulder. I stopped her midway, placed her on the ground and removed her leash.

"Do you know why you're here, Mr. Steele?

"Not really, we were placed into the Cultivation Squad so—"

"You mean your grandfather did."

"Umm, not really. The Animal Bridging Council voted and made their choice as a group."

"A council in which your grandfather just happens to be the president. Correct?"

"Yes, but what does that have to do with me here?"

"We're keeping an eye on you, Mr. Steele. A very close eye. Your father and grandfather made this Squad their playground, something I will not tolerate to happen with you. I've asked you to come here today for several reasons. Firstly, your pay. Notice the contract I have in front of you on my desk. See anything missing? We were unable to receive a signature from you on your first day."

"Well, I was a little preoccupied in the infirmary, after taking a beating in front of the squad."

"I know, how unfortunate," she said sarcastically. "Anyway, we have a payment plan that I did not properly have the opportunity to explain to you one on one."

"Okay, so what's my starting rate?"

"You'll start with $50 a day. Payment is provided every two weeks on a Monday. That is the standard for a level one member of the Cultivation Squad. The more time you spend here the higher your level and base pay will be. But you cannot simply lounge around, you have to work at it. You have to rise in level in order to increase your pay."

"How do I do that? Challenging people?"

"No. In your case, as a Farmer there are a variety of different ways to rise in level. Each level you achieve will add $1 to your overall base pay. Level increases for Farmers occur every day depending on your squad. Squad Three is located in the croplands, as I'm certain you're familiar with. If the crops you provide from the croplands perform well in the market, you will rise another level. Squad Two is located in the Green House and is the science involved with learning to create medicinal remedies. The more medicinal creams, treatment, and pills you create, you rise another level. Lastly, Squad One is located in the wheat and cornfields about a mile north of the camp. If you're able to plow an entire acre of land successfully, you rise another level. Do you understand?"

"I think so, but what about the Hunter's Camp?"

"Hunters have a completely different system of payment. One that you don't need to concern yourself with as of yet."

"Please. I've got six months before I challenge them again. And you better believe I'm going to win."

"If you say so, for members of the Hunter's Camp level one also begins at $50 a day for their base pay. Hunters climb in levels when they win their challenges. Challenges occur each day but can only happen once a day per member. If you win that challenge, your level and base pay rise by $5. Hunter's Camp is also paid based upon the number of bounties you collect."

"Bounty hunting."

"Correct. But as I previously stated, this is not something you must concern yourself with. Not yet."

I signed the contract and handed it over to Miss Peterson to file and submit to the WT. Coco continued to sniff out the room and approached the small pond. The platypus was old and groaned loudly at Coco. She was frightened and quickly retreated to me, climbing up my jeans and up on my shoulder again. I clipped her leash back on her harness while Miss Peterson's platypus submerged under the water.

"Is that it?" I asked.

"Not quite. Secondly, Justin, this camp is dangerous and requires consistent focus. If you lose sight of your objective at any point, it can cost you and your partner your lives. Just keep your head down and fight. Fight every day to get yourself closer to accomplishing your goal."

I nodded in understanding. "Thank you, Miss Peterson."

"That will be all, Mr. Steele. Thank you."

I slowly rose from my chair and made my way back outside to Sammy and Ruby. My brain was running wild with all of the potential opportunities that resided within the Cultivation Squad. I needed to rise in ranks, defeat Todd, join the Hunter's Camp and begin writing my story the way I wanted it to be told.

After finishing up our work in the croplands, the four of us rejoined Davis and Cameron in the dining hall for dinner. We shared stories on where we were from and how we ended up at the Cultivation Squad. All of them were from South Ignacia originally and even attended the same high school. We enjoyed a large protein-based dinner with turkey, spinach, squash, and asparagus. Coco enjoyed a variety of fruits, vegetables, and a chicken drumstick.

We then said our goodbyes and returned to our separate safari tents. Once inside, Coco immediately jumped onto the bed and curled into a ball. I removed my red hat and threw it on top of her. My partner immediately grabbed my sweaty hat and began tossing and turning with it on the bed. I grabbed my shower supplies, locked the door, and made my way to the bath house in the middle of camp.

The building resembled more of an old zomorodi wash drive-thru. It was wide, open, and bleak with little color. I walked through the men's entrance and noticed 20-30 guys walking around the shower stalls. I fast-walked through the space and kept my eyes to the floor. I found an empty shower stall and an empty bench across from it.

The water drain was clogged, and I had never been more thankful for shower shoes. I quickly found a plunger next to one of the toilets and unclogged the drain. Once the water went down I claimed the small stall, placed my belongings down on the bench and started my shower. The hot water felt great and was incredibly relieving after a long day in the hot sun. I shut my eyes in the luxury of a steamy shower. My wounds were healing rapidly. The soap slightly burned as it cleaned each crevice from my head to my toes. I heard someone approaching my direction, and I apprehensively opened my eyes.

A trainer and his rabbit walked past my stall and placed his belongings down in the stall next to mine. Guys from across the room started yelling, "Watch it!" and "Take it outside!" Members from both camps were given access to the same bath house. Of course, Hunters were almost never seen using the outdoor facilities. They had their own private restrooms, showers, and baths inside their apartments. I was paranoid because I wasn't used to sharing such a private space with any other people. I made it a mission to clean what I needed to clean and get out fast. It was the last place I wanted to spend a significant amount of time. I got out and reached for my towel to dry off. It was an older, large, red towel I'd brought from home. I wiped myself off and realized I'd forgotten my shirt. I threw on my boxers and some loose gym shorts so I could waddle back to my tent. After I left the Men's portion of the bath house, I saw Todd walking with Roxanne out of the dining hall.

I walked faster, hoping neither would see me. Suddenly I heard a young woman's voice behind me. "Justin! Justin, wait up!"

Roxanne and Diego jogged after me while Todd and Al paused and watched in the distance. I hesitated and then turned around to face her. "Hey, Roxanne, what's going on?"

"Hey, you're out! How's the Farmer's Camp?"

"It's okay. A lot of cool people. Staying busy in the hot sun. What about you? How's the life of a Hunter?"

"Pretty strict honestly. Rigby puts us through a lot of drills, combat training, and then late hours on border patrol."

"Gotcha." I looked to Diego. "Hey, Diego, you're looking good, bud." I scratched the top of Diego's head as he nestled into it.

"How's Todd been treating you?"

"Not bad, surprisingly. After seeing what Diego and I can do, I think he's a little intimidated by us."

I laughed. "As he should be. That's awesome!"

"Yeah, but I think we may have been wrong about him."

I stopped laughing. "What makes you say that?"

"I mean, yeah, he's Todd, but he's not all bad. He's actually been very sweet."

"Roxanne, the guy took a chunk out of my arm and my leg."

"You challenged him, though, right?"

"What's your point?"

"I'm just saying he was probably doing the best he could to stop you. You have your gift, and all he had was his ability to fight."

"Along with some smoke bombs, but yes, I get it. Roxanne, have you challenged anyone yet?"

"Well, no not yet."

I turned to leave. "Then you don't know how it feels to lose." I proceeded to get back to Coco.

"Where are you going?" Roxanne yelled after me.

"Back to my tent. Have a good night in your apartment, Roxanne."

It was an embarrassing sight, as I attempted to retreat away from Roxanne; my shower shoes squeaked loudly with an obnoxious slippery sound during each step. I tried my best to refrain from turning around, but eventually I succumbed to my own curiosity. The sight of Roxanne's disappointment made me instantly regret what I had said.

She and Diego were accompanied back by Todd and Al. The four of them continued back through the Hunter's Camp entrance. I paused and watched them leave. Todd's eyes flashed back and met mine. He had the same snickering grin he had when he had beaten me and Coco. I could tell he was starting to develop feelings for her by the way he watched her. It was strange watching Diego and Al walk alongside each other with no problems.

Maybe I was just being stubborn.

A part of me had hoped Roxanne would've been a little more upset that Todd had beaten one of her closest friends to a pulp. I suppose she, too, was in a new place and needed every ally she could find. Todd came from money; he had a predator and a lot of potential in The Hunter's Camp. I overheard in the dining hall that Todd had defeated another challenger earlier that day, one that was bigger and more experienced in the Hunter's Camp. Todd was now a level four hunter, making $70 a day while Al continued to grow more every day. He was becoming more lethal with each passing day. Something had to change if we were going to stand any chance against them.

Back at my tent I pulled out a pen and piece of paper and began to write.

Dear Lyza,

I just found your note and I'm happy to know that you and Ivan made it there safely. Things have gone a bit differently from what I had originally planned for me and Coco. Moving into a new place with new people hasn't been easy. Luckily, I've been fortunate enough to meet some kind people. A luxury I hope you too have experienced. When I arrived for my first day, I was informed I would have to challenge another Hunter in order to join the Hunter's Camp.

I challenged someone I recognized from my past. Somehow, I let my emotions get the better of me and I lost. But, I haven't given up. In six months, he, and I will have a rematch. I'll continue to train with Coco every day and stay focused on the task at hand. Coco and I have to push on, regardless of the outcome.

So, for now I've been placed in the Farmers Camp with some new friends: Sammy, Davis, and Cameron. It's not exactly what I had expected or anticipated but it's nice. I've been learning about crops, the history of Ignacia, and how to properly harvest.

I'm pretty sure the Cultivation Squad would be a lot better if you were a part of it. Even though now that I think about it, there isn't a body of water close enough to the camp for Ivan so maybe you wouldn't like it as much. I wish you and Ivan both the best of luck for what lies ahead. I'm excited to hear about the many adventures you two will experience.

Sincerely,

Justin and Coco

CHAPTER 13

The Awakening

The following four weeks flew by, and before I knew it, the cool winds of fall were upon us. The trees and their leaves all rapidly changed colors before my eyes. Each day we'd watch them fade from green to orange.

Coco and I continued to push ourselves to grow and change just as the leaves did. We wanted to learn something new every day and go beyond our physical limitations. To push ourselves harder, to jump farther and move with quickness and intensity in our actions. One that'd cause my body to appear as a blur to the naked eye.

I was determined to dramatically improve in every way possible. Coco and I started each day with an early three-mile run around the camp, a two-minute body plank, and one hundred pushups. The more we moved, the faster we became. The vivid memory of Todd's speed on the challenge field haunted me.

The fear of failure was a constant reminder of how we had to get bigger. It wasn't long before we'd grown accustomed to our weekly routine.

We'd spend Mondays and Tuesdays in the croplands with Sammy and Ruby. Wednesdays and Thursdays were spent creating and crafting medicinal applications with Davis and Sam in the Green House. Then on Fridays we were placed with Cameron and Rudolph in the corn fields. We'd push our muscles as hard as we possibly could plowing two acres of cornfields.

Saturdays and Sundays were always spent training. There was a gymnasium located on the south side of the shared bath house. Most members just took the weekend off to travel, go home and visit family. Some would venture out and travel across the country. However, neither was really an option for me. Grandpa was busy, my father was busy, and Lyza was unreachable. I must confess a part of me was not ready to return home.

Coco and I spent our weekends together training on the challenge field and lifting weights in the gym. Sometimes we'd take a shuttle to the town close by and go to the movies. Coco was never crazy about going to the movies, though. She had the attention span of a squirrel and would not allow herself to relax unless she was sleeping.

During the week, we'd spend the hottest time of the day avoiding the sun and meeting inside the Green House. We'd meet from 1 p.m.-3:00 p.m. for lessons and allow everyone to review their numbers. Herb called it our "daily classroom get-togethers."

We reviewed the number of products we'd created and sold, and he awarded new levels to members in our camp. Within the first week I gained three levels, and the following week I gained another four. I developed a system and knew how I would get to where I needed to be. Supposedly if you change to a different camp, your level stays with you, and your pay is never reduced. It was a fun fact I planned on taking full advantage of.

New members began showing up weekly and challenging Hunters in attempts to make it into the Hunter's Camp. Amongst the latest batch of new recruits, there was a girl named Terra. The new member had a serval, a meticulous cat known to be slender and tall with longer skinny legs. They were ruthless cats and could hunt a variety of rodents, birds, and even small reptiles.

However, they were relatively smaller cats that did not receive the automatic approval of the Hunter's Camp. Terra hesitantly chose to challenge

Kevin and his gray fox. Kevin and his partner began their journey as Hunters the same day Coco and I had arrived. The young Hunter appeared to have gotten much stronger after four weeks of training under John Rigby.

Kevin was a tank that had muscles bulging out of his Cultivation Squad shirt. For some reason he started wearing a red bandanna across his head. His gray fox growled at the young serval before the two faced off. The two partners shared a common mentality, power, and confidence. It didn't take long for them to defeat Terra and her serval. They ran circles around her, and Kevin never even touched her. The fox pinned the serval down as the young woman submitted to defeat out of fear.

I was shocked how quickly Terra had given up, but who was I to say anything? We'd lost just a few weeks prior, and the wound still felt fresh. I could see the love Terra had for her partner, it radiated from her eyes. She started to cry as Mr. Rigby declared Kevin the victor. As time went on, it became an unavoidable pattern. The more omnivores and smaller predators that arrived at the camp, the more victories the Hunter's Camp gained.

I was intimidated and became more fearful at the hindering thought that I would be stuck as a Farmer forever and that Todd would continue to grow stronger and remain victorious. In spite of that fear, a growing agitation sprouted like a weed in the back of my mind. He and Roxanne seemed to be spending more and more time together.

I was bewildered at the thought of the two of them dating. Not out of jealousy, not even on Russel's behalf, but because it didn't make sense to me. Todd was an ass, he was rude, obnoxious, and a bully to anyone that challenged him in passing. Roxanne was a force to be reckoned with. Why would she settle for such an arrogant prick?

Of course, Lyza and I continued to exchange letters two to three times a week. It was crazy how much she and I kept in contact. She'd share her greatest fears and her riveting adventures into the depths of the ocean. Lyza and Ivan had already fought off a great white shark together.

It was pretty crazy. I missed them both very much. I mentioned the idea of possibly visiting her, but she said she wouldn't be reachable for at least another four months. If I could just see her for the holiday season, not only would it give me something else to look forward to, but it would be the highlight of my year.

Coco was growing more each and every day. Her muscles grew stronger because of her active lifestyle and dietary choices. Regardless of what I'd present to her in the cafeteria, she always wanted what I was eating. Which led me to start eating more chicken, salad, and fruit.

We literally shared everything, even the same mindset of becoming stronger in order to protect one another. Thankfully we completed her off leash training just a week prior and we were deemed off leash certified! Coco was allowed to roam nearby and follow me off leash because she knew to always return to my side. She'd run with me every morning until she couldn't run any more.

Friday afternoon we walked wearily back from the corn fields with Cameron and Rudolph. Coco and I had just finished plowing through another acre of soil together and were ready to be done. Sweat trickled down my cheeks and stained my hat as Coco rapidly panted.

With the power of my armor and Coco's combined strength, I was able to complete an acre in the morning and another one in the afternoon. It became a successful way to end the week with two additional levels. Cameron and Rudolph pulled the plow together and finished one acre a day. With the two new levels, that brought me up to level fifteen!

We were walking past one of the ecosystems in the distance which was under the protection of the Hunter's Camp. Coco was panting loudly as she rested on my shoulder, that was until she sniffed something in the air. She immediately leaped onto the ground and scurried across the colorless wheat field overlooking the ecosystem. Three Hunters and their partners appeared in the thick green vegetation walking into a clearing. It was difficult to see who two of the trainers were, but I recognized the same snide sneer from a mile away. It was none other than Todd.

I quickly kneeled, yelled, and slammed my hand on my thigh, "Coco, come back now!"

She paused for a moment and looked back at me. There was something in the air that smelled like death. Something was wrong and I could feel the internal conflict that raged inside her mind. Coco turned back to face Todd, she remained focused and faced forward. She'd disobeyed my recall and remained fixated on the three Hunters.

"Oh, no."

Todd walked out from the forest alongside two of his new allies, Victor, and Hogarth. Both were older, stronger trainers who had made it their personal mission to take Todd under their wing. The three of them had been placed on patrol for that specific ecosystem close to camp.

Victor had an ocelot named Benny for a partner. Hogarth had a wolverine named Paxton. They all walked out of the woods with smug looks as they laughed at one another. Al had grown significantly and was approaching the size of Dusty. I examined Al closer and saw that the aggressive crocodile was carrying a motionless coati in his jaws. My eyes grew big when I realized what Coco had smelled.

The coati's body appeared limp and lifeless. Coco had paused but decided to move closer as she scurried through the wheat field until she stood just twenty yards from the Hunters. She forced her tail down to the ground as she attempted to stand tall and observe the predators over the wheat field, similar to a meerkat. I bolted after her and quietly stood five feet behind my partner.

A small squealing sound was coming from the Hunters. I knew that sound well; it was the first sound Coco made when the caretakers pulled her away from me. It was a scared baby coati, and hearing the sound again felt like sandpaper to my skin.

Todd's eyes met Coco. "Is that another intruder on the premises?"

Victor glanced over and saw me. "Nah, it's just Justin and his little friend."

"Such a shame! They do seem to resemble one another," he yelled back to me. "You're trespassing in ecosystem number five. You have to leave."

"Shut it, Todd. We aren't trespassing. Do us a favor and let the coati go."

Victor and Hogarth laughed.

Hogarth proudly announced, "Not a chance! We caught ourselves an intruder trying to sneak food from this enclosure. It has to be removed."

"They have to be removed. Both her and the baby," Todd added.

"The baby. That's what she smelled." I whispered. I stared back at Coco as her panting and squeaking increased.

Todd grabbed the small squeaking baby from Al's jaws and held the coati in his hands. The baby was shaking and scared.

Cameron and Rudolph caught up with us shortly after.

Cameron asked, struggling to breathe. "Hey!" He wheezed as he quickly inhaled and exhaled. "What'd I miss?"

"Todd caught a baby coati and its mother," I whispered.

"Really? Where are they now?" Cameron asked.

"Go on, boys, dig in!" Todd yelled.

"Oh no," Cameron mumbled.

A brief still frame appeared in my mind as my thoughts ran ramped and formulated an idea of what was about to happen. I heard the sound of three predators pulling the mother's body apart. I heard bodily fluids splatter along the ground as the predators engorged themselves on what they claimed to be a "disturbance" in their area. I looked back and saw the baby coati in Todd's hands who appeared to be just two months old. The orphaned coati squirmed in attempts to break free from Todd's clutches. She was frightened, alone, and searching for her mother. The kit searched for the same mother that helped raise, feed, and protect her. She looked down and went into shock as she realized her mother had become a shared meal.

A large metallic bell rang inside my chest that shook my rib cage, letting me know that this was wrong. No rule in the Cultivation Squad handbook would tell me differently. I looked over at Coco as she continued to watch. Her point of focus remained on the Hunters. I felt a small ball of red, aggressive energy begin to grow within the pit of her mind. Coco's rage quickly multiplied and engulfed her completely. Her fight or flight mode had been activated. She frantically scurried back to me and jumped up my arm. My brave coati pressed down on the transfer button and quickly leaped off. I glanced over at my shoulder and noticed the transfer button was adjusted to "9" and was set to animal. Coco simultaneously sprinted toward the Hunters and rapidly grew in size. She announced her pursuit of the predators with a loud roar. My metallic energy had been drained and was powering Coco up in her eyes, teeth, but especially her hands and nails. The transfer left me struggling after she'd borrowed so much energy.

"No, Coco, stop! Come on, Justin, do something!" Cameron yelled after her.

My eyes peered up as time began to slow down. I saw Coco sprint toward the three predators and three Hunters. Aggression pulled her away from me, but it was the pain and fear she felt for the baby that caused her to react on her own terms. I was shocked she had memorized the transfer process so quickly but was proud to watch her rush into battle and protect the other coati. I couldn't stop her like this. Who was I to come between her and her fighting spirit? Coco was braver at that very moment than she ever had been. However, I had to think about our place in the Squad, and I had to remember the big picture. If I didn't do this correctly, things could go from bad to worse very quickly.

I exhaled deeply. "You're right. I have to do something."

I adjusted the dial to ten and was ready to transfer the power back to me, but then I noticed all three Hunters were struggling to respond and adjust their transfer dials. Time was running out and I was out of options. If I didn't do anything, the three predators were going to rip Coco and the baby apart. I turned back to Cameron and laughed. Without hesitation, I pressed the adrenaline button on my partner patch and chased after Coco. The energy rushed through my veins directly into my heart. I felt invincible, but I only had a few minutes before the effect would wear off. I lowered my head and dashed forward faster than I ever had before.

"Come on Cameron, help us out!"

My friend nervously watched us rush into battle as we prepared to clash with the Hunters and predators. We could've been running to our deaths and Cameron didn't wish to see us fail. He became hesitant and doubtful of his ability to lead both himself and Rudolph into another combative scenario. Rudolph came up behind him and rested his chin on Cameron's shoulder.

"AGH! Okay, fine. Let's go help our friends."

Cameron adjusted his partner patch to "9," selected the transfer to "animal" and pressed down on his transfer button. Rudolph and his antlers began to grow in size as he launched himself after me and Coco. Cameron also pressed his adrenaline button on his partner patch and sprinted after us as well. The four of us were running on fumes after a full day working in the fields. I realized we were about to break at least three or four rules of the Cultivation Squad, but I didn't care. The only thing I cared about was helping Coco accomplish her mission.

All three trainers finally adjusted their patches and sent their power to their partners. Al, Benny, and Paxton began to multiply in size and in strength. I knew in my heart that Coco would not back down. She was ready to face all of them alone, but luckily, she didn't have to.

Rudolph zoomed past me and quickly caught up to Coco. The two clashed with the three predators simultaneously. Paxton and Benny lunged after Rudolph while Coco leaped on top of Al. Rudolph bucked both predators off his body, scooped each one off the ground and flung them into the air. Victor and Hogarth quickly ran after their animals to make sure they were okay. Coco forced her nails into Al as he opened his jaws. The remnants of coati quickly fell out of his mouth. I felt her fear as it creeped up behind her in the pits of her mind, but she remembered the baby that needed her help. Suddenly Coco's left claw began to shine brighter than I'd ever seen as she slashed Al across his head. The impact was powerful, as blood started oozing from Al's head. The crocodile cried out in pain and retreated to Todd.

I successfully maneuvered past Coco and Al fighting and landed behind Todd and brought back my right leg. My body was drenched with sweat, and my hands were worn and covered in blisters. It was Coco's mixture of courage and animosity that allowed me the power to follow through. I clenched my fists, kept my momentum, and performed a roundhouse kick in the back of Todd's left leg. Todd quickly dropped to the ground and dropped the baby coati. Coco ran after the baby and scooped it up.

I grabbed Todd's left arm and somersaulted forward in order to slam him deeper into the ground. I quickly forced my legs on top of Todd's throat into a dragon choke, so he was unable to move. After trapping Todd in an arm bar, I pulled his right arm tightly with both of my hands while my thighs forced his neck into the ground. "When are you going to learn to stop being such an asshole!?" I whispered.

My hands continued pulling as hard as I could until I heard a loud pop. I'd somehow broken his arm entirely. I jumped on top of him and forced my knees on his shoulders. I gripped his Cultivation Squad shirt with my left hand and pulled it upward. I raised my right hand and clenched it into a fist. Luckily a small amount of metallic pigmentation grew and covered it.

"This is it. This will teach you," I whispered.

Just as I was about to follow through, I felt a large hand reach down and grab my forearm. I was stopped in my tracks and unable to move. My body was beginning to lock up as I slowly turned around and saw my father standing over me. I looked over to the right and saw Shadow had pinned Al to the ground while Coco carefully held the small coati close.

I was gasping for air. "Dad?"

"It's time to calm down, son."

My body had stopped moving for too long, and the tiredness and physical depletion caught up with me. Cameron and Rudolph soon returned to their regular forms as Cameron ran toward me. I drifted from side to side before falling off Todd and passing out. My father scooped me, Coco, and the baby up and carried us all back to the medical wing on the third floor.

When I came to, the sounds of Miss Peterson reprimanding the Hunters echoed in the background, once she had learned what the three of them had done to the mother coati. My eyelids briefly opened during a screaming match between Cameron and the Hunters as they attempted to shift the blame. I tried to move and open my eyes more, but I was too exhausted. I felt helpless and powerless once again.

It was my fault, I could've stopped them, but I wasn't quick enough. My body fell into a dark pit, shackled by the defensive rage that lay dormant inside me and Coco.

I woke up hours later alongside Coco back in the third-floor infirmary. I was breathing hard as my legs shook, I was sweating profusely, and I had an IV bag linked to my right arm. My father sat on a chair next to the left of my bed with Shadow standing close by.

Coco woke up empty handed and began to stress about the baby. Coco turned around and found herself nose to nose with Shadow. The large lion snorted and started to smell Coco, but the small coati backed away fearfully and quickly climbed on my head to hide. Shadow saw this and retreated to the large window overlooking the Cultivation Squad entrance.

My father laughed. "Oh, I see these two haven't met yet. Shadow, this is Coco. Coco, this is Shadow. He's what you call a lion."

My eyes opened as Coco frantically scratched at my head in fear. She looked to me with fear while I attempted to wake up.

"She's a real fighter, son. Even when she passed out she would not let go of that baby coatimundi."

"Dad? The baby? What happened to—"

"She's safe I promise, I gave her to your friend Sammy. She said she'd return the coati to the same band outside of Ecosystem Five."

My hands reached out as I calmly scratched my partner's fur. "Shhh, Coco. It's all right. She's been returned home. The other mother coatis will babysit and raise her. We'll go and visit when we get out."

Coco started to sniff around my face and exhaled deeply. She then slowly laid back down in my lap and curled into a ball.

I glanced back at my father. "Thank you. Pops, where have you been?"

"Well, we wanted to be here, truly we did, but work has become more complicated as of late."

"Dad, I spent my entire life training for this. For the Hunter's Camp. I finally made it here, and I lost. Now I'm a freakin' Farmer."

"It's not forever Justin, and you know that. Tell me what you were doing to those Hunters?"

"It wasn't me. It was Coco. But it felt strange. She disobeyed me and ran off when she smelled the kit and mother coati."

My father placed his hand on my shoulder. "Son, she did the right thing. Coco decided to go after those in need and protect them. Mrs. Peterson was in here earlier and really let those other boys have it."

"What about Cameron?"

"Who?"

"The Farmer with the buck, he's my friend. Is he okay?"

"He seemed okay, pretty worn out but you both seemed pretty dehydrated."

"What's new? We work outside in the sun all day. The life of a Farmer."

My father watched Shadow look out the window, "Did you know Grandpa started off as a Farmer?"

I was confused. "What? No, he—I don't remember that. He would've told me. Even with a partner like Dusty?"

"Yep. He got cocky because of his powers and challenged a level fifty hunter."

"What happened?"

My father sighed. "He got beaten pretty badly. The entire camp gave him a hard time for losing, and he struggled to make a name for himself. He found himself living in the shadow of the one who defeated him for the next six months."

I remembered Grandpa's stories about our ancestors. "Who beat him?"

"Jericho Zhang. The same man who became his best friend and partner in the Hero Regime."

My eyes grew big. "Wow. I suppose that makes sense."

"He and Dusty were doing exactly what you're doing now. Training and fighting every day. But you can't do that by breaking rules. If you want to beat that kid, you have to challenge him."

"I'm still five months away from my rematch."

"Then you better get back to training."

The nurse walked over and interrupted, "First thing tomorrow. You won't be doing anything tonight."

She presented me with several pills to take with a glass of water.

I reached for the pills and began taking them. "Am I in trouble?"

The nurse gritted her teeth and turned her head to the side. "I was informed Miss Peterson will be by later on once you've recovered. After she's talked to you, you're allowed to return to your quarters."

I rested my head back on my pillow, "Great."

The nurse gestured to the other side of the room, "It won't be so bad. Not as bad as those other boys. I heard they were reduced ten levels each for what they did." The nurse gestured across the room where Todd and Al laid in their own separate beds.

Todd sat on his hospital bed reclined with his arm propped up. Al lay sleeping on a larger bed alongside Todd's. The medical bot was sewing up the wound along Al's face while Todd slept next to him. The nurses came over and tended to Todd's arm. They wrapped it in a quick solvent cast. They'd already realigned the bones, but the quick cast would restore the bones in about two days.

My father looked back at me. "That's a good-looking hat by the way."

I quickly took it off and placed it on top of Coco. "Thanks, it was a gift." Coco quickly pulled the hat over her and snuggled with it.

"A lot of good times in that hat. Quite a few victories, too."

"Yeah, well, it didn't do me any good last month."

"Justin, this power you have. You can't be like Grandpa. He learned over time how to use it, but it took him many years to do it. You have to learn what it takes to fight with Coco by your side and without your powers."

"Why would I waste my gift?"

My father grinned. "I became the leader of the Hero Regime because of how well both Shadow, and I worked together, and you don't see me with any special powers."

My arms crossed as I glanced outside the nearby window. "I bet you wish you had them though."

"I'll admit there was a time growing up when I thought I'd be just like Grandpa. With his wisdom. His drive—"

"His cooking skills?"

"Where do you think he learned how? He found a passion for food during his time as a Farmer."

I smiled, nodding. "Huh. Yeah, he found a passion."

"You and Coco should do the same."

"I found someone I am passionate about. Is that the same thing?"

"Ha, no... What's her name?"

Just at the thought of her name, I became weightless. When I closed my eyes it was as if she was standing right in front of me. I envisioned the shine of her smile, and the dark shades of brown that laid within her soft hair. I felt the warmth of her hands as I admired the adorable tiny creases around her nose when she smiled. "Lyza," I whispered.

"Is it the same girl you completed the WT application with?"

"The very same. She has a dolphin as her partner, Ivan." I leaned up out of bed.

Noah laughed and pointed at his temple. "That's right! Well, a little word of advice. You've got to watch out for those Exploration Squad women. They'll drive you crazy."

I became nervous and hesitant as we approached dangerous territory and tiptoed around the topic of my mother. The same woman who had no place in my life just as I had no place in hers. She was the same woman who always found a way to ignore her only son for years at a time. I was in no mood to pretend.

"How is it that I never see you, yet somehow, we always end up having these conversations?"

"I have to make up for lost time somehow."

Shadow walked back over to my bed with his mouth open. He rested his head on the pillow high enough for me to scratch his mane. He began making joyful groans and growls.

"We have to get going, I just wanted to stop in and see you."

"Thanks Dad."

"You know the Hero Regime will be here in the spring looking for new recruits. Regardless of level, they'll be looking at everyone in the Hunter's Camp. I need you to be ready."

I nodded in understanding. "I will. I promise."

"We'll see you in April."

CHAPTER 14

A Shining Star

My Dad and Shadow swiftly departed the third-floor infirmary. I saw Shadow growl at the crocodile as they walked by Todd's hospital bed. I wished that I had time to train with my father, so he could show me how to get stronger. But he had to return to The Capital and report back to Hero Regime Headquarters.

The following day Miss Peterson seemed to arrive just moments before Coco, and I were going to exit. She had interviewed multiple sources about the altercation that occurred in Ecosystem Five and asked Herb, my direct supervisor, how he wished to proceed.

After consulting with him, she then came to me and asked my perspective of the situation. I was honest and informed her why we did what we did, and somehow, she did not seem frustrated or upset. I was reduced two levels: one for not handling my partner correctly, and another for causing harm to another member outside of the challenge field.

Coco was required to wear her original leash and harness again for another week. Miss Peterson informed me that Cameron would receive a similar punishment and was also reduced two levels.

"If you are involved in another altercation outside of a challenge, your punishment will be doubled."

I felt as though Miss Peterson wanted nothing to do with me. She and I could speak professionally for the sake of the job at hand and by law of the Squad. However, on a personal note, she seemed to care less about my health or safety. She and her platypus swiftly departed from the third-floor infirmary and passed by Todd without acknowledging his existence. The nurse came to my bedside and helped remove my IV. I carefully stood up from the bed and placed Coco on the floor. My legs were sore but had returned to a relatively normal state. The only pain I felt was my empty stomach. I'd used so much energy before the fight that my body was spent.

Coco and I carefully made our way out of the room until I heard a subtle voice call my name.

"Justin." Todd winced in pain.

I stopped in my tracks and slowly turned my head to face the coati killer. "What do you want?"

He sighed deeply and looked me in the eyes. "I'm sorry."

"You're what? You're sorry? You ripped apart an innocent mother, you scarred her child, and you're sorry?"

Todd leaned forward. "I was wrong for what I did. Please, just let me explain."

I turned to leave and scoffed. "Explain it to Miss Peterson."

Todd sighed. "I did, and you know what? I feel like a piece of shit for it. One second we were on patrol, surveying the area, and the next thing I know Al has a coati in his mouth. I looked closer and found the baby unharmed so I immediately pulled it out! The mother was gone instantly."

"You mean once Al got ahold of her."

"Justin, please. I thought at that point it wouldn't make much of a difference what we did with the body. We should've removed it properly instead of feeding it to our partners. I understand that now. It was never my intention of harming the kit or fighting you."

I shook my head and turned around to face him. "I can understand that, but the damage is done. You had an almost newborn coati in your care that you should've turned in immediately. Instead, your two friends spoke about disposing of it!"

"That's what I was trying to do. I swear. Victor and Hogarth were making stupid jokes on our way out, and then we saw Coco. I know you and I have a history, and it's not the nice kind. But there once was a time when we were friends."

"Yeah and then you ridiculed me in front of the entire school."

"Because you didn't want to be my friend. You said you outgrew me."

"Todd, you wanted to become me. You wore my clothes, changed your hair, and acted like me all the time."

"You weren't just a friend. In a way, you became my role model, Justin."

His response left me speechless for a moment as my eyes remained glued to the floor. "I'm sorry I broke your arm."

Todd chuckled. "Thanks. They put it back together. Should be back out there in a few days."

"What're you up to, Todd? What do you want?"

Todd sighed. "Believe it or not, I want to fix this. I know we've had a rocky start, but I think we could help each other out."

"Because you like Roxanne?" I asked with confirmation.

Todd nervously stammered, "Wha—no, no. I mean, we're friends, but I don't know if she would feel—"

"Todd, why else would you want to be friends with me?" The momentary sympathy I had for him vanished.

Another awkward pause lingered between us. "She talks about you all the time. You've been friends with her for years, and nobody knows her better."

It was true, Roxanne and I had a lasting friendship with a lot of history. Though I hadn't seen her in weeks, she remembered the relationship she and I had built over the years.

My patience was wearing thin. "Todd, we can be friends. But when our rematch arrives, I'm coming for you."

"And we will forfeit."

"What? No! Why would you do that?"

"It's what you want, isn't it? We'll forfeit so you can join the Hunter's Camp. We'll put up a fight and use our same moves from the last challenge so you can come in and pin us to the ground. If and only if, you help me with Roxanne."

"No deal."

"Then I'll refuse your challenge."

"Ha, no, you won't." I started to leave as Coco followed.

"Yes, I will. I'll purposely injure myself the day of your challenge and will be unable to accept any challenges. You'll have to fight someone completely new."

The frustration and volume of my voice began to increase. I felt my blood begin to boil.

"I won't help you date her. Not because you're the most undeserving person on the planet, but because if you want to be with her, you should give her the decency and respect to be honest with her. There was a time when I thought I did, but I wasn't who she wanted, and I wasn't enough. Do you want to know the secret to her heart? It's funny because it's not Rus, it's not even her Dad, it's Diego. She loves that jaguar more than anything or anyone, even more than she loves herself. And if you want to be a part of her future, you'll have to figure out how on your own.

I turned to leave but glanced up and saw Roxanne and Diego standing in the doorway. My childhood friend was in shock and was carrying two plates of lunch from downstairs. She'd left her post early in order to bring me lunch. The surprise stopped her and I both in our tracks as we stood in place, stunned and unaware of how to react to one another.

"Ro-Roxanne!? How much of that did you hear?"

She stood frozen while Diego walked over to me and nestled his face on my knee. She dropped the plates of lunch on the floor.

My eyes grew big as she timidly walked forward with tears forming in her eyes. She picked up the pace and walked faster until she reached my arms. Once Roxanne reached me, she placed her hands on my neck and gently pressed her lips to mine. I was shocked and unsure of what to do. So, I stood still for a moment and allowed her to kiss me. A part of me had waited for this moment, but the other part immediately thought of Lyza. I took a step back and pulled myself out of the embrace.

Todd's face filled with frustration as he got out of bed and hobbled to the restroom down the hall while Al remained sleeping on his hospital bed.

My eyes closed as air slowly exited my lungs. Of course, when I reopened them, I was met by Roxanne's large hazel eyes. It was the way I had imagined Lyza gazing at me in my dreams. She stepped forward and placed her hand on my face, gently rubbing the right side of my cheek as the stubble on my face rubbed against her hand.

She smiled. "Justin, you are enough."

After clasping her hand with mine, I gently brought it down to eye level. I looked down to the ground and back into her eyes, worry and concern covered her face.

"I have to go."

Without wasting a moment, I picked Coco up and placed her on my shoulder as we took the metal staircase down to the first floor. During our descent Coco continued to sniff my mouth as the different scents lingered across my face. She sniffed and chirped at me, in an apparent demonstration of disapproval. We continued our walk into the cafeteria to pick up some lunch for the two of us.

"I know, I know. You disapprove."

She then placed her nose alongside my lips and reached her hands inside as she attempted to pull my mouth open and sniff the inside. I laughed and slowly pushed her hands away from my mouth. "None of that, please. Thank you."

Sammy, Cameron, and Davis all sat together eating lunch at our usual table. Once my partner and I grabbed a mix of chicken, veggies, and fruit, we joined my friends, and I informed them of everything we had just experienced.

It was comical how each of my friends reacted to the recent encounters with Todd and Roxanne. Each of them paused and had different responses to the information. Cameron buried his face in his hands, Sammy's eyes grew big as she placed her hands on the table, and Davis spat out his food with a parent-like concern look.

"Justin, that's messed up," Sammy muttered. And she wasn't wrong, the situation itself left everyone feeling rattled and uncomfortable. Each of my friends seemed unsure whether or not they should offer their perspective or call for a therapist.

"Which part?"

"All of it! Between the stunt Todd pulled with the coatis and then wanting to use you?"

Davis cut in, "Not to mention, Roxanne. What's going to happen with you two?"

The cafeteria grew surprisingly silent as if the nearby tables had heard my retelling and wanted to hear how I would move forward. I glanced around and examined the four nearby tables before whispering my response. "I don't know. I've been talking to Lyza for a while now, but Roxanne and I have history."

Sammy yelled across the room, "Mind your business, there's nothing to see here!" The surrounding Farmers continued talking and eating as if nothing had happened. Everyone in the Farmer's Camp respected and adored Sammy, but they also would never cross her. She and her cow Ruby were well known for their strength. Underneath her kind smile sat a mountain lion ready to pounce on anyone who would dare hurt her friends. She was a true and loyal friend.

"History? Is it the good kind?" Cameron asked jokingly.

I laughed. "Well, not really. As a matter of fact, she did date my best friend on and off throughout high school. I was her go-to friend when she couldn't talk to Rus."

Each time she and Rus would hit a rocky patch, Roxanne used to call me, crying and asking if Rus was still interested in her. I would hear her out, offer my friendly insight and try my best to be there for her. But she never once considered anything more than friendship with me. Sometimes, all I was to her was a shoulder to cry on.

Cameron sighed. "I understand, but you should go talk to her. If you're serious about Lyza, just tell Roxanne the truth and that you aren't available right now."

"It is possible to be emotionally unavailable for someone as well," Sammy offered.

I leaned forward trying to talk lower. "I know, but what about Todd? He was trying to mend a bridge between us, and now he's upset with me again because Roxanne is into me." I knew I couldn't trust Todd especially after the scene that had unfolded right in front of his hospital bed. As far as I was concerned, the sight of Roxanne kissing me was just fuel for the fire. If Todd was serious about friendship, there was still much more he and I needed to unpack before we could move past this.

"Don't worry about that boy," Sammy continued. "You can't let him control how you feel or react to someone. He should be the last thing on your mind."

"He said he'd forfeit on purpose."

Davis laughed. "What? There's no way he'd do that. Right?" I'm pretty certain Davis was only half listening. He seemed much more fixated on his chicken pot pie and mashed potatoes that sat half eaten in front of him. Davis and his partner Sam shared a particular lack of focus in multiple social situations. The pair's lack of awareness was indeed comical but very sincere. I'd hate for the two to actually step into any form of real combat.

"He's too proud. Remember how he acted after your fight?" Cameron muttered.

"Actually, no, no, I don't," I responded sarcastically. "Cameron, you and I were both stuck in the infirmary for three days." I replayed that fight in my head for three days and used every thought, every move, every impact Todd made on my face was a reason to fight and get back out to the camp.

Then again, I was thankful I had the opportunity to get to know Cameron throughout those three days. If I didn't have Cameron there I could've lost my mind.

"Three days? Really?" Davis asked. "I thought it was one at least. Anyway, he was really smug. He loved the attention, and he flaunted his victory as if he'd won the lottery."

"What's your point?"

Davis lifted his finger while he finished chewing. "My point is, the dude will not lose on purpose for some girl. Not when there's pride and money involved."

He had a valid point. There was too much on the line for Todd to damage his image. I knew he'd be upset by the actions that just unfolded, so much so that he had to remove himself from the room. I had to take this new-found information and proceed with caution. I needed to fix things with Roxanne and remain friends. This was no place to have a girlfriend especially with everyone constantly getting into each other's business.

Coco and I finished our meals and continued to hang out with our friends in the dining hall until it was time for dinner. Since it was Saturday, we all had dinner together and decided to go our separate ways for the evening.

On our way back to our tent, Coco paused and looked west into the nearby forest. Our safari tent was just a hundred yards from the forest along with the portable restrooms. It was pitch black in the forest, but I could tell Coco could smell something. I sensed her overbearing sense of curiosity, the same one that she kept with her everywhere she went.

She suddenly launched herself forward and started running into the forest. I dropped the leash but quickly, kneeled and attempted to call her back. Coco continued forward, refusing to listen. I was concerned why she continued to disobey me. I thought maybe she'd seen the coati she'd rescued. Maybe she heard her fearful cry in the woods? Regardless, I ran after her shouting her name.

It wasn't long before Coco reached the forest and ran in headfirst. By the time I reached the entrance to the woods, I found heavy vegetation and thick vines blocking the way.

I pulled out my hedge shears and began slicing my way through the forest. I'd cut, trim, and sever the ties between the vegetation in order to find Coco.

"Coco! Come back, Coco! Where are you?"

After twenty yards of cutting and slashing my way through the forest, I saw a clearing in the distance. There was a steep hillside with a large tree that stood at the top. I could see a variety of small eyes sitting in and around the tree.

I watched Coco make her way up to the top of the hill as she approached the tree. I put my shears away and started after her up the hill.

The full moon lit up the sky and continued shining bright. It illuminated the hilltop and revealed each of the small creatures' faces. The coatis from nearby ecosystems surrounded Coco. Almost thirty white nosed coatis sat watching as the moon revealed their dark brown fur and white faces. They were curious about Coco and confused by what she was doing up there. I kneeled down a safe distance away to watch the interaction unfold.

The white-nosed coatis surrounded Coco and continued to sniff around her while one larger male coati dropped down from the tree and faced her. He appeared to be the alpha male of the bands.

Usually, larger male coatis were more isolated and traveled alone. I was confused as to what his purpose was for his presence in the band. Coco stood still and lowered her head with respect. I felt her heartbeat harder and faster. She was intimidated by the number of coatis, and I was confused as to why she'd run to them so suddenly in the first place. She began making her nervous chirping sounds until I heard a smaller squeaking sound from the tree branches above her.

A smaller coati made its way down the tree and scurried to Coco's side. It appeared to be the same baby Coco had rescued. The baby rushed to her side, sniffed her, and leaned into her as Coco began grooming and scratching the baby's fur. The band of coatis saw this and became more comfortable with my partner's presence. Coco stopped grooming the baby and stepped forward as she raised her right hand high. Suddenly a younger male coati leaped down from the tree and made his way over to Coco. He stepped closer to her, sniffing her extended hand carefully.

He paused and slowly backed away. The young male turned around and let out an aggressive screech at Coco, baring his fangs. Coco stepped in front of the baby, slammed her hands into the dirt, raised her tail and revealed her fangs as she screeched back louder.

I clenched my fists and prepared to run in to defend her. The larger alpha male stepped forward and growled at the young male. The young male coati retreated as Coco calmed down and carefully stepped closer to the alpha male in order to sniff him. After a moment, she raised her right-hand high once more, as the moonlight started to reflect off it.

Coco's nails began to grow into long claws as her hand started to shine with a variety of different colors. It resembled a prism, one that refracted the moon's light rays into a rainbow of different colors. I was confused by the marvelous spectacle. Glancing over, I reached for my partner patch to see if my power had been sent to her, but it remained untouched.

This was not the protector's armor; this was something else. The coatis stared at her with awe and amazement. The sight sent my body into shock which caused me to lose balance and fall backward. Coco transformed into the same alpha male coati that stood before her. It was incredible how she successfully changed her entire body into a mirror image of the alpha male coati. She stood tall and held her head up high to the moon. Her hand continued to shine while she transformed back into her regular self.

"She-She's–She's a crystal claw!"

My hands latched onto the grassy terrain as I crawled back up the hill. The band of coatis started to circle Coco, watching her intently. She was surrounded by babies, mothers, and other curious coatis. It was as if they could not understand what had just happened or what they'd just seen. Coco saw me in the distance and leaned into the baby coati once more before breaking away and returning to my side. One of the surrounding mother's retrieved the baby and placed her on their back as they scurried back up the tree. Coco ran back to me and climbed up my body until she reached my shoulder. Coco started chirping from atop my shoulders as the nearby coatis chirped back. The legendary ability had returned, and it lived within my own partner.

Once we successfully made it down the hillside I stopped to further examine Coco's right hand. Her hand was clear and shined brighter than my armor. The uncertainty of how or when this gene had been introduced to Coco started to bother me. When did she know? Who else knew? Before I knew it, questions circled my headspace like a broken merry-go-round that would never end.

My partner could feel the load of questions begin to grow as she nestled her forehead into mine.

"All this time, and you never showed me what you could really do."

It was as if she knew how surprised I was by her newfound power. I placed her down on the ground at the foot of the hill. My eyes carefully examined her fur, her tail and all over to see if any part of her appearance had been altered.

"So, all those stories Grandpa told us about—that, was you?"

Coco was confused and was clearly unaware of what I was saying. She tilted her head to the side each time I attempted to question her about her origins.

"No. No it couldn't have been you. That was Cici. Wait! Are you Cici?"

The young coati blinked and continued to watch me.

My brown cleats squished into the wet grass with each step I took as I paced around her.

"No. No you're Coco. Cici must've been your great great grandma or something? GAH I don't know! How did this happen?"

My body slumped to the ground as I sat with my legs crossed and placed my face in my hands. My small partner scurried over and sat in my lap comfortably. Coco pressed her nose up from underneath the bill of my hat as she checked to see if I was okay.

"You are amazing. So, how does this work? You can just transform into any animal?" I smiled and scratched her chin.

The young coati reclined in my lap as she closed her eyes and enjoyed the chin scratches.

I lifted her off my lap and stood in front of her. "Let's try this. All right, how about ... a white tiger? Transform!" Both of my hands flew up immediately, fingers spread wide, as if I was a magician dramatically performing a fantastic act.

It quickly became clear that Coco was lost and unaware of what I was asking her. She then squeaked and continued to tilt her head with confusion.

"No, of course not. You don't know what that is. Maybe I have to say a certain word? Yeah, you need a term associated with a word or something that you know. Or someone? Let's try something. Coco, come here!"

My partner stood up straight and faced me with an energized stance. Her arms and legs in a wide stance as she appeared fully focused on me.

I placed my arms in front of me to mimic an alligator mouth. "Dusty. Transform into Dusty. Remember Grandpa's partner?

Coco blinked for a moment and raised her head. She became fixated on the night sky as the small coati stretched her right hand upward to the sky. Suddenly, her hand started to glow as Coco's body flashed with a multitude of rainbow-like colors and multiplied in size. I stepped back and examined the animal in front of me as she appeared to look just like Dusty.

My jaw dropped. "Oh, wow. WOW! Coco, that's it! Well, done!"

Coco's Dusty form started flashing as she suddenly returned to her normal size and form. Once she successfully returned to her original state, she started swaying back and forth as if she were off balance or tired.

"Coco, are you okay?" Without wasting a moment, I bolted to her side and caught her.

She fell into my arms and almost immediately fell asleep. Her transformations had taken so much out of her that she had little to no energy left. My partner hadn't been this tired since we first started running three miles together.

I slowly lifted her sleeping body up and cradled her in my arms. My fingers gently scratched her forehead as we walked back to our tent.

That night my smile shined as bright as Coco's right hand, and it simply would not go away. She was an amazing partner, with an incredible gift, and the power that my family had pursued to reclaim after decades of fighting had finally returned. We were on top of the world, but in the back of my mind I had a painstakingly obvious question that continued to poke my brain.

"Who else knows?"

When we returned to our tent, I carefully tucked Coco into bed and placed her under the covers with my red hat. I pulled out a pen and a clean sheet of paper as I began to write down my thoughts. I needed to get all of my thoughts out and sorted into one place so I could begin formulating the answers I needed.

Questions for Coco
Where did she come from?
Does she know Cici?
How does she transform?
When does she transform?
What does she need to transform?
What do we do now?

My thoughts began to run wild as I nervously sat on the edge of our bed contemplating what I should do. Of course, there was Sammy, Cameron, and Davis that I could talk to and share this exciting news with them. But the news would spread, and the word would be out all across the Cultivation Squad. The idea of calling my father or calling Grandpa was a logical option, but I wasn't sure how they'd take the news.

What if it fell back on me and became an even sadder excuse as to why I couldn't get into the Hunter's Camp? Who was someone trustworthy that could handle this information and keep it safe?

Lyza.

I ripped another piece of paper out from my notebook, but then I paused and thought of the potential consequences.

No. What if the Exploration Squad was reading each letter I sent her? What if the Cultivation Squad screened each letter before they sent it out?

The risk of this written information about Coco getting out was too high. If the country discovered what she was, then she would never be safe. Trainers from all over would be gunning for her and trying to take control of her. We weren't strong enough to protect ourselves, not yet. The situation called for a different approach. My phone sat untouched on my nightstand. I couldn't resist opening my phone, scrolling through my contacts, and locating the number Lyza gave me. In a previous letter, she decided it would be best to have her number in case of an emergency. The situation seemed relatively close enough.

I nervously exhaled the breath from my lungs and attempted to relax. My thumb pressed the call button as I listened intently to the line before it went straight to voicemail. Instinctively, I decided to hang up and call again to see if the line was off or busy. The phone rang multiple times. It must've been on "do not disturb" mode. It rang four more times before going to voicemail.

I raked my hand through my hair as I heard Lyza's voicemail message. "You have reached Lyza. Sorry I missed your call. Leave your name and number and maybe I will get back to you."

A brief pause occurred before a small beep was played.

"Hey, Lyza, it's Justin. I know I just sent you a letter yesterday, but I needed to tell you something I couldn't afford to write down. I was out following Coco tonight and she just transformed into a different animal. She did it so effortlessly, just raised her right hand in the air and it completely changed color. Then she transformed right back. It was incredible! But I don't really know what to do with this information, and I don't know who it's safe to tell. Anyway, give me a call sometime. Thanks, Lyza. I miss you."

As my thumb selected the "end call" button, I couldn't help but feel like an idiot. Each word, phrase, or sentence seemed worse than the last. My mind began to toy with me, as I convinced myself once she listened to my voicemail she'd never want to talk to me again. What was I thinking? The nerves and fear accumulating from the newfound discovery seemed to consume me. I should have taken a moment to calm down before calling. My body collapsed across the bed trying to think and urgently hoping for a return call.

For the next few days that followed, I continued to watch for mail and kept my phone close by as I waited to hear from Lyza. Three days passed, and I still never heard from her. I endlessly questioned my actions as I longed to hear Lyza's voice, to get lost in one of her letters and reminisce in one of her action-packed stories of adventure.

One night, Coco and I returned to our spot in the woods at the foot of the hill. We needed to test our limits and learn more about her newfound ability. Only then could we assist Coco in achieving a level of mastery with her transformations. The moon shined down from the star filled sky which allowed me to read off the questions from my same scrap of paper.

Once I sat my partner down along the grassy hillside, I decided to begin my interrogation of Coco. We stared each other in the eyes as I asked, "Okay, let's start with an easy one. Where did you come from?" Coco tilted her head to the side again as she stared at me with a confused look.

"Right, I'm talking to a coati. Okay you came from the WT where you were assigned to be my partner. Which means you were born in the WT. Interesting. So, maybe they knew?" *Who* knew? And what did *they* know?

I glanced down at my paper. "Okay, next question. Do you know, Cici?" Coco sat on the ground and nonchalantly rolled into a ball. "I'll take that as a no."

My eyes studied the next question and read it out loud. "How do you transform?" My partner continued to sit on the ground and remained curled up as a ball of fur. "Coco, stay focused. Now how do you transform?"

Coco rose and started climbing up my leg. She continued to sniff me all over until she reached my face. My partner stuck her nose in my eyes and my lips as she sniffed my mouth. Luckily, I was able to pull her off my face and into my arms.

"What are you doing, Coco? Sniffing? Why are you–Ohhhhhh. Okay, I get it."

It was a fragile situation, and we had to be cautious. I knew I didn't want the world to know about Coco, not yet at least. We physically weren't ready for that kind of attention. We continued to run exercises, performed drills that Grandpa taught me, and we wouldn't end our evenings until we were soaked in sweat.

After we finished our evening training, each night was the same. Coco sat atop my shoulders as we walked back to our tent. We threw down our belongings and ran ourselves over to the bath house for a quick shower and we'd turn in for the night.

We stayed up entirely too late, but I needed to stay even more active and focus on Coco in order to get my mind in the right place.

Not hearing from Lyza made me feel empty and confused. My emotions continued to get the better of me as I started to wonder where things went wrong. The situation filled my heart with regret and anxiety. For my own good, I knew I had to put the internal struggle to rest. For weeks everything I had ever written or said to Lyza was in question. But I knew I couldn't afford to look down on myself or question my actions. There was only one clear decision left to make, I had no choice but to remove Lyza from my head and from my heart in order to move on.

Nothing would stand in our way, no matter how painful it was.

We would push ourselves until we achieved perfection. With a single mantra branded to our brains. "Work all day and train all night."

CHAPTER 15

Our Darkest Day

A week had gone by since Coco revealed her new power to the bands of coatis. After careful consideration, I decided to keep her ability a secret. Aside from the voicemail I left Lyza. I didn't want to unveil who or what Coco was until we both had a better grip on her special abilities. I gave my partner specific instructions to not transform unless the sun was down. Then again, Coco had a track record of disobeying my direct instructions.

Regardless, we needed to invest more time in training while everyone slept. The only time available in our busy schedule to practice Coco's gift was in the evening, but we weren't going to stop until we achieved a confident level of mastery.

Coco and I continued forcing ourselves to lift heavier weights, to run harder than we ever had, all the while meditating to focus on our breathing. That week we upped the ante on our usual workout routine. We'd complete one-hundred and fifty pushups, plank for three minutes, and a daily four-mile run. We'd work out, work, eat, work, eat, and finally train. It was the same thing for five of the seven days a week.

My partner and I continued plowing corn even on the weekends to help us get ahead. The long hours of consistently pushing ourselves was overwhelming and exhausting. We were always sore, we slept deeply and soundly each time our heads hit the pillow. Each time we slept; I'd dream of Lyza. Visions of swimming down into the depths of the ocean to save her as if she were trapped. Lyza's voice called out to me as if she was searching for me.

When I woke up, my heart was hurting, and I became desperate for the opportunity to hear from Lyza once again. I used my inhaler much more frequently than I used to. It became a nervous habit of mine each day in order to keep pushing myself. Our friends saw how hard I was pushing myself and became concerned for my well-being. Sammy would yell at me to stop or take a day off. After we survived the first hardening week, Coco and I had never felt stronger. It was an intense process, but the work was showing us the results we needed. My abs were always tight, my arms were bulging out of my sleeves, and I'd never felt stronger.

Our stamina had rapidly increased, we were able to push ourselves constantly and for longer periods of time. I was moving at a higher speed than I'd ever experienced before. Everything was moving along in a timely manner with our training. Coco was reinstated for her off leash privileges which allowed her to move freely again.

Friday night, we were on our way out of the dining hall to do some late-night training, that was, until we overheard the breaking news around 7 p.m. Each of the six large televisions scattered throughout the dining hall were showing something big. They usually just broadcasted the weather, cartoons, sometimes a movie, but this was something different. I turned around, walked back over to where my friends sat inside the dining hall and rejoined them.

Bright red borders outlined each TV as they read, "BREAKING NEWS". A tired newscaster attempting to catch her breath appeared on the screen.

"We interrupt this program to bring you the latest news on everything WT. I'm Laurie Panninskee, and tonight, one of the Exploration Squad vessels has been compromised. Reports say it has been hijacked by several members of the AFA. Reports say they forced themselves aboard and apprehended one of the larger submarines. Eyewitnesses have stated that hundreds of members and partners are being held captive aboard the sub. The Hero Regime has been notified and is closing in on the scene alongside several other subs from the Exploration Squad. We take you live to our field reporter, Brad Haywood. Brad, what all do you have for us?"

"No. This can't be happening." I whispered aloud.

Brad appeared inside a small submarine. "Thanks, Laurie, I'm about two hundred yards from the scene. The submarine that has been apprehended is labeled the ES *Sandpiper*. The Exploration Squad currently have four other subs surrounding the—"

Everything around me became blurry. I tightened my jaw as I inhaled deeply through my teeth. I begged and pleaded for it not to be true. The one submarine name that I made it a mission to remember since the last time Lyza and I spoke.

The ES Sandpiper was the submarine Lyza and Rus were aboard. I bowed my head and closed my eyes. I pulled the bill of my hat over my eyes while I slowly brought my left fist up to my mouth to help cover my face. I closed my eyes and went immediately back to my dream of Lyza screaming my name inside the sub. My friends noticed my frustration.

Sammy reached over and placed her hand on my shoulder while Coco placed her nose onto mine. I turned to face the table and saw everyone staring back at me. My face was as red as my hat as a million thoughts raced through my head. My fight or flight mode had been activated and my friends saw it immediately.

Davis suddenly glanced up from his food. "What's wrong? Why are we looking at Justin?"

Cameron nudged him in the side. "Because Lyza is on that sub. You know, his girlfriend."

"You mean the one that hasn't been responding." His eyes grew big as the gears began to turn in his head. "Ohhhhhh. What are we going to do?"

I stood up from my seat and started walking out. "I'm going to make a call. Coco, on me."

I slapped my right thigh and recalled Coco. She followed closely as we departed the hall. My friends peered over at one another with worried looks after I left the table. Most of the Cultivation Squad remained inside and watched the news intently while every ounce of me wanted to go save Lyza. Once I reached the dining hall staircase outside of the exit, I felt a hand reach out and grab my left shoulder from behind.

"Justin. We'll come with you," Cameron offered.

"I'll be all right, Cameron. I'm just going to call my dad and grandpa," I lied.

"I understand, but Rudolph and I would feel a lot better if we escorted you back to your tent."

"Why?"

Sammy came up behind him, "So you don't do anything stupid."

"Guys, come on. You know me better than that. You think I'm going to steal a vehicle from camp and drive north until I reach the Exploration Squad docks? It's like 10 hours away. What could I do?"

"Justin, that's exactly something you'd do, " Sammy said.

I looked at her, disappointed in her lack of faith in me, but she was right. Sammy saw right through my façade.

"Well. Technically we're only an hour from the South Shore Docks. We could board a submarine there and use it to sail north. It'd be a lot faster," Davis offered. He approved of his idea and smiled. "So yeah."

I paused and examined my friends. I stepped off the staircase and pulled them all aside. "Guys, you don't want to do this. Why do you want to help me? You don't even know Lyza."

"Because you're our friend and you can't go alone. Things could take a turn for the worst. You could die," Cameron whispered.

I sighed and surrendered. "Then I won't go, all right? This is out of the question. None of us should go. It's dangerous, and we're only Farmers. I'm sure my dad and the Hero Regime are already on it."

"Then we'll stay with you. You shouldn't be alone right now," Sammy offered.

Coco climbed up my leg and scurried up my arm until she reached my shoulder. I scratched her head and smiled. "I'm never alone. Coco and I have some training to do. We'll catch up with you guys tomorrow."

My partner and I started walking away while my friends cautiously dispersed. After a moment, I took a quick look back and watched as everyone went their separate ways. As soon as they were out of sight, I sprinted back to my tent to gather supplies. I didn't know what I was going to do when I got there or how I would be able to help with the Hero Regime already in pursuit. But I couldn't forgive myself if I sat back and did nothing while Lyza was in danger.

It took an hour to gather snacks, tools, backup clothes—everything I thought I might need to take on the AFA and stop that sub. I packed up my backpack with my gardening tools and waited until there was nobody in my line of vision. We quietly made our way to the only accessible vehicle at the camp, an old, run-down, electric, pick-up truck. Its only use for the Cultivation Squad was delivering soil throughout both camps. We quickly reached the truck but found two Hunters on patrol. The truck was parked on the southwest side of the camp where it could charge overnight. I opened the door and jumped in before the two members detected our presence.

They stood just a mere twenty feet away and were on high alert with their partners as they surveyed the area. Kevin and his fox were patrolling with Roxanne and Diego. The two trainers were talking amongst themselves.

"Do you remember when Rigby got onto Victor and Hogarth a few weeks back?" Kevin asked.

Roxanne sighed. "No, I guess I missed that. How bad did they get it?"

"Bad. He was threatening to kick them out of the program, all over a dead animal."

"That's a bit extreme. What about Todd?"

"What about him?"

"Wasn't Al the one responsible for their situation in the first place?"

I placed my bag on the floor in front of Coco in the passenger's seat. She allowed me to quietly buckle her in the seat belt, in which I kissed the top of her head and thanked her. My hands searched through the inside of the truck looking for the keys to the ignition. I couldn't seem to find them anywhere, until I opened the glove compartment in front of Coco. The keys sat perfectly laid out in the box. I smiled, picked them up, and closed the glove box much louder than I should have. Diego looked over and made direct eye contact with me. He suddenly growled and opened his mouth to roar. I ducked down before Kevin and Roxanne examined the area intently. Diego guided Roxanne over to the truck, my heart started to race, and I was unsure if I would be able to escape with the Squad's vehicle.

"Justin?! What are you doing in there?"

"Oh hey, I'm just uh practicing my driving. You know it's been so long."

"Haha, oh. You kinda can't be in there. Can you come on out for me?"

Kevin's shadow entered the rear-view mirror as he moved alongside the trunk of the vehicle.

Coco pressed down the lock button for the doors. "I'm really sorry about this."

Without hesitation, I turned the key to start the ancient truck and put it in drive. My foot slammed on the gas which caused us to bolt past the Hunters. The four Hunters took a moment to digest what had happened before bolting after us. Diego and Roxanne were gaining on us, but the intense speed caused two heavy buckets of soil to fall off the back of the truck, tripping the four of them, and causing them to fall into the dark dirt face first.

Roxanne pulled her face out of the watery black soil and screeched, "JUSTIN!"

We rolled down the old vehicle's window and waved back, smiling, "Sorry!"

I turned around and glanced into the rear-view mirror that revealed the bed of the truck. Surprisingly, a large blue tarp remained untouched and securely fastened. With my sights set solely on rescuing Lyza, I glanced over at

Coco, "Davis said the South Port Docks had a sub we could use to get up north. So that's what we'll do."

After taking the old vehicle on the interstate, I could tell this was the most it had been driven in a long time. The electric engine would short circuit if I tried to go over 80 miles an hour, so I drove down the interstate at 79 mph. People would honk at me and hover over me in their zomorodis. I started getting weird looks for the fossil I was driving.

After an hour and a half of dodging the police and driving much slower than the speed limit, we found the interstate exit for the South Port Docks. We quickly pulled off, made a brief turn, and came face to face with a large metal gate blocking the entrance. Coco and I quickly got out to investigate the chained barrier. It was an industrial padlock, steel enforced, and unbreakable. Time was of the essence so I adjusted my partner patch to seven, selected "Trainer" and pressed the transfer button.

Suddenly, some of Coco's strength transferred into my body. My muscles were even tighter, my energy intensified, and I felt as if I could destroy a building. I held the lock tightly in my left hand as I focused all my energy into it. The protector's armor grew to cover my entire left hand, wrist, and forearm. My fingers squeezed the lock as hard as possible. I closed my eyes and pulled the lock off completely. Coco stood and watched me while I ripped the metallic gate in two and tossed it to the side.

I glanced down at my partner as she sat waiting. "Well, are you coming?"

Coco ran back up my arm, selected the animal option on my partner patch, and pressed the transfer button, initiating another transfer for her strength to be returned back to her body.

Once the transfer was completed, I examined my partner patch again as she sat on my shoulder. "You're getting pretty good at that. A little too good."

We jumped back in the truck and drove past the broken gate. I noticed there were two older zomorodis parked in the parking lot alongside a brand new, hot rod red, zomorodi XL. We parked our truck, got out and approached the small entrance. The old wooden office was tiny, barely ten feet high and fifteen feet wide. It almost resembled a large, wooden shed.

The Docks just north of The Capital was bright, vibrant with state-of-the-art technology while this one appeared old and forgotten about. We timidly approached the entrance. The structure itself was surrounded by a thick hedge of green bushes. The lights were on outside and shining around the building but once we walked through the front door, we stepped into a pool of blood. I looked down and saw two people lying dead on the floor.

Coco sniffed the blood from the floor and climbed back up my shoulder. There was a dead body sitting behind the desk while another was lying on the floor next to a supply cart. Both appeared to have been shot while on the job. One was counting money while the other was stocking shelves with snacks and memorabilia.

I heard an angry voice in the near distance, but it sounded familiar. I stared through the shop's screen door and saw a man outside pacing around the water. The faint lights outside illuminated my past and in an instant, I had fallen back into one of my nightmares.

The bald man shouted aggressively in Russian into his phone.

It was Fedrov and his monster of a grizzly bear, Magnum. The giant bear swam close by in the water searching for fish to eat. A day had not gone by without seeing the image of these killers destroy my drone. The situation didn't feel real; my body was starting to shake, and my breathing was becoming difficult. I stepped away, pulled out my inhaler and took a deep breath.

There was no question as to why Fedrov was second in command of the AFA. He and Magnum were one of the deadliest partnerships in the country. He was a warlord who wanted every opportunity to bring the WT to its knees. The lingering image of Magnum haunted my nightmares, but I wasn't alone this time.

"Yes! Pick me up, you measly mongrel," Fedrov yelled. "There is no sub here. We will go south until we hit latitude 33.9249° S and 18.4241° E. That's where we'll STROIT!"

"Stroit? What does stroit mean?" I whispered.

He continued to shout at the criminal helmsman of the *ES Sandpiper*. Dad and Grandpa needed to know where I was and who else was here. I quietly pulled out my phone, took a quick picture of Fedrov to send, but forgot to turn the flash off of my phone. The bright flash illuminated my position as it went off. We instinctively hid inside the shop, tucked away behind the isle of knick-knacks to avoid being seen.

Stress enveloped me as I mentally assumed the worst and awaited the grizzly to plow through the screen door. Luckily, both Fedrov and Magnum had not seen the flash from my phone or the photo I captured. This was undeniable proof that needed to be sent to The Hero Regime.

Out of fear, I occasionally glanced back as the frightening man paced along the edge of the water. The giant stood seven feet tall with muscles bulging out of his sleeveless leather jacket. Fedrov resembled a hippopotamus that could walk on two legs. Enormous, weighty, and deadly. I examined him closer and saw he had a tattoo of a grizzly bear on his right arm.

I attached the photo of Fedrov and Magnum and sent the message to Dad and Grandpa, "SOS, South Port Docks, Fedrov and Magnum. Saying something about Stroit! PLEASE SEND HELP!"

"Then remove them! We only allow loyal ones to join the cause," Fedrov yelled into his phone.

Five minutes passed as I debated on how to escape. I couldn't go back the way I came because of the blood all over the floor, the wide array of obstacles and the likelihood of slipping, falling, and giving away my position. Suddenly, a loud "PING!" went off from Fedrov's phone. He pulled the phone away from his cheek to view the message.

The South Docks was a tall, narrow, wooden structure built to include a variety of broad openings. It made entering and exiting difficult for someone who did not wish to be seen. We dropped to the floor as I slowly opened the poorly painted screen door. A small squeak started to escape from the door, causing me to freeze. I knew that any sound would give away our position. If the stakes weren't high enough already, this decrepit docking bay had a ridiculously loud backdoor! This obnoxious screen made sneaking around Fedrov almost impossible, but I had to push my luck to escape undetected. My right-hand secured Coco in one arm and crawled out of the wooden structure with the other. Our goal was to hide behind the tall hedge of bushes and retreat to the parking lot. Coco sat close to my chest as we began to inch our way behind the hedge and return to the truck.

Suddenly, without warning, Coco sneezed which caused me to instinctively launch our bodies behind the hedge to avoid being found. I turned to protect Coco from hitting the ground causing my right shoulder to strike a large root. The impact alone bruised my shoulder which created more discomfort.

I lay on the ground, holding Coco tight, and tried not to breathe. There was no change in the air, and I couldn't hear Magnum getting out of the water. It seemed our position was not given away, and we were safe for the time being. We needed to get back to the truck and wait for my father and Grandpa to arrive.

As we started to crawl, I noticed an opening in the middle of the hedge wall. Goosebumps multiplied over my skin; my palms were covered in soil as I adjusted my line of vision through the small opening to examine Fedrov. The giant man looked up from his phone and looked to where I had stood.

"Ah-ha, Mr. Steele, I presume?" Fedrov laughed and yelled out.

We immediately froze in fear as my heart stopped. Somehow or another our position had been compromised. He knew I was there, and he knew I wasn't far.

"You are not strong, Noah Steele, or old Herschel Steele. You are little Steele, yes?" He laughed to himself. "How did you find me? All eyes should be to the north, but not you. No, no, no you, go to the south. Why is this?"

His heavy footsteps started to approach as he moved up the small incline of the hillside outside the screen door. I lay still and silent praying he did not know our immediate location. Coco could feel my heart begin to beat faster which caused her to start panting loudly.

"Shhh, Coco, stop."

Fedrov stepped away from the water and approached my previous position. He smirked as he walked closer to the back door where I made the mistake of standing too tall in order to capture a photo. I listened as Magnum exited the water and shook furiously. He revealed his true height as he stood on his back two legs and roared. The vibrations that came from the roar of that aggressive grizzly were truly terrifying.

Droplets of sweat began to form on my forehead. I cautiously remained in place, afraid to move. I knew that if I could get to the truck I could drive away. I started to inch through the hedge again and back to the front of the structure. I was almost home free.

"Patience, Magnum, I know you are very hungry. We will find a meal here for you very soon," Fedrov called out.

It wasn't until Cameron and Rudolph barged in from the other side of the hedge and announced themselves that I realized they had stowed away in the back of the truck. The two emerged from the left side of the building and stood in the opening of the hedge alongside the water. Cameron entered, wiping the excess dirt off his uniform. Rudolph raced in behind him and shook his head to get the soil off his face while remnants of the blue tarp lingered on Rudolph's antlers.

"Justin, we're here to–" Cameron quickly found himself standing behind one of the deadliest pairs of the AFA. "Ummm, never mind."

He stared at the two large beings as he fearfully backed away. Cameron suddenly slipped; his foot plunged into the water. Both Fedrov and Magnum stared at Cameron and Rudolph as if they were a piping hot meal. My heart pounded out of my chest, growing louder with fear and helplessness.

"Well, this is a surprise. You are not Little Steele," He snickered with a sinister smile as he and Magnum stepped closer to Cameron and Rudolph. The young Farmer and his buck shook in fear. I knew that if I stood around and did nothing, Cameron and Rudolph wouldn't be able to escape. I had to face my fears and challenge Fedrov. A dry swallow of fear traveled down my throat as I stood up from the hedge with determination. I was ready to face off against one of the top criminals of the country.

I bravely stepped out from the hedge with Coco on my shoulder. "No, but I am."

Fedrov turned around and smiled. "Da. Of course. Not so tough without your family to help you."

"I don't need them. I'm going to stop you myself."

Cameron fed off my bravery. "He's not alone. We're going to beat you and stop that submarine."

Fedrov laughed maniacally before examining us. "Pahaha do you know who I am? A coati and a deer, huh? What is this program coming to? You are just a couple of Farmers. So, what will you do? How are two little weaklings going to stop me?"

"The only way you're leaving here is in handcuffs," I yelled.

I slammed down on my partner patch as Coco started to grow. She leaped off my arm and activated her steel nails and fangs. Even after the transfer she was still not as large as Magnum. My partner patch was adjusted to six and set the transfer to animal. I stood with most of my strength left, thinking it was enough to have a chance against Fedrov.

Coco and I ran toward the top members of the AFA. I clenched my fists as my metallic powers activated in my hands, wrists, and forearms. We reached Fedrov as I launched several powerful blows. I punched and kicked Fedrov's chest and rib cage as he stood in place and took my full-frontal attack. He didn't flinch or wince from the pain. My punches seemed to do little to no damage.

Fedrov pulled a pair of large black gloves out of his pockets and placed them on each hand. The gloves resembled cement casts but seemed to run off electricity. Sounds of tiny electrical surges pulsating through his gloves gave off distinct sounds of static. He pulled his arm back and was about to throw a punch as I brought my forearms up to protect myself. As soon as he made contact, I was forced five feet backward as my metallic armor on my forearms cracked. I could not defend myself from the amount of brute strength Fedrov delivered with just one punch.

Coco made it to Magnum and slashed off more of his fur with each swipe. The grizzly lunged at Coco but had no luck making contact against my quick coati. Coco jumped at his leg and bit into Magnum's fur. Her bite was strong enough to remove a layer of fur and puncture Magnum's skin. But the bear seemed unaffected by his bleeding wounds and continued to attack Coco with unstoppable ferocity and vigor.

Cameron and Rudolph jumped into the fight after he transferred the majority of his power to Rudolph. Rudolph rammed his antlers into Magnum's back, causing the angry grizzly to cry out in pain. Instinctively, the monstrous bear turned around and swiped at Rudolph. The large buck attempted to kick the grizzly with his back legs.

Magnum quickly dodged and delivered a harmful swipe to Rudolph's back-left leg. Magnum had punctured Rudolph's leg as the buck limped back to Cameron. Coco jumped on top of Magnum and inhaled deeply as she bit into his neck. Magnum extended his arms behind him, grabbed Coco, drilled his claws into her fur and threw her back into the hedge atop the hill.

I looked back and saw Coco's body fly through the air and heard her body hit the side of the building. She fell into the dirt behind the hedge. Magnum refocused his energy on Rudolph and ran after the limping buck. Cameron stood in place and attempted to fight off the grizzly. He activated the adrenaline button on his partner patch and ran circles around the bear. Cameron delivered a variety of quick punches to Magnum's mid-section. Each time Magnum would try to counter, Cameron swiftly dodged the grizzly's attacks by leaping the opposite direction. Magnum was starting to slow down, but once the fearful trainer dodged to the right, the deadly grizzly delivered a deep slash and cut into Cameron's chest. My friend sank into the hardened clay ground in pain. Both trainer and partner were injured and bleeding.

I knew I needed to help Cameron. I peered up at Fedrov as he looked down on me and laughed. "Come on, Little Steele. Show me how you will beat us."

He wasn't even trying! Fedrov was just toying with us as if we were flies annoying his breathing space. I twisted my patch to 9 and switched the transfer to myself. I felt all of my power return to me. My metallic muscles started to bulge through my shirt as Fedrov took off his leather jacket.

"You want a fight? You've got it."

"Now I will show you what real power looks like."

I sprinted toward him, and our fists collided. I'd slam into his ribs with each hit harder than the last. Fedrov started to wince in pain as the attacks were starting to affect him. My protector's armor grew in strength but when our fists clashed I noticed something about his gloves. They felt like little leeches sucking energy out of my hands as if they were drilling into my armor. I attempted to pull away as I dodged his punches and delivered powerful blows to his jaw and face. Sparks continued to fly from his knuckles each time they clashed with mine. I could feel his power growing as if he were feeding off me. The gloves penetrated my armor, and his combined strength was on another level.

Blood began to stream down his nose, but Fedrov laughed. "Ha, is that all? The son of the great Noah Steele." He spat blood on the ground. "Pathetic."

He brought back his right fist and slammed it into my chest. The hit sent me flying backward through the hedge and I collided with the small wooden structure and landed alongside Coco. My lungs struggled to function after he knocked the wind out of me. I examined Coco's fur and saw a mixture of dirt and blood covering her body.

"Coco? Hey, Coco, are you all right?"

She remained still as a faint breath came out of her mouth. She slowly forced herself up and started to sway in place. I'd seen her like that just a week prior, and I could tell she was about to pass out.

My forearms trudged through the soil, pulling my body closer to her which allowed me to pet her. "Gah, you're alive. Thank the lord. Just stay with me, Coco. This can't be the end." The hedge provided immediate cover which allowed me to sweep Coco up and pull her into my arms. Oxygen levels were dropping, and my vision was starting to blur. After making sure Coco was safe, I fished my inhaler out of my pocket and took a hit.

Magnum's claws had punctured her body in a variety of places. Without hesitation, I adjusted my partner patch and returned the borrowed power to my partner. I struggled to move while Magnum and Fedrov turned their focus back to Rudolph and Cameron.

"We're out of options, Coco. You need to stay here and rest. I'll take it from here."

Coco forced herself up and out of my arms. She walked over to the opening in the hedge and sniffed the air as Fedrov laughed at Cameron. My brave little coati stared back at me and blinked. I knew what she wanted. She turned around and observed the ongoing chaos brewing near the water. I could feel her heartbeat start to race as she became fearful for her friends.

"No, Coco. You need to stay here."

I could hear Cameron yelling in the distance, "STOP. Please. JUSTIN!"

Magnum cornered Rudolph and Cameron at the edge of the water. The giant buck stood tall, willing to die to defend his partner. The buck turned back and glanced at Cameron, as if he knew it would be the last time he would get to see him.

Rudolph faced the grizzly as he dug his hooves into the dirt as if he were a bull ready to charge. The giant grizzly stood on his back two legs and attacked, lunging forward toward the young buck. Rudolph seized the opportunity and charged into Magnum. The monstrous grizzly was surprisingly able to dodge to the right with great speed, as he grabbed Rudolph's body, and pulled him into the water with him. The two disappeared under the water as they struggled. Cameron was just a few feet from the action but felt afraid and powerless of what he could do in the face of danger.

"STOP!" Cameron cried out as blood covered his chest. The scared Farmer pushed himself off the ground and stood, trying to breathe.

I had to try to save Cameron and Rudolph, I couldn't let my friends die. I punched the ground and forced myself to stand. "I'll save them, I promise."

Coco exhaled deeply, raised her right hand high and suddenly transformed. She continued to grow more and more in size into the creature I'd seen in my nightmares. Coco successfully transformed into the same giant brown grizzly bear, Magnum. She forced herself through the hedge, stood on her back two legs, and let out a piercing, thunderous cry, "ROOOAAARR!!"

I studied Coco's newly transformed Magnum form. "Okay. We'll do this together."

The same terrifying shrill carried down to the water that sat beneath the old wooden docks. Magnum rose from the water irked from the challenging cry. Cameron and Fedrov were stunned by the sound of Coco's

Magnum form. She stood at the top of the hill showcasing her new temporary appearance.

"A crystal claw. Damnit," Fedrov whispered in fear and wonder.

"Is that... Coco?" Cameron gasped in confusion.

Magnum rose to the surface, inspected the top of the hill, and exited the water. He placed all of his focus on Coco and roared back.

Rudolph soon surfaced from the water and started swimming back to Cameron. He exited the water bloodied with deep scratches all over his body. Gasping for life, he lay on top of Cameron. My friend caressed Rudolph while soothingly speaking to him, trying, hoping, and praying to keep him alive. The two both started to bleed more and more.

Coco and I stared aggressively in the face of the enemy.

I smashed my metallic fists together and yelled down to Fedrov. "I told you, you can either leave here in handcuffs or not at all."

Fedrov glared back daringly and smirked. "Now that is a challenge. We will see who leaves here today, Justin Steele."

"No. We'll beat you; save our friends and then I'll save EVERYONE."

"Da. Let's finish this," Fedrov laughed.

I activated the adrenaline in my partner patch and sprinted down the hill as Magnum and Fedrov ran up to meet us halfway. Magnum sprinted toward Coco, but moments before the two clashed, I slid in front of Magnum and swept his right leg from underneath him. The large bear quickly changed his focus to me, which provided Coco the perfect opportunity to strike. She charged into Magnum and knocked him backward. Coco landed on top of Magnum and began clawing and biting at his stomach. Once I made sure Coco was protected, I turned around to find Fedrov standing over me. I quickly moved moments before he threw a multitude of rapid-fire punches at me.

I swiftly dodged each punch with intense focus. I remembered the punching bags, ducking low, high, to the right and to my left. I glanced back over and saw Cameron and Rudolph out of the corner of my eye as they appeared weakened and fading fast. Fedrov kept after me and raised his hand directly for my mid-section. Time began to slow down as I watched Fedrov throw a strong right fist toward my ribs. Rage began to grow within me as it developed into a chemical reaction inside me. The rage, adrenaline, and armor created a new level of power that I'd never seen or experienced before. I watched my armor begin to darken until it altered the metallic pigmentation to a dark shade of black. I could feel the power race through my veins as darkness raged inside me. I felt as if I could breathe smoke.

I leaned forward and prepared to catch Fedrov's heavy blow. A moment before his fist made contact, I maneuvered my left forearm over his fist and placed my right hand under his fist. I clenched my hands together as my power began to grow. I felt the power of my armor grow as it covered each inch of my fingers up to my shoulders. I opened my hands and grabbed his fist as tightly as I could. I began to pull his hand apart in opposite directions. I pulled harder than I had ever pulled anything in my life. I felt his bones begin to crack as his glove tore into two separate pieces. The exposed wiring caused the glove to short circuit. The more I pulled the more skin I saw was being stripped from his hand.

"AGH! RELEASE ME YOU FREAK!" Fedrov cried out in pain.

"No. Now you'll suffer."

He attempted to pull his hand out from mine but was unable to break free. Out of fear he brought up his left hand and grabbed me. Fedrov reached for my left shoulder and squeezed as hard as he could. My armor was holding steady until it slowly started to crack. The glove was drilling into my armor as his strength, combined with the glove, squeezed my shoulder. The pain was more excruciating than anything I'd ever experienced. It felt as if he shattered my armor as well as my left shoulder.

I pulled away in pain as both me and Fedrov stood ten feet away from one another panting heavily. I glanced back and saw Magnum and Coco facing one another. Coco was gasping for air, as bloody scratches and bite marks covered each of them. It was the hardest she'd ever pushed herself and time was running out. Coco couldn't maintain her transformation much longer. We had to wrap this up. My eyes shifted forward as I witnessed a blur of Fedrov's left fist approaching my face. With no time to react he landed a direct blow and sent me flying backward and up the hill once again. Blood dripped down my nostrils. The blurriness intensified as I desperately tried to determine which way was up. Fedrov turned around and saw Cameron whispering to his partner who was no longer moving. Rudolph was gone. He had passed on in Cameron's arms. The pain of accepting that his partner was gone had been too much for Cameron to bear. Both partner patches fell off and rolled into the clay.

Fedrov looked down and examined the deceased buck. "Poor little Farmer. No partner to save you now," he said while gasping for air.

Something in Cameron snapped. "You did this. You BASTARD."

Cameron pulled out his foldable hedge cutting shears from his pocket and ran at Fedrov. He ran at him with rage, sadness, and defeat in his heart. All Cameron wanted was revenge for his partner. "DAMN YOU!" Cameron yelled. Fedrov quickly caught his hand and removed the shears.

I peered down and saw Fedrov holding Cameron in the air with one hand and Cameron's cutting shears in the other. I swallowed my pain and slammed my fist against the ground once more. I punched myself up out of the grass. Every part of me wanted to save Cameron and if I could remove Fedrov, Magnum would follow his partner.

"Give up Steele. You lose, and you have nothing left. The deer is gone and so is the boy." Fedrov raised the shears to the middle of Cameron's chest and began to drive them into his sternum. Cameron brought both of his hands up and caught the shears in between his hands. He struggled to hold the shears as Fedrov looked back to watch what I would do.

"Get out of here Justin. GO!" Cameron yelled.

Goosebumps covered every inch of my skin; the situation had escalated more than I ever thought it would. It left me with no choice. I had to move faster than I ever had before to hit Fedrov, rescue Cameron, and distract Magnum. Everything I'd ever done had led up to that very moment. It was my fault Cameron was there, it was my fault that Rudolph had perished. I could never forgive myself for the torment I caused him, but I would do anything to save his life.

I remembered Grandpa's teachings. I closed my eyes, inhaled deeply, leaned forward, and launched myself toward the giant Russian monster. My legs moved faster than I'd ever seen. I slowly exhaled as time began to slow down. I heard Grandpa yelling at me from inside my head. "Plant your feet. Find the strength inside. Put your heart in your fist. Don't just strike a heavy blow. Strike fear into your opponent and finish them!"

Every step I took, Fedrov's shears were closer and closer to penetrating Cameron's sternum.

I finally reached Fedrov as I turned the side of my body and brought back my right fist at the last moment in order to inflict as much pain as possible. I became completely fixated on delivering the most excruciating punch I'd ever thrown. I didn't care if it broke every finger on my hand, I was willing to do whatever it took for Cameron. I turned in place as I clenched my fist and activated all the metallic armor energy I had left. I blinked and watched the same ball of light I'd seen in my dreams as it enveloped my right fist.

"Finish them!" I screamed out.

I released the full extent of my attack into Fedrov's stomach. The point of contact created a cacophony of cracking noises as my fist sank into his midsection. It sounded as if I'd broken every rib in his body. My punch launched Fedrov fifteen yards backward out into the water. Cameron dropped to the ground as his shears sat pierced inside the wound Magnum had given him. He began bleeding more and more from his chest. The adrenaline was still pumping through my body as I turned and faced Magnum.

"GO AWAY!" I yelled.

Magnum watched Fedrov fall in the water. He stood alongside the water and faced Coco but was torn as to what he should do. His fight or flight instincts were activated and was about to lunge back at Coco until the ES Sandpiper surfaced in the distance. The ceiling hatch opened, and a small ladder was thrown out. Magnum turned around and retreated as he followed his partner into the water toward the submarine.

Coco immediately transformed back to her original form and fell over. The young coati passed out instantly from the amount of blood, energy, and strength she'd used. Not to mention the number of wounds she'd received. After transforming into Magnum, I didn't know how she was able to maintain the transformation as long as she did. I could feel her breathing and was thankful to know she was alive. I fell into the clay knees first with Cameron and attempted to see what I could do.

I pulled Cameron out of the clay as my black steel started to fade. "Cameron? Cameron, can you hear me?" I put my hand on his motionless chest. He felt cold and empty in my arms. Cameron's eyes looked up and eventually found me"Justin?"

"Cameron. Cameron, we did it, man. Fedrov is retreating." My eyes began to water.

"I tried to keep up. I'm sorry."

"No, no it's okay. You'll be back on your feet in no time."

"Not this time."

"Cameron."

"I won't be able to keep up my end of the bargain."

"No. Come on, you can get through this. Please!"

"Take care of her." Cameron's eyes closed as if he were drifting off to sleep.

Both his and Rudolph's eyes were closed as their partner patches lay on the ground, disconnected from their bodies.

"Cameron? Hey. Cameron! Don't do this, man. PLEASE. COME ON."

I began to cry as I looked back at the water and saw Fedrov staring back from the giant submarine. Fedrov grinned ."Another day, Little Steele. We'll play again soon."

Lyza was on that submarine and there was nothing I could do to save her. I failed her and Ivan, I failed Cameron and Rudolph. Coco was hanging on by a thread, but I knew, even then, after all that training we'd done, it didn't matter. I still wasn't strong enough to save everyone.

Tears streamed from my eyes, and I cried in agony. No person alive was around to hear me scream, but it traveled across the water surface all the way down to the depths of the ocean. The howl wasn't filled with anger or intimidation. It was a damning call to the darkness for reaping Cameron's unfulfilled soul. I paid the price and lost. I held Cameron's lifeless body in my arms. I was the one solely responsible for what happened. There was so much blood on my hands, I was drowning in my own suffering. I would never forgive myself for gambling on Cameron and Rudolph's lives. The loss was too great.

I called the police immediately after. I held Coco in my arms as members of the Hero Regime and police arrived on the scene. Suddenly a small escape pod was shot out of the sub before it submerged once again. The pod was full of members from the Exploration Squad from the ES Sandpiper. It had about five members along with their partners that swam after them. I saw Rus walk up onto the wooden docks and watch me from a distance. He and his Exploration squad members all wore black and blue wetsuits. They appeared agitated and glared at me as if the entire attack was my fault. I rushed to Rus as I gently carried Coco in my arms. I had questions and concerns, not about the sub or what he'd experienced. But what happened to Lyza?

"Rus, you're all right? Where is Lyza? Have you seen Lyza?"

"Justin, what happened to you? What happened to Coco?"

"We faced off against Fedrov and Magnum... And uh, we lost." I exhaled deeply as dried tears remained on my face.

"How are you still alive?"

"Never mind that, where is Lyza? She was on the sub with her dolphin Ivan. Have you seen her?"

Rus exhaled deeply. "No, no, I haven't. I haven't seen her in two days. We were lucky to escape with our lives, let alone our partners."

"No... Lyza and Ivan, they-they were there too. They were down the hall from you. She told me. She was there!" I shook my head and yelled,

"Justin. I don't know where Lyza is. I haven't seen her in a couple days. I'm sorry," Rus said calmly.

My father arrived soon after and ran to my aid. He arrived just a half hour after the submarine was out of sight. Dad picked me and Coco up and escorted us back to a nearby ambulance to receive first aid.

I looked in the distance and saw Rus speaking to a policeman with a notepad. Rus remained at the dock with his Exploration Squad crew and their partners as they swam in the water close by. Rus and a handful of other members of the Exploration Squad survived, but the rest were either kept or removed. He did not know what came of Lyza. She was nowhere to be found. Maybe she joined the AFA for the sake of her survival or maybe the option was taken from her. My heart couldn't fathom the thought of Lyza being taken from me. Either way, I didn't have any leads on how to locate the truth. One way or another she was gone, and I had no idea of how to find her.

Coco and I received top tier medical attention. She had several fractured bones and was dehydrated and exhausted from overexertion. Her right hand had been splintered. A medical bot placed her back on a hover stretcher inside the ambulance. I sat by her side patiently as the medic bot performed realignment surgery, wrapped her wounds, and applied an IV into her body to regulate fluids and medications. Luckily, Coco's secret remained secure for the time being. The two of us were asked to stay in an ambulance and wear large anxiety blankets until the rest of the Hero Regime could record as many clues from the crime scene as possible. I had bruised ribs, a black eye, a broken nose, fractured fingers, a bruised sternum, a shattered rotator cuff, a concussion, and overall overexertion. They investigated the shop, the dock, the hedge, and Fedrov's red zomorodi XL. It wasn't until the sun started to rise that Grandpa finally arrived on the scene.

We approached the early hours of the morning when two members from the Cultivation Squad showed up to speak with me. I was surprised to find Hunters from the Hunter's Camp to investigate the crime scene working separately from the police. I'd heard rumors about a separate unit dedicated to hunting down Fedrov. They approached me about Fedrov and questioned me as they wanted to know every detail of the attack.

I sat inside the ambulance with Coco as the two trainers stood outside the vehicle. The taller slender trainer stepped forward and introduced himself. "Good morning, my name's Josh, Josh Hollington. I can see you two had a rough night. I'm sorry for your loss."

The shorter man stepped behind Josh and whispered, "Josh, that's Justin Steele, Noah Steele's son. He's a Farmer."

Josh turned around as his mouth dropped. "Ah, mhm, I see." He turned back to face me, "Well, Mr. Steele, you too are a member of the Cultivation Squad. So, you know why we're here. We have a few questions about the attack if you could kindly assist us."

I sniffled and wiped my nose. "Of course, you want to know about Fedrov?"

The shorter gentleman spoke, "The name is Dashae Finnek, we're part of the AFA investigation unit of the Hunter's Camp. When you initially approached Artem Fedrov, what was he doing precisely?"

I carefully scratched Coco's head as she lay unconscious on the stretcher. "He was on his phone, and he was speaking Russian. He was waiting for the stolen submarine when he gave out coordinates for somewhere. I assumed it was for here, but he kept saying the word, STROIT!"

Josh made eye contact with Dashae. "Stroit. He's building something. Did you hear anything else? What were the coordinates to?"

I shook my head. "No, he was quick. I took a photo of him and sent it to my Dad and Grandpa."

"Can we see the photo?" Dashae asked.

I slowly stood and took out my phone from my pocket, noticing a new large crack down the center of the screen. I presented the phone to the two of them as they examined the photo and whispered amongst themselves.

"Yep, that's definitely him," Dashae whispered.

"Magnum has gotten fat," Josh observed. He looked back at his partner. "We're going to need to do some more weight training. Isn't that right, Darwin?" Suddenly a giant black bear, the size of Magnum, stood on his back legs behind Josh.

"So, you engaged with Fedrov? Just you and your...?" Josh asked.

"Coatimundi."

"Coatimundi, sorry."

"No. We had help from Cameron and Rudolph. Fedrov murdered my friend, Cameron Sykes and his partner, Rudolph. They fought by our side until the end."

Josh and Dashae stared at the ground unsure how to respond.

"I'm sorry, Justin. We want to find this man, but in order to do that we need to find out everything that happened," Josh sighed deeply.

Coco's secret was on the fence, and I became nervous on how I would respond accordingly. There was no way a simple Farmer and his coati could go up against a top officer of the AFA and live to talk about it. There had to be an important detail to draw their attention away from my partner.

"My family had a legendary gift. One that's been passed down for generations. It's one I received from my Grandfather. It's a sort of metallic armor that—"

"The protectors' armor?" Dashae asked. "Of course, that makes sense, after all you're a Steele! Wait." He paused for a moment as he examined me from head to toe. "How did you become a Farmer?"

I turned around to face Coco as I sat back down near the stretcher.

"Pride."

Josh smiled. "I know something about that. Look, if you can remember anything, anything at all, please let me know."

He handed me his card.

"Cameron and Rudolph were my friends. They died heroes who wanted nothing more than to bring Fedrov to justice, but really they just wanted to bring me home. If you find anything out, please keep me informed."

"Just leave the hunting to us," Dashae scoffed.

Josh frowned and stepped in front of Dashae. "I'll keep you in the loop. You have my word."

"Thank you."

The two trainers and their partners made their way back to their black zomorodi and exited the scene. The medic bot finished with Coco and started working on my left shoulder. Grandpa and Dusty returned to the ambulance alongside my father and his partner Shadow.

"Anything new?" I asked with urgency.

My father sighed. "Well, it looks like the current is going south. We've reported to the Exploration Squad, and they should be in hot pursuit of the vessel."

Grandpa placed his hand on my right shoulder. "Tell me what's going through your mind."

My eyes were drawn to the sky. I placed my hat over them. This loss had become more consuming than when Todd beat me.

"It's my fault Cameron's dead," a faint whisper emerged from my lips.

"Don't say that," Grandpa said.

Tears filled my eyes, and I removed my hat. "It's true! He wouldn't have even been here if I hadn't driven that stupid truck here. I wanted to get a submarine and sail north. I wanted to go after Lyza and now. Now, I've lost them both."

My father knelt down to the ground so his eyes could meet mine. "Hey. Lyza is strong. She's a fighter. If she's with the AFA, she won't let that stop her from doing what's right."

"What matters is that you're alive," Grandpa muttered. "One thing I'm slightly concerned about. How did you fend off Fedrov?"

"I used the armor, our gift. But it was different this time. It was like I got so angry that everything turned..."

"Black?" Grandpa asked.

"Dark. But yeah, how'd you know?"

Grandpa exhaled deeply. "Black steel. It's the next level of power for the protector's armor. Took me years to figure it out, but even longer to master. After using it I learned how deadly it can be. You can't use it, Justin."

"Why? I never felt stronger than when I—"

"Because it kills you. It absorbs your life force and ultimately, takes years off your life. If you use it for too long, you could lose your power forever. That's what happened to your great-grandfather. What's done is done. We can't take anything back. He was a nice boy, but your friend is gone, and you have to let him go."

A grimace enveloped on my face as I stared at Grandpa and wanted to slap him. "How can you stand there and say that? You met him, you shook his hand, and saw him fight. Cameron was my friend. And black steel or not, I wasn't strong enough to save him."

Grandpa stepped forward and grabbed my chin, "Look at me. This is the job. People live and die every day. I just hope the lessons I've taught you are enough to keep you alive."

I was emotionally distraught at the moment and couldn't see how Grandpa held his true emotion behind his eyes. He looked at me with anger because he had to fight to get through to me. He was thankful I was alive. I'd been stubborn and refused to listen to him because I thought Cameron and Rudolph deserved to be mourned. Still, I couldn't let this loss provide an excuse to be reckless, and Grandpa saw that. He made sure to put a stop to that way of thinking before it had a chance to bury its roots into my mind.

My father pulled Grandpa's hand off my face. "Come on, Dad. Knock it, he's just a kid."

The medic bot sat me back down and continued working on my shoulder. It quickly sewed up my shoulder and applied a cast.

"And so were you. Did you become number one by sitting around and sulking?"

"I had my rough nights. But I suppose you wouldn't know anything about that."

I coughed to clear my chest. "Stop. Please. Let's just say goodbye and go our separate ways again."

The medic bot completed my procedure, and I slowly stood and carefully hopped out of the ambulance. I turned around and directed Coco's hover stretcher toward the truck. I placed my hat back on my head and spit more blood on the ground. I threw my anxiety blanket over my good shoulder and the other onto Coco.

"Are you sure you should be driving right now? What are you going to do?" My father asked.

"I'll be fine. This doesn't change a thing. I'm going to become a Hunter."

Grandpa followed me and squeezed my right shoulder. "That's my boy. Dusty and I will come and visit soon. I promise."

I got back to the old truck feeling like a lifeless ghost. I pulled down the tailgate of the truck to find the tarp gone, but what was left behind were a few hoof marks and footprints in the soil like a dried-up crop. A flower that never had a chance to grow. My hand covered my mouth to stop myself from crying. Instead of giving in to my emotions, I forced the tailgate up and walked back to the driver's seat. Coco's hover stretcher floated through the opened door and safely lodged in the back seat. All of my emotions had been removed from my body. The sadness in me had been absorbed into a black hole which was now my heart. But I was alive and still had a single mission. I knew what I had to do. We had to use this loss to double our training, push ourselves harder for us and in the memory of my friend. Cameron deserved to be a Hunter, and if he had his chance ripped away, then I'd do it for the both of us. We were done playing games. I'd show the world what Coco and I were truly capable of.

I drove the electric truck back to camp. I apologized for my actions and informed the faculty of everything that had occurred. Coco and I were demoted a single level as punishment and remained in the infirmary for a week to rest. It was a lonely, silent healing process, one that made me miss the sound of Cameron's snoring.

CHAPTER 16

Five Months Later

An eerie fog encompassed my mind as a hazy memory surfaced. The words continued to play in my head over and over while my body remained still.

"Let's do it together," Cameron whispered.

"What do you mean?"

"Join the Hunter's Camp! That's what we're here to do, right?"

"Right."

"So, swear to it," Cameron challenged me.

I sighed. "I swear."

"I can't hear you!"

"I swear!"

A sudden flash blinded me.

The alarm on my phone started blaring and woke me up in a hurry at 4:30 a.m. With blurred vision and most of my body still asleep, I jumped out of bed and knocked out my morning pushups. Coco slowly stood, stretched, and jumped onto my back. After I hit 200, I stood tall and reached for my inhaler. I looked at the new mirror in my room and saw my muscles bulging. I'd added twenty pounds of muscle within the past few months and was extremely proud of my progress.

I quickly changed into my green running gear and ran out the door. Coco ran alongside me as we entered the misty fog. Coco had grown into a large, beautiful coati. All of her wounds healed nicely. She had a longer stride, and her tail was twice the size of her body. My partner was much faster, more powerful, and she had earned a heightened endurance with masterful stamina. Coco was able to keep up and continue running with me for all five miles. We returned to the bath house where we cooled off with a quick shower. I wanted Coco to look and feel her best for our big day. After we were clean, I held her close in my arms as we walked back to our tent. She maneuvered into a more comfortable stance as she sat perched on my shoulders.

I quickly changed into one of my short sleeve Coati Cultivation Squad uniforms. My hands pulled up my black compression pants with my gym shorts over them. I securely tightened my black running shoes with double knots. My black and green Level 100 Patch sat proudly on my left shoulder. I remembered the hours spent collecting crops, creating medicine, and plowing countless acres of cornfields. With each acre, I always pushed myself past my limit and would not allow myself to stop until the job was finished. For the past month, I averaged four acres a day. My hands bled as my skin began to peel off my palms, but they slowly healed and grew back callused and more durable. I'd grip the plow as hard as I could and lose myself in my own mind. Days would pass when I wouldn't talk to anyone but Coco. The still frames of Cameron lying alongside the water, lifeless, haunted me in my dreams and Sammy and Davis saw it.

Coco and I made our way to the cafeteria where Sammy, Davis, and Roxanne sat eating. We rejoined our friends at our usual spot inside the dining hall. The same unbalanced, unproportioned brown table sat full of loving and supportive trainers and partners alike. Sammy greeted Coco. "Good morning! Are you ready?"

I exhaled. "Let me think about that for a second."

Coco jumped down onto our usual table as I turned around to get in line. She socialized and sniffed Diego, Ruby, and Sam while I fetched our food. When I returned, I'd brought back the breakfast of champions: a breakfast bowl of quail egg yolks for Coco and an omelet for me. Finally, my body sat still and reclined on the wooden bench before I faced Sammy with a fork full of eggs. I nodded calmly. "We're as ready as we'll ever be."

Roxanne rubbed my forearm. "You're going to do great, just wait."

I forced a smile and swallowed my food. "Thanks, Roxanne. I know Coco is ready. We were up late practicing some new combinations. It's incredible, she's really something."

Davis patted my shoulder. "Well, I'm excited to see you and Todd go at it. The way you've been training is insane! My money is on you."

Sammy looked at Davis and scoffed, "You aren't gambling on Justin's fight!"

Davis looked at Sammy confused. "Why not? Everyone in the Hunter's Camp is doing it. I want to get in on the action!"

A young Farmer and his ball python wrapped around his neck entered the dining hall yelling, "Bets here! Get your bets here! Todd the Terrible vs Justin the Just!"

I took another bite and laughed. "Ha! No way those names will last."

"So, Justin, how are you feeling? Really?" Sammy asked.

I placed my fork down and stared down at my plate for a moment. My eyes started to water, and I knew I was on the verge of tears. I laughed and wiped my face. My eyes glanced back up at Sammy. "I'm okay. You know? I can feel his presence. Cameron is here. And today, we'll win it all for him."

Sammy reached across the table and grabbed my hand as tears began to form in her eyes. She sniffled as she turned around and rubbed her face against Ruby. The large cow buried her face into Sammy's.

"Maybe that fella with the snake wasn't too far off. 'Justin the Just'... I like it," Roxanne whispered.

Davis remained quiet and sat across the table eating his eggs and hash browns. I could tell he too missed Cameron.

I looked at Roxanne and placed my hand on hers. "Justin the Just, it is. Remember to get a good spot to watch." I turned to face the table. "If you guys are ready, let's get a move on. We don't want to be late."

Roxanne leaned in and hugged me before she stood to leave. "Good luck! I'll see you out there."

We finished our meals. I took one last swig of coffee and stood alongside Sammy and Davis as Roxanne and Diego exited the dining hall. I stopped in my tracks and remembered to recall Coco to my side. She finished her bowl of quail eggs and scurried across the breakfast table before leaping onto my shoulder. I walked out of the dining hall more nervous than I had been in a long time. I clenched my fists as goosebumps crawled up my arms. I could see the challenge field in the near distance. I knew today would change everything for the better and would allow us the chance to get back on track to pursue our dream. My friends discarded their trash and followed us out the door. A thick blanket of assurance covered my body knowing they were right behind me every step of the way. Outside the dining hall, hundreds of members from the Cultivation Squad made their way to the challenge field to find a good seat.

John Rigby stood in the middle of the field with his arms crossed and his sunglasses on. The director was wearing his referee outfit again just for the occasion. John and I had a bumpy relationship when it came to training with our partners. He'd been telling me to lay off the training and to relax. Each time we saw each other in passing, he'd remind me to take breaks and not push myself too hard. Every time I saw John or Todd, it made me want to get bigger that much more. I hugged Sammy and Davis before we entered the enclosed rocky terrain. More members of the Cultivation Squad arrived and circled the outskirts of the field.

John Rigby took an old microphone from his pocket as I met him in the center of the field. "Is this thing on? Okay, well, look at this, ladies, and gentlemen, we've got ourselves another Challenge Day!" Applause rained down from across the field, echoing loudly in our ears.

"Today we have our redemption match for Mr. Justin Steele. Now, Justin, as of yesterday you achieved level one hundred. This redemption match is completely up to you, which means you can face anyone at the Hunter's Camp, myself included. If you win, you will become a Hunter."

Josh and Dashae stood close by examining me. I hesitated for a moment before grabbing the microphone from Rigby. "Firstly, I'd like to dedicate this match to my departed friend, Cameron Sykes. Today was supposed to be both of our redemption challenges. Cameron, this is for you."

A pause resonated throughout the crowd.

"We'd like to face Todd Ramos," I proudly announced.

The crowd of trainers applauded cheerfully. Hunters drummed on cement; Farmers applauded as I watched everyone out of the corner of my eye. I was nervous to be back on the field. The same rocky terrain traveled from under my shoes and into the air. "You got this. We can do this," I whispered to myself.

Suddenly, Josh and Dashae stepped aside and revealed Todd. He made a grand entrance as he casually walked out arm in arm with Roxanne. My challenger dipped Roxanne backward and kissed her passionately before he and Al entered the field. Al was fully grown and was about twenty feet long. His jaws were massive, and his teeth appeared to be sharpened. Coco jumped off my shoulder ready to face off against the giant croc. I could see the scar she left him on his left eye and the one on the top of his jaws.

I remained silent studying his posture, his shoes, his stance, along with the overflowing cockiness that defined him. He smirked and slowly paced back and forth.

Todd threw his Hunter's jacket back to Roxanne and pointed at me, "I've been waiting a long time for this."

Rigby examined Al and gestured back to me. "Are you sure this is who you wish to challenge?"

I stared back at Rigby and looked dead in his eyes as I nervously exhaled.

"Yes, sir."

I stretched my legs and pulled my arms over my chest without breaking eye contact with Todd. Al let out a giant growl, followed by a mean hissing sound. My feet carefully bounced in place as Coco stood in front of me. My coati stood just ten yards away from the intimidating croc. I felt no fear from her, only immense focus. I remembered how fearful and angry this croc had made her in the past. She was able to put everything aside and remember our training.

Rigby stepped up in between Coco and Al. He confidently stood in the middle of the field as his wolf, Raven, lingered behind him, studying both trainers and partners.

"There are only three rules to remember. One. Only the challengers and their partners are permitted to face off on the field if you leave the field you are disqualified. Two. You cannot kill the other challenger or their partner. Three. If you or your partner cannot carry on, you will be asked to forfeit. There is no dishonor in knowing your limit. Are we clear?"

I nodded confidently. Todd snickered and reached for his smoke bombs, carefully positioned in his pockets.

John Rigby placed his black whistle in his mouth, raised two red flags, looked back at the two of us, blew his whistle and dropped the two flags on the field.

Time started to slow down, but I used it to my favor. Goosebumps ran across my body as I traveled across the field in the blink of an eye. My heart was racing, my blood was pumping, and I wasted no time in launching myself across the challenge field. In a brief blur, I carefully landed behind Todd.

All those miles of running, waking up extra early every day, just for this moment. Todd saw me appear out of the corner of his eye as he attempted to turn around. His eyes grew big with fear. I released my excess speed into my fist and launched into his face. My knuckles ricocheted off his mouth as the impact caused blood to drip from his lips. Todd fell backward onto the challenge field as Al growled aggressively and lunged at me. I caught the killer crocodile's jaws with armored hands. I activated a small portion of my armor solely in my hands and forearms in order to pry Al's mouth open.

"NOW, COCO!"

Coco moved from her position and leaped onto Todd. She quickly performed a variety of harsh scratches and slashes to his skin. She moved with extreme speed and slashed at him repeatedly until Todd was covered in layers of scratches. Todd attempted to dodge and block her claws but was unable to keep up with her speed. After four or five seconds, he successfully reached for the smoke bombs inside his pocket and slammed them onto the challenge field. I instantly threw Al to the side and dove into the smoke, searching for Coco.

My right hand connected to my thigh to signal my partner as I yelled out, "Coco, on me!"

Her small hands and feet dug through the rocky challenge field as she approached me. It was the same sound I heard every day during our morning runs together. After training together for months, Coco had memorized my scent and could locate me even in the smoke. We'd prepared diligently how to handle these types of measures.

I closed my eyes and held out my left arm. Coco found me and leaped onto my arm. She secured herself atop my right shoulder as we jogged to the outskirts of the challenge field. Quick steps and loud thumping came from the center of the field.

Instead of fleeing the smoke we decided to make use of it and plunge into the center for a surprise attack. My right fist approached the target but was stopped by a pair of hands that had successfully blocked my punch. Todd stood over me in the white smoke at first, but his physical appearance started to alter. It was unlike anything I'd ever seen as a black shadow covered him.

Roxanne had mentioned Todd had been experimenting and working on something new, but I had no idea what it actually was. It was as though his body was encompassed safely within a dark foggy shadow, one that was pulled right off the ground. The black silhouette grew until it stood over me and started to overpower me.

Todd's shadow form held my fists tight as he yelled out in a dark distorted voice, "Now, Al! Take him down!"

The large crocodile dashed toward us from behind. Coco quickly leaped off my shoulder as I instinctively opened my fists and grabbed Todd's forearms. Two small mechanisms sat comfortably under his wrists which sounded like small fans. I flexed the muscles in my arms and activated my armor. My fingers wrapped around his wrists as I squeezed and crushed the devices. Bits and pieces of mechanical hardware crumbled into the field as I side stepped to the right and swung Todd's body to my left. With careful precision and timing Al's attack correctly, I launched Todd's body into the large crocodile before he could make contact. The two slammed into the ground and sat motionless. I arched my back, lifted my hands high, brought my elbows back, and clapped hard enough to blow Todd's smoke away, the same way I had during our first challenge.

Coco stood still, calm, and motionless as she continued to closely watch both Todd and Al. Todd's shadow form dissipated as remnants of each device fell off each wrist. He returned to his regular form and slowly started to rise. He wiped the blood off his chin. "Not bad, Steele. Seems like somebody's been practicing. Huh?"

I exhaled. "You have no idea."

Todd smirked. "Then I suppose it's time we turned things up a notch."

He adjusted his partner patch to 9 and slammed down on it. Al suddenly started to grow larger, heavier and had an evil red look in his eyes. The same shadow that once covered Todd now covered Al.

I looked over to Coco as she stood beside me. "He must have some device placed on Al as well. You know what Coco, let's start off with Dusty. Just like we practiced. Go get him," I whispered.

Coco inhaled as much air as she could before she ran toward Al. The massive shadow crocodile opened his jaws and roared loudly. Coco continued running toward the deadly set of jaws but jumped in the air before she came in contact. She raised her right hand in the air as it began to shine. The sun reflected rays of light, radiating the colors of the rainbow. Suddenly, she transformed into the mirror image of Dusty, Grandpa's legendary alligator.

Todd's mouth dropped while everyone in the crowd was shocked by the transformation.

"My God," John Rigby whispered.

"So, the rumors are true? Fantastic!" Herb yelled out.

"GO, COCO!" Sammy and Davis cheered.

"A crystal claw. He did it. He finally did it," Miss Peterson whispered.

While Coco was in the air, she twisted and somersaulted forward as she slammed on top of Al. Her point of impact crushed the small mechanical device located on top of Al's head. Coco's Dusty form opened her massive jaws and clamped down onto Al's head where the device was originally placed. She squeezed and began to spin and roll her body rapidly. Her strength was enough to flip the crocodile over completely and slam him into the ground. I remembered way back when Dusty fought off the giant liger, Aries. I was a paralyzed with fear, and an inexperienced student back then. Fortunately, I was no longer that same person.

Hundreds of members of the Cultivation Squad were moved by what they had just seen. Hunters stood in awe with their hands on their heads and mouths on the floor. Farmers cheered and began pointing, shouting, and jumping up and down.

Josh watched alongside Dashae with their arms crossed from the Hunter's Camp side of the field. They both carefully hid their smiles. Josh started to laugh under his breath as they both pretended to be surprised. After months of training with Josh, he finally saw what Coco and I were capable of. Now the world knew who we were. We kicked off the new era of the crystal claw.

I ran into the middle of the chaos as Coco's Dusty form moved away from Al. I jumped in front of Al to deliver the final blow as I clenched my right fist and brought it down on top of Al's jaws. Al suddenly collapsed onto the ground motionless and passed out from the critical blow. I looked up at Todd as he watched Coco move closer to him. Coco hissed with the same animosity Al used to hiss at us. Todd stood in place as his hands began to shake.

Todd kneeled on the ground. "How? You-you didn't even use your partner patch?"

"We didn't need it."

Todd sighed. "Okay, I suppose my time is up." He reached down to touch the ground.

I zoomed over and kicked his hand away from the dirt.

"Don't you dare. Look around you. Everyone is watching. You give up now, and everyone will ridicule you. Is this really the way to restart our friendship? How are we supposed to work together after this?"

Todd laughed. "Ha, I suppose you have a point. What would you have me do?"

I sighed. "Just hit me as hard as you can."

Todd struggled to stand back up. "Thank you, Justin. Maybe next time, crystal claw. But for now." Todd slowly walked backward and stepped out of bounds before dropping to the ground.

My eyes grew big in shock and awe. I wasn't sure if Todd was overwhelmed by Coco's public transformation, or if he were scared, or if he genuinely felt defeated. Either way, I was thankful for his actions. It was what I'd been fighting for the past six months.

Rigby blew his whistle. "That's it! There you have it, folks! It looks like we have our winner. Give it up for Justin Steele, the latest member of the Hunter's Camp, and the new crystal claw trainer of Ignacia!"

Members from both camps stood and erupted with excitement at the historic event. Applause broke out in crisp claps, cheerful howls, and high-pitched whistling. It was all happening for me and Coco. I scanned over the sea of people and saw many trainers and their partners clapping. Herb, Miss Peterson, Sammy, Davis, Roxanne, Dashae, Josh, even his partner Darwin. The memory of Cameron's words played in my mind like an anthem. I thought of how proud he would've been to see us achieve our goal. We'd pushed ourselves for months in order to climb up to the next level and that's where we stood.

I took my hat off and watched the clouds sail by as I stood hoping Cameron and Rudolph were looking down at us. The positivity that radiated off every member of the Cultivation Squad sent shivers down my spine. That moment was the real start of our journey, one that pushed us further than we ever could have imagined. Coco transformed back into her coati form and leaped onto my shoulder.

Both Josh and Dashae hoisted us atop their shoulders.

"Don't you think that somersault was a bit much?" Dashae asked.

"No, I think they were brilliant," Josh countered.

"They fought better than you did."

"Well, Justin is a quick learner!"

I laughed. "Thanks, guys."

"We're going to have to look after these two," Dashae muttered to Josh.

Josh smiled. "The Hunter's Camp will be happy to have them."

"You realize now that the entire country will be coming for these two."

"Everything will work itself out. We'll be by their side every step of the way. And as you can see, I think Justin can take care of himself."

My partner placed her front hands on my hat as she stood on the back of my neck. Coco looked out at the sea of people cheering for us before I pulled her down for a big hug. She licked my face and buried her forehead into my shoulder.

"We did it, Coco. We're Hunters. Get ready because we're just getting started."

Happiness, encouragement, and acceptance filled my heart. These feelings were what I'd been searching for my entire life. This was just one of the trials that would prepare us for the many challenges to come. Happily, I laughed holding Coco up affectionately.

Buried deep in the Atlantic, Fedrov and the Dark Trainer stood admiring their newly built underwater utopia.

"You smell that, Fedrov?" the Dark Trainer asked. "Breathe it in. The sweet smell of success."

Fedrov exhaled a thick cloud of cigar smoke. "I have to admit, at first, I did not think you could do it. You said a giant city underwater, and I thought, 'Oy vey. A modern-day Atlantis.' But here we are." The Dark Trainer laughed. "Yes, here we are indeed. Two thousand meters beneath the surface and we are finally free. An entire civilization created and led by us. Cherish this, Fedrov. We built this city, one where trainers and animals may live together in harmony. No alternative implications, and no mechanical attachments. It's up to us to protect it."

Fedrov inhaled his cigar. "I suppose it is a good thing I kept the boy busy so we could use the tech from Sandpiper. Of course, we succeeded, you hired the right guys for the job."

"Suits will do anything to feel a part of something."

Vladimir Mathias entered the velvet room, as he coughed and stood offended. "Do we now? May I remind you; I make one phone call and I have the ability to retract our entire deal, right now. It's a simple contract, we supply the structure, you supply the partners and the land. But you believe it is us who are so desperate? Should we go ahead and withdraw our contribution?"

"Nip it Vlad, you know what I meant," the Dark Trainer snapped. "Fedrov, how's your daughter coming along?"

"We have good days and bad days. She longs to venture out into the blue. She and that damn dolphin." He exhaled another cloud of smoke from his cigar.

"Always longing for the unknown. Use that to your advantage. And her partner patch?" the Dark Trainer asked.

"Taken care of. Still, she and her dolphin remain close. The bond is true."

"Good. We're going to need her."

"Now we go back for the boy. I told you he was a crystal claw!" Fedrov stood and demanded.

"I must admit, he is becoming something of a spectacle. One that must be dealt with immediately. His power grows daily, and everyone in the camp is expecting him—"

Fedrov growled as smoke departed his mouth. "Nobody listens to me. You have kept me too quiet for too long, old man."

The Dark Trainer turned and advanced toward Fedrov. "Watch your tone. Remember who you are speaking to. Nobody needs to worry about Justin Steele. In time, he will become the guiding light, and lead the way for the next generation for a new AFA. Mark my words."

Fedrov slammed his fist into a table and sat down defeated. "I had him in my grasp. He got lucky and pushed me into the water!"

"Broke four ribs if I remember correctly. But neither of you should worry about Justin Steele anymore," the Dark Trainer commented.

Herschel Steele removed his hood. "You leave him to me."

END OF BOOK ONE

ACKNOWLEDGEMENTS

I extend my deepest gratitude to the remarkable individuals who have played pivotal roles in shaping and supporting me throughout my writing journey. Their influence and encouragement have been instrumental in making this endeavor a reality.

First and foremost, I am indebted to Miss Betsy Creveling from P.K Yonge in Gainesville, FL, my earliest inspiration in Language Arts. Thank you, Miss Crevling, for instilling in me an undying passion for creative writing during sixth grade.

In my senior year at Richland Northeast High School in Columbia, SC, Dr. Dean Roof you became my dedicated literary mentor. Dean, your belief in my work and guidance as my first developmental editor has been invaluable. This piece owes much of its existence to your unwavering support.

I express my heartfelt appreciation to my father, Emerson King, whose influence has shaped my character and overall approach to life. Thank you for imparting essential values, business acumen, and a steadfast voice of reason. I aspire to emulate the legendary figure you are, and I am grateful to call you my father.

To my younger brother, Davis King, whose constant presence, and reliable support have been a lifeline during challenging times—I extend my deepest thanks. Your kindness, logic, and patience have been indispensable, and I am proud to have you as my brother.

A sincere acknowledgement goes to Mr. Torron Grimes for your impactful training, guidance in anger management, and introducing me to the world of free-verse poetry. Your generosity, including the memorable black and red notebook, will forever be cherished. Stay breezy, good sir.

I express gratitude to Gaal Almor, a dear friend from Richland Northeast High School, for his kindness, belief in me, and genuine friendship. G-money, your support means the world to me. I will always cherish our time together in the theatre department at Richland Northeast High School.

Joshua Hollington, my unofficial big brother from Winthrop University, you have been an authentic role model and positive source of inspiration since

2012. Thank you for imparting lessons of honor and gentlemanliness. I look forward to witnessing your continued journey and coming to visit in Charleston!

My appreciation extends to Samantha MacFarlane, a cherished friend from Marineland Dolphin Adventure. Thank you for your honesty, kindness, generosity, and lifelong friendship. I am truly fortunate to have you in my life and will always call you my sister. Love you lots!

I am thankful to Miss Natalie Hughes, Miss Deborah Warwick, Miss Lindsay Ehrlich, and the entire team at The St. Augustine Wild Reserve for allowing me the opportunity to volunteer and work with such incredible creatures every Saturday. Without you all I would not have received the inspiration to bring this story to life.

I want to take a moment to thank my mother, Lisa King. For your consistent support over the years and allowing me to express myself creatively. Though we have not always seen eye to eye, you have always made an effort to love, care, and attend my theatrical productions over the years. I love you.

Thinking back to each employee, team member, and friend that have supported me from Marineland Dolphin Adventure over the years. Felicia, Cait, Roque, Kristen, Jodi, Jill, Ashley, Terri, Terran, Alyssa, Tess, Emily, Keith, Wes, Michelle, and everyone. I'd like to recognize and highlight your kindness and professionalism. Thank you for always greeting me with a sincere smile and bringing your optimism and positivity to the workplace.

And I could not forgive myself if I did not pay tribute to the team at Kookaburra Coffee Store 312 located on US 1 in St. Augustine, FL. Julianna, Jayden, thank you both for allowing me to write this story in your store and making the best coffee!

Lastly, the love of my life, Maria King, your consistent support has been the bedrock of my strength throughout this process. Thank you for your critiques, edits, opinions, and ideas after reading my manuscript multiple times. I am blessed to call you my darling bride, and I look forward to building an amazing life for us together. Thank you for being my guiding light throughout this adventure. My heart is yours, from this day until my last day.

ABOUT THE AUTHOR

Meet the author, Gaston (Trey) King whose lifelong fascination for animals has shaped a rewarding journey immersed in the world of diverse creatures. From domestic dogs to exotic big cats, from endearing critters to majestic marine mammals, King has marveled at their unique behaviors and personalities. Recognizing that every animal possesses its own distinct way of navigating the world, King emphasizes the importance of understanding and appreciating these individual traits are essential to forming a genuine and lasting connection.

Currently serving as the Marketing Specialist at Marineland Dolphin Adventure in St. Augustine, FL – the world's first Oceanarium – King plays a pivotal role in showcasing a remarkable array of species, including red-footed tortoises, sand tiger sharks, and captivating Atlantic bottlenose dolphins. Among them, 'Oli, a dolphin that King first encountered as a 2-year-old calf during his early days at Marineland in 2017, has grown into a 7-year-old companion, holding a special place in King's heart.

Each Saturday, King still dedicates his time to The St. Augustine Wild Reserve, where every morning involves cleaning habitats, feeding animals, and visiting Maya, a cherished coatimundi. The bond formed with Maya began during her early days at 2 months old in 2019, exemplifies King's deep connection with coatimundis. Encouraging readers to experience the wonders of these establishments firsthand! Marineland Dolphin Adventure and The St. Augustine

Wild Reserve, King highlights their commitment not only to pampering their residents but also to their championing conservation causes.

For those intrigued by King's literary endeavors and eager to follow his journey with Marineland Dolphin Adventure and The St. Augustine Wild Reserve, stay connected on different platforms for future updates. Join King on an enriching exploration of the wild side, where a world of awe-inspiring creatures and conservation advocacy awaits.

You can find Gaston King's socials listed below:

Website: **www.gastontking.com**
Facebook: **www.facebook.com/gastontking/**
Twitter: **www.twitter.com/gastontking**
Instagram: **www.instagram.com/gastontking/**
YouTube:**www.youtube.com/channel/UCJhu3sFvPCmFvjskF8GFqWg**

Thank you all for your support!